# O MY
# AMERICA!

HARPER & ROW, PUBLISHERS

NEW YORK

Cambridge
Hagerstown
Philadelphia
San Francisco

London
Mexico City
São Paulo
Sydney

*1817*

# O MY AMERICA!

## A NOVEL BY
## JOHANNA KAPLAN

Grateful acknowledgment is made for permission to reprint:

"For Everyone" by Alistair Reid. Copyright © 1969 by
Alistair Reid. From *Pablo Neruda: A New Decade* by Pablo
Neruda, and translated by Alistair Reid. Copyright © 1969 by
Grove Press, Inc. Reprinted by permission of Grove Press, Inc.

"Turn! Turn! Turn! (To Everything There Is a Season),"
words from the Book of Ecclesiastes. Adaptation and Music by
Pete Seeger. TRO—© Copyright 1962 Melody Trails, Inc.,
New York, N.Y. Used by permission.

Excerpt from *Democracy In America*, by Alexis de Tocqueville, translated by Henry Reeve, revised by Francis
Bowen, and edited by Phillips Bradley. Copyright 1945 and
renewed 1973 by Alfred A. Knopf, Inc. Reprinted by permission of Alfred A. Knopf, Inc.

Excerpts from *Collected Poems*, published by Harper & Row,
Publishers, Inc. Copyright 1922, 1950 by Edna St. Vincent
Millay and Norma Millay Ellis. Reprinted by permission of
Norma Millay Ellis.

Portions of this work originally appeared in the January, 1976,
issue of *Commentary*, under the title of "Not All Jewish Families
Are Alike."

FIRST EDITION

*Designer: Gloria Adelson*

Library of Congress Cataloging in Publication Data

Kaplan, Johanna.
  O my America!
  I. Title.
PZ4.K17330ac [PS3561.A56]    813'.5'4    79-2649
ISBN 0-06-012289-7

80 81 82 83 84 10 9 8 7 6 5 4 3 2 1

*O my America! my new-found-land . . .*
—JOHN DONNE

*Thus not only does democracy make every man forget his ancestors, but it hides his descendants and separates his contemporaries from him; it throws him back forever upon himself alone and threatens in the end to confine him entirely within the solitude of his own heart.*
—DE TOCQUEVILLE

# O MY
## AMERICA!

# 1

THERE was only one policeman, very young, his hands already on the steering wheel, by the time Merry got down to the police car. Holding out a pack of Chiclets, he said, "Want a piece of gum?" as if he were a casual acquaintance, someone's friend or downstairs neighbor agreeably giving her a lift because they were going in the same direction.

Much too quickly Merry said, "No, thanks," and because she was sure there had to be *some* protocol, *some* formality that would relieve them both of this strained unreality—slipping so rapidly through familiar city streets—she said, "I'm Merry Slavin. His *daughter.*" Because on that point there had already been enough confusion.

The policeman, practically a parochial-school kid, redhaired, with the painfully fair, blue-white iridescent skin of redheads—the same color skin as Isobel's, though Isobel had never, even as a child, she said, had red hair—the policeman nodded, but did not really look at her. Glancing through the rear-view mirror, he said, "Sorry about the noise here, but it'll give us speed, and that's the purpose." The sudden sound of the siren and the smell of his peppermint gum fell through the car simultaneously; Merry turned and stared out the window, her eyes continually catching and keeping signs and stores as if it were a movie whose subtitles she could easily assimilate, but whose internal sense she would never really grasp.

The purpose: only an hour before, Merry, dressed to meet her father for dinner and waiting for his phone call, had fallen asleep on the living room sofa. She had changed early on purpose, hoping that by putting on a new dress she would prevent herself from falling asleep. This dress, which was Indian, and dark blue, with the customary intricate, multicolored Indian embroidery across the front, would annoy her father because it was a dress and therefore an implicit bourgeois demand; because it was Indian, thus taking jobs away from mere subsistence-level American workers and encouraging the exploitation of Indian ones even poorer; and because its embroidery was machine stitched—a once vital folk craft now brutally cut off from its real source, and so cheapening to a whole culture. But the dress itself, now wrinkled and sweaty, had not stopped her from falling asleep, an old habit she could not break. "Somnolence is a primary symptom of anxiety," was one of the first things her analyst had ever said to her, and Merry felt this to be true. She did not like it herself and yet could not stop it. Waking up from an undesired sleep in the late afternoon always left her with a detached gloomy sourness that did not go away for hours. Her father looked at it differently, however, having written of certain Impressionist paintings, particularly Cézanne's, that they gave you the same unique sensation as did waking up from a nap: out of a haze, you suddenly saw ordinary everyday objects as if only half formed. They were in the process of being born; it was a discovery, you saw them newly. Not that he especially cared about Impressionist paintings, or art of any kind, for that matter. What he valued above all was the sense of seeing something as you had never seen it before: through child's eyes, a discovery.

This was exactly what Merry knew he was doing as she waited for his phone call—he was walking slowly, hazily through Manhattan streets he had been through a hundred times before. Maybe this was one of the times he had gotten off at an unfamiliar subway stop by accident, or on purpose. It didn't matter; it would come to the same thing, especially now that he no longer lived in New York. A half smile was on his face as he stared and wandered: he was seeing something old and familiar in a new light, discovering something he had never previously noticed, or—who could tell?—possibly even finding something that was actually new. In a little while, over dinner, his eyes glazing with delight behind his glasses, he would be telling Merry about a new discount drugstore in the East Twenties or a new library in the West Sixties; they would both have been there for years. It was what Merry called to herself his Rip Van Winkle syndrome, and she had once told this to Isobel, who, in keeping with her nature, had merely shrugged. But Isobel could afford to shrug; she had been divorced from Ez Slavin for years.

Where was he now? Probably sitting over a milky lukewarm cup of coffee in an old Automat or an about-to-be-torn-down Bickford's, staring with ingenuous fascination at someone's left-over racing form, or happily fingering what he temporarily regarded as an ingenious new ketchup dispenser. With the clothes he wore and the way he looked, he would fit right in—and this was Merry's worst fear: that without trying, without even knowing or caring about it, her father would turn into a Bickford's bum. Especially since she had just finished writing a piece on Potter's Field, this thought put

3

Merry to sleep, and when the phone rang, startling her into partial wakefulness, she saw that the dye of the dress had come off, running purplish blue onto her arms.

But the ringing phone was not her father; it was the police.

"Mrs. Ezra B. Slavin?"

"This is *Miss* Slavin," Merry said, so instantly annoyed that alarm did not reach her. "It is *not* his wife. I'm his daughter."

"There's been an accident, Miss," this police voice said, against a background of terrible noise and headachy buzzing. "Mr. Slavin's been taken to Bellevue. We're sending over a squad car now. It's on special orders."

Once, from a neighbor, Merry had heard a story about a woman who had received a similar phone call, but it was about her ten-year-old son and had come from the police department of the suburban Long Island town to which they had only just moved. It was for the sake of this son that they had moved, the woman was always apologizing: he had been mugged on his bike once too often. On a new bike, in his new town, the boy was run over by a car. When the phone call came at work, his mother had had to take the Long Island Rail Road from Penn Station all the way out to Westbury. "I knew he was dead," she had kept on repeating numbly, when people spoke to her afterward. "They wouldn't tell me anything, but all the time I was sitting there on the train I knew he was dead."

When the police car pulled up at the emergency room entrance, Bea Shestak, exactly the same, still streaky blond and florid faced, jumped out at Merry and embraced her. "Oh, my God," she sobbed. "We didn't even know he was in New York! He wasn't even listed as a speaker! Your *father! Ez Slavin!* He was just *standing* there, just standing on the edge of the crowd. If one of the Peace Committee marshals hadn't recognized him, he might have been lying there for hours. He didn't even have any identification, Merry. All he had was an old library card!"

4

"Well, he doesn't *have* a driver's license," Merry said. "And you know what he thinks of credit cards. Anyway, he's always been against identification, Bea. He thinks it's an intrusion of the state. I only hope he had Blue Cross or something. He certainly can't afford to stay in the hospital."

Staring into the distance, Bea Shestak said, "He died for his principles. He was never any different. He was always, always modest and he never changed his convictions."

"He's *dead?*" Merry said. "Just *dead?* They told me there was an accident."

"There was no accident," Herb Shestak said, stepping forward, nervously fingering his glasses. He was nearly totally bald now, but his beard had grayed only slightly. "Your father had a heart attack. A massive coronary. He was dead by the time he got here."

"DOA," Merry said, and looking around at the ambulances driving up and the crowd of white-uniformed doctors, nurses and attendants walking in and out—one girl with a stethoscope around her neck was brushing her hair as she pushed through a swinging door—she thought suddenly of how her grandfather had died. The police had found him too. "Was your father a man of means?" said the cop who had battered down the door to her father and his older brother, Uncle Bloke. Whispery groups of Chinese children stood in the newly made entranceway; their alien smells had bothered the old man, their tight, slanted eyes reminding him of the Mongolian tribesmen of his whole freezing Siberian childhood and youth, causing him to call out, "Tartar! Kalmuk!" when he saw them from his window or on the stairway. "*Means!*" exploded this uncle called Bloke, a giant, red-faced, crude-featured man, who had acquired his nickname in childhood from hanging around the Irish. "Would a man of means have lived in this shithouse?"

"I'd like to call Isobel," Merry said, having no idea whether or not she was making any sense. "What time is it there?"

"*Isobel?* What is she *talking* about, Herb? What time is it

5

*where?* Merry, darling, you're the next of kin. You have to make the *arrangements.*"

Herb Shestak said, "Isobel Rees—you know, that writer he used to be married to. *The Blood Curtains.* She lives in England."

"She lives in *Italy,*" Merry said coldly. It was Isobel who was cold, her father always said, and she thought of how angry it made Isobel when people connected her solely with that one novel, which, made into a movie, brought her unexpected, temporary fame and permanent public association with a work whose tone and characters she could hardly even recognize. "I just want to talk to her, but not if it's the middle of the night there. Maybe she *would* come here, because she does come sometimes anyway. But I'm not the next of kin."

Bea Shestak began to cry again and hugged Merry so tightly that she could smell her perfume, or maybe it was only lotion or some kind of makeup. Why had Bea worn perfume to a demonstration? Ez did not approve of perfume, of any cosmetics at all; it meant she had succumbed to the seduction of advertising even if she only used blush-on or a little lipstick, which she needed because she looked like him and was sallow-skinned.

Tearfully, Bea said, "I *know* how awful it is for you, Merry. And shocking. But I wish you would cry instead of being so overwhelmed. Because there are things you'll have to *do* now. . . . When Herb's sister died, she was cremated too, so at least that's something we know about. And the newspapers . . ."

"He doesn't believe in cremation, Bea. And besides, I am *not* the next of kin."

"My God, Herb! Look how upset she is! What are we going to do? She's not even *thinking.* Of *course* he believed in cremation, and, honey, Isobel has nothing to *do* with this. They were *divorced.* It's a *legal* thing. That's why those— those other girls—your sisters? Your half-sisters? Paula's

6

girls—*you* know who I mean. Of course, you'll have to call them if you know where they are, but they're not *legally*, I mean, he wasn't actually ever married to their mo—"

"He had a son with Isobel," Herb said. "I forgot all about it."

"Nicky?" Merry said. "I think he's supposed to be in India, I'm not sure. They were hardly even speaking." She was aware suddenly of feeling extremely tired. "I mean Jeannie. That's who I should really call first."

"*Jeannie?*" Bea screamed.

From somewhere in back of her, Merry felt a light tap on the shoulder and a soft, nearly whispering woman's voice, oddly foreign, saying, "Mrs. Slavin?"

"No. *Miss* Slavin," Merry said wearily. "His daughter." And turning around, saw that she was facing a slight, very pretty Filipino girl, no older than herself. A stethoscope was shoved into her pocket; the name tag on her jacket said Concepcion Lopez, M.D. She looked hesitantly at Bea Shestak, and then, to Merry, said:

"There was no question of primary cause. You won't need a coroner. . . ." She stopped abruptly and Merry stood there waiting, caught in the lilt of her voice, which was almost hypnotic. "The seizure was so massive, didn't he have a history? Suspected coronary events? Warning signs?"

"I don't know," Merry said. "I have no idea." Because when would her father have gone to a doctor? He had never believed in doctors, had not viewed medicine as a science. But then he did not believe in science.

The loudspeaker, which had been broadcasting constantly, a nearly unintelligible flat, metallic squawk, now burst out: "Dr. Lopez, Dr. Concepcion Lopez, Dr. Zwerling, Dr. Michael Zwerling, Dr. Lopez."

"Excuse me," Dr. Lopez whispered, and having already stepped away on her equally whispery, tiny shoes, she turned back and with sudden, surprising, shy urgency said, "I saw

7

your father once. In Cambridge. We went to hear him speak, but it was so crowded they put us in an overflow room. When he found out later there were people who didn't get in, he took us with him to a special reception. We—we weren't even invited and he talked to us specially." She looked more and more embarrassed, and said finally, "I'm very sorry."

He slept with her, Merry thought instantly. Another one. He had asked her about the rebel fighters in the Philippines, listened to her lilting, hypnotic whisper, and decided entirely in his own mind that she would return in comradely bravery only to the farthest of the out-islands, a tiny, remarkable, healing heroine.

Bea Shestak clutched dramatically at Dr. Lopez's white jacket, her eyes filled again, and said, "Thank you, dear. He was always the same, the same with everyone. That's why this grief will be so shared. You have to *think* of that, Merry, it will *help* you. Now the shock and pain is yours, but the grief will be shared by so many."

Merry said, "I better call Jeannie. I suppose she should really know first. *She's* the next of kin, Bea. She's his wife."

"That little *girl?* In Massachusetts? The one he brought back from Kentucky? Merry, he wasn't *married* to her. You're not thinking straight."

"He *was* married to her," Merry said uncertainly, because of course there were all those years when he hadn't been. "They have a child, a little boy."

"Herb, did you know about this? Is it true? He got married up there in Massachusetts? And has a son? Is she rational? Maybe we should call up Dave Roizman and he'd give her a tranquilizer. Or *talk* to her. *Some*thing."

"He did have a baby," Herb said slowly. "And I suppose that's with Jeannie. But I didn't know he was married to her. I guess it's perfectly possible."

Perfectly possible. As ambulances careered in and out and sirens wailed, Herb Shestak waved his glasses in the air; it was

8

undoubtedly the gesture he was accustomed to using in front of his classes when he was considering with just, reasoned gravity the varied but perhaps equal claim on truth of two opposing theoretical arguments. After all, on the one hand, but then, there was always, not to be dismissed, on the other: perfectly possible. Merry felt a wave of her father's contempt for Herb Shestak, for academics, for sociologists, for Herb Shestak who had always been this same one thing from a young man on—a teacher and a sociologist—and then recalled that her father had rarely made a living until he had gotten university jobs, and in a field usually called American Civilization or American Studies, not so different from sociology. And how much of a living had he made even then? Merry could not tell. He had found and embraced rural poverty when he met Jeannie on a trip to Hazard, Kentucky, and had lived up to what he considered its truth in a ramshackle farmhouse in northwestern Massachusetts, even these days when his commute had been to Amherst. But this was not entirely fair: he had always preferred being poor to having a real job, and did not care who had to share in his choice without having made it. None of the women he had ever been involved with, from Merry's mother on, had, according to him, truly understood the nature of his choice. Only Jeannie, Jeannie, who could not possibly have known the difference because she had lived all her life in real, dire, unelected poverty, had not minded, and he had elevated what she knew as the sole and natural condition of human life to be its highest form—and moved to the country. And to a remote and isolated place in the country at that. What about urban vitality? The streets and neighborhoods teeming with real life, the community of men?

> Slavin—Ezra Benjamin. Suddenly, in New York City on March 12, 1972. Husband of Georgeanne. Father of Merry, Nicholas and Samson. Funeral private. Memorial meeting to be announced.

What if obituaries were true? Not whether some man whom casual and musing obituary readers did not know had *really* been a beloved husband, devoted father, adored grandfather and dear brother. That much of a romantic Merry wasn't. But what if just the ordinary facts were true? That this unknown mourned man, exactly as the newspaper death notice said, had left a wife, children, grandchildren: those were their names, there was no one left out, there was nothing inaccurate. What, then, should her father's death notice say?

> Slavin—Ezra Benjamin. Husband of Georgeanne Blaikie Slavin, Isobel Rees Slavin Giobbi and the late Pearl Milgram Slavin. Father of Dr. Jonathan Spivak, Merry Slavin, Nicholas Slavin, Francesca Meisel, Susanna Meisel, Samson Slavin. Grandfather of Adam and Miranda Spivak and Mountain Spring Meisel.

What could casual, musing obituary readers make of that?

But they would never have to try, because anyone who did turn to the obituary page that morning would have found a two-column spread with a photograph, headed EZRA B. SLAVIN, ICONOCLASTIC SOCIAL CRITIC, DEAD AT 64.

> Ezra B. Slavin, the writer, editor and social critic who was Visiting Professor of American Studies at Amherst College, died last night in New York City after suffering a heart attack. He was 64 years old.
>
> Mr. Slavin, a frequent contributor to many magazines and journals since the 1930s, was an unconventional and often controversial figure throughout his life. Often associated with and claimed by the Left, both Old and New, Mr. Slavin disavowed specific political ties, saying, "Labels and pigeonholes are useless and distasteful. All they can do is hinder growth and solidify enmities. They bring comfort to all enemies of intelligence and hopefulness." According to his own account, he was by nature and temperament an anarchist and pacifist, and though he shunned the appellation political activist, he often

demonstrated and fought for those causes which reflected his beliefs.

From very early in his career, Mr. Slavin was harshly critical of the anomic trends of urban, mechanized American life, yet his vision of the city as a place of "limitless, tumultuous possibility" was a lyrical, even celebratory one. "I have had a lifelong affair with the idea of America," Mr. Slavin once said. "And when people find that difficult to believe, I remind them of that flintier vision which is bound to result when love is unrequited." A man of wide-ranging interests (he wrote about a diversity of topics ranging from the outlaws of the early West, whom he viewed as forerunners of the Populist movement, to the influence of psychoanalysis in the '50s, "Psychoanalysis and Everyday Life," to the proliferation of fast-food chains in cities and suburbs), Mr. Slavin's essays were always characterized by the insistent inclusion of his personal likes and dislikes. "Unlike journalists and so many intellectuals of his generation, Slavin does not eschew the 'I,'" a *New York Times* reviewer wrote of his last book, *Three Chairs in the House,* "thus happily endowing his work with the indelible mark of the passionately personal." But this very quality did not always win him praise; he was accused by some critics of "iconizing the trivial and profligately idiosyncratic in the name of cultural criticism." To this charge Mr. Slavin responded with a characteristic blend of charm and bellicosity. "I have an ulterior motive," he told an interviewer. "I actually want to move people. To change the way they perceive and live their lives."

Mr. Slavin, whose own life and ideas have often been cited as precursors of those propounded by the New Left and the "new consciousness," was born to Russian immigrant parents on New York's Lower East Side. Noting that he was one of four sons, Mr. Slavin wondered, referring to the well-known passage found in the Passover Haggadah, whether he was the wicked son or the simpleton. Certainly he was a rebellious one, having

11

attempted to run away from home many times. "When I was five years old, I hid in an iceman's wagon, but it was drawn by a horse and he didn't go any farther than the other (Brooklyn) side of the Williamsburg Bridge. By the time I was eight, though, I was a little smarter and I managed to get as far as Connecticut." But his most daring childhood exploit occurred when, at the age of ten, he attempted to stow away on an oceangoing freighter. He was discovered, however, and sent home on a Coast Guard cutter from what was probably Long Island.

Though an unwilling and infrequent student, he was a graduate of P.S. 12 and De Witt Clinton High School, at that time located in Manhattan. He later attended City College, but he did not complete his studies and never received a degree. After a brief apprenticeship in photo-engraving, a trade he was to work at at various times in his life, Mr. Slavin found employment in the Writers' Project of the WPA. It was at this time that he acquired the reputation for having what a colleague recently described as "the original crash pad," and even many years later his Upper West Side apartment was very often a stopping place for several generations of friends, students and admirers. It was not until the mid-1960s, however, that he emerged from relative obscurity, becoming a figure of widespread appeal, especially to the young. He did not find this role entirely congenial, explaining that though he had always throughout his career urged governments, groups and individuals to "simplify" in the interest of truthfulness and clarity, too many of his young students appeared overwilling to simplify ideas and history, unwittingly pursuing what he termed "that great American goal, fake pragmatism." Mr. Slavin also deplored his sudden loss of anonymity, a condition which he viewed as an absolute prerequisite for "an honest day's thought."

Mr. Slavin's first book, *Outlaws and Citizens,* was a study of such frontier outlaws as Jesse James, the Dalton brothers, Belle Starr and Billy the Kid. He was also the author of several collections of essays: *A Career in Itself, The Aboriginal Name, Stranger in the Land* and, most recently, *Three Chairs in the House.*

He leaves his wife, the former Georgeanne Blaikie, a daughter, Merry, and two sons, Nicholas and Samson.

*Three Chairs in the House:* "I had three chairs in my house; one for solitude, two for friendship, three for society" (Henry David Thoreau, *Walden*). There were three chairs on Ez Slavin's torn screen porch on the day the photograph that accompanied his obituary was taken. Not one of them had cushions or offered comfort of any kind, though Francesca Meisel, not yet the mother of Mountain Spring, had spread her quilted sleeping bag over the hard wooden seat and cracked ladder back of the chair on which she was sitting. Ordinarily, of course, she would have sat on the floor as Peter, her boyfriend, was doing, but Ffrenchy had just had an abortion and she could not seem to make up her mind exactly how much attention she wanted paid to it: abortion was about to become legalized in New York State. Also, as it happened, it was Ffrenchy's third abortion, and her mother, Paula, with whom Ez had had two daughters but whom he had not married or ever really lived with, was running out of sympathy. This was part of the reason Ffrenchy had come up to see Ez in North Darby: her mother was nagging her constantly to settle on some form of birth control, and her adopted father, Al Meisel, was a doctor—obviously *he* couldn't possibly be expected to understand. Anyway, he was extremely dogmatic and bullheaded, Ffrenchy said; in fact, he was a Taurus, and she saw no point in getting into arguments with him.

It occurred to Merry that Ffrenchy, who was beautiful anyway, might be even more beautiful when she was pregnant. She resembled her mother in a certain open-featured, lusty look, but while Paula's attractiveness came from a faintly sloppy, very dark, exotic quality which she had always

13

cultivated, Ffrenchy was fair, like the Slavins. Except that unlike any Slavin Merry had ever met, Ffrenchy had high coloring: pink cheeks, made pinker now from the sun, and very long, thick, brownish-red hair, almost auburn.

"Tauruses *love* arguments," said Peter, who did not stay crouched on the floor but was constantly getting up, moving around and shifting positions as he clicked his camera. Which was *his* purpose in being there that muggy weekend: he was taking pictures of Ez for the dust jacket of his new book, an arrangement that had been thought up by Ffrenchy.

"This is Peter Honig and he's a *terrific* photographer," she had said when the two of them, with backpacks and sleeping bags, had walked in, neither invited nor expected. "What he's starting to get into is radical documentaries, and he's been very influenced by *you*, Daddy. He really admires your work. I mean, he *loves* it." She beamed but said this "Daddy" tentatively, because to begin with, it was what she had all her life called Al Meisel, and moreover, because she knew that Merry, whose acknowledged and legitimate daddy he was, called him Ez.

She will always hate me, Merry thought, as Ffrenchy looked past the screened porch, and taking in her presence, instantly misinterpreted it.

"*Oh!*" Ffrenchy said bitterly. "*Merry!* . . . I read that thing you wrote about illegal immigrants in New York, those Haitians. What a weird thing to get into. I mean, they could really zap you. *You* know—voodoo."

"Well, I didn't write *against* them," Merry said, glaring and tightening immediately. "I only wrote *about* them."

Peter Honig fingered the camera that temporarily hung around his neck. He had clearly not counted on there being such awkwardness in a weekend he must have been so much looking forward to, but he was determined to stay loose. Very loose, in fact: as he bobbed up and down with his camera, his

14

exposed penis bobbed out before him from the folds of a kimono which he either couldn't or wouldn't close. The kimono was not his; he was wearing it because his own clothes were still wet from his morning in the flooded basement. Early that morning, it was Jeannie who had first discovered what was then still just a puddle, a leak—Jeannie up doing the laundry, Jeannie up feeding the new baby, crying, tiny Sammy Slavin. At breakfast, already looking distracted and entirely disheveled, she stacked dishes in the sink and said finally in a hesitant, unhappy twang, "I think there's something wrong with the pipes? . . ." From her tone, it was obvious that this had happened before—and ended in disaster. Probably they couldn't pay the plumber, Merry thought. And as the baby, who was supposed to be sleeping, suddenly began to cry, Jeannie said pleadingly, "Ez, we *can't* call that plumber in town. And anyway, it's Sunday."

This atmosphere of domestic chaos and helplessness which her father always engendered, but from which he himself could remain remarkably immune, was exactly what Merry could not stand. So she said with false cheerfulness, like a camp counselor, "Oh, I bet there's an emergency plumbing service somewhere. In Greenfield, in a bigger town."

Ffrenchy, who was still drinking orange juice, having recently given up coffee because as an addiction it was as bad as alcohol or nicotine—that was the first point against it, the second point being that all caffeine-ingesting societies, and this included both coffee *and* tea, were into a truly destructive and down trip—Ffrenchy said, "What's broken? Plumbing? Don't worry, Peter can fix it. Peter can fix *anything*."

"Ah, omnicompetent," Ez said happily. It was a word he liked and a concept he was genuinely devoted to.

Peter said, "I don't know . . ." and it was impossible to tell whether he was expressing false modesty, decent and perhaps legitimate doubts, or whether he simply did not know the

15

meaning of the word "omnicompetent." "I mean, I'm not really into pipes. What I'm great with is electricity. Wires."

"You fixed that shower, Peter," Ffrenchy crooned at him. "When we were staying at André's. And I was taking a bath." She offered up a smile of broadcasted intimacies: herself rosy and naked in a bathtub, a wash of wanton sensuality, her lover with high boots and competent hands entering in to fix the showerhead and complete the bath.

Peter scratched at his ponytail and repeated, "I don't know," but he went down to the basement, where he tapped too long at a bursting pipe and got drenched.

Which was why on the porch that afternoon, Peter was bobbing up and down in a kimono, prompting Ffrenchy to giggle gleefully, "Oh, Peter! You're a closet flasher!"

She is torturing me with her sexuality, Merry thought. Because I am seven years older and have never had an abortion. Because I am hardly younger than Jeannie and have never had a baby. Because she knows I am fastidious in these things and was brought up by Isobel. She will always hate me and there is nothing I can do about it. Merry sat rigidly forward; she *had* to, the chair was so cracked and rickety, but it was an exact imitation of the stance her father had so often ridiculed in Isobel.

"You can have another chair," Jeannie said uncertainly as she walked through the porch laden down with the morning's laundry, which she had decided, finally, to hang outside. "From the kitchen?" Her voice slid up into a question when no question was intended; probably it was only her accent, but there was a kind of perpetual worried, birdy nervousness about Jeannie that made her seem, especially when she spoke, like someone who was always asking questions whose answers she knew she wouldn't have time to stay around for.

"Don't worry about it, I'm fine," Merry said. Because the last thing she wanted was a chair from the kitchen. Covered in yellow oilcloth, dirty, sticky and sour-smelling—that particular smell of poverty, old age and slovenliness—the chairs in Jeannie's country kitchen could easily have been castoffs, refugees from Merry's grandmother's apartment on Rivington Street. This grandmother, Ez's mother, was dead for years now, but she had been gloomy and half blind even when Merry was very small and had lived with her. Those chairs so instantly summoned up her whole tiny, fetid apartment— bathtub in the kitchen, cockroaches wherever you turned— that Ez, noticing the look on Merry's face the first time she had seen the kitchen in North Darby, had said, "My daughter Merry, the compleat bourgeoise! It's these chairs, isn't it? Your very own madeleine. . . . If only you could find some joy in the memory, some pleasure."

"How could I?" Merry said irritably. "And since when do you? And you didn't even live there when I did, when she was so old and worn out."

Ez turned to Jeannie and said, "That's how it is, parents are always villains. It's an old story."

Embarrassed before Jeannie, Merry said, "I didn't *say* you were a villain. I'm only asking for a certain base line of honesty." And thought: I'm only asking for *what?* From *whom?*

"*Base line,*" Ez repeated sourly, his features contorting as if he were struggling suddenly with a surprise attack of indigestion. "Base line! My God, Merry! The gobbledegook of social science! Is that why you went to college? To learn to degrade the language? So you, too, could help erase spontaneity?"

"I didn't know you were the French Academy. And what are *you* doing, taking the side of purists? I thought you always argue that *they're* the ones who kill spontaneity."

"That's more like it!" Ez said, smiling. He was showing her off to Jeannie, whom he now put his arm around, announcing cheerfully, "In my family, there's never a lack of contention."

Jeannie looked at Merry uneasily and said, "There's only instant coffee? I hope you don't mind it, I just know there are

17

some people who do. From the college? We were having coffee on the porch and they, they . . . well, some people sure do."

On the porch, which three years later had still not been repainted or improved in any way, Peter Honig clicked his camera and Ez's family went on proving its contentiousness.

Ffrenchy said, "I *know* Tauruses love arguments. That's exactly why I wouldn't get into it with him. I mean, why give him the satisfaction? He always gets this *look* on his face—his creepy, boring, uptight look. Like he *knows* he's right. Like there couldn't be any *question*. I mean, *everybody* knows that birth-control pills are bad for you, it's not even a matter of opinion! And he has the *nerve* to sit there with his statistics and tell me that I'm listening to alarmists! And that the danger has been exaggerated. *Exaggerated!* I mean, shit! The man does not care about what happens to my body!"

Which was surely not Ffrenchy's problem: she sat there with her Mexican wedding blouse half unbuttoned and her long and beautiful reddish hair spilling out against the khaki dullness of the sleeping bag, looking, pleading for Ez's attention.

Ez Slavin was sitting on the third chair on the porch, a rocking chair. It was not broken. He leaned back, occasionally rocking slowly, staring, apparently preoccupied, at motes of dust or filtering sunlight. With each careful rock, he varied his expression: he was trying to look natural for the camera.

"I know what you mean about doctors," Merry said, and heard her voice sounding reasonable—reason, the infamous and sickened enemy of passion. "They're always ready to tell you statistics and never mind that you're the one who might turn out to be on the wrong end."

"That is *not* the point, Merry!" Ffrenchy screamed. "I'm trying to explain what kind of *person* my fa—Al is. It has nothing to do with your bullshit intellectual *theories* about doctors!"

18

From inside the damp, reeky house, the baby cried. That baby was the reason Merry was in North Darby that close, hazy June weekend. She had come up to see her newborn half-brother, surprisingly named Samson after a grandfather who, out of all Ez Slavin's children, only Merry had known. But hardly remembered: he had paid even less attention to her than he had to his own children, and spent his last years living alone, separated from his wife of a lifetime, reading and rereading his collection of old Russian books (the *classics*, her father said scornfully), apparently mourning a country which had certainly never mourned him, and bitter against anything which had once interested him. *Yeder mentsh iz a velt far zich alayn*, he had answered anyone who criticized him—Every man is his own world—and had emerged each day dapper and lordly to buy rolls and a newspaper amid the noisy filth of the Lower East Side.

That was one Samson Slavin, Shimshon—Shimsheh, her grandmother had called him—and here now, red-faced and crying, was another. Why had Ez decided to name this son of his old age Samson? What new wrinkle on a constantly reinterpreted past had he managed to come up with for this one?

"Hey, baby. Hey, little baby, baby," Peter said in a singsong, as if he were stroking and talking to an overwrought animal—a horse who had just heard a firecracker or a dog who kept on mistaking an uneasy delivery boy for a mugger. The child's persistent crying was disturbing Peter's concentration.

Ez said, "Poor Sam . . . already wrestling with the Philistines."

"I think it's the heat," Merry said sharply, as Jeannie could be heard running up the stairs, calling out helplessly, "Oh, Sammy, sweet little baby boy Sammy."

Ffrenchy shifted forward, this time looking only in Ez's direction. She said, "Actually, even my mother agreed with me about the pill. It was only him. But then they both started bugging me to get a diaphragm. Well, I *hate* diaphragms, I hate the way they *feel*. It inhibits me, Ez. Do you know what I mean? It's not natural."

Ez turned his chair only slightly; he was still not looking at anyone, but with his face in shadow, continued to stare at ordinary air with such removed and saintly intensity you could easily imagine that an invisible air-molecule morality play was now going on in front of his glasses. Speaking very slowly, reluctantly, as though he could hardly bear to tear himself away from his private entertainment, he said, "Abortion isn't natural, Francesca. In the literal sense. Against nature. Against life."

Ffrenchy shrieked out, *"Daddy!"*

Peter stopped fussing with his camera and Merry said, "I didn't know you were against abortion, Ez. Since when?"

"You don't mean since when have I been against killing, do you, Merry? You don't mean since when have I been unable to oppose an act that's directly against life?"

"Oh, my God!" Ffrenchy howled. "How can you *say* that? What are you *talking* about?"

Ez looked up, wondering, and *click* went Peter Honig's camera. It was that expression, no longer so remote and saintly, but almost boyish in mischief and surprise, that stared out at Merry one morning three years later from the obituary page of the *Times*.

# 2

WHAT is it like in a house that death has come to
unexpectedly? In Merry's apartment, which had once
been Ez's, the sun fell in as if it were midsummer and the
phone did not stop ringing.

"Merry? Be very, very careful," said a breathless woman's
voice, whispering through the wire in the urgent conspirato-
rial rush of people who think their phones are being tapped.
"*This* is the time—the vultures will start coming out of the
woodwork!"

"Charlotte!" Merry said, with genuine surprise and pleasure, though even now she could not hear that voice without
laughing. Charlotte Brodsky Barro (from Barrow Street,
where she had so many years before had her first apartment)
was Isobel's oldest friend in New York, and Merry had stared
at her, mesmerized, since childhood. Charlotte was an actress

and her great talent, in life as in art, was for calamities: her large, dark eyes—always made up with kohl—popped in horror and disbelief, her many chains and strands of beads clinked against one another as she writhed, shuddered and hugged herself, her black, curly Medusa hair flew apart from alarmed self-generated windstorms, and her voice—deep, rending sighs and long, piercing Arab-funeral wails and shrieks—pursued you from one end of the apartment to the other.

But they did not pursue Ez, who had always instantly widened his own eyes in mimicry, and often taking Merry with him, fled the house as soon Charlotte stepped into it. Because of her ringed, popping eyes and overall darkish appearance, Ez called her the Black Frog; it was the same name his father had given, in Yiddish, to a sister-in-law he could not stand. "Ohhh, ahhh," sighed Charlotte, her whole body going flaccid and cow-heavy in dumb despair as she mournfully stared out the window: she had forgotten her umbrella in a taxi and now it was actually raining. Or, "Aaiii, ayeee," she wailed in truly awesome pain and terror—and this was the one where her eyes popped: some people she had been particularly counting on had at the last minute canceled out of a dinner party. Still, Isobel always said, this gift for exaggerated alarm, sorrow and horror—also betrayal—had stood Charlotte in good stead. In a short-running Broadway play in the forties, Charlotte had played the part, a small part, of a maid who unexpectedly comes upon the body of a dead man while she is briskly humming and dusting. The humming stopped and, "Aaaah, aaiii, ayeee," Charlotte had screamed on that stage with such convulsive, terrifying force that her cries had reverberated all the way to Hollywood, and even now, on late-night TV or in revival houses having horror festivals, you could still see a much younger screaming Charlotte, her eyes very big and her mouth wide open. In this way, her face was familiar though not precisely identifiable to many people.

"Listen to me, dear. First they come out of the woodwork, and then—*then*—" Charlotte stopped, her voice was getting too gaspy. "Oh, it's so *ugly*, Merry! How can we ever explain it? Such dark needs of the human spirit! They'll all try to claim their own special piece of the corpse."

"You're right, Charlotte," Merry said into the phone. "Uncannily right. Really, it's already happening." And realized that she had said "uncanny" —a purely Charlotte word. It went with dark needs, ecstatic truths, the mysterious sadness of all things poetic and spiritual—all those happy mainstays of Charlotte's ordinary conversation. Besides which, she honestly believed herself to be clairvoyant, and sometimes, looking at her fixed, staring eyes and intense other-side-of-the-moon expression, Merry believed it too. But that was another story; this time Charlotte was simply right, what Ez used to call "one of her flights into lucidity." Because by this time, Merry had spent hours on the phone, often with people she had not seen or spoken to for years, all of whom had been able to tell her with unswerving, mournful certainty just what it was her father would have wanted. "In the city and working on a new book, he died just the way he would have wanted to." Or, "Standing anonymously in the midst of a demonstration! That's exactly how Ez Slavin would want to be remembered." But what Ez Slavin had ever *really* wanted in life was always anyone's guess, so what could you possibly know now?

Charlotte sighed deeply. "Well, Merry . . ." she said very slowly, suddenly sounding faintly Southern, the accent that came to her for sadness. "Well . . . I do hate to seem so *hard* in a time of grief—you'll think: Kill the messenger . . . but that's what happened when my dear, darling husband died. And I *know* that's what Isobel would tell you. . . . Poor Isobel, changing time zones right now." Charlotte sighed again; it was the kind of sigh that would rend her body and creep up into her face so that she would look exactly like an old-fashioned psychology textbook illustration of severe and incurable melancholia. Poor Isobel? The time zone Charlotte was thinking of, Merry knew, had nothing to do with a jet flying over the Atlantic. Once, in an altogether different time zone—it would have, in Charlotte's mind (and who could blame her?), the illuminated, aching clarity of a folk tale—once she and Isobel had been young, small-town girls starting out together in the big city, their whole lives winking out before them in unknowable, mysterious excitement. So "poor Isobel" you immediately had to translate to "poor Charlotte."

Aloud, Merry said, "Did she send you a telegram? There's some kind of local phone operators' strike in Milan, and the only way I could get through was by wiring Enzo's office."

"Strikes!" Charlotte cried out. "That's what's so *upsetting* about Italians—they're always striking! Do you know that once I was on an Italian train—they say *treno*—sweet, isn't it? Like a toy. Anyway, I *took* that train especially for my screaming, it was supposed to go through a lot of tunnels, which is *perfect*, ideal, and just as we were approaching the big tunnel and I had really worked myself up, gone over everything in my mind—all my anguish, all my frustrations— just as I was really ready to *let go*, the train *stopped*. They said it was twelve o'clock, they were going on strike for two hours, and we would all just have to sit there!"

"In the middle of a *tunnel?* I bet that's when everybody else started screaming," Merry said. And instantly regretted it because Charlotte took her train-screaming theory very seriously, often trying to convert anyone who happened to be around. She had learned it in her youth from an acting teacher and this was it: You boarded a train and when it had gained momentum and was at its noisiest—whistles blowing, engines chuffing, wheels screeching—you screamed as loud and long as you could. It was the perfect release for all pent-up emotions. The near disappearance of train service, Charlotte was convinced, was responsible for the rise of mental illness in America.

She now said, "Oh, no, dear! They were *terribly* sweet, so *personal.* They brought out all their food and wine and just . . . shared it. *Gave it away.* The French would *never* do that. But the Italians! Oh, I've always loved Italians. Of course, I know, I know—*The Garden of the Finzi-Continis* and all that. And even the origin of the word 'ghetto'—*that* was a shock! How would you *explain* it, dear? What do you think?"

The explanation for Charlotte, Merry was sure, would once again lie in the terrible dark needs of the human spirit, so she purposely misinterpreted the question and said, "It was a *beautiful* movie, Charlotte, the book too. What exactly did Isobel's telegram *say?*"

"Oh, Merry!" Charlotte's voice began quavering dangerously. "How can I add to your distress? How can I add to Isobel's? How can I *burden* you both this way?" She was hurtling into full-blown hysteria, an express train skipping even expected stops, so Merry quickly pulled the emergency cord for her and said, "What's the problem, Charlotte?"

Oh, the problem, the problem! What an inadequate word, how inadequate words were altogether—and Charlotte was off again. But here was the trouble: Isobel, poor Isobel, was naturally expecting to stay with Charlotte; she always did when she came to New York. But what could she do? Charlotte's building had just gone co-op and her apartment, which she had been able to buy thanks to the foresight of her dear, darling husband, was being entirely remodeled. Not *her* idea, it had to do with property values and she didn't understand it, but it was now so totally torn up that it was impossible to live in. In the meantime she was staying in a loft, studio, whatever you wanted to call it—the place was one room and claustrophobic—that belonged to a very sweet boy, a sculptor who had gone off to some Greek island and was very glad to have her house-sitting because of all the robberies and vandalism that artists in the neighborhood had been prey to.

Which was another thing about it, of course—it was *so* dangerous: one room, claustrophobic and dangerous. One room, claustrophobic, dangerous and crowded with all his . . . works in progress. It was all right for *him,* she supposed—a great windowed wall of north light (though Charlotte had always understood this was necessary for *painters,* not sculptors)—but terrible for her plants, which needed east or even west light. Particularly her iron-cross begonia.

"Isobel can stay here. With me," Merry said, and immediately felt that heady lift of anticipation, an old, old hunger: I will pretend Isobel is my mother, she lives so far away and will be so happy to see me; I will clean up the house for her, together we will bake cookies in the kitchen and as the sugary aroma floats over us, we will drink cups of coffee and talk and talk and talk. Well, whose mother was ever like that? And since when was that what happened at a father's death? Think of Nicky, whose mother she really is—and exactly how much good has it ever done him? Think of Nicky, in whose face, especially when he plays the piano, there is an expression of such terrible, helpless baby-hurt and unaware gawky weirdness, it is hard to even look at him. Think of Nicky with his smashed, half-paralyzed leg, once pinned between rocks and a canoe in the rushing white water of a Wisconsin river, hoping to gain from his mother the acknowledgment that he belonged to her, to her family, to that long-ago piece of her past where people, *her* people— brothers, cousins, neighbors—did such things commonly. She'd written stories about it, hadn't she?

"Even Isobel's vision isn't *that* simple-minded," Ez had said crankily at the time, though not to Nicky, who lay unvisited in a hospital bed in a town in northern Wisconsin so remote that even Isobel had never heard of it. "All this American-manhood wilderness-conquering!" Ez shook his head in distaste and puzzlement. "Tame it, claim it, carve it

26

up, conquer it!" They were sitting in a Chinese restaurant, Ez and Merry, all the different dishes crowding up the table. "It's all just a kind of latent, disguised imperialism. How *else* could you describe it?" Ez looked up at a nearby waiter pouring tea, and seemed to expect him to take part in the discussion. "It's Manifest Destiny, Merry. I can't imagine anything more alien. Or alienating, for that matter." Because he had always thought of Nicky as Isobel's son, not his, the result of some private, peculiar Protestant immaculate conception.

The waiter, naturally misunderstanding, now came over to their table, saying, "Dessert, sir? Ice cream? Kumquats? Pineapple?"

"No, no, no." Ez waved him away, annoyed.

"For the lady?"

But neither of them ever ate much: long, thin faces, sallow skin and—incongruous, really, in people who were not full-faced—those broad foreheads and high cheekbones, that very Russian look which in an earlier Slavin generation, Ez's mother, went with broody, cryptic peasant dumpiness. "She is not a mother, she's a barrel," Ez's father had often said to his sons of his wife, their mother, once, so long ago, the unclaimed, orphaned girl—older than he, already no prize, illiterate, no dowry, nothing—he had been handed as a bride from a marshy Lithuanian village, a wagon stop on his way from Siberia to America. And she had considered herself very lucky, she had told Merry once, because in her town the big push had been to South Africa, a place where, even *she* knew (though how they had all tried to trick her: cajoling, threatening, telling outright lies, but she *knew*)—the old woman fixed Merry with her crazy eyes—the natives ate you as soon as you got there.

"*'Bais oylem blumen!'*" Shimshon Slavin used to recite—declaim, apparently—as he stared at his gray hairs in the mirror. "*'Vus zeit ihr tzu mir azey frie gekummen?'*" Cemetery flowers! Why have you come to me so early? To *me:*

27

anyone else, okay. Because his hair had turned gray at forty; he dyed it in secret. *She* knew. And this, *this* was the old woman's good luck! Still, she had gotten entirely used to her husband and her reckless, window-breaking sons, looking out at them skeptically, slyly from her heavy-lidded, cataracted eyes, always moving very slowly. But she had never had a daughter and who knows what she might have secretly imagined, wanted? Not Merry, who was above all so *thin*. *"Din und dar."* She would screw up her face in disgust. *"Grin und gel."* Thin and skinny, green and yellow. It was an embarrassment; those little skirts, as small she was careful to make them around the waist, were always sliding down: no flesh. What would people think? Because in this one way she depended on what some people might think: she took in sewing, did alterations for the spoiled and lazy young house-wives in the Knickerbocker houses. From "remnants"—a word Merry had for years believed to be Yiddish—her grandmother made skirts, dresses, sometimes bathrobes, the strange acrid smell of fabric sizing always there on her clothes, in her breath, on her fingers. It clung to dishes, to the furniture; sometimes Merry smelled it in poppy-seed cake, and—another madeleine—any brand-new unwashed sheets or pillowcases could still make her gag.

Ez tapped his fingers on the teapot, looking annoyed, owlish, and said, "It's not that I don't understand the spirit of adventure. But this! It's adventur*ism*. Teddy Roosevelt! Blow the bugle, charge that hill, plant the flag! The roots are certainly the same."

"He's your *son*, Ez. *Nicky.* You're behaving like a mon-ster," said Merry, no angel herself, so guiltily, greedily glad of her father's favoritism.

"And he's your brother! *You* change planes three times and go out there and visit him! . . . Christ almighty! How *you* sound like your mother! The betrayal of the genes—you never even saw her and you sound just like her! The self-righteous, fanatically single-minded Jewish nag. I might just as well be talking to Pearl!"

Which, in Merry's opinion, was exactly what he thought he was doing at least half the time. Yet in what ways she might really be like her mother was very often on her mind—superficially, that she was dark-haired, small and small-boned, with a certain smallness of face and tightness of feature which in Pearl Milgram, according to photographs and other people's accounts, had been almost beautiful, or more accurately, had expressed a kind of vivacity, a liveliness that people tended to remember as beautiful. And which in Merry, when she caught surprise glimpses of herself—a reflection in a bus window or the sudden electric-eye-opened door of a store—gave her the sense of some small, sharp animal warned into a state of perpetual alertness.

"Well, you've always had *that* version—Pearl Milgram as domestic succubus. How about the other ones? Vital, impassioned, in love with ideas, relentlessly curious—Pearl the dead saint? And my favorite: 'She was just a simple Jewish girl.'"

"Let me tell you something about your mother," Ez said, looking up at her shrewdly. "She *did* have a good idea in her life. Once. When she wanted to live on a kibbutz. And not for the reasons that *she* thought, but exactly for the reason she would never have been able to do it. Those people, with all their pathetic, primitive confusion, they understood something about families—their grasping, corrosive, destructive force. In the abstract they understood it anyway. Which is more than Pearl ever did. And don't you come tell me in that stricken, soap-opera voice that Nicky is my son—Isobel's emissary. Because Isobel is another story entirely. There is *nothing*, but nothing, that could deflect that woman from the sacred flame of her art."

"You think it's only Isobel's attention that Nicky's looking for. It's not. It's yours too. My God, Ez! He deserves it. He's

29

only seventeen and he's lying there all by himself."

"*He's lying there all by himself,*" Ez mimicked. "What are you suggesting, Merry? That because Nicky is injured, weak and helpless, I *use* his vulnerability and pretend to create a bond that neither of us feels? Is this your idea of paternal integrity? It's a *lie*, cookie. What are you saying?"

Cookie: Ez Slavin's sweet, long-braided, motherless little girl. But grown up now, with her mother's tongue and—odd, this betrayal of the genes—also her mother's small, busty figure. Talk about bonds!

"If you need to hear me say that I'm sorry this happened, that I'm upset about it—well, of course I am! This afternoon, when I was on the Lexington Avenue bus and I passed the Ninety-second Street Y with that inscription: 'Rejoice, O young man, in thy youth,' I began thinking about Nicky and it was very painful for me. Because that's just what he can't do, he's incapable of it. It's not this accident, Merry, it's *him*. And for me that's the real sadness. . . . Look, cookie, if they move him to Madison, to the university hospital, I *will* visit him. Really."

"Madison? Why?" Merry said. "Are you giving a lecture there?"

"No, I'm going out to see the kids who've been putting out *Studies on the Left*. It's a very good little magazine, though I can see it, they *could* run into trouble, get too sectarian. Or too academic. So far, though, they've done a really nice job. It's very heartening."

"Terrific. Bring Nicky a copy," Merry said acidly. "It's bound to cheer him up."

But nobody visited Nicky: not Ez, not Merry, and not even Isobel, who in those days still would not take planes, though she had already married Enzo and was living in Milan. So that was Nicky at seventeen. And now, seven years later, he was limping his way around the Indian countryside with a tape recorder and a music notebook, looking for certain isolated hill people: after so many years of wanting to be a pianist, he had become interested in music ethnography.

"I don't know about all this," Ez said edgily, putting on his scarf and shaking his head in a way that was supposed to convey scrupulous thoughtfulness, but instead felt exactly like ordinary grudging disapproval. They—Ez and Merry—had just been taken by Nicky to see the Satyajit Ray film *Days and Nights in the Forest*. When they had gone in it was midafternoon, still light, but now, standing outside the First Avenue Cinema in the too early twilight of a bitter winter day, ejected from the familiar and comforting darkness of the theater and the unusual compelling force of the film, Merry, hearing the shrill, echoing cries of children still outside playing and the quick-step bustling sweep of people leaving offices and stores, was overcome by a thin evening loneliness so bone-old, separate and awful that it suddenly recalled to her the Yiddish word *umetik*: lonely. A child's dark, chilly loneliness, *umetik*, because it was the first word for it she had ever learned. Perhaps Ez felt it too: he hunched his shoulders against the wind and, taking off his glasses, began nervously squinting up and down this peculiar piece of First Avenue: unbroken rows of old tenements standing in the gloomy shadow of the Fifty-ninth Street Bridge, now become an uneasy and unlikely fringe of high-gloss fashion. There was a chance, even, that this was what Ez had in mind when he came out with his cranky, querulous "I don't know . . ." Because here, almost as if these simultaneously dismal and glittery streets had been set up for him on purpose, was progress, particularly urban progress in its most hideous aspect: all these coy, overpriced stores and garish, airport-like apartment houses sneaking up on and displacing what had not even been blight. Where could you find a more perfect example of such a favorite Ez theme—and in this case, Merry couldn't even disagree with him. But she knew how easy it would be for him to connect all this with the movie and in a winding, leisurely way, manage

31

to finish with an attack on Nicky. How? Well, probably something like this: Here before us, my children, staring us right in the face, are Technology and Commerce, those satanic Siamese twins whose ghostly, terrorist messenger is Violence. In fact, of course, Violence is really a double agent, necessarily amoral, and even less readily understood, necessarily insidious. Which was its awful, hypnotic appeal (and here Ez would turn on Nicky an intense, prolonged, accusing stare). This was true both internally and externally, in Western countries and Eastern countries. Take, for example, India (with an outstretched, offering arm, he would be as generous with his insight as with an entire subcontinent)—the India of this film, in fact. The urban vacationers, those pretentious, denatured bureaucrats, aping Western ways, but uneasy, and in their uneasiness drawn inexorably to the "primitive" tribesmen. What else could occur but violence—violence and corruption? And it was not just the men from the city who were guilty of corruption, because of course, in their own way, the tribespeople had corrupted the vacationers. All so sad, all so inevitable; and by the way, how did Nicky think (Ez would not be studying a signpost or craning toward a newsstand: he was, after all, only expressing a passing, neutral curiosity)—how did he think he was *different* from these urban vacationers in this project of his? Also, his being American—mightn't this *complicate* the legitimacy of his presence, not to mention his intention?

Positive that something like this was on its way, and also because she felt lonely, Merry reached out for Nicky's arm, Nicky's *skinny* arm—he was so thin, still, and also so tall that she barely came up to his shoulder—and resting her head against him as they stood in front of the theater, Merry realized how easy it was for them both to slip back into the fluid physical intimacy of childhood. Why? Because he had once been Baby Nicky, a sweet, smiling, chubby baby sitting on the lap—this was even in a photograph—of his already too-serious-looking big sister Merry, who sat with a handkerchief pinned to her blouse for elementary school neatness? Because for a few years they had been brought up together, in apparent equality, as brother and sister? Of course, she was his *half*-sister. Though Isobel, to her credit, had been scrupulous about showing him no favoritism. *Too* scrupulous, it could easily be argued: Merry, already a schoolgirl, did not need changing in the middle of the night, carriage hours in the park, or bottles at inconvenient hours; she did not get croup or wail unaccountably. Out of the house for so much of the day, she was just not the same kind of interruption.

And the other half of the supposed equality, Ez? Well, Ez had never claimed an interest in babies, that was one thing. ("Babies just cannot engage his mind, you can't expect it," Charlotte, who had no children, had told Isobel.) For another, what was already engaging his mind by that time was Paula Meisel, and he often took Merry along with him, a confused and unhappy accomplice. But his real objection, or anyway, the one he frequently managed to voice, was that Nicky looked, not so much like Isobel herself—he didn't—but nearly exactly like people in her family. Father, brothers, uncles, cousins: all those people she had worked so hard to leave behind, braving, really courting, disapproval and what amounted to emotional disinheritance, and here was Nicky, with that same look—and in baby pictures especially, that same little face. Even now Nicky retained that Rees family look: long, thin, thin-featured, narrow and vulnerable around the eyes, tight through the lips and chin, oddly austere and fragile at the same time. These days, the resemblance was curiously magnified by fashion: Nicky, with his rimless glasses and muttonchop sideburns, had the exact old-timey look of the people in Isobel's photographs. Had he sought it consciously? Was he even aware of it? Merry had no idea; altogether, there was not too much she and Nicky really knew about each other now. In fact, he even misunderstood her gesture; his voice high with disbelief and excitement, he said, "Oh, great, Merry! You really liked the movie! What about the music—*that's* why I wanted you to see it. What do you think?"

Why should he care what she thought? Why? "It's terrific, Nicky!" Merry said. And then in a half whisper she did not want Ez to hear, "I'm really surprised—it's very erotic." Because God only knew what Ez would make of that one: milky-pale, reedy, tentative Nicky, who could not stride out joyfully into his own destiny but would be lamely dragging around the world *writing down* someone else's erotic music! Luckily, Ez did not hear; he had been staring up and down First Avenue, and now, briefly looking over at Nicky, who was becoming almost gawky with pleasure, fumbling with his knapsack and scarf, Ez said, "Well, you won't be in school anymore, *that's* something. No more aimless courses. And none of that graduate school dissertation bullshit. I'm glad you didn't crumble." Ez nodded and began walking off, slowly ambling northward as he spoke—they were all supposed to be going out for dinner—and Merry, horrified, stared out at her father's jaunty, sauntering figure. He *knew*, he had to know, about Nicky's courses, that he was in a graduate program in musicology. It was the point of his going to India: he was hoping to get material he could use toward a dissertation. "Of course, your sister chose something genuinely useful. . . ." Ez, apparently musing, trailed off: he was referring then to Merry's part-time job in a neighborhood poverty program.

"You son of a bitch! You lousy bastard!" Nicky threw down his knapsack; his voice, wild, broken with anger and tears, rang out on the dark, empty street. "There is *nothing*, not a Goddamn thing, I'll ever ask from you again!"

"Nicky, *please*," Merry begged. She bent down to pick up his new cassette machine, which had fallen out onto the sidewalk, and louder, "Ez! Come back!" A passing cab slowed down, stopped, and caught in the glare of its headlights,

Merry was blindly turning and calling from one to the other.

"Get away from me, bitch!" Nicky screamed. "I don't *want* him back. That motherfucker—I don't ever want to see him again!"

And that was it: he never did. Now, almost two years later, in that same famous Slavin apartment where she and Nicky had once lived with Ez and Isobel, Merry sat on an old kitchen stool—probably Isobel had bought it—and talked on the phone with Charlotte. "That's just what happened in my dream, Merry! Isobel came back and stayed with you. In her old apartment. She was standing alone in the hallway as if she didn't know what to do and when she opened up her purse—remember that wine-colored purse she had?—the only thing in it was her old key. She really *could* do that, couldn't she? Isobel could still use her old key!"

"No, she could not," Merry said shortly. "I had the locks changed when I moved in." Which had nothing at all to do with Isobel.

"I am *deeply* disappointed in you, Merry," Ez had said when she explained her intention. He spoke slowly, somberly, shaking his head and looking away. Because he did view it as a betrayal, there was no question.

"You don't believe in parents being disappointed in their children, remember? No child ever asked to be created, so no parent can ever ask for *his* expectations to be fulfilled. 'How can there be a ledger book for parents and children? What does "owing" mean? Between the generations, with all our wrong-headed anguish and dead-end heartbreaks, this is the blindest. Because think of it, Sam, false debts are—can only be—false feelings.'" This was from an essay ("A Letter to Sam, a Letter to Myself") in the form of a letter to a friend of Ez's whose son, after a very serious suicide attempt, refused to see his father.

"Go ahead, quote me out of context. I suppose I shouldn't be surprised." Ez sighed uncharacteristically and once again

35

shook his head in dismay, apparently determined to keep this tone of more-in-sadness-than-in-anger. "Merry, I don't know why you're doing this. If I were the kind of father who believed in forbidding things, I would forbid you to have the locks changed."

"If you were the kind of father who believed in forbidding things, you wouldn't want me to have to live this way. And you know exactly what I mean. Practically everyone you ever ran into, and their friends' friends, have a key to this place. It's *dangerous*, Ez. I don't *want* people walking in in the middle of the night! Because some guy had a fight with his wife. Or some kids are too stoned to drive back to Brandeis. *I'm* paying the rent now and I'm not running a shelter for a bunch of grubby strangers."

"*Paying! Grubby! Dangerous!*" Ez spat out. "What *is* this? Who am I talking to? Or would I rather not know? Could it *be*, Merry, could it really be that your trust in people is so minimal, or your suspicion so great, that all you have left is this pathetic, frightened name-calling?"

"Look at it this way, Ez. In school, I always had roommates, people were always sharing and borrowing things. In college, in boarding school. Now, if I have my own apartment, I really want it to be my *own* apartment. It's just a matter of privacy. Is that so hard to understand?"

"Oh, I understand it, Merry, I understand. It's all too clear. Lock the doors, change the keys—you're hiding yourself, *burying* yourself in those six dark rooms."

"The six dark rooms of my childhood," Merry intoned, but was distinctly uneasy. Because it was not as if he was describing a Martian, and he knew it. Still, she said, "Oh, come on, Ez! *You'll* still have a key. *You* can bring in the life and sunshine. And anyone else you want."

"Where does this *cynicism* come from, Merry? How can you talk this way? Tell me—and think about this. Because I'd really like to know. What do you think would free you?"

He means his own death, Merry thought, that's the answer he's looking for. He's trying to goad me into saying it. Instead, she said, "*Free* me? From *what?*"

"Oh, no, cookie. No, no, no. Not even the right question. . . . Not *from* what. *For* what."

Eight years later, forced suddenly into that peculiar and unseemly freedom which she was so sure Ez had once had in mind, Merry listened to Charlotte, whose voice kept floating on in sighing, cloudy rapture—as if any minute now she would turn into a daffodil. "It's at times like this, Merry, that I so much envy Isobel for having Vito."

Vito? *Vito?* This, probably, was what came from so much Italian-loving, Merry thought. Enzo, Vito—it was all the same.

"Whatever we think of men, dear—I know in your generation nobody believes in them—still, there are times, Merry, there are times. . . . Don't you agree?"

"About *what?*" Merry snapped, worn down finally by Charlotte's impermeable theatrical vagueness.

"Men, dear," Charlotte fluted. "Men."

"They are not bread and butter," Merry said testily, and heard herself answer in Isobel's voice.

# 3

JULY 18, 1944

Dear Editor,

I am asking for your advice because I am afraid that with my heart pulling me in such different directions, whatever I do will be a mistake. Less than a year ago, my son's wife died after she gave birth to her second child, a little girl. The older child, a boy of five, was immediately taken by an aunt, one of his mother's sisters. But the baby nobody wanted to touch, I don't know why. It's true, they have their own children, their own worries, and now especially, because so many in their family did not get out of Poland and for five years they have heard nothing. My son, in the meantime, before his wife was even cold in the grave, was already living with a Gentile woman, a real Jezebel—always with a cigarette in her mouth—who does not like children. I have already warned my son many times: when you die only dogs will go after you. But it's no use. So only I alone am left to take care of this baby granddaughter and though it's

38

certainly true that a child brings back some of the light and honey of youth, it cannot bring me back a young woman's energy and strength or even a young woman's eyesight. This is why I feel I cannot take care of the baby much longer, and yet I don't want to give her away to strangers, make a real orphan out of her, because this was the bitterness of my own young life, and to this day I haven't forgotten it.

Also, I have very bad feelings about this child's mother, my son's wife. I didn't like her and didn't want him to marry her because she was a *grinneh*, and the kind of *grinneh* who thought that because of her education and her family's *yichus* she was too good for me. But I never suspected that she was sickly, and now I am bitterly ashamed that I always showed how much I didn't like her.

Please tell me what to do.

With thanks in advance,
A perplexed grandmother

ANSWER: We were very moved by this grandmother's plight, and we believe it is not her problem alone, but the problem of a whole family. The grandmother must go to other members of the family, in-laws as well, and explain her situation to them just as she has explained it to us. Above all, the child's father must understand how serious his responsibility is in this matter. Certainly the death of a young mother is a tragedy, but when there are other close relatives living, there is no reason to add to the tragedy by sending a child to live with strangers. As for the other problem this grandmother mentions, we regret to say that her prejudice against a *grinneh* is not unusual, and as she can now see for herself, such foolish prejudices only make everybody suffer.

"Look, Merry! Here comes your father! See? Here he is," her grandmother said to the unkempt little girl who had been running back and forth, forth and back, on the grayish-blue kitchen oilcloth all morning. Except, of course, what she actually said was: *Bald kumt der Tateh! Zeh? Ut iz er!* They were leaning, both of them, against the very narrow sill of the kitchen window, which looked out onto the front, the street.

39

And there, slowly making his way down that crowded noisy street, weaving around garbage cans, racks and stands of outdoor merchandise, women with bundles, and children yelling and playing games, was Ez Slavin. He did not remember to look up toward their window, but Merry waved anyway, she waved in a frenzy, finally calling out, "Tateh!" and jumping up into his arms as soon as he reached the top of the landing. And then what? Did Ez smile in a distant and abashed way, saying, "Hi, cookie," and then irritably greet his mother, "For Christ sake, Ma! Isn't there someone around here who can speak to her in English?"

"A big girl talks to me in English," Merry said. "A colored girl. In Sara Delano Park. She makes my hair in *tzepelach*."

"*Braids*, cookie. Braids! The colored girl doesn't say *tzepelach*."

"No, she's a *big* girl. She goes to school already. *Real* school. With books!" And wriggling out of her father's arms, Merry climbed onto a kitchen chair, and in the loud, strong, fervent voice the big girl had taught her, began singing:

> "I looked over Jordan and what did I see,
> Comin' for to carry me home?
> A band of angels comin' after me,
> Comin' for to carry me home."

"Who gave you a Paul Robeson record?" Ez asked, smiling, forgetting or disregarding the fact that his mother did not have a phonograph.

"It's not a record," Merry said. "It's from Sara Delano. With the big children. When I sing." And this was a story from Merry's past that she really did remember: herself standing on a park bench, surrounded by a crowd of older, black children, as she held on to the hand of her friend the "big" girl, and sang and sang at the top of her lungs. Once, on a Sunday morning, these kids had wanted to take Merry with them to church, and catching a glimpse of this strange springtime sight—a milling group of black children dressed up in their Sunday best and tiny Merry riding the crest of their arms—the ground-floor neighbor, Mrs. Glick, a tiny woman with the odd, chirpy voice of a canary ( a little hopping yellow canary even sat in a cage on her window sill), had piped out from her open window in alarm, "Esther! Estherkeh! Come quick! The Negroes have stolen your granddaughter!" Who could have come quick? Not Merry's grandmother, Bubby, who was so fat and always went everywhere so slowly. And certainly not Mrs. Glick, who stopped after every few steps; she wore big black bunion shoes because her feet always hurt her. *"Meineh fees! Meineh fees!"* Mrs. Glick cried out piteously in her little canary voice every time she climbed up the stairs to visit Merry's grandmother. And *"Meineh fees! Meineh fees!"* Merry would call out after her with no pity at all; her father laughed every time he heard her imitation.

But there was no stealing. Why would Merry go anywhere with the big children on a day when she knew her father was coming?

> "Swing low, sweet chariot,
> Comin' for to carry me home.
> Swing low, sweet chariot,
> Comin' for to carry me home."

"Look how excited she gets when she knows you're coming! She's up singing and running around before it's even light out! How can you do this every time, Ezra? What's the matter with you? Why can't you get here a little earlier? You can't leave your treasure to light her own cigarettes?"

"*'Tayereh malkeh, gezunt zolst du zein.'*" Merry sang even louder now, climbing from the chair onto the table. " *'Gis un dem becher, dem becher mit vei-i-in. Bim bam bam bim—'*"

"And who taught her *that* one? The colored girl in the park?"

"*'Shayn bin ich shayn!'*" Merry practically screamed.

" '*Un shayn iz mein nomen. Red'n mir shiduchim mit—*' "

"Sender," said Merry's grandmother above the din. "Joe Sender. You know them. The bakery downstairs . . . You know, Ezra, they would take her for a weekend sometimes. Or a holiday. They're good-hearted, his wife too. Not like the rest of them." Not like the rest of them: because Joe Sender was Pearl Milgram's second cousin.

"It hurts me to see Pearlie's little girl like that," Joe Sender often said, lifting Merry up onto the slatted wooden back part of the counter. He would give her an end piece of bread, the heel—probably it was what his own daughters had preferred—and shake his head as Merry pulled apart little pellets from the center, rolled them around and around in her hand instead of just taking a bite of the bread and eating it.

"You know something, Merry?" Joe Sender would say. "When I was a little boy a long, long, long time ago, your mother and I lived in the same town for one year. She was just as old as you are now, maybe a little bit older. For one year"—he held up one fat, floury finger—"she came and stayed in our house and slept in the same bed with my sisters. How do you like that?"

"In Russia!" Merry would say, swinging her legs against the counter. "*Kleb!*" Because *kleb* was the Russian word for bread, and sometimes when her grandfather came around, he would stick his head into Sender's store and for the fraction of a second that the door was open, manage to call out contemptuously, "*Ah! Der klebnik!*"

"*Kleb!*" Sender said, laughing, his face red from the heat as he rushed out fat brown loaves on a heavy tray. "I give you fresh warm delicious *kleb* straight from the oven, but do you eat it, little one? Do you eat it? What you want is cookies." But Sender's bakery did not have cookies; he baked only bread, *kleb*. In fact, Sender himself looked like this word *kleb*: round, doughy, almost always flour-stained. The smell and look of yeasty bread rising and baking and the bakery's small, bare indoor warmth were forever confused in Merry's mind with the word *kleb* and the person Sender. Also, his wife, Merry decided, looked like honey cake.

"And then," Merry said in the singsong of a child repeating an often heard story, "and then she ran out of your house into the street and ran and ran and ran, far, far away from all the soldiers."

"Who? Your mother? Where she ran was in *her* town. That's why her mother sent her to stay with us. Where we lived, we didn't have any soldiers. Anyway, we didn't see them."

"How did the soldiers look?"

"How do I know, little one? I just told you—we didn't see them."

"On horses!" Merry screamed. "You *know* about the horses, that's why she couldn't run fast enough."

"The *whole* story, Merry? Again the whole story? So you can tell it to me backwards again? . . . Here: When your mother was a little girl in Europe, the town where she was living all of a sudden had two armies. Two different armies, and they were supposed to shoot just at each other, soldiers with soldiers. But people in the town worried because they used to hear the shooting, so all the mothers told all the children not to run around anymore and just stick close to the house. But your mother was then only a very little girl, she didn't even go to school yet—in fact, she first went to school a little when she stayed with us—and probably she was just used to running around when she felt like it. Anyway, one day she went out in the afternoon, and for hours after, her mother waited for her but she didn't come back and didn't come back and then, when it was already dark, somebody—a neighbor, I don't know who—came running to their house with a terrible story. They said that they saw your mother playing and running near the soldiers' horses, all of a sudden there was a shot, and they didn't see your mother anymore. Well, as

43

it turned out, about five minutes later she walked right into the house, and there she was—perfectly fine. But that's when her mother decided it would be better for her to go stay with us in Minsk, where it was safer. And that's how I first saw your mother—very little, very skinny, just like you."

"With *tzepelach*," Merry said, clutching at her own braids and completing the ritual. "Just like mine."

Ez Slavin said, "Sender! Of course! How could I forget? Joe Sender, the Mighty Fist of Judah!" He laughed, but that was when he had liked Joe Sender—not when he was a baker, but in his youth, when he had been or tried to be a boxer, wearing as his special trademark blue shorts emblazoned with a huge gold Star of David, inside which there was embroidered, also in gold, a poised, muscled boxer's fist. This same symbol had also decorated the robe he wore into the ring, which was striped and multicolored: Joseph's coat of many colors. In this outfit Sender had once gotten as far as Montreal, the city of his single spectacular triumph, so that when he came back, he immediately had leaflets printed up in English and Yiddish, saying: "Joe Sender, the Mighty Fist of Judah. HE TOOK CANADA BY STORM."

"Cheap! *Prust!*" was supposed to have been Pearl Milgram's reaction to this, according to Ez, and she had turned up her nose at what in anyone else's family she would have been the first to recognize as poignant, a poor boy's dreaming ambition. But that wasn't why Ez liked it. What had appealed to him was what he called its noisiness: that in those days Joe Sender had been a real wild man—wild, impatient, clamorous and, yes, vulgar. Absolutely vulgar. Was that what Pearl, with her European *gymnasium* snobbery, objected to? Was it? Because he, Ez Slavin, American, celebrated that vulgarity, that noise. And as much as he abhorred brutality, he had loved hanging around the boxers' gym on Hester Street where Joe—and this was years and years before he had met Pearl—used to practice. The noise, the smells, the energy!

"And do you think there's only one kind of energy? He's an ignorant man, Ez, from an ignorant family. They lived among peasants and became no better. I saw it even as a child. Do you know what they hung over their cradle? A hand, to ward off the evil eye! My mother was horrified." And Pearl had shrugged in horror herself at these crude peasant superstitions, always regarding this branch of her family as practically Kallikaks. Which was exactly the conclusion that Ez came to when Joe Sender, no longer a boxer but a baker, had moved with his wife and two daughters to a two-family house in Far Rockaway.

"Ah! The landlord!" Ez Slavin always said of this venture, in exactly the same tone in which his father had once said, *"Der klebnik,"* but he never stopped Merry from visiting them, and her own first memory of that house had to do with the tenants.

"Shh!" said Sender's teen-age daughters, Rozzie and Vivian, whenever they walked through that part of the downstairs hallway that belonged to the tenants. "Make believe you don't have shoes on. She gets headaches."

"I get headaches too," Merry whispered. "It's from when you stay in the sun too long and throw up"—a matter very much on her mind among the Far Rockaway beach-loving Senders.

"That's not why *she* gets them," whispered back Rozzie, who already wanted to be called Shoshana, and she pointed to the spot on her own arm where the tenant's wife had a number. Because the tenants were refugees, when you went to knock on her door you had to listen very carefully to make sure she was not crying. Of course, Merry never really wanted to knock on that door, but the tenant's wife, from her dark, narrow downstairs apartment, sold blouses, so that in those years, each time she went to Far Rockaway, someone in the Sender family, often the Mighty Fist's wife, Dora, would put three dollars in her hand and tell her to go down and buy a blouse.

"Don't be afraid. She *likes* you, she likes children," said

Dora, who stood against the sink, busy, comfortable and plump in a flowered housedress. Oh, the order of that house! It was always hot, it was always Sunday. Dora chopped celery, onions and green pepper: tuna fish for lunch. "Vivi, put down the book and slice me some cucumbers. And what else does the little one like? Tomatoes—the little Italian plum tomatoes." What else would be on that table? Corn bread, rye bread and onion rolls from Sender's bakery; pot cheese, cream cheese and muenster cheese from the butter-and-egg store next door; a bowl of radishes for Sender—he loved them scooped up with some salt and a little butter, it was the way he had eaten them in Europe as a child—and for Rozzie-Shoshana a dish of crinkled, briny olives and one of her own homemade yogurt, *leben*. They were both foods she did not actually like but was trying to accustom herself to for the new life she was planning on in Israel, then just born. She closed her eyes, popped the shrunken, mottled olives in her mouth, and with a shivery half smile, tasted the salty excitement of coming deprivation.

"Go ahead! Just knock on her door and don't worry." Dora nudged Merry in the direction of the stairs. "You'll see! She'll give you Kool-Aid."

But Gitta's Kool-Aid was no attraction; it was not even cold. She would mix it up at the last minute, as soon as she saw Merry at the door, and for Gitta—so skinny, big-eyed and nervous—even this stirring up an envelope of Kool-Aid seemed to be a big project. Barefoot, she swayed and stumbled around her dark little kitchen, stopping frequently, the confused slowness—it was not languor—contrasting so oddly with the terrible thinness of her face and body and the tight, jerky gestures of her hands. Sometimes a very long black hair from her ponytail would get floated in with the sticky, sugar-grained warm red Kool-Aid. Almost always she had the rumpled, unfocused look of someone who had been sleeping, not, as Rozzie and Vivian had warned, crying. And in fact, only once did Merry see Gitta cry: it was when she had just decided to sell nightgowns as well as blouses, and going to the closet to take out all her plastic-encased merchandise, suddenly couldn't find them. She untied bundle after bundle of grayish plastic, her fingers becoming so shaky that she could no longer retie the narrow strings. "I want only to *show* them," she kept repeating. "Only to show."

"It's okay," Merry said. "I don't want any nightgowns, I just want a blouse." But it was too late: Gitta, with one hand pressed against her eyes and forehead, had begun crying hysterically. Merry threw down her three dollars, grabbed up a sleeveless blouse—yellow, terrible for her sallow skin—and calling out, "Good-by, Gitta," ran up the stairs.

"Already? So quick?" Dora said. "Didn't she read you a story? You know how she loves to read children stories, it helps her with her English. You should see how she's always begging the kids around here!"

And that was the worst of all: sitting next to Gitta on her lumpy living room sofa bed, always sticky, giving off the feeling of days that were perpetually damp and muggy. In the close, nearly airless downstairs room, the smell of Gitta's perspiration was overwhelming, and whenever she turned pages, the blue number on her arm stood out in the air like ugly jewelry. She read Merry the story of Rapunzel: In a little town somewhere in Europe, a woman who for years had wanted only one thing, a baby daughter, knew one day that all her wishing had finally done her some good. Everything would have been perfect, except that she had a bad habit of looking out her window, staring straight into a garden that belonged to a witch. And in this witch's garden there grew a certain vegetable, rampion, which the woman got so hungry for—she remembered how she used to love it scooped up with butter and dipped in a little salt—that she cried to her husband if she couldn't have some she would die. Her husband went out and stole her some rampion, and from that minute on not one good thing happened. Since the witch was after all a witch, there was no way you could expect her to be nice about it. She said, Okay, I'll let you have my rampion as long as you let *me* have your baby daughter. How could they have agreed? Why didn't they just take the rampion and move? Were there soldiers in the way? Horses? Who would want to keep on living next door to a witch? And how much did that woman really want a baby daughter in the first place? Gitta wanted a baby daughter. Once, in Europe, she had had one, said Rozzie-Shoshana, but it died, was killed, and now Gitta so much worried that she would never have another one that she kept hugging and touching any little kids she could get her hands on with her long, thin, bony witchy arms, trying to trap them into her tiny dark apartment with awful stories and sickening Kool-Aid. Meanwhile stupid Rapunzel grew up thinking the witch was her mother, never once wondering who else had once had two long braids down her back—for sure, the witch didn't—or why she had to live locked up all by herself on the top floor of a castle in one room. She just stood there on a chair by the window, singing all the songs she knew, and before she knew what was happening, the witch cut off her braids and fixed things so that Rapunzel's happy ending was getting married to a prince who was blind. Happy-ending Rapunzel and the happy-ending prince wandered around the forest looking for berries, which was exactly what Gitta and her husband had once had to do when they were first hiding in a cave. Gitta's story did not have a happy ending. The smell of the cave remained with her: that awful, sour perspiration which ran down her arms and onto Merry's clothes, especially by the end of the story, when Gitta hugged her closer. Why did Rapunzel's mother get so hungry for rampion that she forgot about everything else? How could she have forgotten all the other, terrible things the witch was famous for? This story of Rapunzel and her mother gave Merry such nightmares that she paid no attention to the look

Dora exchanged with her daughters and said, "I only like *Isobel* to read to me."

And this had always been true: on all those weekend days when Ez, invariably late, would come to pick her up at his mother's, small Merry with her long, dark *tzepelach* would be waiting with the special Isobel book.

"Are we going to your house? Can we go see Isobel?"

"Not now, cookie," Ez said. "Isobel's working."

"Working!" Ez's mother laughed. "*Oich mir* a worker! Is she cleaning the house? Sweeping up cigarette ashes? . . . Listen here a minute, Ezra. Celia was here. With Jonathan. They brought him."

"They? *They?*" Ez repeated magisterially.

"Leo waited downstairs, he came up only a few minutes."

"Ah, a busy man, Leo Spivak," said Ez of the man to whom he had given up his right of fatherhood, and with whom since that time his sole exchange had been, "A lot of roofs caving in, Leo? A good time for roofers? Busy? Busy?" "And what would you know?" Leo, a short, red-faced, blustery man, had answered him. "You, who never worked a day in your life!" But Celia Spivak was Pearl Milgram's sister, and Jonathan, that strange, squinty, scowling boy, Merry's brother, though she did not know it at the time.

"This is how Jonathan talks," Merry giggled. "I d-d-d-don't w-w-want a-a-any c-c-c-coffee candies."

"*She* laughs." Merry's grandmother shrugged. But the Spivaks had laughed at Merry. First Celia had pushed her fat, soggy face into Merry's small one, and turning her all the way around as if she were about to play pin the tail on the donkey, pinching and pulling Merry's clothes and shoulders, she finally turned her face away in disgust, saying, "Ucch! So thin! Couldn't you ever make her some oatmeal?"

"I don't *like* oatmeal," Merry said, and pointing to the candy dish on the table next to Jonathan, "I like *raspberry* candies."

49

"You like! You like! What's the difference what you like?" Celia screamed. "A tiny little *pischerkeh* like that and she already thinks she can go around liking!"

"Celia," Leo said, suddenly rousing himself from his newspaper and cocking his head in Merry's direction. "Listen how she speaks English." He smiled slyly. "*What* kind of candies do you like, Merry?"

"Raspberry candies," Merry said. "The round red ones." Except, of course, what she said was "Rrhezberrhy" and "rrhound" and "rrhed."

"Did you hear? Did you hear?" Leo had gotten so excited that he stood up, and pointing to the oilcloth with his newspaper, said, "What color is the floor?"

"Gray," Merry answered, but was saying, "Grrhay."

"And the curtain? The curtain? Look at the window and tell me what color is the curtain?"

"Green," said Merry, but it came out "Grrhin."

"Grrhin. You said it, girlie! Exactly like a *grinneh!* Some big shot, that Slavin! Big shot American, big shot writer, and his own daughter talks an English like someone just off the boat!"

"You're surprised?" Merry's grandmother said. "Who do you *think* she takes after? What was her mother?"

Isobel read the story about the two children who lived on a farm. She always wore her pretty opal earrings, she always read in a calm voice. It was the book Merry brought her every time: the two children got up very early in the morning, they ran out to help their father milk the cows, they stroked the coat of the woolly lamb, they fed grains of corn to the clucking chickens and a lick of sugar to the baby horse. In the hot afternoon, while the animals grazed and drowsed, the two children sat on the steps of the shady porch and nibbled on pieces of bread with maple syrup that they had tapped from their own trees in the springtime. Their mother was baking apple pies in the kitchen, and when the pies were done, she set them out on the window sill to cool. They smelled the pies even though they knew they could not eat them till much later, and watched them to make sure a tramp did not come by. Their mother called to them as she passed them a pitcher of lemonade from inside the cool kitchen. She always smiled and wore the same flowered apron.

"Why do you always ask Isobel to read you *that* book?" Ez called out irritably. It was evening, they were already in the subway on their way back downtown. Merry was ducking under the turnstile, but Ez, yards ahead of her, was pacing back and forth along the platform, staring and scowling at billboards and candy machines. "It's a terrible book, cookie. A tramp stealing apple pies! I don't know why you like it."

"Isobel lived on a farm like that," Merry said. "When *she* was a little girl."

On the uptown side, an express train was rushing by. Merry put her hands over her ears, but could still hear her father say, "She did *not* live on a farm. Isobel never told you that! She lived *near* where there were many farms. And she knows a lot about farm life. . . . If *that's* what you like, you should ask her to tell you some true stories."

True stories? In the train, Merry let go of her father's hand—he always leaned against the dangerous doors, which sometimes just jerked out and opened—and grabbing onto a pole instead, told herself this true story: When Isobel was a little girl, she ran away to a farm nearby because she wanted to see the horses. But she was too little to ride them, so the two children who lived on the farm said, "Here. Why don't you give them some sugar?" Then they all ate bread with maple syrup while they sat on the porch and watched the cows and the lambs. Just then the farmer's wife, who was the two children's mother, came out of the kitchen with her flowered apron. She smiled at Isobel and said, "Don't worry. There aren't any tramps coming. Why don't you stay with us and eat some apple pie? You have very cute braids."

51

Outside, the streets were now as dark as the subway. Ez said, "Have we got everything? Is this it? Just your sweater and the book?"

Merry said, "When Isobel was a little girl, she had two long braids down her back just like me. She *told* me. She combed my hair and she told me."

"I think I better get you something to eat, Merry," Ez said. They were now so close to his mother's house that they had reached the knish stand which was just on the corner. "Come on, I'll get you a knish. It's very late, your grandmother'll ask if you had supper."

"I wish Isobel was my mother," Merry said, and running up the four flights of stairs to her grandmother's house, immediately threw up.

could she be prey to it? There she was: so possessed by order, routine, by *things*, that these things of her mind took on the power of the primitive! Although that wasn't fair. Because he respected the primitive, the *true* primitive. Greatly respected it. In fact, that was probably what had originally drawn him to Pearl Milgram. He had sensed it in her immediately—never mind the facade, never mind the education—that girl was a true *shtetl* primitive! And this was how Ez would go on from the bedroom in the middle of the night, while Isobel, like a wraith in an old terry-cloth bathrobe, would be wandering through the house, pacing from room to room, opening drawers, closets, the medicine chest, touching things, taking them out and replacing them. With her hand clenched over her mouth, always her gesture of worry, she would stand over her packed but still opened suitcase, and finally, smoking one cigarette after another, in the glare of a streetlight, just look out the window.

Did she do this still? In another life, another continent? Merry imagined her as she had been the night before in her apartment in Milan. The building was supposed to be on the top of a hill, so that even though it was the middle of the night, somewhere in the streets below or perhaps in a far-off valley, there was the unruly winking of tiny pinpoint lights and the still, ghostly presence of a golden-ocher church cupola. All these sights which had once been strange to Isobel were now precisely what was familiar and dear to her, just like espresso. Wearing a pale-colored flowing and expensive negligee (*Isobel? expensive? negligee?*), she stood staring through the tall Renaissance window, now simply her living room window and not a century's, and with her hand clenched over her mouth, shivered in the night air. "*Ma che cosa c'è, tesoro?*" This was Enzo, who had been wakened by Isobel's pacing and closet-opening, and was now astonished at the look of desolation on her face. He lit a cigarette for her, and in the brief flare of the light, his resemblance to the actor Raf

Vallone was remarkable. *"Non so,"* said Isobel miserably, and she shrugged in the style of disaffected Italian actresses made famous by the films of Fellini and Antonioni. *Ho perduto . . . Ho dimenticato . . Davvero, in fine, non so. . . ."* And then, just as the faint strains of melody recalling some foreigner's bittersweet childhood could be heard echo-like in the empty, but not soulless, night streets, she turned to Enzo with a look of confused and vulnerable vacancy that had absolutely nothing to do with the real Isobel.

In the meantime, the real Isobel, wearing her glasses and looking absolutely drained, sat on the couch, her stockinged feet tucked under her; she was leaning forward, her shoulders hunched as if she were cold, though she was drinking brandy and had draped around her an overbright red mohair shawl. Me, me, me, Merry thought: that's who that shawl would look good on, it's only overbright for her because she's so fair-skinned that any bright color always looks harsh—but on *me!* Merry stopped herself. What was the point? Isobel did what she could, gave what she could; you couldn't expect her to turn into someone she wasn't. Nor was it fair to call her—Ez's favorite accusation—the ice mother. This particular description was one he fastened on the first year Merry came to live with them. Already at her grandmother's, she had been prone to bouts of throwing up that were followed by violent headaches. What if Isobel doesn't know what to do for me when I throw up? Merry had worried then, praying that it would never happen. But because it did, there was Isobel, woken up in the middle of the night, standing at the bathroom door, watching.

"Merry, what did your grandmother do when you got sick like this?"

"She gives me a wet washcloth," Merry had told her, "but you have to keep on getting it cold again." But her grandmother had stood over the sink with her, pressing the wet washcloth to her forehead. Disappearing from the room,

Isobel had come back with a much more practical solution: an ice bag. You filled it up with ice once, and there you were. She said, "Much better, don't you think?" and in fact, Merry had become used to it very quickly. But, "An *ice bag!*" Ez had stormed the next day. "An ice bag! How can you give a *child* an ice bag? Isn't it bad enough that she learned throwing up from my mother? Is ice all she'll ever learn from you?" But who was he to criticize? He never even got out of bed himself.

Aloud, now, Merry said bitterly, "He didn't even *die* decently. . . . My God, Isobel, I'm an orphan!"

Isobel took off her glasses, and rubbing her eyes, reached for another cigarette. The pack in front of her was empty, but already—and Isobel had been in the house barely an hour—there was an unlit cigarette neatly propped on an unused ashtray. Oh, Isobel! The same rituals, the same old habits: she had always hated the fumbling involved in opening a new cigarette pack, the awkwardness of digging out the first cigarette, so what she did instead was open new cigarette packs at her leisure, take out the first cigarette and put it in an empty ashtray. Single unlit cigarettes would sit in ashtrays all over the house, resembling some out-of-place piece in a mysterious still life—a glass filled but barely drunk from, a table laid, with no sign of why the guests had unexpectedly been forced to leave. It had the look of an intimation of disaster, but was merely one of Isobel's rituals of order, and Ez hated it. "Constipation!" he snorted. "And that's exactly how the dinosaurs died out! They *died* of constipation." Well, this was true, but only indirectly, and only according to one theory—that a climactic change had caused the death of vegetation which had been the dinosaurs' roughage. It was a typical Ez Slavin charge.

"Forgive yourself your neuroses," Isobel wrote in her letters to Merry, and unquestionably meant it; she had certainly forgiven herself her own—and so what? Did it make her life easier? Maybe. She was still afraid of flying, so she rarely took planes. She was still made anxious by disorder and the disorientation of certain kinds of change, so she arranged to minimize it. She did not like vacations, so she didn't take them. And she had come to realize that she had no taste for the unrelenting high drama of constant argument and emotional accusation, so she married Enzo—very handsome Enzo, true, but what she had once said to Merry was: "If what you want is marriage, you're looking in the wrong direction. Marriage is *not* for romantic excitement. It's to give you some domestic peace so you can get your work done." And this was the marriage about which Ez had said, "Ah, Isobel! The chilly child of the North drawn irresistibly to the passion of the South." And also: "Typical Isobel! Too much Henry James."

Make peace with who you are is what Isobel meant when she wrote, "Forgive yourself your neuroses." And also: There is no point in struggling against the grain of your own nature.

"Every American generation always orphans *itself*, Merry. Surely you know *that*," Isobel now said, and they both laughed because it was exactly the kind of answer Ez would have given. Laugh, Isobel, laugh, Merry thought; you *did* orphan yourself, and so did he, you both *decided* to—and it's like deciding to be poor when you don't have to be. But are you really never sorry? Are you never even curious?

Almost as if Merry had said this aloud, Isobel pulled out some papers from her purse, stationery marked "Alitalia": on the plane she had begun making notes, jotting things down for a eulogy, for the memorial meeting. Think of Isobel on that plane: in a numb and icy panic, darting occasional shuddery glances out the window at the endless clouds, worrying about her luggage, about changing money, trying to read and failing, paging through an address book and thinking suddenly that it was the wrong one, rummaging frantically for her sunglasses or her cigarettes, and feeling, in her awkwardness, the pressure of other people's eyes and genuinely puzzled expressions: *Ma che cosa c'è, signora?* Do you see? There—

the American woman is distressed. My God, I am making a spectacle of myself, thought restrained and disciplined Isobel, even though she had forgiven herself her neuroses. Because the other passengers were playing bridge, chatting or drowsing, and the stewardesses, the stewardesses had the childlike, easy pleasure in their own appearances that had so amazed Isobel when she first saw it in the faces of Italian women seated around her at a beauty parlor. So much had it amazed her, in fact, that she had written a story ("La Bellezza") about an American girl, an art history student traveling in Italy, who becomes so obsessed with trying to achieve this look—the ease, the complacency—that she spends part of every day in a different Italian beauty parlor and part in a museum or gallery as she is supposed to. Finally, she is unable to look at or write about paintings without thinking about changing the various Madonnas' hair styles, and has had her own hair done, cut and bleached so many times that she is barely recognized by her family and her fiancé, who have come to meet her plane. The story was full of staring: staring into mirrors, staring at paintings, staring at faces, expressions and gestures—all in the heat, all in an eerily dazed and hypnotic pull into senselessness. It was a creepy and morbid story, and in this way not characteristic of Isobel.

So there was Isobel sitting in that Alitalia plane, hurtling through the sky from one part of her life to another, so fidgety with her lighter and her glasses that she was suddenly reminded of her grandmother sitting in a disliked neighbor's parlor, caught stranded without her knitting. I must *do* something, Isobel thought, I must put my mind to some use. So she caught the attention of a passing stewardess and in her accented but excellent Italian asked for some paper. This was the paper she now showed to Merry: mostly it was jottings, notes, not really legible—and certainly not Isobel's famous perfect sentences, or what Ez had sneeringly called her "fine writing," but by the time she got to the third page, what had come to her mind was the Welsh inscription on the grave-stones of all her family: "Out of the mud and scum of things, always, always something sings."

On the very humid August night in 1939 when Isobel first met Ez Slavin, she had walked into the party late, so that from all the way down the hall, singing was the first thing she heard.

> "*Viva la quinta brigada!*
> *Rumba—la—rumba—la—rumba—la!*
> *Viva la quinta brigada!*
> *Rumba—la—rumba—la—rumba—la!*
>
> *No tenemos ni aviones*
> *Ni tanques, ni canones*
> *Ai, Manuela!*
>
> *No tenemos ni aviones*
> *Ni tanques, ni canones*
> *Ai, Manuela!*"

"You're not singing," said a man who was striking a match as he leaned back against the high sill of a completely opened window. "You won't sing because you refuse to let the agony of Spain become the casual night music of Manhattan."

"No!" said Isobel, jumping in astonishment that he was speaking to her, uneasy anyway in the noisy, smoky crowd which she had just entered, and high from the gin she and Charlotte had been drinking to give them both the courage to walk into this party.

"Well, then you won't sing *that* song because you cannot forgive what the Fifth Brigade did to the anarchists."

"No," Isobel said again, and thought: He's making fun of me because he can see what a hick I am. I should never have come; I should never have let Charlotte convince me. But because he continued to stare out at her directly, half smiling from his perch on the sill, she said, "It's the dampness, that's

59

why your matches won't light. It's too humid." And getting braver now, smiling back at him, "*You* weren't singing either."

"I *am* an anarchist," said Ez Slavin, changing his tone and standing up suddenly. "And I will *not* sing the song of a Communist brigade," and scooping up his cigarettes and matches, he walked away.

Tears welled up in Isobel's eyes and the color rose in her cheeks; from behind her, a man practically yelled in her ear, "It's tactics! I told him and I'm finished telling him—tactics, plain and simple! If he can't even give Russia that much credit, then let him . . ."

Isobel pressed her hands over her ears, hoping it would only look as if she were trying to fix her hair or her earrings. It was a gesture about which Ez would often say in later years, "Ah *hah!* Someone is taking up space in the privacy of Isobel's head—and they're not paying rent!"

> No tenemos ni aviones
> Ni tanques, ni canones
> Ai, Manuela!

"Isobel!" Charlotte whispered excitedly, her beads and spidery Mexican necklaces clanking as she made her way over and grabbed Isobel's arm. "What did he *say* to you? What were you talking about? Don't tell me you don't know who he is! Ez Slavin! *Outlaws and Citizens!*"

"I *thought* he looked familiar," Isobel said. "But at times like this I begin to think they *all* look familiar." And thought: Oh, my God! She'll think I've said something anti-Semitic.

"Familiar!" Charlotte's eyes grew very wide, approaching the popping stage. "He's brilliant, Isobel. How can you be so blasé? Ez Slavin's a genius!"

"Some genius!" said a smallish, short-haired girl, who was so badly sunburned it was apparent even in the ill-lit loft. She picked at her peeling skin, saying in a careless, sour singsong,

"The Party wouldn't touch him and I happen to know he was interested."

Isobel said, "He just told *me* he was an Anarchist."

The girl shrugged. "Did he tell you he was married?"

"*Was?*" Charlotte demanded in her deepest, most commanding British-actress tones. "Or *is?*"

"Is," the sunburned girl answered emphatically as she called out and waved to someone all the way across the room. "And to the absolute *worst* social Fascist reactionary. I happen to know that when the Revolution comes, Pearl Milgram will be one of the first to go! 'Strung up' is what this person said."

"Pearl Milgram?" Isobel said. "She's written some very good essays."

The sunburned girl looked at Isobel pityingly and said, "He *only* talked to you because you're pretty and you're from out of town. You *are* from out of town, aren't you?"

"*I* think," said Charlotte, once again drawing herself up to the presumed stage splendor of Sybil Thorndike, "that it is *extremely* bourgeois to be concerned about whether or not a man is married. Isobel and I are *artists*."

But the sunburned girl had walked away, and Isobel said, "Oh, it doesn't matter, Charlotte. He didn't *really* talk to me anyway. And he certainly wasn't very nice."

"Nice!" Charlotte glared at Isobel. "Nice! *Now* who's being bourgeois?"

Not Isobel. Oh, surely not Isobel, who had come to New York from Spring Green, Wisconsin, and had spent all her adolescent years dreaming about the triumphant day when she would live in what she then called "Green-wich" Village.

> We were very tired, we were very merry—
> We had gone back and forth all night on the ferry.
> It was bare and bright, and smelled like a stable—
> But we looked into a fire, we leaned across a table,

> We lay on a hill-top underneath the moon;
> And the whistles kept blowing, and the dawn came soon.

"What *you* should do, Isobel," Charlotte said, "is send him one of your stories. After all, you've read *his* book. It's only a courtesy. Send him something of yours."

"I haven't actually read his book," Isobel said stonily. She was tired of being bullied by Charlotte, tired of being instructed how to dress—peasant blouses and shawls were one thing, but Isobel could not, *not* wear the jewelry—tired even of the oddly angled Barrow Street apartment which, with its batik hangings, India throws and partly rounded windows, had at first seemed so exactly what Isobel imagined of New York that its perfection made it practically Paris. But it was not perfect. It was small and sloppy, *Charlotte* was sloppy; Isobel had no privacy, there was no door she could close when she wanted to work except finally, in frustration, the front door—something she found herself doing more and more often. Slamming the rickety downstairs door, clearly the door of a firetrap (why had this not been clear before?), she walked and walked through the streets of New York, the *unyielding* streets of New York, till her legs and head grew drained and dazed with the simple and familiar sweetness of physical fatigue.

> We were very tired, we were very merry—
> We had gone back and forth all night on the ferry.
> And you ate an apple, and I ate a pear,
> From a dozen of each we had bought somewhere;
> And the sky went wan, and the wind came cold,
> And the sun rose dripping, a bucketful of gold.

Why was it not like that? How could it continue to elude her so? For even though Isobel did this almost every day—walked all through the Village, and then uptown, first west, then east, so that the hectic order of streets and stores, parks and buildings, were no longer at all strange to her—on the whole, she knew where she was going; still, the real life of the city seemed entirely closed to her, she was locked out. The purposefulness of people's strides, for example, or the chaotic quickness of ordinary speech: it was not that she found New Yorkers unfriendly exactly, or even unhelpful; it was not that. But they seemed oddly, perpetually, uncontrollably *busy* in a way that she could not connect with any sense of purpose or hopefulness inside herself. Buying a peach at an outdoor fruit stand in the high heat of lunchtime or slowly circling around the graceful stone and city greenness of Gramercy Park in the changing light of late afternoon, Isobel was overwhelmed by loneliness and it shocked her. What had her loneliness been about all her life if not that she belonged elsewhere? And here she was—in the very particular else-where she had always had in mind—and again, *again* she did not belong?

> We were very tired, we were very merry,
> We had gone back and forth all night on the ferry.
> We hailed, "Good-morrow, mother!" to a shawl-covered head,
> And bought a morning paper, which neither of us read;
> And she wept, "God bless you!" for the apples and pears,
> And we gave her all our money but our subway fares.

"You don't *look* well, Isobel," Charlotte now said. "What's the matter?"

The excitable-voiced man in back of them once again erupted into Isobel's ear like a machine gun. "So what? So what? I *did* say it—it's tactics, it's realism. And what's wrong with that?"

"I think I'll just find some water," Isobel said, and pushing her way out of the vast, noisy room, was suddenly in a darkish, narrow passageway that led to nothing but a peculiar, makeshift, bamboo-shaded closet. It was not exactly a closet, however, but was apparently intended as a room divider, because behind the uncovered rack of clothes and an overhead shelf that held items as various as towels, a hot-water bottle and an umbrella was an alcove containing the rudiments of a kitchen. And there in the light of a gooseneck office lamp, which was placed precariously on the edge of a chair, a tall, dark-haired woman bent over the sink; she was bathing a baby. The sleeves of her peasant blouse were pushed up, and as she moved and bent over, her hair kept slipping out of a low bun. Her cheeks—high cheekbones in an oval face—were pink, flushed, from the hot water, from her effort, and her eyes had the faintly Asiatic cast common to Russian-Jewish faces of the Slavic mold, but this was a look not yet familiar to Isobel, so it seemed purely exotic. And all this, all this, while the unshaded lamp cast its shaky shadow round, white and traveling as a full moon glimpsed from a train, and the smell of soap and soapy water rose and floated. Isobel, behind the bamboo shade, stood staring, hypnotized: she had come upon this scene like a child in a fairy tale wandering into the secret room of a castle. In just this same dreamlike way she had once watched, through a screened porch, a girl doing rosemahling: with her head bent in concentration, the girl's long blond hair fell onto the blond wood board as she worked, and as she slowly filled in the pattern of colors, it seemed a reflection of the rose-gold color in her face. I have let myself become so distracted, so carried away with agitation, Isobel thought, that I have forgotten the quiet of *things*. Which exists everywhere. Just then, there was a slightly louder splash from the sink, the baby cried out, and the woman began screaming piercingly, uncontrollably, "Oh, my God, Al! I don't know what happened—I was holding him, he just slipped. Al, the baby's *head* is bleeding! He'll bleed to death! Oh, my God!"

Isobel, the closest, rushed in. There was blood all over the sink; the woman, entirely white-faced, cradled the wet, screaming child against her. Her eyes were wild; the blood from the baby's head had already soaked through her blouse, and as it ran down her arms, she kept shrieking brokenly,

"Oh, my God, he's bleeding to death. My baby is *bleeding* to death!" She is hysterical, Isobel thought in recoil, but grabbed a towel, and pressing it firmly against the baby's head, shouted into the woman's face, "He will *not* bleed to death. The skin has been broken and *that's* why he's bleeding."

"But his *head!* My baby's *head!*"

"Yes," Isobel said very sharply, and felt that her own voice was slapping at the woman, in distaste. "Head accidents are always very bloody. You just have to stem the flow of blood."

A slight, mustachioed man darted in, saying, "Take it easy, Selma. Take it easy. We'll get him to a doctor, he'll be all right."

From the crowd behind him, the sunburned girl called out, "A doctor! You'll never get a doctor on Sunday at *this* hour. You better go to the hospital. It's not that far to Bellevue."

"Bellevue!" Selma moaned. "I'm not taking my *baby* to Bellevue. Where's Dave Roizman? *He's* a doctor."

Al said, "He's not here, honey. Take it easy." He turned around uneasily, saying, "Is there anyone who can drive us? Or get us a cab and we'd come right down?"

"I'm not *going* to Bellevue!" Selma cried out desperately, and her sudden shrill pitch seemed to stimulate the baby all over again; his tiny body twisted with agonized shrieking, and his face grew redder and more distorted. "Oh, Elliot, Elliot!" Selma wept over him, sobbing as if the child were actually dead. In the midst of all this weeping and shrieking stood Isobel, her hand pressing the towel on the baby's forehead. The lamp was still casting its erratic, moony shadow, but now sometimes it fell on Isobel's face and she could not free her hands to shield her eyes from the glare or her ears from the noise. She was caught in the chaotic center of what she had only minutes before been regarding as a framed and perfect vision of the serene and ordered wonder of all created things. "There's a hospital right on Sixteenth Street," Isobel said, thinking of the dark red brick building opposite a small park she had often passed by on her walks. "Beth Israel Hospital."

"Beth Israel! That's right! She's right!" Al said, and apparently noticing Isobel for the first time, gingerly put his own hand on the towel, releasing her.

"Beth Israel! It's *kosher!*" the sunburned girl practically hooted, as Isobel began edging her way out of the makeshift kitchen. "That's the only hospital my *mother* would go to!"

Isobel heard Selma cry out, "Oh my God, Al! My blouse! My blouse! Look at me! I'm drenched with *blood!*" Someone in the crowd nervously sang out, " 'The workers' flag is deepest red . . . .' " Charlotte, her eyes enormous, pounced on Isobel. "How did you know what to *do*, Isobel? How did you *know?*"

Embarrassed, Isobel shrugged. "Oh, my brothers . . . When they were little, they used to fall a whole lot. They were always climbing and falling. Especially near the creek, where it was so rocky."

"Crick?" said a man's voice behind her. "Crick? . . . And where are *you* from?" It was Ez Slavin; he was staring down at her with the same mocking, insolent smile.

"A very small town in southern Wisconsin and you wouldn't have heard of it," Isobel said crisply; this time she just wanted to get away from the party, leave.

"Oh, it's a very interesting, *unusual* little town," Charlotte rushed in, fluting. "They're all Welsh. And they had to escape for religious persecution—I mean, *from* religious persecution!"

Ez drummed on his cigarette pack and said, "Then your last name is Jones. Or was that your mother's maiden name?"

"My last name is Rees," Isobel said, laughing despite herself. "And my mother's maiden name was Griffith. But there *are* a lot of people in town named Jones. And I *am* related to some of them."

"Well, Miss Rees-Griffith, Miss Griffith-Rees . . ." Ez

nodded, approving, and then, stopping suddenly, said, "Wisconsin . . . Wisconsin . . ." He squinted and peered into the distance as if he were an explorer who had just come upon the place and was now attempting to name it. "Then how did you know the nearest hospital? How did you know it was Beth Israel?"

"I take walks," Isobel said. "And I read signs."

## Reading Signs: Toward a Lawless Future
### by Ezra B. Slavin

*"This idiosyncrasy of a nation is a sacred gift."*
—Theodore Parker

There is a new kind of madness afoot these days: people are talking back to their radios. "No!" they shout to these machines which have managed to gain in so short a time such a peculiar hold on our souls. "No! Impossible!" they shout, and it is *not* madness. Because daily the news from Europe is *so* bad, it is above all so *invasive*—a cacophonous, immoral symphony of war drums and countercharging bugles. We hear treachery in the minor mode and confusion and despair in every movement. So there is no gainsaying it: the news from Europe is *very* bad, but when has it ever been otherwise? October 1917? July 1789? If Europe, with its centuries of oligarchic oppression, had proven itself capable of providing us with "good" news, would we—a cataracted promise still in our eyes—be here? Any of us? After only 160 years, we are far too young for our memories to be so dim, and yet . . . and yet we seem to be behaving, in our discussions, both private and public, like an amnesiac nation. "We will take their wisdom joyfully," wrote that prescient Abolitionist minister Theodore Parker, "but not their authority, we know better; *and of their nonsense not a word.*" (My italics)

Not a word, said Parker in 1852, and here we are in 1939 talking about voluntarily embroiling ourselves in still another of Europe's endless convulsions by repealing the Neutrality Act. Did the

American government repeal the Neutrality Act for the valiance of Spain? The pathos of Czechoslovakia? Certainly not. Yet on whose behalf does it now wish to act? In whose hands is it now deemed safe, *necessary* to place weapons? In the hands of clerical Fascist Poland! And should our sympathy fail to be stirred by this peculiar plea, well, then, come the bankers, the steel magnates, the munitions-makers (for surely, *surely* their kind of war must be our kind of war)—well, then, they soberly adjure us: think of England, think of France, so long honorable, so long democratic. Honorable, liberty-loving England—what a wonderful proposition this would be to discuss with the Mahatma!

But do we have to go so far from home to remind ourselves that in all its dealings, Europe has always shown itself to be decadent and class-ridden in a way that specifically precludes the spirit of liberty which it was once our national—and natural—genius to seize upon? Seize upon, but in generations of misbegotten plunder, sadly betray. "Often enough have the mights of men been organized," Parker declared in his touching hopefulness, "but not the rights of man." And he goes on to tell the story of a European nobleman who became infuriated when a "Yankee stagedriver . . . uncivilly threw the nobleman's trunk to the top of the coach. 'I will complain of you to the government!'" this nobleman threatened. "'Tell the government to go to the devil!' was the symbolical reply."

Symbolical? That poor stagedriver would be a shuddering ghost on the highways of our bankrupt cities, coughing and choking in the dehumanized fumes of those engines of mindless acquisitive squalor and decay. So we have turned our backs on what he knew, building roads of dross and rubble he had never intended us or himself to travel on. But because the germ of his vision, his affirming spirit, lies somewhere buried within us ("Tell the government to go to the devil!"), it is in our hands now to make sure we are not led even further astray. For it seems obvious, inescapable that if we are to become involved in Europe's wars as if they were our own, we will be unable to avoid taking on Europe's characteristics: they will *become* our own. We know that a country at war becomes a rigid and repressive one; we have once trafficked with such authoritarianism in the World War, and could not again plead innocence. Our potential for lawlessness is our buried natural gift: "sacred," as Parker has it, because it was once our "great idea" to do away with the old-world authoritarian order of imposed, artificial law—imposed from without, from "above"—to create instead communities whose foundations are the rights which emerge and flow naturally from within. Clearly we have not succeeded—bloat and decay, bloat and decay. Even in the communities of small towns, even in the vast unruly West, where the real fruits of the promise have intermittently surfaced, the madness of money-making, Babbittry and iron conformity have crept through the trees and hills like poison gas. "We began our national career by setting all history at defiance," says Theodore Parker, ". . . and refused to be limited by the past. . . . Human history could not justify the Declaration of Independence and its large statement of the new idea: the nation went behind human history and appealed to human nature."

*Refused to be limited by the past!* Every time we have let ourselves be limited by the past, by that Europe whose rigid canons and disordered senses we left behind, we have willfully discarded all the best possibilities in ourselves. Now, in a sense, this is happening newly every time we turn on the radio. For now we know from direct radio broadcasts exactly what is happening, exactly how it feels to live in numberless European capitals—and this has fostered a spurious sense of identity. We have succumbed even further to the loss of ourselves. For we do *not* know—after all, there is no disembodied voice to tell us (must there be? have we so far slipped our moorings?)—what is happening and how it feels to live in the towns of our own country. We have lost touch with the real life of a farm community in the prairies, a mining town in the West, a fishing village on the New England coast, and even, yes, even with the streets and neighborhoods of our own cities. But it is disingenuous to find this last surprising. It is only natural that among us in the large cities, with their taut frenzy and human disconnection, the premise of our promise should have suffered its greatest stunting (after all, for how many years now have we, both readers and writers alike, been enlivened and embittered by what is essentially a European controversy, a European idea?).

Only recently, I was at a party in Manhattan where the hard truth of this observation was brought home to me. Almost all the guests were American, almost all the guests were New Yorkers; they could have and in fact did, with great vivacity and interest, discuss events taking place in Spain, in Russia, in Ethiopia, in Austria. They were all well intentioned, they were all well informed. Toward the end of the evening, however, there was a minor accident which made it necessary to take the hosts' child to the nearest hospital. In that great room full of people, people who knew and could speak knowledgeably of streets in Moscow and Madrid, parks in Paris and Vienna, there was nobody who could think of the name or location of the nearest hospital. Nobody but a surprising young guest only recently arrived in New York City from a small town in the Midwest. With the wholesome freshness of the country in her cheeks, and its hopeful innocence in her eyes, she alone, from a *community*— where perhaps neighbors still retain the dream, the memory of helping one another at harvest time—she alone was able to provide her new city neighbors with the name of a hospital only a few minutes away. When I asked her how she knew, she answered simply, "I read signs."

"They come murmuring little of the past, but moving in the brightness of their great idea. . . ." We must read signs, the signs all around us, for only in their premonitory light can we once again attempt that hope, that idea: our own and lawless future.

"Isobel! Isobel!" Charlotte breathily shouted over the phone. "Have you seen Ez Slavin's article? Do you know that you're—"

"Yes, I know," said Isobel coolly. She was sitting on the sofa bed of her new apartment, smaller but her own, and draped in a towel, was staring into a round mirror propped on the pillow beside her. She stared at the country freshness of her cheeks, the hopeful innocence of her eyes, and letting the towel drop, at all the rest of her body, to which she had never previously given so much thought. *Oh, I am a dangerous woman,* Isobel thought. It sang in her head, for it was to this new apartment that Ez Slavin came almost every night now: *Oh, I am a dangerous woman, I am living with a married man.*

# 5

WHEN the notorious Eleanor Boland Hughes was accused and acquitted of the murder of her husband, it *was* reported in the papers—Isobel had even seen a picture captioned DEB HEIRESS LEAVES COURTHOUSE—but Ez had simply missed the whole thing. This was not really surprising; during the months the case dragged on, these other things occurred: the Germans invaded Poland, the Neutrality Act—despite Ez's polemic—was repealed, in December the Russians invaded Finland, and finally, about two weeks before Eleanor's acquittal, the Germans invaded Norway. Still, because Ez had known nothing about it at all and was now on a train on his way to visit the woman, he said irritably to Herb Shestak, sitting opposite him, "What do you mean—*made an effort to hush it up?* Did you go to Miss Periwinkle's Academy too? Hush it up! Those bastards probably bought up every Goddamn judge and newspaper from Maine to California!"

Herb said, "It really *was* self-defense, Ez. There was never any question about that."

"Naturally! Naturally! Is there some *other* kind of defense people like that would know about?"

Haughtily, Bea said, "The Boland family did use its influence just to cut down the publicity a little. And I don't see how you can blame them."

"Tell it to the Scottsboro boys," Ez said, leaning back against Isobel, but he was no longer really interested. It was Bea who was responsible for this whole business in the first place: she and Eleanor had been classmates and then friends at Barnard College, where Bea, then Beatrice Kadish, had been a scholarship student living at home, and Eleanor Boland, just back from a finishing school in Switzerland, was a girl in rebellion against her family and looking for interests.

Bea said defensively, "She was *never* just some silly rich girl, Ez. I don't care *what* you think! In her family, it was absolutely expected that she'd go to Wellesley and she—well, she just refused!"

Ez said, "Ah, bravo! Bravo! What a spirit! Isobel, where are the apples?"

Isobel tore herself away from the train window—she was sitting on the seat facing backward, which increased her sensation of disembodied trance and private happiness: houses, trees and fields flew by in the chilly, pale painter's-green cloud of early spring. Pressing against Ez to reach into the bag of apples, she thought: But my happiness is *not* private, it's because of Ez. And then the smell of the apples, so high, winy and dreamlike, made her feel entirely separate all over again. It occurred to her to say, "Did you know that Chekhov always kept an overripe apple in his desk, for the smell, to start him working?" But this only drummed up her own anxiety: she had done next to nothing for too many weeks; she was in an erotic haze. It was just this erotic haze which had led Bea to remark the week before within Isobel's hearing, "A little fey, isn't she?"

Isobel was not at all fey. She understood that Bea looked at her with suspicion: if Isobel had gone after one married man, what was there to stop her from pouncing out at another; that the Shestaks, both, were uneasy about her coming along on this weekend but could not admit it to themselves—it would seem unworthy of their advanced opinions. She understood all this, but there was a wildness, a giddiness inside her and she didn't care.

"*You* know what I mean, Isobel," Bea now said. "For someone from Eleanor's background, that *showed* something. She's got a very determined streak."

Am I supposed to have some special understanding of Eleanor because she's not Jewish? Isobel wondered. Because she's a murderess and I'm an adulteress? Because it's something only women understand? Or is it because I'm a writer and presumed to have an understanding of anyone?

Isobel responded with the exact degree of remoteness she felt: she smiled and nodded as if she were a foreigner and exempt from conversation. What she wanted above all was to hold on to the trance of the train window. Besides, she had read the paper, she had heard Bea discuss it before. Eleanor Boland, always so independent and rebellious, had married, in her senior year, a Harvard divinity student—what Bea kept on calling "a young curate." Her parents were greatly relieved: David Hughes was acceptable in all ways. As it turned out, though, he was crazy—literally crazy: always silent and moody, he would disappear for days at a time and offer no explanation. But worse than that, he began having unpredictable violent rages, breaking furniture and striking out at Eleanor. Hours after, he would cry and plead for forgiveness. It was said that David Hughes was undergoing a faith crisis, but their friends could see it—Eleanor was always black and blue. This went on for months and still David refused to agree to a separation. Finally, Eleanor could stand it no longer, so one morning after David had finished his coffee and gone off for the day—or longer—she left a note and moved out, *snuck* out, she felt, really, not back to her parents' house, her old home of comfort and unease, but to her sister's. This was perfect because her sister and brother-in-law were in England for the month. It was not perfect because it meant she was there by herself and that much more vulnerable when, after about a week, David turned up at the door, begging to speak to her. She heard the whine in his voice but let him in anyway; they were going to be civilized. And so, in the late afternoon of a clear, chilly fall day, she served her husband, the young curate, tea from her sister's flowered Spode as they sat together in the large empty house in front of the fire. Civilized? This scene, revealed first in the tentative, affectless whisper of Eleanor's testimony, described again with the bald and lively relish for scandal of newspaper accounts, and told still again in the peculiarly awed, proprietary hush of Bea's voice, retained for Isobel the pure, ordered clarity of an English murder mystery: *in the late afternoon of a clear, chilly fall day, she served her husband, the young curate, tea from her sister's flowered Spode as they sat before the fire.* But it was not an English murder mystery; there was no arsenic in the teacup. Instead, David Hughes went berserk. Neighbors and a passing grocer's delivery boy heard raised voices, crashing china, heavy rumbling thuds, a scream, but there were no witnesses, only Eleanor's testimony. Enraged by her refusal to go home with him, David, she said, had knocked her down—something which she was now publicly forced to admit had happened before. But this time, as she lay gasping on the floor in front of the fire, that fire she had built to take the chill off the air, he suddenly lunged at her from behind: her husband was trying to strangle her. Eleanor reached out for something, anything—it was a poker—and struck David in the head. He did not die instantly, but it was at this moment, with the blood gushing out of his head and onto her sweater, actually her sister's sweater, that Eleanor let out the

75

was it? The Menominee? The ones he thought spoke some variant of Welsh?"

Herb Shestak suddenly took a hard look at Isobel—it was his sociological look—and nodding solemnly, said, "I didn't realize you had such an unusual background, Isobel."

Ez beamed again through the chilly, gray gloom of the train, and extending his hand toward Isobel like a stage magician who had just pulled a rabbit out of a hat, exclaimed, "Pockets of authenticity! You see that, Shestak? They *exist*. Of course, I'll grant you—it takes some looking, but when you find it, when you really *find* it, you've struck gold."

"I don't see why that's so much more authentic than Eleanor and the Bolands," Bea said huffily. "It's just a different *kind* of authenticity."

Herb said, "Ez didn't mean that, honey. He just meant—"

"I know what he meant and I don't care!" Bea turned her face away, and glaring at some total stranger on the other side of the aisle, muttered, "Poor Pearl! Even though she *does* have the most peculiar politics . . ."

Outside the train window now, Isobel saw two houses— small, tumble-down "grandmother" houses, their sides and fronts overgrown with Catawba vines. The huge, dark-green, heart-shaped leaves fell one upon the other till the houses themselves, as in a children's picture maze, were almost hidden. It was the green, dreaming peace of the countryside—familiar, rejected, but alluring like a sweet, magical poison draught. Outside these houses, in the summer, there would be hollyhocks: you could pick them, upend the petals, and in the high summer sun after lunch, make hollyhock dolls. Isobel pulled herself back from this pocket of authenticity—it was blind and foolish nostalgia—and said, "The Preacher Rees Ez is talking about was actually my great-uncle. My father was a schoolteacher."

"Farming, preaching and teaching," Ez said, still smiling and marveling. "That's all they believed in. Nothing else improves the moral condition of the community."

And that's why I left, Isobel thought, but did not say: suddenly it seemed too much of a betrayal.

"What's my favorite quote? 'Those contribute most to the community who give the best they can to those nearest them.' Is that right, Isobel? I wish we had that pamphlet with us!"

"What pamphlet? What pamphlet?" Herb asked. The idea that there was printed matter he had missed out on was making him jumpy.

Isobel said, "Oh, a cousin of mine wrote a kind of family history. He had it privately printed and sent one copy to each member of the family at Christmas."

"See that?" Ez said. "Stern but free." He raised his fist and nodded in approval. "That was her Christmas present. Dedicated to—what was it, Isobel? Christ, I wish we had it now."

At Christmas, they had both laughed about it. Now, thinking of the frontispiece, a photograph of her great-uncle Owen, with his broad, white beard, large frame and stern expression—as massive and forbidding-looking in the picture as he had always appeared to her as a child—Isobel answered with icy clarity. She said, "'To that distant gleam which is always the guide of high human endeavor.'"

Herb said, "Fascinating, Isobel. I'd love to see it."

"My God, Herb! What do *you* want to see it for?" Bea screwed up her face in distaste. "It sounds so . . . so *religious*."

"Terrific stuff, Shestak, isn't it? Huh? Terrific! . . . Isobel, what was the 'untrammeled' business?"

"That was in Wales," Isobel said coldly. "They felt that their religious impulses couldn't be given untrammeled expression. I think that was actually your favorite." She felt, as she spoke, that her eyes had narrowed and that she was suddenly looking at Ez with a terrible and lonely detachment. The sentence in that little book which she now remembered precisely was this: "All human relationships must be tried in the crucible of rationality."

Ez said, "Of course, they always had a very strong anti-urban bias. It runs all through."

"That's what Eleanor has now," Bea said, "and *I* think she's making a terrible mistake. Of course, she's had a *harrowing* experience, I understand that. But what's the good of her just staying in Vermont all by herself? She should get involved with other people."

"*Look!*" Ez said, suddenly leaping to his feet and rapping on the window. "My God! Look! The dark Satanic mills!"

But Isobel had already seen it and was staring. They were on the outskirts of a town, and there, rising above it on the riverbank, dwarfing the scatter of lumberyards and rickety frame houses, was a massive dark-brick abandoned factory. On one side of it was a high, rock-strewn waterfall, on the other, a blackened iron footbridge. It was dreadful; it was majestic; from the dingy windows of the moving train it looked, in the gray light, like an island prison fortress.

"Talk about untrammeled expression!" Ez said bitterly. "The only ones in this country who ever had untrammeled expression were the bastards who built those mills!" And taking in the look on Isobel's face—she was transfixed by the smokestacks, the enormous, blind windows, the whole raw, grimy, awesome mass—he said, "Yes, I know. It *is* beautiful in a way. In the sense that all power is beautiful—and also ugly. No, *I* didn't say that, Isobel. It's Sherwood Anderson— he was describing the mills in Elizabethton, Tennessee. . . . He said he thought the mill girls were half in love with the machines they worked at. For just that reason."

Isobel looked up at Ez and thought: How could I have doubted him? Why was I getting so annoyed? Aloud, she said, "It looks like a prison," and immediately thought of Eleanor Boland Hughes.

"Exactly!" Ez said. "They were built like prisons—that's the whole point! All over New England, they built mills from the exact same architectural plans as the state prisons. . . . What's the matter, Shestak? It surprises you? *You've* heard of Yankee ingenuity!"

Quickly, Herb said, "No, no, I *know* about it, Ez. The most famous example is in Manchester, New Hampshire. But I don't think this one actually *was*." He pointed out the window. "You see? It doesn't have a wall."

"And for you that changes something? If you don't literally *see* a wall, it's somehow a different story? Scholarship is a wonderful thing, no question about it! *Look* at that building!" Ez punched the window so that other passengers turned to look. "Just look at it! It doesn't tell you all you need to know about the travesty of technology? The lies, the destruction, the human waste! . . . My father worked in a sweatshop. Every day of his life that man has made buttonholes. He sits in a row—twelve men, twelve machines. But there's no wall, Shestak, there's no wall."

Isobel was amazed: she had never before heard Ez even mention his father.

Irritably, Bea said, "My God, Ez! Nobody *disagrees* with you. That whole structure just reeks of child labor."

"Only child labor? That's all you see here? In Barnard College you once read a book about the industrial revolution? What about all the generations of this region it ate up and spewed out? It took them off the land, tied them to machines, made them miserable and useless for anything else, and then, when the mills closed, they just spat them out again. You didn't see the mill owners on bread lines. What do they care?"

"Oh, my God!" Bea jumped up, panicky. "The abandoned factory! That's the *landmark* Eleanor said to watch out for! We're here! It's not a regular stop, we have to tell the conductor!" And quickly darting over to the other side of the aisle, Bea looked out the window and shouted, "There she is! See? Waving to us! Eleanor! Eleanor!"

Isobel looked out too, and there, standing on the top of a muddy incline, was a slight, boyish figure in slacks and a plaid lumber jacket—once again she was wearing clothes that were too big for her—unquestionably Eleanor Boland Hughes. With one hand she waved; with the other—a quick, nimble arc—she flicked away a cigarette. It was a quirky, self-disparaging gesture; at the same time, as she narrowed her eyes in the wind, she had a certain placed, self-possessed look.

"Let me get this straight now," Ez said crankily as they jumped off the train. "What is she doing here exactly?"

Isobel whispered, "She's *living* here. Shh!"

"What do you mean—*living* here? Where, how, what, why? I thought she *lives* in Boston."

Bea said, "Oh, it's just a family property. The Bolands've always had this house in Vermont, and no one was staying in it."

"Ah!" Ez said. "A *family* property. Of course. How dense of me to have asked, and I do hope you'll *excuse* me." And then, suddenly noticing Eleanor's car, a new maroon station wagon with wooden sides, he said in a voice loud enough for her to hear, "Henry Ford's best. How delightful!"

Eleanor said, "Yes, it's *wonderfully* roomy, but it's my fault—I've just got stuff all over the place. It's not mine, though, it's for the new calves at Ascutney Farm." And smiling rosily, glassily, she turned to Bea and said, "Oh, Bea! They're *so* sweet, but two of them just aren't thriving, so when I went to the vet with Maggie, I told him about the Ascutney calves and he gave me some things to take along for them."

Bea said, "Oh! Maggie! How's Maggie? Where is she?"

"Poking around somewhere," Eleanor said happily. "The

81

country is *so* good for her, it brings out her old hunting instincts after all this time. That's why I had to take her to the vet—I think she must have tangled with a woodchuck."

Ez said, "Never mind animals! What happened to the people who used to work at the mill?"

Eleanor looked puzzled. She said, "What mill?"

Nervously, Bea said, "You know—the one we passed. The one you told us to look out for as a landmark."

"*Oh!* The old factory. It's closed. Nobody's worked there for ages."

"Nobody worked there for ages and nobody worked there for wages, and what did you think I was talking about! What *happened* to those people? What became of them?"

Eleanor turned white, and in the voice of a chastened small child, said, "Oh! Are you an organizer?"

"Only organizers are supposed to be concerned with what happens to people's work and people's lives, is that it? Otherwise, as far as you're concerned, the whole business out there"—Ez gestured past the empty, rutted road at an invisible pinch-faced, hurrying crowd—"otherwise the whole thing is just a shuffle of human furniture."

"I didn't *mean* that," Eleanor cried out. "*Please* forgive me. I know how selfish I must have sounded." And she looked genuinely distressed, Isobel thought, the pleading alarm in her eyes and her face, just like the oversized country clothes, so pathetically invoking her cloudy, child-like vulnerability. It forced you to hear the cell door clang shut, the matron's keys and footsteps echo through an empty, awful distance.

Bea said, "And who has more right than you to sound selfish right now? My God, Ez! Think of what she's been through!"

"Oh, no, Bea!" Eleanor begged. "Please don't say that, that has nothing to do with it. Absolutely *nothing*."

"But it has *everything* to do with it, Eleanor," Ez said. He leaned forward as if to touch her, grasp her, and was suddenly speaking very kindly—like a father putting a child to bed, and purposely choosing this moment of comfort and intimacy to explain a difficult but necessary truth. "Look . . . The experience that you had—and I know it was shocking and terrible—but just *because* it was, it gives you the chance to change your whole life. To understand everything in a new way and live differently because of it. And that chance, Eleanor, that chance is there for a few seconds' worth of time. It's like a light going on after hours in a store you would never go into. Not *you.* So you can either push open that door and learn something totally surprising, or you can walk right past it—the light will go out anyway, it only came on by accident, a mistake—and keep on walking home the way you always do and never ever think about it again."

"I *do* think about it. And I know there are people around here who are very poor. . . ." Eleanor's voice trailed off in confusion and she looked as if she were about to cry.

Bea said, "Oh, I'm so glad! I knew that Ez was *exactly* the right person to talk to you! But not now, because you have to keep your eyes on the road—*look* at it! We're driving on a piece of *ribbon!* What the hell happened here? A tornado?"

"Oh, it always floods when the snow melts," Eleanor said breezily. "Only this one was the worst in years. *Everything's* been washed away. If any people were out on the road, *they* would've been swept away too. It's all that rain and high wind." And she finished in a breathy rush which was itself like a high wind, Isobel thought: a child delighting in someone else's mischief.

Herb said, "Was all this damage done by water? Those trees, for instance. . . ." He pointed at trunks and branches which were caught rushing down the blackened, silty stream. "That many trees were knocked out by one flood?"

"Don't worry, Shestak," Ez said. "They'll turn them into paper faster. Before you know it, you'll have a whole new library, toilet paper included. . . . We're just city provincials, what do we know? Country people are used to these eruptions of nature, they know what to do. Right, Isobel?"

Isobel said nothing; she had never before seen such a sweep of primitive devastation. Because of the uprooted trees, the eroded hillsides had become bald faces of dark, jutting rock and from the craterous road there was a sheer drop to twisting, clay-covered stream beds which gave the whole landscape the look of a place thrust out of earth before its time. This forced on Isobel the idea of time itself and made her think: Why have I done no work for so long? And why am I sitting in this debutante's station wagon?

"Oh, Isobel!" Eleanor smiled. "I didn't know you were from the country. Then you won't mind the mud."

It was not the mud which bothered Isobel, but the cold. Downstairs, in the kitchen, there was a Franklin stove, and the living room had a fireplace, but the upstairs bedroom where Eleanor had put them retained a musty chill so damp, raw and penetrating that Isobel peeled off her clothes as if she had come in from a drenching rain. She flung herself onto the high, old-fashioned bed and pulled the down-quilt comforter over her. Leaning over her on the bed, Ez traced the lines of her body on the quilt and said, "I don't know why you won't go downstairs and help her build a fire. She's afraid the logs got too damp and they won't catch."

"Not me." Isobel laughed from beneath the quilt. "You know what happens when Eleanor Boland Hughes gets too close to pokers."

"No respect for the judicial process, it's appalling," Ez said, as his fingers, now underneath the quilt, circled the whole of Isobel's body so that even the idea of chill and discomfort belonged to a distant place. "After all, the woman was declared innocent by a jury of her peers."

"Tell it to the Scottsboro boys," Isobel teased, cradling his head, and even though she was whispering, felt that her laughter was ringing throughout the whole cold, dim house.

"*That* I will not let pass!" Ez ripped off the comforter, and

Isobel, uncovered, saw Ez leaning over her in an old blue and maroon plaid bathrobe she had never before seen. It shocked her: Ez, smiling, in her bed, in her arms, was wearing a bathrobe that for all these months had never even hung in her closet. Pearl must have bought it for him, she thought, probably years ago, when she was new at her job as a court interpreter. Pearl must have brought it home for him as a gift, and this thought once again gave her the uneasy double feeling of possessing another woman's husband, and yet—in these small, daily, homely ways, ordinary pieces of his clothing which she had somehow never seen—hardly even knowing him.

"Oh, Isobel," Ez said heavily, suddenly holding her tightly. "I can't stand it. Pearl's pregnant again. I can't *stand* it. . . . Maybe she'll lose this one too."

Isobel sat up rigidly. "What do you mean—*too?*"

"She's miscarried twice since Jonathan was born. She wants children—*nobody* wants children now. Who do you know who wants children? With so much uncertainty, with the world in such chaos"—Ez shrugged—"*she* wants children. She wants to drown me in diapers. That's what I come home to—diapers and Palestinians. Baby food and the White Paper. It's no accident the Arabs rioted in 'thirty-five, that's the year Pearl was in Palestine. . . . I can always tell when she's been to her Zionist meetings—there's a smell of cigarette smoke in her hair."

"What's the matter with you two?" Bea banged on the door, shouting. "Dinner's on the *table*. We've been waiting for almost twenty minutes."

Dazed, Isobel said, "We'll be right down," but heard again and again in her head: *I can always tell when she's been to her Zionist meetings—there's a smell of cigarette smoke in her hair.* Because it forced into her mind the picture of Pearl, whom she had once seen, her dark curly head bent over the sink—perhaps she was washing diapers—and Ez coming into the room unexpectedly, sneaking up behind her, impulsively catching her around the waist and burying his head in her hair.

Downstairs, Eleanor looked up from her seat at the creaky farmhouse table and said, "Oh, Isobel, were you taking a shower? I meant to explain about the hot water, but of course, you're from the country, so you would *know*."

Herb, greedily, happily spooning up scrambled eggs and macaroni—it occurred to Isobel that he ate like a baby—grabbed a piece of bread and said, "Eleanor's just been telling us about a fascinating place they've got buried in the woods up here—a cemetery that dates all the way back to the Revolutionary War!"

Crankily, Ez said, "Why is it buried in the woods? What are they hiding?"

"They just don't *use* it anymore, Ez," Bea said. "That's what Eleanor was telling us about. It's called the Revolutionary Cemetery and she only found it by accident one day when she was trailing around after Maggie."

"Maggie?" Ez frowned. "Who's Maggie? And what was *she* doing there?"

Isobel nudged him under the table, whispering, "The dog, Ez. She tangled with a woodchuck. Remember?"

Herb said, "I think it's safe to assume that where it is was once right off a main road, especially since we know it adjoins an old church. And then, for some reason, probably local politics, say the arm-twisting of some influential local merchant, when they built the paved road, this place got bypassed. So people stopped using it, and over the years it became so overgrown that by now it's very hard to get to."

Eleanor turned to Ez, and smiling—not the least bit poignant now—said in a high, thin voice of clove-and-cinnamon sweetness, "Didn't your mother ever tell you that *all* good things are hard to find?"

"My mother? I don't think she believes there *are* good things. And when you think about it, why should she?"

Eleanor looked shocked. She said, "Oh, you don't *mean* that, Ez. You don't agree with it?"

Between swallows, Herb gulped out rapidly, "That's a very different background, don't forget. You have to take it into consid—"

"Of *course* he doesn't, Eleanor!" Bea, making coffee, shouted over the running water. "He's just trying to give you a hard time. . . . I can't wait to put on my walking shoes and go see the Revolutionary Cemetery! I just hope it doesn't rain."

"Did you bring walking shoes too, Isobel?" Eleanor smiled her gingery, cat-like smile. "Or aren't you coming? Of course, there are so *many* Revolutionary cemeteries all over New England. But you've been so quiet, I don't even know what *part* of the country you come from."

"I'm from Wisconsin. And we *don't* have any Revolutionary cemeteries."

"Exactly!" Ez said, pounding his fist on the table and suddenly coming to life. "Maybe they haven't buried all their revolutionaries yet. . . . Will you just think of what that's supposed to mean—'the revolutionary cemetery'? Is it a cemetery arranged in a revolutionary way? It *could* be. . . . Or does everybody call it that so easily because that's what this country has become? A graveyard for revolutionaries?" Ez nodded. "The only good revolutionary is a dead revolutionary."

Impatiently, Bea said, "Oh, you *know* what they mean, Ez. It's only shorthand. Not that I disagree with your point—what else would this society be comfortable with?"

"But that's the tragedy, Bea. Because it wasn't *meant* to be that way. And it doesn't have to be."

"You see, Eleanor?" Bea said happily. "Not only does he believe there *are* good things, but he always sees a way to work for them. And that's just why I wanted him to talk to you."

Eleanor smiled. "Why don't we have our coffee in front of

the fire?" she said, and picking up the cream and sugar, walked out.

Ez said, "What's the difference where we drink coffee? It's warm in here, there's nothing wrong with it in here. Besides, I thought she said she *couldn't* make a fire, the debutante Girl Scout. I thought she said the logs were wet. Isobel, what do you do about wet logs?"

"You don't *do* anything," Isobel said, half laughing. "The fire'll just be smoky," and giddy suddenly from the querulousness in his voice, she ran off into the living room with the wild, quick running steps of a child. Because any minute now, she thought, languor would overtake her totally: Isobel was once again feeling the odd, sweet curtain of her private erotic haze, and didn't even care that she would be alone in the room with Eleanor. Sitting there watching the fire and watching Eleanor, all through such a sieved distance, it seemed to Isobel that just as she had felt this way on the train and at odd moments she could never account for—walking to the bakery, for instance, or waiting for a bus—this feeling she called her erotic haze had nothing to do with Ez at all, but came from herself entirely.

Bea said, "What a wonderful fire, Eleanor! It's not smoky at all, and I love the *smell.*"

Dreamily, Eleanor said, "Would anyone like some home-made blackberry brandy? I helped Mrs. Giddings—the little brown house down the road—and *all* the berries came from this hillside. This summer, if I help her pick 'em, she'll show me how to make blackberry jam."

"Eleanor," Bea said, shaking her head, "this is all very nice, but *I'm* not going to let you get away so easily. What do you think you're doing? You make blackberry jam, you help a farmer with his calves—all right, it's sweet, it's *very* sweet. But my God! You can't keep this up! You can't just stay up here alone in the country, alone in nature like—like some D. H. Lawrence heroine. You have to come back to real life, be with people, *do* something for people. You have to make a contribution. Right, Ez? Isn't that what you meant before?"

"Before *what?*" Ez muttered. He was staring moodily at the stuffed deer's head above the fireplace.

Eleanor said, "Actually, there *is* something I've been thinking about doing. Someone sent me the most wonderful article by a woman who's a court interpreter in New York. I don't know if they've even got any in Boston, but I studied languages and I certainly know what it's like to be in court. And that article was *so* wonderful, I even remember how it starts. It's what someone said to her when she was first looking for a job. They said, 'In America, all girls become *typewriterkehs*.' Isn't that a funny, wonderful word?"

Uncomfortably, Bea said, "That just means secretaries."

Isobel stared at the fire; she could not breathe. It was Pearl Milgram's essay, and everybody knew it.

# 6

A young woman in a white drawstring peasant blouse and silver filigree Yemenite earrings is setting a table for dinner. The sensual clarity is almost shocking: the starchy snap of the clean tablecloth, its unfolding high whiteness, are like a newly made bed to someone in fever. But soon there is the repeating pattern of blue-rimmed plates and funnel-shaped wineglasses, then napkins and silverware, and suddenly from a round wooden bowl comes the smell, the fruit-store delirium of imported oranges. Is there bread? Yes, crusty bakery white bread, still smelling of the oven, delicious the next morning with sweet butter and milky coffee. Are there candles? Maybe. Is it a Friday night? Above the table and just where the young woman is bending, there is a small curtained window. It holds not only her reflection but, from outside, the sallow globe glow of a streetlamp. This, in early winter evenings, is one of the most melancholy sights in New York, but not to the woman setting the table. She dashes off into the kitchen—there is a smell of frying onions—and the expression on her face is not the humming, peaceful busyness of domestic pleasure; instead, in her eyes especially, there is a look of excitement, of anticipation that cannot be accounted for by anything she is actually doing. In Merry's mind, this is Pearl Milgram. Because how could she know?

"I can't see why you're asking me *now*, Merry. *Today*," Ez said. They were having dinner together to celebrate Merry's twenty-seventh birthday; also, Ez had to be in town for the taping of a panel discussion on public television. "Doesn't it seem to you slightly morbid to associate your birthday with the anniversary of your mother's death?" Ez shrugged. "I suppose you're being encouraged by that psychoanalytic quack. . . . But this what-was-she-really-*like* business! It's unworthy of you, really. It sounds so—so journalistic, so *cheap*. Besides, you *know* what I think she was like."

"Yes," Merry said, "and I can't imagine you would want me to stop being interested in the extraordinary variety of your answers."

"*That's* what she was like!" Ez pounced. "Just like that! Intolerant, argumentative, relentless in her made-up bourgeois domesticity—'the *chil*dren the *chil*dren'—and her senseless, pathetic obsession with the Jews. She *drove* me away. How could I stay there?"

"I never asked you that, Ez. I never reproached you."

"Christ! If you could hear the sound of that smug suffering, the sanctimony! At least, *she* never gave me that. *She* was a fighter."

"If you think I do sound like her, it's no good, and when you think I don't, it's even worse. What do you want of me?"

"What do *I* want of you? What do *I* want? That's what's so wrong with all this, Merry! What do you want of yourself, *for* yourself? That's the only question ever worth asking."

"Did you think I was your television audience? Or one of your fan-letter groupies? I'm your daughter, Ez, and I asked you a question about my mother. What was so *wrong* with her bourgeois domesticity? What was made up about it?"

From a neighbor's apartment came the sound of some-one—a child, probably—practicing the piano, playing with a child's unphrased tentative energy one of the simple Bartók Slovakian folk pieces. It was a piece that both Merry and Nicky had once played, and hearing it now, Merry had a feeling of almost unbearable family intimacy.

Ez said, "Because she didn't believe it, cookie. She didn't believe it for a minute. She *wanted* to believe it—why, I never really understood—and she threw all her energy into that one enormous piece of self-deception. Pearl the Wife and Mother! And how did I fail her? I refused to turn into Ez the Husband and Father. I *did* refuse, that's true. I could not be part of her self-delusion."

Uneasily, Merry said, "She probably just wanted you to make a living. And behave as if you really lived there."

"Yes, but that's never who I was. I never pretended. *She* was the one who changed. Or pretended to change. Merry, she became unrecognizable. She was living a lie and she died of it."

"What are you saying, Ez? She died because she disagreed with you?"

"It had nothing to do with me, Merry. It never did. The battle was only inside herself, and she never understood it. She, who understood everything, who could look out at the world with such clear eyes! Suddenly to become so blind—and turn back and back in her blindness, and willfully cut herself off from who she was and what she was meant to be . . . She was *afraid*, Merry. And you could *not* discuss it with her. If you said, 'Pearl! Look at what you're doing! You're not your mother. You *can't* be, you *shouldn't* be. What for? Is this why they sent you to *gymnasium* in Warsaw? So you

92

could turn yourself into some kind of Jewish Madonna? *Stop* it, *stop* it.' Do you know what she would say to me? Do you know? That I was a child-murderer and an anti-Semite. What could I do with that? So I gave up, it's true, I stopped trying."

"Why was it so *wrong* that she wanted children? What was so reprehensible about that?"

"Wrong! Reprehensible! Merry! How can you use words like that? Why does it have to be put in a *moral* context? That's just what *she* used to do! What has that got to do with it? How can such a thing ever be right or wrong?"

"All right, then, why were you so against it?"

"I was *not* against her having children—*our* having children. After all, they were my children too. What I was against—what I fought till there was no point fighting—was her crazed eagerness to turn herself into a Mother in some blind atavistic way. It had nothing to do with the reality of her life and her nature. . . . She was trying to turn herself into somebody else. Out of fear, Merry. Out of fear. And that was it. Because from that fear came inauthenticity and then there's no way out. Because I swear it to you now and I told it to her then: inauthenticity kills."

"But she died of a heart defect, Ez. You told me that yourself. From some sickness she had in Europe as a child."

"Being in Europe *was* the sickness she had as a child," Ez said bitterly. "She lived in a village of mud streets, surrounded by superstition and constant threat. . . . Do you know that when we were on the subway together, if she saw a priest or a nun she still shivered. And if there was a drunk—my God! All she had to do was see someone stumble and she was ready to change trains. Once there was an old Italian—he was *reeking* of wine and smiling from ear to ear. Merry, you couldn't miss it—the man was *smiling!* He leaned over her and said, 'Bella, bella!' I tell you, if there had been an open window, she would have jumped right out of it! . . . Actually, you know, she did jump out of a train once, she told me. A moving train, too. It was on her way to America; she had to get to Hamburg—Bremerhaven—some port city to get the boat. She was by herself, I guess, a provincial kid on a train, all wrapped up in scarves because she'd just had mumps, and her papers weren't in order. So some Polish soldier in her compartment, a kid himself, I suppose, took pity on her when he saw there were some officials—border guards coming around to check—and he said, 'Look, Miss, if they find you they'll arrest you. Get off now. Jump!' So she did."

Exactly what had she done? Merry wondered. Instantly, painfully, slithered through a half-opened window? Or purposely casual—sauntering, as if she were merely stretching her legs or looking for a toilet—made her way through the rocking carriage, and from its high edge—there would have been no steps—tumbled onto the coarse brown grass of a frozen field? A frozen Polish field? A frozen German field? Would she have known where she was, this provincial kid, with the scarves wound around her neck and face to disguise the swelling of her childhood sickness? And what about those scarves: mightn't they have got caught—on a wheel, on the track, on a branch as she jumped in the high wind? All right, she was not Isadora Duncan, not Anna Karenina: Merry saw the romanticized confusion in her own mind. Still, the lonely terror of this incident gripped her like an awful bedtime story—a frightened, sickly young girl leaping off a train into God knows where: a swamp of ditches, dogs and peasants— and this was in her face and her voice as she said, "My God, Ez! What *happened* to her then? What did she do?"

"Oh, I don't know." Ez shrugged, and having taken in the panic in her voice, he leaned back with exaggerated carelessness. "Probably waited around for the next train and then hopped right on up to the Vistula Sunset Limited."

"Oh, excuse me, I forgot—you're Paul Bunyan. Or is it Casey Jones? Tell me, what do you hear from John Henry?"

"All right, all right, *enough*, Merry! Enough! For Christ sake, you're no different from her!"

Outside, someone was shoveling snow, and the muffled, metallic clatter ringing through the air from so many stories below was a sound Merry always loved: it was the lively and remote renewing promise of the city in snow. But the someone doing the shoveling was probably some super's helper, and cruelly far from the tropical assurances of his own youth. This was exactly the kind of thought that Ez had always claimed to value most in Pearl Milgram.

Merry said, "I *am* different from her. I was *not* on my way to a whole new world at fifteen—and neither were you! I don't know how you even dare tell me that *that*—*that* is your idea of someone done in by fear!"

"Oh, cookie." Ez shoved away his plate. "Do you really think it costs me nothing to say it? To have lived through it and watched it happen? *You* don't know what she was like when I first saw her. You don't *know*. . . ." He was speaking, and had now stopped, with such bitter forcefulness that Merry said, "When she was first working in the courts, you mean?" Because she was shaken.

"No, no." Ez smiled. "That was much later, when I really got to know her. I mean way, way before then, when I first actually *saw* her. When she was working for her uncle— cousin—whatever he was. Gorelik, the jeweler. She was living with them too, I think, uptown somewhere, but his store was on Eldridge Street and she used to work there after school."

"What were *you* doing in a jewelry store?"

"It wasn't exactly a jewelry store. He didn't *sell* jewelry, he repaired it, Pearl explained it to me—if some rich woman had a necklace, say, and it broke, she would bring it in to her own jeweler. Well, of course, *he* wouldn't be able to fix it, he wasn't a *craftsman*, so Gorelik used to send Pearl around to all the different jewelers. She would pick up the pieces for repair

95

and then return them." Ez stopped and suddenly started laughing.

"I don't see what's funny about that," Merry said testily, instantly envisioning a thin, black-cloaked girl, briefly admitted to the gleaming stores of the rich, only to hurry back in darkness to the entrapping confusion of the Lower East Side. "She was his errand girl, Ez. He probably exploited her—just took advantage of her because she was young, an immigrant and his relative."

"*Probably?* I don't think he even paid her, that was her room and board. But that's not why I'm laughing. When Gorelik went himself, he was always being robbed, pickpocketed. That's why he needed her so badly."

"So in addition to everything else, it was dangerous!" Merry said.

"Not the way *she* walked, Merry. That's how I first noticed her—that's why *everyone* noticed her. All the kids, all those bums I used to hang around with—every time she came whipping up the street on those tiny feet, they used to call out, 'Here comes the racing shoes girl! Watch her put the streetcars out of business!' I used to say it too, but really I wanted to talk to her, make an *impression* on her. I didn't want her to think I was just one of those kibitzers, but I didn't know what to say. It's *true*, Merry, don't look at me that way! I was a kid, what did I know? All right, I was going to CCNY, and I had my own way of flirting with girls, but it was all kibitzing." Ez shrugged. "Not for a girl like her. . . . What I wanted was to say to her, 'You're beautiful,' and I wanted to say it in Russian. Because what she looked like to me, even though she was half covered by that red shawl, and carrying her schoolbooks, and walking so fast—she had a very serious, very foreign look—she looked like the illustrations in one of my father's Russian books, his old Russian novels. *Russki knigi!*" Ez shook his head. "He used to comb the city, that's all he ever read, the contemptuous old bastard. Well, that and his union stuff. . . . Anyway, I suppose I *could* have asked my father. I even thought about it. But can you imagine—*my father? My father?*" Ez stood up, and holding himself very erect, began miming his father's elaborate theatrical gestures. "*Okularn,*" he said, and on top of his own actual glasses put on, with drawn-out, ritualistic splendor—each earpiece separately, and in place—an imaginary pair as his father had done. "And now perhaps I can sit down." He stared at the chair with disdain, and haughtily lowering himself into it, hitched up first one pant leg, then the other, and smoothing them each down slowly, carefully, he checked to ensure perfect alignment with the floor. Finally, he brushed off the edges of the chair with palms so exaggeratedly turned in, it was as if the crumbs or dust were vermin and he a velvet-clad visiting noble.

Merry laughed; it was an imitation of her grandfather that she had seen Ez do many times, but it was in fact close to the way Ez himself sat down when he was ill at ease or among strangers, and precisely what he did when he was being interviewed on television and shifting around in his chair.

But Ez hadn't finished. He sighed very deeply, a sigh of terrible disappointment, and with the whole upper part of his body very erect, like a soldier standing on parade, stared ahead of him with an expression both mournful and dismissive, and began singing with the sturdy, resonant, basso solemnity of a Russian male chorus: " '*Bourem glorem, n'ye-eh va chorem. . . .*' " It was the one line of the song that Ez knew, and Merry had heard it before; the song was about a blizzard, and because it really was snowing outside, Merry and Ez both laughed.

Ez said, "And that was above all what Pearl couldn't stand about him. She used to say to me, 'What's all this *Russian*-loving your father indulges in? This nostalgia? What for? *I*

97

have no nostalgia for Poland. How could I? What *were* Russia and Poland for the Jews after all? What can he possibly be nostalgic *about?*' "

"His youth, I suppose," Merry said. "The hopes he once had—whatever they were."

"She was *right*, Merry. He was a terrible snob. He used to look at his sons and say, 'Bums! Illiterates! What have *I* got to do with *you?* American street bums!' And we *were!*" Ez said defiantly. "The old man was absolutely right—that's exactly what we were!"

"Come on, Ez, you just said yourself you were going to college."

"Ahh! My father never made that mistake. *He* knew better. . . . Did *I* read novels? Did *I* memorize poems? Did *I* spend every Saturday morning in a different synagogue so I could find the *chazan* who could *really* make me cry at *Kol Nidre?* In short, did I ever give any sign, ever, of having been touched by a 'finer feeling'?" Ez shook his head. "He used to see me coming home with books—textbooks, of course, not novels—and say, 'You behave like a bum, you dress like a bum, and someday you'll lie in the Bowery with them together.' Oh, yes, the cocoon, the celebrated warm hearth of the immigrant Jewish family!"

"You never did get to speak to her, then?"

"To Pearl? Of course I did! Do you think I'd let that bastard stop me? What I did was ask a kid in the John Reed Club. He was always hanging around the lunchroom, carrying on about the spirit of the Russian people and the beauty of the Russian language, so one day I said to him, 'All right—give me an example. How do you say "beautiful" in Russian? "You're beautiful"?' Well, he got very excited, that schmuck, because he said I'd picked the perfect example. That in Russian the word for 'beautiful' was the same as the word for 'red'— *krasnyi, krasnaya.* It turned out he was wrong, but what did I know? So one afternoon—and it was *bitter* cold—because the cold made her walk even faster, and the wind made her cheeks flushed, ruddy, and her eyes so bright that she looked, especially all wrapped up in that red scarf—Merry, she looked *exactly* like the girls in those illustrations. *You* know what I mean: the burning eyes, that radiant, intense, hellbent expression—the works. I went up to her and I said what I thought I was supposed to say: 'Vy krasnaya.' She stopped, turned around, and glared at me. So help me, she glared at me as if I were an idiot, and said, 'I speak English perfectly, thank you. And I certainly know the color of my own scarf.' And that was it," Ez said. "The next time I talked to her, she was that girl out of nowhere who had just written that remarkable article about working in the courts."

# 100 CENTRE STREET
*by Pearl Milgram*

> Q. *Will you tell the Court in your own words, Mr. D'Onofrio, what was in your mind on the night in question?*
> A. *Mind? It had nothing to do with my mind. When Bradford's fired me after all those years, suddenly something went wrong with my eyes. It was my eyes. Suddenly I couldn't see straight.*

"In America, all girls become *typewriterkehs*," everyone told me when I first arrived in this country. They said it to me as advice, they said it as simple observation; they said it with surprise that anything else had crossed my mind, and finally, with undisguised condescension for an immigrant girl, who, so pitiably unlike their own daughters, could barely even speak English. Well, I knew I could learn English, but how could I be a *typewriterkeh?* Typewriters, then, seemed to me like subways and elevated trains: confusing American machines—noisy, clattering, disjointed. It was plainly impossible. Besides, in Poland I had already been a student: the pride of my parents and of my little town, I was sent off to a *gymnasium* in Warsaw at the age of twelve under the sponsorship of a rich Warsaw family. Their own daughters attended this school, and the D. family was known all over Poland not only for their wealth but for their cultivation and particular philanthropic interest in the education of deserving girls from the poorer, backward Jewish villages. So they paid my fees, invited me to their house (servants, flowers, a telephone, and most remarkable of all, exotic imported fruit casually set out and casually indulged in) for family musical soirees, which they did actually call "soirees," and one memorable night, took me to the opera. It remains especially memorable to me not only because of the opera itself, but also because of the dazzle of lights and luxury—all the scented, languid ladies, their self-satisfied, crisply elegant husbands, and the whispers in French.

This glimpse of Warsaw high life, a spur to a kind of precocious lust for the West, was not precisely what my parents had in mind when they sent me off. (Although thinking back on it, my father must have had some inkling of this possibility: as a very young man, he had been expelled from a rabbinical seminary in Minsk for reading, in class, a Russian translation of the stories of Maupassant, and reciting to a gathering crowd the poems of the Hebrew poet Bialik.) But his acts of secular recklessness had the ironic effect of pushing him back into just that hopeless small-town mire from which he had tried to escape. That's what he wanted for me, then, in Warsaw: an education for a profession that would free me from Eastern Europe—either to a civilized city like Vienna or Budapest, or since it was to be a *useful* profession, to Palestine. (America was not in his mind at all: a natural haven for the crude and ignorant, single-mindedly besotted with the dream of money.)

My father wanted me to become a pharmacist, an *aptekarka*. I was easily caught up with the romance of this vision: a knowing, cold-eyed lady, possessed of obscure but specific knowledge and clad in a white smock. But though I dutifully struggled with mathematics, with formulas, with charts of elements and combinations of chemicals in test tubes, it was soon apparent to my teachers, and to me too, that I had no aptitude for science; I would never be a pharmacist.

At Hunter College, all girls became schoolteachers. But even before I had the chance to begin imagining myself seated in stern authority at the head of long rows of New York City schoolchildren, I was told that as a practical matter, it was absolutely impossible. Because of my foreign accent, I would never pass the teachers' speech examination, and would never be hired—except perhaps as a teacher of foreign languages. So I majored in foreign languages, read À la Recherche du Temps Perdu, I Promessi Sposi, some medieval German plays, and became an interpreter for the New York State Court of Appeals.

Q. Will you tell the Court in your own words, Mr. D'Onofrio, what was in your mind on the night in question?

A. Mind? It had nothing to do with my mind. When Bradford's fired me after all those years, suddenly something went wrong with my eyes. It was my eyes. Suddenly I couldn't see straight.

On "the night in question," Dominic D'Onofrio was finishing up some work in the stockroom of Bradford's, a wholesale hardware distributor, where he had worked for twenty years, when he was interrupted by Joseph Cleary, a nineteen-year-old payroll clerk. Though it was not payday, Mr. Cleary handed him his pay envelope and a layoff notice. According to Mr. Cleary's account, Mr. D'Onofrio at first seemed merely puzzled, asking, "What's this, kid? Huh? What's this?" But when Mr. Cleary answered, "I don't know. It's from the front, it's from the boss," D'Onofrio suddenly lunged at him, stabbing him repeatedly with the knife he used to open packing cases. Dominic D'Onofrio was found guilty of attempted murder and sentenced by Judge Francis T. Cahill to fifteen years at Sing Sing Prison.

For Adam Waskiewicz, it was not a night in question, but a morning. He was at home on this Wednesday morning in question, just as he had been for the past six months, since the ball-bearing factory in Long Island City which had employed him had closed down. Two of his sons were at home with him, one a five-year-old not yet in school, and the other an eight-year-old, who had come down with a bad ear infection. His wife had left the house at seven-thirty that morning as usual to go off to her job as a cleaning woman in a midtown office building, a job she had taken only a month before, very much against her husband's wishes. Mr. Waskiewicz had just finished clearing away the breakfast dishes; in fact, he was still wearing an apron—his wife's apron, which hung on a hook beside the sink—and had just begun making the beds when his older son, seeing him this way for the first time, called out, laughing, "Hey, look at Papa! He looks like Mama!" Mr. Waskiewicz knocked the child to the floor, fracturing his skull, and repeatedly pummeled him with his fists till several ribs had been broken and the boy lost consciousness. Neighbors called the police. Adam Waskiewicz was charged with assault in the first degree and sentenced by Judge Thomas J. Riordan to five years at Clinton Reformatory.

And what was in eighteen-year-old Leon Malinsky's mind on the Friday afternoon in March when he walked into Friedlander's cleaning and dyeing store on Avenue A and pulled out a gun? The gun belonged to his oldest brother, who had worked the docks during Prohibition, but Leon Malinsky pointed it straight at Abraham Friedlander, and said, "You owe me, you bastard! You owe me." So he made off with a week's receipts, but since Friedlander had never even seen him before and certainly did not know him, what was it that he owed him? That morning, Malinsky had learned that a job which had been promised to him for almost a year had now, at the last minute, not come through. The job was at a women's clothing factory called Friedlander's. In court, Malinsky's mother cried out, "He was the good one—ask anyone, I swear it. He was my best son, he even finished high school." Leon Malinsky was found guilty of armed robbery and of violating the Sullivan Law and was sentenced by Judge Adolph Mossbach to ten years at Sing Sing Prison.

Criminal acts are pieces of a tragedy, always, and what these men have in common with each other is clear. But what have they to do with my life, my account of my own vocational rambles? We say commonly that we've fallen into a job—and perhaps that's true. But when we've fallen out of it, or—as is now so frequently the case—been ripped out of it, we have fallen out of the grace of ordinary life and out of that moral sense which gives it meaning.

---

From *Down and Out: American Writers Witness the Depression,* edited by Ronald J. Teplitsky and Sanford Spaiser.

EDS. NOTE: Pearl Milgram (1912–1944) wrote this account of her experiences as a court interpreter in New York City in 1935, the exact midpoint of that tumultuous decade. "100 Centre Street" was her first publication, and is typical of Depression writing in its outraged, anguished portrayal of the dilemma of the powerless, victimized ordinary citizen. It is atypical because of the writer's perspective as a European immigrant, a perspective which perhaps enabled her to link the effects of the economic breakdown of American society with what we have since then come to think of as the "existential" dilemma or the quality of life. Miss Milgram's early essays bear compassionate witness to the everyday trials of the "common man"; at the same time, they are invariably informed by a marked anti-totalitarian bias. Toward the end of her life, Pearl Milgram seemed to turn away from the immediacy of the American situation *per se,* becoming increasingly concerned with the plight of the European Jews.

---

From *Land Where Our Mothers Died: Five Generations of Radical American Women Speak,* edited by Jessica Ruthdaughter and Cathy Raines.

EDS. NOTE: Pearl Milgram was born in 1912 in Poland and died in 1944 in America. In the first sentence of this, her first published essay, she tells it all: "In America, all girls become *typewriterkehs.*" Well, she didn't, and what a terrible price she paid for this act of daring and defiance we can see from her dates alone. In 1936, she married Ezra B. Slavin, and though everyone knows who *he* is and how *his* career has flourished, how many of us have even heard of Pearl? Male writers have always had the societal support to adopt the defensive strategy of "silence, exile and cunning." That is not what happened to Pearl. For even though she did continue producing occasional beautiful right-on pieces throughout the thirties, her fate, not surprisingly, was a different one: silence, childbearing and death.

A young woman in a white drawstring peasant blouse and silver filigree Yemenite earrings is setting a table for dinner. Above the table and just where the young woman is bending, there is a small, curtained window. It holds her reflection, and to her eyes, perhaps simply because she is bending, the peasant blouse seems to billow. It's the billowing look of pregnancy, and because she's no fool, this young woman, and it's been a long time since her husband came home for dinner merely as a matter of course, what she fears is that this twilight imagined reflection of pregnancy is just about as far as she will get. And if this should turn out to be true, she knows how she will feel: that she, too, has fallen out of the grace of ordinary life.

# 7

OH, the lively disorder of the coffee table, its hectic, laden pleasures! Rum-browned coffee cake sliced on a grainy board, walnuts and almonds cracked and half shelled, tilted fruit knives and sinewy, sectioned tangerines, a cream pitcher between the coffee cups, and just beside a thimble glass of cognac, just to the left, there so exact and perfect on a plate, the whole spiral peel of one round red apple. So much did this resemble an Impressionist still life—dark-toned, but happily shadowed with certain comfort and nearby life—that Merry sat staring at her own coffee table, unable to move, clinging to it as if it were an exotic charm.

The night before, it would never have occurred to her that this sight, her own coffee table, might offer such dream-like enchantment—practically the feeling of a Fauré song. The night before, she had just come back by subway from

Brooklyn: she was doing a piece on victims of crime, and had interviewed the neighbors and family of a seventy-six-year-old man clubbed to death behind the counter of his music store in East Flatbush. The small group of people in the store, mostly neighboring storekeepers, had appeared embarrassed—not so much by Merry's presence, as she had feared, but because the murdered man had been so old, and as it happened, cancer-ridden, they all seemed to feel a certain illegitimacy in complaining about his death. The next-door merchant, a liquor store owner, said, "He never put in an alarm, he never locked the door. Not even a buzzer. What do you expect?"

And the wife of a fish store owner, a tiny, tough-looking woman, still wearing a bloodstained, fishy coverall, nodded. "He used to *walk* home. From here, walk! Can you imagine? Of course, he never had a penny in his pocket, but that's what gets them angry. . . ." She gestured disdainfully toward the strewn-about sheet music and dusty guitar strings. "Anyway, what did he ever take in here that they could rob and make it worth their while?"

Finally, the victim's son, a man so disheveled, burly and red-faced that he looked dangerous, straightened up from behind the counter, where he had been picking up pieces of glass, and burst out, "Is this a way to *die?* Is this a *reason?*"

The dismal familiarity of this scene, its sour, pinched anger, clung to Merry's skin and whined in her head as the train swayed and rattled through unfamiliar Brooklyn, so that as soon as she got home, she put on the radio. And turning the dial, trying to find some music, there suddenly was her father's voice: ". . . and I'm *much* older than you are, so don't you talk to me about your friends giving up! *I've* never given up."

The interviewer, very young-voiced, perhaps a student, said, "Well, I don't mean . . . I don't mean . . . giving *up*. I just mean . . . well, you know, people getting their heads into other scenes. Spiritual scenes. *Inside.* Because for a lot of people—I mean, a lot of people sort of feel that that whole political trip was really a bummer. Like they were really into it. I mean, these are people who even did the whole political process Democratic Convention number, okay? And now, I mean, shit! *Nixon!*"

"But, Jeff, you don't think that Nixon will last forever, do you?"

"Well, not Nixon himself. Right. I mean, the man's just collected too much bad karma. But, well, Agnew, Kissinger . . . the whole Middle America Silent Majority John Wayne death trip. I mean, when you *know* that's what's out there, like where can you go but inside?"

"I'm not sure I understand your inside/outside split—*dichotomy.*" Ez laughed. "If you'll forgive me a word from the Academy that feeds me . . . What I've always found so heartening—exhilarating really—about your generation is that unlike your elders, you've understood, and understood instinctively, that politics is not something that happens *out there*. In newspapers. Or in some distant other realm. And of course, the passion of politics is just that: its intimate and undeniable connection with all of us, and all of our lives. *We* belong to it, and *it* belongs to us."

"Yeah. Right. Well, I think that a lot of that, uh, activist political commitment scene was something *you* turned us on to, Ez. I mean, we could really relate to what you were saying. *Plus* all that other really beautiful shit going down in the black community—Eldridge and Malcolm. And of course, the NLF . . . And if you want to be academic and historical about it and *really* go all the way back, I guess Cuba. And Berkeley."

Ez said, "Yes. You've had the enormous good fortune to be living through very exciting times. And what I find so admirable is that you've *seized* upon them, *acted* on them. Not become spectators. *There's* something history teaches us every time: the danger of spectatorship. . . . Imagine, for instance, if in nineteen fifty-two, in some small town in Wisconsin, someone—a farmer, a lawyer, anyone—had decided he *could* buck the dairy interests and run for the Senate. And with that daring and faith had won! There would have been no Senator Joseph McCarthy. Imagine!"

"Hey, wow, Ez! That's terrific! That's really far out! I love it. And I love *you* for saying it. I really *love* you."

"You don't have to *love* me," Ez said uncomfortably, and Merry could see him pulling at his trouser legs and shifting about in his chair. "What you have to do is think about what I'm saying."

"No, accept it, man! Accept it! Go with the flow! I mean, I know it's heavy, but I have to feel that I can really be upfront with you. Because otherwise, how'm I—I mean, shit, there are things I have to say to you that aren't so—so— Oh, wow! I'm really having trouble here! . . ."

Ez said, "Are we about to have a confrontation? Through the good offices of the FCC?"

The interviewer laughed. "You really *are* beautiful, that's why I know I can say this, okay? I want to go back to what we were into before. Because I don't feel that we really . . . I mean, you were sort of—well, maybe I didn't exactly . . . I guess I'm just really not into that whole macho media journalism tough interviewer trip. I mean, I don't get off on it. . . ."

"I hope you weren't thinking of going to law school, Jeff."

He laughed again and said, "You mean, like I'm not Perry Mason?"

"I mean if you want to ask me a question, *ask* it."

"Well, it's not exactly a *question*, it's more like, uh, a whole *attitude*. A head trip. Okay? . . . A lot of older people— parent types, teacher types—and I don't mean *you*, Ez—"

"That's all right," Ez said. "I am a parent. And I'm a teacher too, God help me."

"Well, I *didn't* mean you. But a lot of people like that—

older types, okay? They were always putting us down for . . . well, for going outside the system. That we weren't being *constructive*, that we were into our own like separate *power* trips, separate *ego* trips, and we weren't *really* working for change . . . all that garbage. . . ."

"In fact, the old charge of the arrogance of the young," Ez said.

"Hey! Wow, Ez! That's beautiful, that's really right on! I mean, I never thought of it that way. But you . . . you really. . . . Yeah!"

"And why shouldn't the young be arrogant?" Ez said. "If not then, when? In arrogance there is so much daring, so much hope!"

"Yeah. Right. So we were always hearing these 'you have to work inside the system' raps, okay? And *now*, this time, for a lot of people, it was . . . well, it was really going against all their own gut instincts—I mean, it was actually *violating* them. But we *did* it. I mean, like I was giving out leaflets in Riverdale! *Riverdale!* Like my parents still live there . . . and . . . and shit, that place has *very* bad vibes for me. It was really heavy. . . . Standing on Henry Hudson Parkway, with the *sun* in my eyes, and all those cars zooming past, it was—it was like my whole *life* was flashing in front of me! I mean, I just kept *flashing* and *flashing!* And I've been burned with bad acid, but nothing like that, man. Nothing! And then, the sound truck! Riding in the same sound truck with all those Bronx Democratic machine Fascists! I mean, boxcar to Auschwitz! It really freaked me out. . . . *But.* It was for a purpose, right? Means and ends and you gotta crack some eggs? So we did it. Only, shit! After all that—all those really *low* games and humiliating scenes—*Nixon? Richard M. Nixon?* I mean, what is the point, Ez? What is the point?"

"I think there again, Jeff, you're making a distinction between inside and outside that I don't believe in, I don't accept. I don't think it makes any difference whether you work inside the system or outside the system—as long as you *do* work. And don't give up. Because it seems to me—now, I really hope I'm wrong—but it seems to me what you're saying is that because you've lost one skirmish—*one skirmish*—you're just ready to get up and walk away."

"Hey, come on, Ez! Shit! That sounds like . . . I mean, are you . . . Well, it sounds like you're trying to lay some *guilt* trip on me! Some really heavy instant-gratification guilt trip!"

"Maybe I am, Jeff. Maybe I am. . . . But look, don't you feel . . . don't you ever have the sense, maybe in reflection sometimes, that you have been—and still are—young during very exciting times? A time of questioning and upheaval and vitality— Of course, it's not without pain, that goes without saying. But a time that's *alive*, almost electric with change and trial and possibility. Don't you ever get that sense?"

"Well . . . maybe in music. You know—the rock scene."

For the first time, there was a long silence, and then finally, in a stunned, small voice, Ez said, "My God. When I hear things like that! . . . Jeff, I can see I'm going to have to make a confession to you. I've often—*too* often—been very envious of young people like you, my students, my young friends. Because nobody likes getting old. But when I hear things like that, what you've just said, I know I would *never* want to exchange my youth with yours, the experiences of my generation with any other. Because when I was young in the thirties, the time itself seemed charged with excitement. We were living through a time like no other and we *knew* it. It was *special* to be young then. And we felt it."

Oh, my God, Merry thought, that's it, he's finished, they'll kill him. No more "young friends," no more adoring students, they'll stop buying his books, he'll lose his job. So that when the phone rang, she was sure it was someone calling to say, "Your father's on WBAI and you won't *believe* what he just said!" But instead, it was a woman with a very foreign voice, saying, "Please, I am speaking with the house of Mr. Ezra Slah-vin?"

"Yes," Merry said hesitantly, since this was no longer strictly true. "But he's not here now. He's in Massachusetts."

"Mass-a-chu-setts!" She sounded desolate. "I am not here so long to travel."

"I'll give you the phone number and you can call him. It's area code four-one-three—"

"No, no! Please. Not to *call*, to *see*. I want really—what I wish is to see his son."

"Oh, the *baby*," Merry said. "You want to see the baby. Well, that's where he is—in Massachusetts. That's where they live now."

"No. Not a baby. A grown son. A man."

"*Nicky?* You want to see Nicholas?" Because when would he ever have given Ez's phone number as his own? Merry said, "I'm sorry, I'm not sure where he is myself. His mother would probably know, but she's in Italy."

"Impossible! Not a mother in Italy. No. . . . Forgive me, please, that I am so forward, and also that I am—I have, ah! *cómo se dice*, jet *lag*, yes? But you, you know well Mr. Ezra Slah-vin? You are perhaps a friend?"

"I'm his daughter," Merry said. "Why don't you just call in Massachusetts, I'm sure he'll be happy to answer any of your questions."

"His daughter," the woman said, very slowly. "His daughter . . . Please, I must ask you—in two days I am again returned in Buenos Aires, so I *must* ask you. . . . Your father, Mr. Slah-vin, he had once a wife named Milgram? Perla Milgram?"

Stunned, Merry said, "That was—she was my mother."

"*Your* mother? *Your* mother? Then it's *you* I want to see and not a son at all! Shall I come to you? Or you will come to my hotel? What you prefer, what you prefer—it's for me no difference."

"Look, you don't understand. You're very welcome to come here, but there's nothing I can tell you about her. I didn't know her."

111

"But *I* knew her! *I!* In Warsaw. That's why I must see *you*."

"Warsaw? Then you must have . . . did you go to school with her?"

"Of course! Yes! To school. And to my house. Very often she was to my house, very often! My parents—ah, but please! You must forgive me. I have just—*cómo se dice me he invitado? m'inviter?*—invited myself to your house and you don't know even who is this person! I am now, from my husband, Halina Zylberschlag, but I was then Halina Dubrowska."

Dubrowska, Dubrowska . . . The D. family! Merry thought. "Was it your parents, your family, who took her to the opera?"

"The opera! . . . Of course! Yes! Zylberschlag! *Ella me ha recordado de algo que*—but how can you *know* such a thing? How is it possible?"

"She wrote about it," Merry said. "It's in an article she once wrote. And I've read it."

"Ah! Yes! She did already write something then once when I have seen her in Palestine. But I was then very much—*cómo se dice*—*boba, naïve, farouche.* Yes, really! Do you hear? Zylberschlag laughs! He thinks it's what I am yet, *siempre.* Well . . . So I will come to you tomorrow, yes? And you will have something to show *me*—what it's written about my family, even so, I will need *traducción.* And *I* have also something to show to you!"

Merry said, "You knew Pearl—my mother—in Palestine too?"

"It's the last time I saw her. In nineteen thirty—thirty-*five* yes. Ai! How much I was miserable then there! Because I—tomorrow I will tell you. But you know, it's funny—*pas drôle, extraño,* yes? Because it's where I'm just coming from now, Israel. Only last morning I am still in Haifa. And now—*now* I love Israel. I love it! I can be *every* day—every, every day—with only Polish. And *such* good Polish! I bath myself. It's how I have seen the photograph I will show to you. Ai, now I am very much excited!"

I don't *look* like her, Merry wanted to shout into the phone. Everyone says she was very pretty and I don't—

"Tomorrow evening, nine o'clock, yes," Halina chirped. "*Ciao!*"

Here is one fact about Pearl Milgram: she had very thin wrists. In an old envelope with the purple-ink letterhead "League for Labour Palestine," there was the face of a watch, a single earring and a tiny tarnished silver bracelet. Only the clasp was broken; otherwise, it was a perfect fit.

And how to entertain a woman brought up in the way Pearl Milgram's essay described? Pretending this was her only real concern, Merry spent the day trying to remember the luminous, winy after-dinner table sets of certain French movies. And as if Halina had actually just stepped out of one, she arrived on that raw, rainy night dressed in a beautiful mauve wool suit and silk scarf, and was carrying flowers. Standing in the dim entranceway of the old Slavin apartment, her blondish-gray hair lighting up the narrow space, she immediately cried out, "Look how small you are! Just as she was! Tiny! Tiny! Zylberschlag, *mira!*"

Behind her, a very thin, stooping, long-faced man with a tan that made him look yellow extended his own hand, and bending over Merry's as if he intended to kiss it, said, "Eliezer Zylberschlag. Pleased."

Thank God Ez isn't here, Merry thought. For him this would be a Marx Brothers routine. But she said, "I didn't realize that you had known my mother too, Mr. Zylberschlag."

"No, no!" Halina cried out, alarmed. "Of course, no. We have met only in Sibir, Zylberschlag and I. *He* is not from Warsaw. Not at all, not at all!"

Merry smiled. "My mother wasn't either. She was from

some backwater little town." And thought: They won't know "backwater." But Halina grasped Merry's arm, and exchanging a glance with her husband, suddenly turned to Merry with a very odd look.

"You don't *know?*" she said, staring into her face. "You don't know even the *name?* To find out what happened?"

*What happened:* Here was a total stranger, she had barely put down her flowers and closed her umbrella, she was dressed with the careful, scented elegance of a Parisian matron, with the look of a woman whose greatest problem in life had been making a beauty parlor appointment, and already she was invoking the ovens. Involuntarily, Merry's eyes went to Halina's forearm.

"No," Halina said. "I have no number, I was not in the camps. I was in Sibir, a labor camp, very different. You see"—she shook her head—"this is what comes from not knowing."

I *do* know, Merry wanted to shout into her face. I know what happened. But instead, she said, "I suppose my father might know the name of the town. If he remembers."

Halina waved her hands as if she were shooing away a crowd of tropical insects. "It doesn't matter for your father— forgive me, please, that I say it. He has perhaps another wife—wives, it doesn't matter. It matters for *you. Always* only I want to see the children."

"This is how she has been in Belgique," Halina's husband burst in proudly. "And almost even Australia!"

"*Almost.*" Halina smiled. "Almost, almost!" Laughing like a schoolgirl, she turned to Merry conspiratorially, her eyes very wide, and said, "I have made him to get assignment—he is journalist, Zylberschlag, *political* journalist for a Yiddish journal in Buenos Aires—I have *made* him to get assignment to Australia. Ai! What I have done! I have made strings, I have made politics, everything!" She did the purposely devious hand gestures of a marionetteer. "And then, in the end, I

114

have found that the sons—both? *les deux*—are in England. Much, much more simple, I had only to stop on the way to Israel. But the daughter I didn't find. Also, they have told, in Europe, not Australia. Maybe Firenze, because she is studying to be—" Halina, with her chubby, beringed hands, deftly made the motion of a chisel against stone. "She is studying to be *sculptreuse.* . . . But now you understand, now you see, this is what I so much feel: to see the children. Brothers, sisters, even husbands, wives—I don't care. You will maybe think I am, *cómo se dice, dura, callosa*—you have this word? But it's what I *feel:* always to see the children! That's why, when I have seen in Israel this time the photograph, I have thought: I must find, I must see Perla's child. So, then, Zylberschlag has gone to make some . . . some researches about the town."

"Then you *do* know what happened to the town my mother came from?"

"I beg you please for my English." Eliezer Zylberschlag stepped forward tentatively. "You have Spanish?"

*Comidas criollas, gran ventas* and *prohibido fumar,* Merry thought, but she said, "Very little, I'm sorry. In school, I learned French—and I do know some Yiddish, but it's really child's Yiddish, kitchen Yiddish, from my grandmother."

"I, too, know only very little Yiddish. And also, only from my grandmother." Halina shrugged, and picking up an apple, began easily peeling it in the spiraling European manner. It was the way she must have once learned in that house in Warsaw so filled with flowers and servants. My mother would have eaten apples that way, it suddenly occurred to Merry, and caught in this thought, did not immediately realize that Eliezer Zylberschlag, his head bent forward intently, was really speaking to her.

"*Ce qui s'est passé en ce petit village, c'était, je crois, un peu exceptionnel. Parce que—*"

"Ai, Lezer! Look how he worries for his English! *I* will tell

115

to her, *I* can tell! *Et en tout cas, Lezer, je ne le trouve pas tellement exceptionnel! Qui sait? Vraiment! Qui sait?"* Turning to Merry, Halina said, "What happened in that town he thinks was . . . *exceptionnel.* I don't know, maybe. But anyway, because the town was very much west—west, west"—she gestured in the direction Merry always thought of as California—"it was finished very fast. *Very* fast. September nineteen thirty-nine. First came the German army, just soldiers, then special S.S. with—yes?—special orders. It was September—Rosh Hashanah? Yom Kippur?"

"*Sí, sí,* Yom Kippur." Halina's husband nodded.

"Yom Kippur, yes, so all the Jews were ordered to be in the synagogue. They would be there anyway, except maybe some . . . some *athées,* but in such a place, how many? Ai, Zylberschlag! *Yo he recordado!* There was one! I remember Perla told this, because in Warsaw for the first time she has met so many Jews who have said they are *athées.* And she was . . . she was very shocked. She told that at home, there was one, he was the . . . ah! The *boulanger,* and he used to *fume,* yes?" Halina made the abrupt motions of a man smoking a cigarette. "He used to *fume* before everyone on *sábado.* He waited for the people to go out, at *midi,* from the synagogue and then, *then* he would begin to *fume!"* She had stopped and was still smiling when her husband said, "*Mais, en trente-neuf, dans cette situation-ci, vous comprenez, même les athées—"*

"Yes, yes, of course," Halina said. "In that time, with such orders, *everyone,* even the *athées,* would be in the synagogue. So all the Jews were there, the S.S. group has come in, and they have shot them. Just shot. And it was finished. So, yes, it's possible to say they didn't so much suffer in that town. *Par exemple,* they were not in the camps. But they had no chance to run, for *échapper,* to *cache* themselves. And they had no chance to fight."

"Did *she* know?" Merry said. "If all this happened in nineteen thirty-nine, my mother could have known about it—her parents, some of her brothers and sisters. . . ."

"But no! Of course not, she didn't know," Halina said. "No one knew. *No one. Personne.* Because if we heard such things, we didn't believe. *We,* who were still in Poland, didn't believe. And I especially didn't believe, I believed *nothing.* Because I was then crazy, crazy in—"

*"Personne ne croyait, personne ne savait, parce qu'ils ne voulaient pas savoir!"*

"Ai, Lezer!" Halina shook her head as if she were admonishing a child. "Because we didn't *want* to know, he says. It's true, yes. But *he* doesn't want that I will tell about myself. *This* he doesn't like!" Halina smiled, and with her eyebrows raised, had the slightly smug, doll-like look of an adored and coquettish wife who had just bought something so outrageously expensive that for a while, at least, she would omit mentioning it to her husband. This look could not possibly have originated with the taut, stooping man who was actually her husband, Merry thought: It must have come from her father.

Aloud, she said, "Maybe he's afraid it would be too upsetting."

"For *him,*" Halina said. "Not for me! It's my life, it's my *jeunesse,* how can I be upset for it? I *liked* my *jeunesse.* Yes! Really! I *liked* it."

Eliezer Zylberschlag sighed, and picking up his cognac glass, walked over to the bookcase, where he began picking out books from the long, packed, disorderly shelves.

Suddenly, Halina grasped Merry's wrist, and with her eyes very bright, whispered, "He doesn't want I will tell, but how I was then crazy I must *explique.* I was not *really* crazy, but crazy in love—with a German. Yes, really! He was the son of a general and so, so *beau*—my God! I know it sounds now *unglaublich,* but it *was.* For all my *jeunesse*—from when I am sixteen till even the war. I *remember,* even *now* I remember, when I am sixteen and I have first seen him. How he was

117

playing and singing, especially singing with so much beauty and feeling, so much *tendresse*, I thought: Oh, my God, I will die. I will die from love!"

"Almost she did," Halina's husband said. "But then it was nineteen forty."

"Ai, Lezer!" Halina shook her head, and quickly turning back to Merry, said, "You see, he was very often coming in my house. *Very* often. He was a friend of my brother, they were together students. They didn't *study* music, but they have found, each, that they love it. Because in my family, you *have* to love music. If you are born in that house, you *must*. From the blood, yes? *Les gènes*. But really, also they did, everyone. *Sauf moi*." Halina laughed. "I didn't care about it so much at all, until when I have heard Heinrich sing. So Heinrich was singing, my brother Vladek was playing the piano, and I was sitting, *just* sitting, so, so quiet that my parents were then very pleased. They didn't yet understand. But I was sitting and—*this* is how you are crazy when you are in love—I was thinking two things. Two—two things! One, I was thinking: He is singing to *me*, only to me—every, every song! And also I was thinking: He doesn't *know* me, he doesn't *see* me, not even to *look* at me. Because who am I for him? Only Vladek's little sister, a baby! But . . . He did look, he did see, and when my parents have understood, they have become very much worried, especially my father. Because he knew, he *understood* how I am *farouche*, yes? So they have sent me to Palestine. And ai! How I was so much miserable! All the time—only, only miserable."

"That was in nineteen thirty-five? When you saw my mother?"

"And how I *cried* to her when I saw her! I have run and embraced her, and then I have cried because it was everywhere *so* ugly, *only* ugly! Hot and brown and sand, and ugly little *houses*, ugly little *trees*. *Nothing* pretty, nothing *gai*. And such *terrible* cuisine, my God! And all the while, you see, *I know* Heinrich has promised he will take me in Italia—Bellagio, Como—with everything, everything beautiful! Blue and green and *beautiful*. And instead, I am there in Palestine with everyone—boys, girls, *everyone*—*running* and excited, *talking* and excited, *working* and excited. Excited, you understand, yes, but nowhere *gai!* Just talking, talking, talking—only such high talk! The land, the future—only *such* things. They didn't *care* it is ugly, they didn't *know* it is ugly, they didn't *suffer*. They think because they have made themselves to be so *dirty* and *wet* and *exhausted* from—I don't know—planting some trees or—or a field that they think for them it is beautiful. *It was not*. And you know, now, for me this is *really unglaublich! N'est-ce pas*, Zylberschlag? Because now, in Israel, exist pretty places. Yes, really! Lezer, *Comment s'appelle le kibbutz que nous avons visité? Près de Haifa? K'far qué K'far Giladi, sí?* It *is* pretty now, what they have planted. But then—*then! Stones* and *brown* and nothing, nothing! My God, I must tell, it was *affreux!* And I, *I* was all the time crying and desesperate. So one day Perla said, 'Come, I will show to you something.' And she took me to a very old—*cómo se dice*—*pardess. Orangerie.* Very old—planted, I don't know, by Rothschild maybe. And it was full, full in bloom with such round, *grandes* oranges, and also the trees were very green and the sky not hot, but blue, blue. And she said—because she knew what Heinrich has promised to me—she was looking at me and smiling and she showed with her arm the whole *pardess,* all the trees, she said, '*Land wo die zitronen blühen.*' You know this—what Goethe has said about Italia, yes? So she smiled and she told, 'Oh, Halinka, only look! Also here they bloom!' . . . Well, it *was* pretty, yes, and it made me to be there more calm. But sometimes I think of that day, and I think what was *really* beautiful was not the *pardess,* but Perla standing there with such a smile—small, small Perla with her arms out *so,* standing and smiling *en face de tous les arbres.*"

"*Mais le photo, Hala! Le photo!*" Mr. Zylberschlag said over his shoulder. "*Encore tu ne l'as montré le photo. Montre-le! Montre!*"

"*Ah, sí, sí! Le photo!*" Halina leaned over Merry to reach her purse and whispered, "You see? He doesn't want now I will continue. Because what I did? I have then returned in Warsaw, to Heinrich, and how I lived? Every day, every week, every hour—only, only for my *rendez-vous*. You understand, this had to be for a secret to my parents. Even so, sometimes I think they maybe knew. Because I was all the time so happy, only happy! And many people—students together with me, my friends and Vladek's friends—are becoming already worried a little. And then, after Munich especially, everyone, *everyone* was completely gloomy, *only* gloomy. Not for the Jews, but that it will be the end of Europe. So everyone was going around this way with such long, sad faces—*sauf moi! Still* I was happy and only waiting for my *rendez-vous*. Even after, when Heinrich has returned in Berlin for the army to be an officer, I have thought: It's for his father only, *c'est une famille militaire,* he is *laughing* at Hitler, I *know* it. And even still after, in nineteen forty, when Poland was already finished, and Heinrich has returned in Warsaw a *Hauptmann—capitain*—because he knows well Warsaw and also Polish, *still* I didn't believe he is a Nazi. Because he has promised to me, to my parents, that he will get for all of us visas—to Sweden, to Santo Domingo, to Shanghai. We didn't know, we didn't care. So my parents have given him everything—money and jewels and paintings and papers for the house and, I don't know, some properties. To watch it for us, guard it until we can return. He promised, yes, and also he told for the visas he must have *more* money, and that we must be immediately prepared to leave for when they will come. But Vladek didn't want to go. He didn't want to go out from Poland. He wanted to stay and fight. With the partisans—Polish partisans, he was very Polish, Vladek, and blond, blond like me—also my mother has looked this way. So he has gone to Heinrich to *explique* he doesn't want any more the visa, and also to ask him to help for some— some—what we are calling 'good papers'—*cartes, documentes officielles* that will say he is Polish, *only* Polish, so he can go through. And what Heinrich did? He has laughed, only laughed to his face and told, 'You think you don't look like a Jew? You are right. You look like ten Jews. Ten!' And *I*—I couldn't believe that Heinrich has said such a thing, so I have gone, at night, to see him. And he told, oh, he is now too much busy, even he cannot speak with me, but tomorrow, all the day, he will have for a holiday, so we will go for a drive in the country, someplace very pretty that he knows, and it will become maybe more cool near the evening so I must bring a warm coat. Well, because he has said evening, in this way, you understand, I didn't tell to my parents where I am going, and I have just gone . . . gone out from the house."

"And she didn't any more see it *et ça suffit!*" Halina's husband said firmly. "Hala, *por favor, querida! Bastante!*"

"So we have gone in his car," Halina said, "and I have brought a little—*cómo se dice*—basket, yes? *Panier*. With some foods and a cloth, so we can stop somewhere, in the country, in a field, and have, I don't know, some—some little *dejeuner alfresco*." Laughing, she said, "You see how much I was romantic! Because still I was happy for the *rendez-vous*, still I was excited. . . . But Heinrich was all the time very quiet, very grave, and he didn't want to stop. He was only driving, driving, driving very far, very fast. And I said to him, 'Heinrich, where are we *going?*' Because I see already we are so much east, it's not any more my Poland, what I know. It's only forests and marshes and muds, and such *very* poor, poor little houses of peasants—more poor than how I am accustomed in the country near to Warsaw. And also the shrines, the churches are not any more *Catholique Romain*, but they have such little round onion tops of Russian churches. So I said for a joke, a pleasantry, 'What is this? It is like Bielorussie, what the Soviets are always demanding.' And this, about the Soviets, I have said for a joke. Because yes, even so there *are* Russians—the peasants living there—for *us*, how we thought then, it was still Poland. East, yes, but still *our* Poland. But Heinrich didn't laugh. He said, 'Yes, you are right, we are now in the Soviet *partie*, and here it will be safe for you.' And because *still* I haven't understood, I said, 'What do you mean? *What* are you talking about?' He didn't look at me, and he told only, 'Oh, I am now very tired from so much driving. Let's just go out from the car for a little, to use our legs.' So we went out from the car and we are walking and walking more, and I see still he is very strange, very nervous. But he said, 'You have the coat? You have the basket?' And I thought: Good! *Enfin!* Now we will sit, we will eat some— some foods, and I will ask about what he has told to Vladek. Because I was from this *so* much upset! So I have put out the cloth, and I see on the top of the basket are some . . . some papers—a *carte d'identité* with my photo. But it's *not* my papers, I *know* it. So I said, 'Heinrich! What *is* this? Why have you put my photo?' And he told, 'Oh, *verdammt!* Look what I have done! I have left in the car my cigarettes and now I must go back and get them.' So he got up, he went away to the car, and . . . well, he just didn't any more come back."

"But you didn't even know where you were!" Merry said. "Did you think you could somehow find your way back to Warsaw?"

"Oh, no! No, no! This even *I* knew. Because how can I pass? It will be first Russian lines, and then German lines, how *can* I? With Heinrich, in the car, we have had no difficulties because he is a German officer, and it was then in the time, you know, when the Nazis and the Soviets are—are kissing yet. It was still nineteen forty, October. And what Heinrich knew, I am now sure, is that very soon in Warsaw, in some days or

weeks, all the Jews will be closed in the ghetto. *If* he knew more, I don't know. If he *cared* more, also I don't know."

"*Il savait tout! Tout! Evidemment! Ce n'est pas une affaire de conjecture!*" Halina's husband turned to Merry and said, "Forgive me, please. I regret. But when she tells this way, I am become so fru*strat*ed!"

"Well, but it's because of this that we have met!" Halina said, smiling. "He must be glad. Yes, really! I mean this! We have met, you know, because we are both in Sibir. Zylberschlag the Soviets have sent to Sibir because he is a Bundist, and I, *I* because I am *bourgeoise.*"

"And this she is still!" Eliezer Zylberschlag came across the room to his wife, smiling. "*Siempre.* As you see."

"He laughs, but I mean this really!" Halina said. "It's because of what Heinrich has done that I remain! I am the only one of my family, even so I have some—some cousins in Israel, and Zylberschlag has also a cousin in Denmark, but still! It's what I thought again when I have seen this time in Israel the photo which someone has found, that I will show to you. Because it is of the girls who were in my class in the *gymnasium*—not all, you understand, but we who were friends together. And I am looking at it and looking at it and not speaking *anything*, and *enfin*, I told to Zylberschlag, 'Of all these girls in my class, of all my friends, only two—two—remained. Only I and Perla.' "

"But she's been dead for almost thirty years!" Merry said, "What are you *talking* about?"

"But *you* are here! *You!* Don't you understand? Because of this, she was not—cut off! Because of *this!* Come, I must show the photo."

I don't want to see it, Merry thought, maybe I'll be lucky and she won't be able to find it. And then suddenly, with the picture—actually a postcard—thrust in front of her, she heard herself cry out, "My God! I *look* like her!"

"Yes. She was your mother. How can you find it so much strange?"

"I don't mean I look like her *now*, but in some of my childhood pictures—"

"Ah, she *was* here a child only." Halina nodded. "It's true. For us, the baby. Yes, really! It's how we thought. Because she was anyway always little, little, as you are, but here in this photo, we are all, I don't know, fourteen, fifteen—big, grown—and she is only, oh, I think perhaps twelve. You see, she wears here the clothes of the school, the *uniforme*—this blouse and such a blue *jaquette*—"

"Yes, she's wearing a smock." Merry smiled, reminded suddenly of the schoolchildren in Italian movies, and yet staring in amazement at the clearly foreign-looking girl who had once sat before a camera in Warsaw with her own face. She looks like me because she looks depressed, Merry thought, but then they all do. Because the picture had the look of all European Jewish photographs of that time. The people, camera subjects, so solemn, distant and still achingly familiar, stare out with faces that already seem to hold within them the fate which only the onlooker knows; and at the same time, in a certain momentary glimpse of dreaminess or obstinacy, they are merely people sitting in a meadow or a schoolroom, knowing nothing, impatient for their lives to go on.

"I don't know why she wears here the clothes of the school," Halina said. "She is the only one. . . . Oh, no! Here also Fruma Shperling wears it, you see? This plump girl who has in her hair the ribbon? She also came from such a poor, poor terrible little *shtetl*, like Perla. Maybe such girls didn't have so much other clothes, I don't know. But Fruma we didn't love; she was only all the time looking in books, books and studying, studying, but I don't know—she was not really clever. Dull, you say?—*ennuyeuse*—and she didn't like me. Because, you see, here *I* am—so *blonde, blonde* with such a

124

beautiful dress, so much *à la mode*. Because I am *bourgeoise*, yes, Zylberschlag? And because I am *bourgeoise*, you see, I wear here also this little *collier*—gold, very much delicate. From my father, I remember. He has given it one day when he has returned from Frankfurt. And ah! Here, *here* is my friend Irena—also very pretty clothes, and you see, such a laughing face. She was what we call now *chica. Muy chica.* And always, with me, getting into mischiefs from the teachers. And here, this one, *never* getting into mischiefs, but other troubles, yes, because she is so *serious,* so grave! Look how she wears even here for a photo only such dark, dark clothes—with *nothing* pretty, nothing! And of course she holds here a book, and of course it must be, I am sure, *Das Kapital,* this is Liba Margolis. Of us all, the great, great *athée* and *agitateuse.* And then when she has met Perla's cousin Leszek, the great *communiste*—even as a boy, really, already he was—Liba has become so much only *looking* at him and so much always *following* him that *we* started to call, from the letters of her name *en français,* L.M.—*elle aime!* Every, every time we were calling after her, 'elle aime, elle aime,' and every, every time Liba was becoming so—so red and angry, and only telling to us speeches—about the workers and—and *la commune de Paris,* and that *we* are the ones who are thinking about love, we but not she, because love is *bourgeois.* And *she* will be like Rosa Luxemburg. . . . But she *did* love Leszek." Halina smiled. "A schoolgirl love, you understand, but she did. Because he was, well, not to say *beau,* this not, but very much"—she made a fist and a swaggering gesture—"very much strong. Brave. Sure—like a fighter. Very much what we are calling *macho.* In the end, of course, he *was* really brave. And fighting. Everyone who remains has said this—from all parties."

"So that was the cousin who fought in the Warsaw ghetto?"

"Yes, of course! This was Leszek. In the end, he *was* fighting, but not a class war, not the war he was always waiting and telling. . . . But you know how I think sometimes? It's better he has died this way. Yes, really. Because what would be if he remained? First, he would be staying in Poland, and because Leszek was always, *always,* from a boy, *so* much *communiste, so* much *idéologue*—you have this word *idéologue,* yes? Well, he would be, I am sure, first *apparatchik* and then going higher, and *enfin,* when Gomulka has removed all such high Jews, he must go then in Denmark to stay and be miserable. This I know, because I have seen. *Par exemple,* Zylberschlag's cousin, but many are like this. *Many.* They will not go, because of *idéologie,* in Israel, and also the same they will not go in United States, so they are sitting in Denmark, *beautiful* Denmark, with nothing to do, and are only miserable. *So* much miserable, my God! So much bitter."

"Hala," Mr. Zylberschlag said tentatively, "I regret, but it's late now, I think. *Il nous faut partir.*"

"Ah, you see? You see this? He doesn't like now what I am telling about Leszek! To say it was brave how he died because he was fighting. I *know* how Zylberschlag thinks. Because it's for us already a long, long argument. *He* thinks it's not—not right, not *juste,* for all who have died to make this as a difference. To make in this way classes of the dead—that these were brave and fighting, and all others not. *He* believes to tell this way: If they have died, if they have suffered, this is also brave—and it's enough."

"*Oui, parfaitement,*" Halina's husband said. "*Parce qu'autrement c'est comme ces gens qui disent qu'ils sont morts comme les moutons.*"

"Ah! That it's the same to say they have died like sheep. No, I don't find it's the same, *I don't!* And it's also *my* family, Lezer, so I can speak! I don't make of those who were fighting big, big great heroes and all others *nothing*—sheep. They didn't make *themselves* to be big, big heroes—*pour la gloire.* They were fighting, yes, because they were young, and this was natural. Not *exceptionnel*, but natural. Because they were young and so much full with life and *ardeur*. And this—*cómo se dice*—*característica*, this, what is a natural character for all *jeunesse*, it's a *good* thing, Lezer, a *better* thing, even. Yes, I think so. Better."

Because when *I* was young in the thirties. . . . What was it Ez had said on the radio? But how was it the same 1930s?

Halina said, "Well, we won't now finish this argument, I think, and it *is* late really—for us, for you. . . . Of course, I invite you to come and stay sometime with us in Argentina, but you won't come. No, no, no, you *won't* come. Why should you? You have no reason. It doesn't matter. I travel."

"There's something I'd like to ask you: how did you find this phone number? How did you know my father's name?"

"In this, as you see, she has become brilliant *detectiva!*" Mr. Zylberschlag said, smiling.

"Do you see how he makes such romances? And he is calling *me bourgeoise!*" Halina shook her head. "Of course, sometimes, I must make some—some researches, but for this, not at all. Because I have had letters from Perla—not so much often, but letters. That she is married and of course with whom. That she has had a child—but you know, I thought, *really* I thought it was a son! And also . . . also that he will have to be older."

How to explain about Jonathan? That Ez had, in effect, simply given him away; that Jonathan had been raised by Leo and Celia Spivak, and regarded them as his parents—*them* and no one else. So Merry settled on saying only, "I was her second child."

"Second, *ah!* Then you are born in which year?"

"Nineteen forty-four."

"Nineteen forty-four! Nineteen forty-four!" Halina cried out. "This is *maravilloso! Zylberschlag, tu l'as entendu? Elle est née en quarante-quatre!* But this is a great, great thing! For a Jewish child to be born in nineteen forty-four, it's a *great* thing. It makes you to be, I think, very . . . lucky."

"My stepmother wasn't Jewish," Merry said in a rush, and instantly regretted it.

"Stepmother . . ." Halina said slowly. "Was she kind to you?"

There it was, even in the phrasing of the question: Isobel, whom Halina would never know, never see—fastidious, delicate, well-meaning Isobel as evil stepmother. Guiltily, Merry said, "Yes, she was *very* kind. Always. She's been kinder to me than to her own son."

"Ah, yes, this happens. I am familiar. It's not so much *exceptionnel.* But still, you see, once again, then, it makes you to be quite lucky. . . . Well, so, you have now the photo—to keep, and I wish also you will have—this." From the lapel of her suit she removed a flowered pin.

"Oh, no, I couldn't. I can't keep *that.*"

"Yes! You *can!* Of course you can! It's why I am giving it! I have *many* like this—many, many. It's nothing. These little jewelries I am making myself. Already from when I am little. You see what it is? It's a flower. So I am taking the flower and I am—*cómo se dice—preservar?* I am preserving it, yes, and then, *then* I am making, like this, some little jewelries."

"*Elle accueille des fleurs partout! En tous pays!*" Mr. Zylberschlag nodded proudly.

"Yes, that I'm taking flowers always when we are going in a different country. It's how I like to do. So I have—from every travel. Only *this* flower"—Halina held out the pin, squinting at it—"this one, I don't remember where I took it. And what it is"—she shrugged—"I don't know at all. It's only some— some pretty flower, and I have many, many such, so you must take it." She picked up her umbrella, and suddenly, in this stance, ready to leave, Halina had once again become an elegant, remote European matron—poised, formal, charming—and surely not anyone Merry would ever have expected to know.

"I regret to say good-by," Mr. Zylberschlag said, once again bending over Merry's wrist.

Halina smiled and drawing Merry toward her as if she were kissing her good-by, instead urgently whispered in her ear, "That flower? I have taken it in Schweiz. And why? Because it's *this* flower every, every time that Heinrich was bringing me. So—if I would have a daughter, I would give it for her. But I don't. So I think now it's *propre* that you will have it."

# 8

EVERY day at about three o'clock on Madison Avenue in the Seventies and Eighties, there is a long, uneven parade of young mothers pushing baby carriages. They keep looking in store windows as they walk, and every so often you can hear them call out, "Seth! Rachel! Jeremy! That's *it!* I've *had* it! I'm *going!*" And very soon, from somewhere not too far down the block, a little child comes stumbling back, crying, "Joshie's mother said . . ." or, "But you *promised* I could. . . ."

Some of these mothers walk singly, and some of them are in pairs, but almost all of them are very well dressed, and where they tend to linger longest are the store windows filled with imported shoes. And they can afford them, too. Because usually they're the wives of doctors whose offices are right nearby—say, just around the corner from a famous French bakery, or else maybe across the street from a new gourmet shop. So through this unusual cloud of heady smells—baking croissants and fresh-roasted coffee beans—they keep ambling along in their private, winding after-three parade. And this is the strange part: there they are, moving in the sulky glow of young and affluent health, and yet they somehow manage to look, at the same time, both smug and squintily disaffected. Unfair? Well, one of these women was Merry's sister-in-law, Laura Spivak. But which one? Which one?

> Laura Beth Ragovin, daughter of Mr. and Mrs. Bernard J. Ragovin of Hewlett Harbor, L.I., was married yesterday to Dr. Jonathan Spivak, son of Mr. and Mrs. Leo Spivak of Forest Hills, N.Y. The ceremony was performed on the lawn of the bride's parents' home by Rabbi Sherwin Zaslow of Temple Adath Israel of Hewlett. The bride was attended by her sister, Andrea Lynne, and the best man was Dr. Sanford Bienstock.
>
> The bride is a graduate of Brandeis University and holds a master's degree in social work from the Columbia University School of Social Work. She is a psychiatric social worker at Hillside Hospital. Her father is the president of Rainbow Yarns, Inc., of New York City and Grey's Ridge, South Carolina, of which her grandfather was the founder.
>
> Dr. Spivak, a first-year Fellow in the Cardiology Department at Mount Sinai Hospital, is a cum laude graduate of Columbia College, and received his M.D. degree from the New York University School of Medicine. His father is the owner of Guaranteed Rite-Away Roofing of Long Island City.

"Laura Beth Ragovin! Laura Beth Ragovin!" Ez had said at the time this announcement appeared in the *Times*. "Oh, Laura Beth Ragovin, darling little suburban dumpling! Can you imagine? That a son of mine should have come to this!"

Merry said nothing. Neither she nor Ez had been invited to the wedding, but they had received engraved cards more than a week after it had already taken place. In a way, it was surprising that the Spivaks themselves hadn't just cut out the newspaper announcement and put it in an envelope: it was the method they had long ago settled on for communicating, like blackmailers in murder mysteries, Merry always thought, or kidnappers sending ransom notes. When Jonathan graduated from high school, Leo and Celia had sent an item from the *Times* headed STUYVESANT YOUTH PLACES FIRST IN REGENTS AWARDS. They circled Jonathan's name in red and, further obscuring the tiny print of other names, wrote in: "Jonathan will be able to use his State Scholarship because even though he also made Harvard he decided to stay home with us and go to Columbia." And when he had graduated from college, they sent along a clipping headed SIMCHAS, and circled this paragraph: "We extend our heartiest congratulations to Leo and Celia Spivak on the graduation of their son, Jonathan, from Columbia University. Not only did he graduate with the highest possible honors, but he is bringing them yet even added *nachas* by his acceptance at NYU Medical School. We remember Jonathan from those long-ago days when he attended our Talmud Torah, and of course, had his Bar Mitzvah in our Main Synagogue. We know that in but a scant four more years we will be joyfully welcoming back Doctor Jonathan Spivak!" And for all Merry knew, that's just what they did, because the next communication from the Spivaks was a clipping from the *Mount Sinai News.* It was a list of the interns who would be starting in the coming year; naturally, there was Jonathan's name circled in red, and Celia had written: "Whether you know it or not, Mount Sinai happens to be a top internship to get. It was Jonathan's first choice, but if he wanted he also could have had Mass. General."

"Oh, Laura Beth Ragovin, adorable little kewpie doll of upstanding Bernie J., who's worked so hard, *so hard* just to keep you in orthodontia and private riding lessons that even Grey's Ridge, South Carolina, could not remain untapped! Grey's Ridge, South Carolina, Merry! Do you realize what that must be like? The kids there have probably never even *seen* a dentist! And braces, to them, would have to mean those funny, stringy things that hold up Grandpa's pants on Sundays. . . . Well, cookie, I don't know. . . . It's just incredible. This is my son. This is your brother. *Your own brother!* I'm really sorry. I only wish there was something I could say."

Merry said, "I think I'd like to send a present."

"Present?" Ez said. "Present?"

"*You* know—those things that come in boxes and you put wrapping paper on them and take them to the post office."

"Why would you send them a present? What—what *object* could they possibly need? You don't imagine that Mr. and Mrs. Bernard J. Ragovin of Hewlett Harbor, L.I., would *stint* on this joyous occasion of their daughter's marriage? Or deny her anything for her first household, do you? Or wait a minute, wait a minute! Do you mean that because she's no longer strictly *his*, the old man'll turn into the cheap, cheating bastard he's always been in his business dealings? Oh, that's a *very* interesting idea, cookie. I'm proud of you. I never would have thought of it and I bet you're right!"

"I don't think they'll *need* anything, Ez. That's not the point. I'd like to send them a present because—well, partly just to show the Spivaks. Because they've always been so rotten to me. I'd like them to see that *I'm* still capable of civilized behavior. Jonathan is my brother, he just got married, I will send him a present, I will do the right thing."

"The right thing!" Ez exploded. "The right thing! My God, Merry! Bernard J. Ragovin has spent his whole life doing 'the right thing'! He's despoiled an alien landscape, he's made sure to hire where the labor isn't unionized, he's exploited and connived even in his sleep—but I'll guarantee you that that man never once forgot to send out Christmas cards to his business associates or anniversary presents to his wife!"

"You left out about his slum buildings—Bedford-Stuyvesant, East Harlem, the South Bronx. . . ."

"Really? Does he? He's a slum landlord too?"

"Oh, Ez! How do I know? But suppose he is? What's it got to do with my sending a wedding present to Jonathan?"

"You're making a mistake, cookie," Ez said. And he was right.

Because standing in the housewares department at Bloomingdale's, Merry fell into the dream of things. Coffee grinders and electric juicers, fish poachers and asparagus cookers, copper teakettles and ceramic French coffeepots, all of them, all of them would fall from the walls of Jonathan and Laura Spivak's new apartment, and seated with them around their dining room table—austere butcher block, but decorated with sunny straw mats and grainy blue-green Mexican glasses—would be Merry Slavin, new-found sister and sister-in-law, joyfully welcomed back. So she sent them an electric food-warming tray, and in an engraved envelope received this: "Dr. and Mrs. Jonathan Spivak thank you for your thoughtful gift." And that was it.

"Why?" Merry said tearily to Isobel. "Why do they have to treat me this way? Why do they always have to behave as if I don't exist? Or as if I've done them some terrible wrong and can never be forgiven? They never even *talk* to me, ask about me. Nothing. Ever. My God, Isobel! I'm Celia's sister's daughter. I'm Jonathan's sister. *Why?*"

Isobel was then in New York—she had come by boat—for the publication of her new novel, *Early Closings*. She was staying with Charlotte Brodsky Barro, but had come over to the old Slavin apartment partly to see Merry and partly just to escape, for a while, from the noise and generally senseless hullabaloo that was always going on at Charlotte's. The phone rang endlessly, waves of people trooped in and out, eating and drinking, scattering their plates and glasses, and Charlotte herself blew back and forth on a confusing round of errands and appointments, each of which she followed with a breathy, frenzied bulletin. Altogether, what it was like, Isobel said, what it reminded her of, was when there was a death in a Jewish family. "Like when your grandmother died," she said to Merry. "When they sat *shiva.*"

There had to be some other Jewish family's *shiva* that Isobel had in mind, Merry decided. Because when Merry's grandmother—Ez's mother—died, Merry, then eight, had already been living with Ez and Isobel for two years. And the *shiva,* which she remembered only hazily, had taken place at her Uncle Bloke's, Ez's oldest brother's. This Uncle Bloke and his redheaded, heavily made-up wife, Nettie, were people Merry had seen only two or three times in her life, and their apartment, somewhere in Brooklyn, was a place she had never before been to. All that hot June Sunday afternoon, their door was left wide open to let in a breeze, and people, all strangers, poured in, bringing cakes, fruit and children. From the kitchen, a radio broadcasting a baseball game went on and on with tinny monotony; from downstairs, the bells of a Good Humor truck rang and rang through the sounds of children skating and shrieking. Pasted in perspiration to her seat on the sofa, and listlessly sipping some warm, flat orange soda, Merry listened to the droning blur of disconnected conversation, and felt that this drone and the drugging, stuporous heat was itself like an illness; perhaps it was something like this her grandmother had died of. Because otherwise, she could find nothing in that place that was connected with her grandmother, and nothing that had anything to do with the new version of her life that she was clinging to: Merry Slavin, no longer just somebody's granddaughter, but the daughter of Ez and Isobel and the big sister of little baby Nicky. Opposite her, in a wing chair, an unknown man smoked a cigar and fanned himself with a newspaper; at a corner window, a boy of about her own age sat on the sill with a bowl of fruit, methodically spitting out cherry pits at the children in the courtyard five flights below. The uneven, jumping dazzle of the sun's rays and the slow, hanging patterns of cigar smoke began to creep into her orange soda. Fearing suddenly that she would throw up, Merry unhooked herself from the damp, heavy arm of a woman she did not know, and whispered to her father, "It's *boring* here." Ez smiled. "Yes, cookie," he said kindly. "It is *very* boring."

As it turned out, this was a sentence Ez never forgot. "It's Boring Here" was the title he gave to a piece about middle-class family life. And how was it surprising, he wrote, that it was a child who had peeled away the soggy layers and bit through to the essence? "In a somewhat different context, George Orwell has written with peculiar ambivalence about this same quality in English middle-class family life, and offers the chillingly evocative phrase 'solid breakfasts and gloomy Sundays.' But characteristically, Orwell manages to find some special virtue in this. Luckily, children are not similarly muddled. For what can the psychologists, the sociologists— all those smug, certain celebrants of our post-atomic 'adjustment'—tell us that my eight-year-old daughter's observation would not disarm? Proclaim it from the television sets and the hi-fis; shout it above the washing machines and the vacuum cleaners, and—why not? Paste it clear across the picture windows! Yes, indeed, my dear, it's boring here."

Well, there wasn't a picture window for miles around, but that was Ez's mother's *shiva*. And how Isobel could connect it to the chaotic goings-on at Charlotte's, Merry could not see. But she said to Isobel, "That was practically the last time I saw Jonathan and the Spivaks. When my grandmother died. At her funeral."

Isobel looked old and tired, and this made Merry furious for no reason she could say. There was Isobel, sitting with her eyes half closed and her fingers massaging her forehead, as if she were trying to conjure up a past that was practically beyond reclaiming. Finally, she said, "Yes, I remember that. . . . He was a very strange-looking child, wasn't he?

But of course, he didn't speak to me. None of them did."

"They didn't speak to me either, Isobel! That's exactly what I'm talking about!"

"But that's *why*, Merry. That's *always* been why. Don't you understand? It's because of *me*. When Pearl died, those two women came rushing into the house like—"

"Which two?" Merry snapped. "Celia and who else?"

"That other sister who had come here. Miriam, I think that was her name."

"Oh, *crazy* Miriam! Who had to be put away. Ez told me about that."

"Crazy Miriam who had to be put away. And who died in Pilgrim State, yes. . . . I'm not *excusing* them, Merry. Really, I'm not. I'm just trying to—"

"Oh, go ahead! Just finish the story. When Pearl died, what?"

"Those two sisters tore through the house like madwomen, I'd never seen anything like it. They didn't cry, they hardly spoke. But the hysteria! It was all over their faces—in their eyes, in their expressions, in the way they moved. They were like a whirlwind, they just *grabbed* at anything that had belonged to Pearl, and threw it all into bags and boxes. They even took things that belonged to me. I remember because they took away my favorite dress, and I couldn't move, I couldn't stop them. They took almost everything in sight. Throwing it, piling it—they just took *everything*."

"They didn't take *me*," Merry said bitterly.

"No, they didn't. Because in their eyes, you were instantly connected with me, with my presence in the house, with Ez's 'other' life. Jonathan had been raised by Pearl, so he belonged to her and they took him. But not you. That was their attitude, that's how Jonathan was raised, and then, of course, during all those years, Ez neglected him totally. So really, it's not surprising. In a way, what else could be expected?"

"But he's my *brother*, Isobel. He just got married and I haven't even been invited to meet his wife. Maybe Ez doesn't care, but I do. What will happen when they have children?"

What happened, three years later, in 1967, was this: "Dr. and Mrs. Jonathan Spivak (née Laura Ragovin) joyfully announce the birth of a son, Adam Raphael." This announcement was sent to Merry but not to Ez. It was an engraved card and could have come from a casual acquaintance. Well, in a way, what else could be expected?

But of all people, it was Ez who had once, in the meantime, expected something different from Jonathan, and this was why when his first grandchild, Adam Raphael, was born, he didn't even receive a printed announcement. It affected Merry too. Because even years later, after Halina's visit, when she decided to call up the Spivaks, Laura, whom she'd never met, said warily, "Jonathan isn't home, and I really don't know how he would feel about seeing you. I don't know if he's ready. I mean, I don't know how much of all that he's really worked out. . . ."

Merry said, "Look. Two weeks ago, a woman came to see me who was a friend of Pearl Milgram's in Europe when they were kids. And she gave me a picture of Pearl as a schoolgirl in Poland. I thought Jonathan should see the picture too. I thought he might want to."

"Well, if *that's* all, you could make a copy of it and send it to him, couldn't you?"

"It's *not* all. I want to *see* him. And speak to him. And I'd like to meet you and Adam." But because Laura said absolutely nothing, Merry went on nervously, "And also, there's a publishing house that's interested in putting out a collection of all of Pearl's old pieces, and they've asked me to write a sort of introduction—since she was my mother. Well, she was Jonathan's mother too, and I thought he might be—"

"Oh, a *book!*" Laura burst out. "God, how typical! What an absolutely typical Slavin maneuver! Listen, Merry, I don't know whether Jonathan wants to see you or not, but if he doesn't, I wouldn't blame him. I mean, you know what happened the last time he saw someone from the Slavin family."

Practically the whole world knew what happened the last time Jonathan saw someone from the Slavin family. Because the "someone" was Ez. And what happened on that day—the Peace Parade of October 16, 1965—ended up by bringing him the kind of widespread fame he had never before had and probably never expected. Not that he was unknown then. In fact, earlier in that same week in October, Merry, then in her senior year in college, overheard this conversation in the ladies' room at the library.

"Did you see that girl? In the green corduroy pants? Who just combed her hair?"

"Oh, yeah . . . I think her name is Merry. She's in Leslie Ettinger's Shakespeare section. You know, that famous Shakespeare section where Rachel Polikoff stripped when they were doing *Antony and Cleopatra?*"

"Forget Rachel Polikoff! Do you know who that Merry stays with when she goes to New York? *Ezra Slavin!*"

"Oh, I don't believe it. Ezra Slavin! It's probably just like Kathy Swerdlow—when she goes around telling everyone that she slept with Fidel."

"No! I just heard her tell it to Abby Gerson. And they're friends."

"So? Kathy told the Fidel story to her friends, too."

"Yeah, but this was different. Abby was inviting all these people to stay over at her house for the demonstration. Because she lives on the East Side and that's where everyone's supposed to line up. And also because her parents are going to the country for the fall foliage, so they'd have all this *space.* Anyway, *that* girl Merry said, 'I can't, I'm staying with Ez. He's supposed to be one of the speakers, so I think I better be around.' "

"What did Abby say?"

"Nothing. Just something like, 'Well, then let's meet for coffee.' "

"*I* didn't know that people were staying over at Abby Gerson's. Are you?"

"No." Merry heard the girl giggle over running water. "How can I? *I'm* staying with Pete Seeger."

But when Merry arrived in New York very late on Friday night and there was no sign of Ez anywhere in the apartment—no clothes, no papers or books strewn around, and no food in the house at all, not even anything for breakfast—she was very tempted to just take a cab across town to Abby's. A cold roast beef and a still warm roast chicken would have been set out on platters by the Gersons' maid, and in the refrigerator, for the next morning, Abby's mother would have left stacked boxes of Sara Lee croissants, and at least five different kinds of Hero jams.

"My God! Do you know where I've been? Do you know what I've just seen?" It was Ez, and he was standing in the doorway with an expression of such heightened internal excitement—that glow of wonder which shone through his glasses and lit up his whole face—it suddenly occurred to Merry that he must be expecting a girlfriend. "Merry, have *you* seen the Forty-second Street IRT station? All the signs and lights and corridors and colors! Blue and green and yellow, it's so beautiful! It's a marvel! You know what I forget every time? What this city *is!* The *life* that it has! I forget it, and I'm away from it, but God almighty, there is nothing like it! That smell—the grit and electricity of the subways? One breath and it's like the rush of euphoria mountain climbers are supposed to feel when they reach the top. It's the energy, Merry! It's the energy, and I love it. My God, I love it."

Because Merry knew exactly what he meant and had felt it herself, it embarrassed her. She said, "It's for the World's Fair, Ez. That's why they fixed up the subway station. All those signs and lights and things—it's for the tourists. So they don't get lost trying to find their way to Flushing."

"But that's just what I mean about the *spirit* of the city! Even from something foolish—worse than foolish, commercial, meretricious—even from something *that* bad, *that* destructive, the spirit of the city itself can wrest something wonderful. It's always self-renewing. . . . We are *wrong* to malign cities. *I've* been wrong." Pacing back and forth through the foyer, Ez now walked into the kitchen as if he were looking for something, so Merry said, "There's *nothing* in the house, Ez. Nothing. We don't even have—"

"But you know something about that kind of being wrong? It's what makes me optimistic, I swear it! I feel now as if I could walk through this city for hours and hours without stopping! From the Battery to Spuyten Duyvil—I just want to *walk!*"

Merry said, "In that case, if you happen to pass a bodega or a deli someplace that's still open, could you please come back with something for breakfast? We don't even have instant coffee."

"Breakfast?" Ez said. "Breakfast? We don't have to worry about that. The Roizmans are giving a big brunch."

"Oh, God, the Roizmans! Is this supposed to be Sybil Roizman's contribution to the antiwar movement?"

Ez laughed. "I suppose you *could* look at it that way, cookie. But I don't know why you'd want to be so cynical."

"Because I can't stand them. I can't stand one person in that whole family. And the only reason *you* like them is that they're always sucking up to you."

"Don't you think this is a conversation you'd do much better to have with Isobel? Dave Roizman is an old, old friend of mine. And for a psychoanalyst, he's very open-minded."

"Open-minded!" Merry said. "You mean he always reads your books and articles and writes you little notes about them—even though they weren't published in psychoanalytic journals."

"Well, for an analyst, that *is* open-minded, Merry. Especially since he knows how much I disagree with the whole outlook of his profession, that's *very* open-minded. It's very generous. . . . What's so terrible about him? What don't you like?"

"I don't like the way he greets people. I don't like the way he says hello."

"You don't like *what?* What's this? From some literature course you're taking? Word-by-word explication? What do you mean—you don't like the way he says hello?"

"I don't like the way he looks when he says it. He always gives you this look as if he's got some very special relationship with you—a private line to your hidden suffering. And only *he* can understand. . . . He's always—he's always doing a commercial for compassion."

"Well, he's known you since you were a little girl. And you're my daughter. I'm sure he does feel some kind of special interest in you."

"Oh, Ez! He does it with *everyone!* It's disgusting. It's smug and boastful and condescending. In fact, that's what that whole family is. Sybil, with her mental-patient poetry and her ridiculous folk-dance counselor outfits! And *Nina*—my God! When she played the guitar in high school, the only teacher who was supposed to be good enough for her was Andrés Segovia. So she went to Spain for the summer. And then when she decided her *real* love was ballet, and everyone told her she was too old to be starting, she said that she was going to England so she could study with Margot Fonteyn!"

Ez said, "Spain, yes, I remember that. Dave and Sybil were terribly upset about her going to Spain. I think they even promised her a car and a whole year anywhere else. . . . But what did Sybil just tell me on the phone? That she's studying acting now—I think that was it."

"In that case, Nina's in England. Private lessons with Sir Laurence Olivier. How else could she study acting—I mean, *theater?* I'm sure Nina doesn't say 'acting.' And I bet Sybil didn't either!"

"And what about Mark?" Ez said. "I haven't heard a word against brilliant Markie."

"I never really knew him, he's the one person in that family I don't have anything against."

"Well, he's the one person who's sure not to be there tomorrow. Dave and Sybil hardly ever see him. There was some big falling-out between Mark and his father. Or as they say in the language of Dave Roizman's profession, it's a troubled and complicated relationship. . . ."

Merry said, "I thought Mark was a doctor. And was doing research at Rockefeller Institute."

"Something scientific." Ez waved his hand in dismissal of the whole unknown enterprise. "But it was antipsychoanalytic—I think that's what the fight was about. . . . Christ, they *are* smug, Merry. I know what you mean. But it's the smugness of money, it's the smugness of success. . . . Look, if you don't want to go tomorrow, of course you don't have to. But Sybil did ask for you specially."

"Oh, I'll go," Merry said grimly, "but I'm leaving early. I'm meeting Abby Gerson across town."

"Abby Gerson! The wide-eyed flower of the bourgeoisie! Talk about the smugness of money and success—how's her fat-cat father?"

"You've never met him, Ez. You've never even *seen* him. How can you talk that way? What can you possibly have against him?"

"A window shade manufacturer? Who lives on Park Avenue—excuse me, *off* Park Avenue? In a ten-room apartment?"

"The Roizmans have a ten-room apartment," Merry said. And that was at least half the reason she wanted to go there.

# 9

FROM the Roizmans' fifteenth-floor apartment on Central Park West, from their high, wide windows, the whole autumn city—full red and gold trees and misty buildings, blind towers and light, vaulting bridges, ridged roofs and shaded windows, buses and cars that stopped and started as far away as Madison Avenue, and traffic lights that blinked and changed beyond a river and among invisible streets, probably Queens, the sense of bustle and removal from bustle—all of it, all of it flew before Merry in the high, thin golden light of a childhood dream. If I lived here, Merry thought, I would never be bored. But this was not necessarily true: Nina had lived there and clearly she was always bored. And Sybil? Sybil, who now came rushing toward Merry, and embraced her through a rhythm-band clapping of wooden beads.

"Merry, darling! I'm so happy to see you! I only wish Nina were here. But she's in Paris. She's studying mime with Marcel Marceau! Of course, I'm sure she'll do something there—at least sign a protest at the American embassy. But I know she'll be very sorry to hear she missed you, you know how much she loves you!" Propelling Merry toward a laden table, Sybil stopped before a squinting young woman in a very expensive-looking wine suede outfit, and grabbing her elbow, said, "Judy, darling, this is Merry Slavin, Ez Slavin's daughter. And weren't we lucky to snag *him* today of all wonderful days!"

Wine-clad Judy squinted, not at Merry, but at some distant point beyond the liquor bottles and the tall vase of autumn flowers, and said, "It's all the smoke in here, I think *that's* what's bothering me, because otherwise I'm really used to my contact lenses. God, I'll die if I have to go through a whole Peace March in my glasses." And then, turning toward them both, she said, "Sybil, that's a *terrible* way to introduce someone. All my life I've been introduced as Barnett Diamond's daughter, I *still* get cramps when it happens and I've been in analysis for eight years! . . . You know, sometimes I think that's the real reason I married Marty. So I wouldn't have to be Judy Diamond anymore."

Firmly, Sybil said, "*Judy*. You realize, sweetheart, that you're projecting. Of course, I understand. But not everyone experiences it that way. And besides, Ez Slavin is a highly unusual man! . . ." She suddenly stamped her foot as if she were performing a folk-dance step and shouted out, "Oh, *no*, Judy! Please! If you're going to do something with your contact lenses, *please* do it in another room! It's the one bodily operation that absolutely makes me squirm! . . . Merry, darling, what can I get you? A screwdriver? A Bloody Mary? Or are you absolutely ravenous and ready for a bagel?"

"Actually, what I'd really like—"

"The Nova's right here—and doesn't it look *scrumptious*

with all those lovely lemons and capers! Here's the cream cheese, *with* scallions and without, there's the beautiful sturgeon. Do you know that a neighbor of ours told me she'd never had sturgeon because it wasn't kosher? I said, 'Nonsense, Yvette! That fish practically wears a yarmulke!' I don't know *where* some people get their ideas from—but of course, she's Belgian. . . . And let's see, what else? Oh! The eggs are coming soon, but it's only omelets. What I *really* wanted, Merry, what I had my heart set on was eggs Benedict. But Dave said absolutely not, it was inappropriate and practically the same as moving to the East Side, so-o, we're having omelets. But I know Verona hasn't started them yet."

"Sybil, what I'd really like is some coffee."

"Oh! Coffee! Well, I just plugged in the urn, so I know it can't be ready, but let's go into the kitchen and see if Verona's still got some left from this morning."

In the kitchen, against a half-curtained window facing the park, a heavy, uniformed black maid was moving pans and bowls from the stove to the sink. Sybil, with her arm around Merry, said, "Verona, darling, you remember Merry, I know you do. Oh, I just love it when all of Nina's beautiful little friends come back! Doesn't it make you happy?"

The maid looked up blankly, and Sybil, suddenly breathless, said, "Just give her a teeny cup of your wonderful coffee, and then I'll leave you two. I know how long it's been, and how much you both have to catch up on!" She blew Merry a kiss, and as she hurried out, could be heard saying, "Yes, of *course*, Frances, darling, I *told* you Ezra Slavin would be here! No, you will *not* be shy. He's an absolute love and you are going to meet him *right now!*"

Merry looked out the window, past the trees and the park, to Fifth Avenue, which would soon be filled with crowds amassed for the Peace Parade. From this distance, and in the natural blur, they might very well look—so many people, all the different colors of clothing—like a peculiar but by no

146

means unattractive extension of the brilliant autumnal park. Only Verona, clearing away the brunch dishes, would be left to take in this view—Verona, who now glanced at Merry, and without a hint of expression, remarked, "Nina in France."

"I know," Merry said. "Her mother was just telling me."

"Yessir!" The maid suddenly livened up. "That girl in Paris, France! I said to her, 'Nina, I ain't gonna believe you *nowhere* if I don't get me a picture postcard with that Eiffel Tower on it!' And you know what that girl done? She sent me a picture postcard with the Eiffel Tower right on it! And Mark? When he had to go on over there for some doctors' meetin' in Holland? I said, 'Mark, I ain't gonna believe you *nowhere* if I don't get me a picture postcard with some of them *tulip* flowers on it!' And you know what *that* child done? He sent me a picture postcard with a whole bunch of them *red* tulip flowers! And you know what else it have? A windmill! Yessir! A windmill! Red tulip flowers *and* a windmill!" Chuckling and banging the pots around in that large, sunny kitchen, Verona, so wide-framed and in her uniform, suddenly seemed to Merry like a maid in a forties Hollywood movie. Well, why not? If Dave Roizman, with his crooning, seductive voice and his stare of pained and penetrating compassion, had made himself into a Hollywood version of a psychiatrist, how was it surprising that he managed to come up with a Hollywood version of a maid?

From the doorway, Sybil was saying, "Of *course* you're not late, Ilse, darling! Let Ernst come whenever he's through. Dave has emergencies too. It's the curse of the answering service. . . . What *I'm* going to do right now is give you a piece of the most *marvelous* Viennese coffee cake—special for you and Ernst. And I'm going to make *you* guess what bakery it comes from!"

Merry said, "Thanks very much for the coffee, Verona," and she was already out of the room, edging her way around the crowded bar, when Verona suddenly leaped out of the kitchen, a large pot still in her hand. *"Now* I remember you!" she called out exultantly. "Miz Roizman was right, I *know* who you is! You that skinny little thing with all them dead, divorced mothers!"

"Oh, you must be Lydia Samet!" said a woman at the bar, looking up. "I *thought* you looked familiar. Don't you remember me? I'm Penny Lustig's cousin. We met in Mexico—the day the bus kept breaking down and there was that adorable family with the chickens and everyone at Franny's went to Taxco. In fact, I'm even wearing the earrings we all got that day. See?" She pushed back her hair and fingered the two hammered silver fish shapes that dangled from her ear lobes.

"I've never been to Mexico and my name is Merry Slavin. Please excuse me, I'm just looking for some food."

"Ez Slavin's daughter! Oh! Tell me! What's he going to say this afternoon? And what about the park? Did we get the permit? Did the bastards give in?"

"You can ask him yourself, he's around here somewhere." But where? Because looking around the Roizmans' enormous living room, Merry did not see anyone whom she knew, not even Dave Roizman. In front of her, as she reached for a bagel, a heavy, baldish man with sideburns was scooping up some black olives and saying, "Christ, Schechter! That schmuck calls *everything* schizophrenia! It's his favorite diagnosis. When Arnie Golub was presenting a borderline with schizoid features—*which* the psychologicals backed up, you know Arnie, he doesn't take any chances—Schechter just stood up, took one look at the history and practically wiped the floor with—"

"Oh, good! Here's my darling wonderful Merry and she's eating! That's what I call an active, successful guest!" Sybil beamed as she pushed through the crowd with her arm around a slight, gray-haired, very reserved-looking woman whom she was propelling in an uncertain direction. "People are always talking about a successful *party*. Or a successful

148

*hostess.* But what human interaction could ever be one-sided? Am I right, Ilse? You have to have successful guests!" The gray-haired woman smiled uncomfortably, and Sybil said, "Darling, I know you'll excuse us. Ilse and I are in quest of the coffee cake. Oh—and, Merry!" Sybil suddenly jerked her arm out, and pointing to the farthest end of the room with the severe and frozen solemnity of an explorer's Indian scout, she called out, "Remember the ruggelach!"

"You don't mean clinically?" the bald doctor now said. "Because in that kind of illness, as soon as you scratch the obsessional overlay, you're smack up against the—"

"Excuse me," Merry said loudly, and made her way to the other side of the room for the ruggelach. No one had yet gotten up to this part of the meal, so the area around the table was empty, except for an elderly couple who were standing beside it all by themselves. In their stance of hunched and nervous eagerness, they looked like somebody's in-laws invited by mistake. The wife, with a tight and hopeful smile, held on to her coffee cup and kept glancing anxiously at her husband, who had just then clutched at the sleeve of a passing guest. "Since five o'clock this morning," this in-law husband said desperately. "What am I saying? Since five o'clock *every* morning. I'm up like a country boy, up with the birds. Ever since my second heart attack. What do you think?"

The bearded young man who had been stopped was awkwardly balancing several Bloody Marys; he looked in the other direction and said nothing.

"I happened to mention it to Roizman in the elevator and you know what he told me? That it's a sign of depression. Could this be true? That just because you get up early it means you're depressed? You're a doctor too, I'm sure of it. In your opinion, tell me, does this kind of thing make sense?"

"Early rising is a classic depressive symptom," the young man said hurriedly, and tipping one of the Bloody Marys, instantly escaped.

Merry bent over the enormous platter of miniature Danish,

and just as she was biting into one with apricot filling, there was the in-law wife, exuding the department store smell of too many different cosmetics, almost on top of her.

"I bet I know who you are!" she said, her smile so eager, broad and forced it looked as if her mouth would break. "I bet you're a friend of Nina's! And not only that, I bet you know her from the days when she was mostly interested in music. Am I right? You're a music major?"

"No," Merry said. "I'm majoring in English."

"You're majoring in English! Isn't that wonderful? Ben, did you hear? She's an English major. Isn't that nice?"

"What's so wonderful about it?" the in-law husband said, looking around gloomily. "Somebody should tell her—she won't be able to get a job. Look what happened to Carolyn. Every time we went there for dinner, before I could even sit down, I looked around that apartment and everything turned black."

"What's the difference now, Ben?" the wife said helplessly. "It's such a long time ago."

"The difference now? I'll tell you the difference now! It hurts me. It hurt me then and it hurts me now. Still. That for all that time my daughter had to live that way! Because she *didn't* have to live that way. She could have—"

"All right, but then when she got married, everything—"

"*Which* time when she got married? Because the first time, with that bum, that loafer, all he did was take her from one slum to another. The cockroaches were their moving men. My Carolyn! With that face and that sweetness . . ."

"So it didn't work out that time. Why dwell on it? Look how *different* everything is now! Just think of all the—"

"Now!" the in-law husband said bitterly. "Now!" As if this lost time, a specific but enormous region, were spread out before him like a road map of the wrong place. "Listen to me, young lady. Don't be an English major. First, you'll never be able to get a decent job, so you'll work for peanuts in a

150

publishing company and you'll live like a dog in a rattrap. And then when you get married, he'll turn out to be a bum. What *he'll* say is that he's a poet, and because he walks around in a turtleneck, with your good heart you'll believe him. Until one day when it's already too late, you'll understand and you'll wake up crying." He looked as if he were about to cry himself, and finished with a stare of such impassioned sadness that Merry actually took a step backward, and looking at her watch said, "Excuse me, but I have to go."

"Don't go," the in-law wife pleaded, smiling frantically. "You mustn't take it to heart what Ben just said. He didn't mean anything, he's only aggravated."

"No, I really do have to go," Merry told her. "I'm meeting some friends across town."

"Friends . . ." the woman said wistfully. "That's what it is to be young. . . . Friends, and coming and going, and meeting and seeing. And whether it's night or day, the phone never stops. . . . Go, sweetheart, go ahead and meet your friends and have a wonderful time! And if what *you* want is to be an English major, don't let anybody stop you. Do what *you* want, believe me. It's the only way you'll have good luck."

"Good-by," Merry said, trying to smile, and from behind her, as she was walking away, heard, "You know what I think, Ben, every time I see a sweet young Jewish girl like that? Good-by my whole young life."

Suddenly feeling a terrible burden, Merry pushed her way back through the crowd.

"Oh, Merry, darling." Sybil, standing in the center of the room, was sucking on an empty cigarette holder and looking around in all directions. "I see you were talking to Lily and Ben." She made a face, and said finally, "They're our neighbors."

"I know," Merry said very quickly. "Sybil, have you seen Ez? I have to leave now and I'd just like to—"

"No, what I mean is they're *just* our neighbors. Of course,

151

they're very sweet people and I'm *extremely* fond of them, but . . . Well, they're not political at *all*, Merry. They don't even go to concerts!"

They're not musical at all; they've never even set foot in a voting booth? Merry said, "Sybil, I've had a *wonderful* time, but I promised my friends I'd meet them early, so I really have to leave right now. Do you know where Ez is? I just want to tell him."

"Darling! Didn't you know? He's with Dave. In the study. And God *knows* how long they've been in there, Dave absolutely kidnapped him as soon as he came in!" She put her arm around Merry, and sighing deeply, whispered through the clamor of the room, "I always told him, all we have to do is be patient. . . . But he was so hurt he couldn't be rational. And my God—Dave! Who is above all *the* rational man. But you know, he just felt that all his values of a lifetime had been, well, trampled on. Thrown out the window. And now, *now* he is just *so* happy, he's a changed man! Do you know what I keep thinking? It's like the opposite of that—what's that quotation? 'In the midst of life we are in—' No, not that one, that's the Christian one. What's the Jewish one? At weddings, when they step on the glass? In the midst of your private joy, you're supposed to remember public tragedy? Well, we're just the opposite. Because here we are in the midst of this ghastly, appalling war, and *we* have this—this incredible occasion of enormous private joy."

Merry said, "Sybil, I don't know what you're talking about."

"Darling! You don't know? It's Mark! Our Mark has come back to us! And it's all because of Ez!"

Still completely puzzled, Merry said, "Did Ez speak to him?"

"Oh, it's not only *Mark* who Ez is speaking to, Merry. It's *all* those children! When Dave went that night with Meyer

Tabakoff he said that's all they saw there. Kids. *Babies,* practically. That's what's so wonderful!"

"What was this? Where was Ez speaking?"

"No, no, no, Merry! *Ez* wasn't speaking. *Mark* spoke, our Mark! That's how we knew he'd come back to us! I'm telling you, if you saw something like that in the theater, you'd never believe it! All because Dave saw a sign somewhere that there was a meeting for doctors who were concerned about the war in Vietnam. So, naturally, he went. And then when he gets there, he finds that his own son—*his own son*—was one of the organizers of the whole committee! Merry, when he came home that man was so beside himself with joy, he could hardly speak! He was up all night. . . . And then of course, two days later, Mark came over for dinner, and what can I tell you? He's our Mark again! In fact, he would be here right now, but he's busy with the committee. And if anyone ever had a better reason for not coming to a party, I haven't heard it!"

"Sybil, that's great," Merry said. "I think I'm just going to knock on the door and—"

"Do you know one of the things that he said? Mark, who does brain scans with computers? He quoted Ez! You know that thing Ez always says about technology? 'When I hear the word technology, I always reach for my slingshot.' Well, when Dave heard Mark say that, that's when he *knew.* For certain."

"I think Ez actually says 'Yo-Yo.' 'Whenever I hear the word technology, I want to reach for my Yo-Yo.'"

"Oh, he's a wonderful man, your father. A rare and unique human being. Sometimes I think he's a saint, I mean it. Except he has faults. Because he *is* human. And that's even *more* wonderful."

"Well, I'll just knock on the door, Sybil. To let him know that I'm leaving."

"Nonsense, Merry! Nonsense! Don't be shy! Go right in

there! We can't let Dave monopolize him forever, can we? He has to *share* good things. Isn't that what it's all about? What we're always trying to— Oh! There's Ernst!" Sybil turned toward a short, spry, quick-stepping older man wearing a beret, and said, "Ernst, darling! The Viennese coffee cake! Of all *days* to have a suicide attempt on your hands! You're going to have to talk to Milt Jarcho, with his theories about timing."

The small man, in a deft, impatient gesture, took off his beret, revealing a Viennese Ben-Gurion haircut, and briefly smiling, said, "Ah, Sybil. I hope that you can forgive me. But you understand, with such things . . ."

"Oh, darling! Forgive you! Don't be absurd! And Milt Jarcho's theories! I mean, he's a lovely, well-meaning man and the place in Shelter Island is a *treasure*. But as Dave always says and everyone knows, it's the analyst *after* him who has to pick up the pieces!"

Merry walked toward the room where Dave picked up pieces. Only this office part of the Roizmans' apartment did not face the park, so that even though it was already noon, the light coming in had a certain filtered, chilly, first-cold-of-the-season feeling. In this austere autumn sunlight, in the sound-proofed hallway just outside the waiting room, Merry stood looking at one of Nina's seashore collages—she had titled it "Not True Green/But the Green of the Mind's Eye"—when the door of Dave's office was flung open and Ez, gripping his jacket and newspapers, came bursting out. Things kept slipping out of his hands as he walked, and altogether he seemed so upset that he went right past Merry, barely nodding—exactly as if she were simply some familiar subway billboard. Suddenly half turning, he said, "I have to leave immediately. I'm going over to Mount Sinai to see Jonathan."

"You're going to do *what?*" Merry said. "To see *whom?* My God, Ez! What are you *talking* about?" Because instantly, instantly she was afraid she knew: if Dave Roizman had just been telling him the miracle story of Mark's return—the estranged son, for so long devoted only to the dehumanized disciplines of the laboratory, now suddenly become an organizer of a medical committee against the war in Vietnam—well, then, Ez also had an estranged son who was a doctor. And why not? Wouldn't he, too, want to take his rightful part?

Ez said, "I don't have time to discuss it now, Merry, but believe me, it's *extremely* important."

Which was just how he approached the girl behind the information desk at Mount Sinai Hospital. With Merry standing beside him (and why? why? what was she doing there? what did she think she could prevent?), Ez leaned over the high plastic partition, as if this leaning alone could obliterate the separation, and in a clipped, anxious voice, said, "Dr. Jonathan Spivak. I have to see him immediately. It's *extremely* important."

The receptionist, a young, very pretty Puerto Rican girl, in a navy-blue uniform inscribed in gold lettering MISS L. FIGUEROA, was absently singing to herself and filing her nails with an emery board. In the shiny, empty hospital space, a corridor as sleek, dead and glassy as a resort for Martians, her partitioned-off singing sounded especially melancholy. But she held out her hand to examine her nails, and said pleasantly, "You know which floor he at? You know which building?"

"My dear Miss Figueroa," Ez said, drawing himself up like a drunken English actor. "How can *I* know that? It is *you* who are enclosed with the Information. It is locked up with *you* behind that . . . that glass cage."

"Yeah, but see, I don't call no doctors. That's not what I do, you know? What I do is—you got someone over here, you got a patient you want to visit, I check out their names and I tell you where they at." She pointed to several loose-leaf binders of cards, saying, "That's the information, you know? For patients. Which floor, which room, which building. That's it."

From somewhere in the ceiling, a tinny disembodied

loudspeaker voice called, "Dr. Brian Weisskopf, dial one-four. Dr. Weisskopf, Dr. Brian Weisskopf."

"Of course! Why didn't I *think* of that?" Ez said. "I'll have him paged! Miss Figueroa, will you please have Dr. Jonathan Spivak paged? Will you please arrange it?"

The receptionist slammed down her loose-leafs, and no longer smiling, said, "Hey! I just told you! I don't page nobody and I don't arrange nothing! You got somebody over here, you got a patient you want to visit—"

"Hey, Luz! What you doin' here today?" A young black orderly raced an empty stretcher past the information desk. "It's Saturday, girl! You got to get yourself ready for some real fine partyin'!"

"You think I'm not ready, Marshall? Just 'cause I don't do my partyin' with *you?*"

"Luz," Ez said rhapsodically. "Is that your name, Miss Figueroa? Luz? My God, what a beautiful name that is! It means light, doesn't it?"

The girl put her hands on her hips and eyed Ez as if she wanted to say, "So?" Instead, she just nodded warily.

"Luz . . ." Ez went on smiling at her distantly, intently. "There was a time, Miss Figueroa—of course, you're far too young to know what I mean—but there was a time in my life when names like that, Spanish women's names, seemed to me the most beautiful names in the world. The *only* beautiful names in the world . . . And perhaps they were."

Oh, my God, Merry thought, in about three seconds he's going to start telling her about the Spanish Civil War.

"Just the *sounds* of those names," Ez said. "Luz, Alicia, Marisa, Graciela . . ."

"I got a cousin her name Graciela, but we call her Gracie. 'Cause Graciela, you know, that's too *long*."

"Too long for *what*, Luz?" the orderly said. "And too long for *who?*"

Ez turned to him, laughing. "You're very funny, I really

156

like that! You're a very clever young man. . . . But you know, you're *so* young, both of you, that you weren't even *born* at the time I'm talking about. Actually, come to think of it, my son Jonathan—that's Dr. Spivak—wasn't born yet either. In fact, in those days, I never even dreamed I'd someday have a son called Dr. Spivak. . . . Oh, look, Miss Figueroa, Luz, I don't want to put you to any trouble, especially on a Saturday. But it really is *terribly* important for me to see him. Isn't there anything you can do to help me?"

Was this the best of Ez? Or the worst? The receptionist, totally disarmed—she began twisting a curl around her finger in thoughtful distress—said, "Well . . . You know which department he in? You know *something?*"

"Dr. Spivak?" the orderly said. "You mean that skinny dude with glasses who always racin' and rushin'? *I* know where he at now. I can tell him you here. Only thing I got to do first is get this stretcher over to Emergency, those dudes over there so *cheap* about their damn stretchers."

"Don't go too fast, Marshall," the receptionist called out, smiling. "You don't want to take away no energy from tonight. For who*ever*."

Ez began glancing through the lobby at the white-coated young doctors who were hurriedly passing by. "Look at that!" he said. "They're *all* skinny dudes with glasses, racing and rushing! And you know why? They're learning to rush out their bills! They're practicing to race each other to their stockbrokers!"

Nervously, Merry said, "Ez, *please*. Don't speak to Jonathan that way. He hasn't seen you for so long, and he might feel—I mean, he might not—"

"Merry, really! I'm surprised at you! What I have to say to Jonathan is *very* important, but it's not at all personal. It's not in any way private. This is an issue that so far overrides all those old . . . family conflicts . . . old childish resentments. I would never *dream* of—"

"You! What are *you* doing here?" A very harried-looking, unkempt young doctor—even his white jacket looked as if it had been slept in—stood glowering in front of them. "What the hell are you *doing* here? I was just told that my father was here! I was given an urgent message! How could you *dare* do a thing like that? How can you even have the nerve to—"

"Jonathan," Ez said, extending his hand. "I'm terribly sorry to have taken you by surprise, but believe me, this is no time for anger or recrimination. I wouldn't have come here if it weren't urgent."

"Tell me! What's the matter? Was there an accident? Is someone sick?"

"No, no, no, not an accident. I don't think *anyone* would call it that. But sick . . . well, yes. Because it's in your capacity as a doctor that I've come to see you. Only it's not just one sick person that I'm talking about; it's a whole society. *Ours.*"

"You came here—when I'm in the middle of working on a *kid*, a twenty-year-old kid who's just gone into cardiac arrest—you came here to tell me *what?*"

"Oh, Jonathan!" Ez said. "When I think of all the things I've said and thought about doctors, and now I listen to you and see your passion, I—I'm just so *ashamed*. I can't *tell* you how ashamed I feel. But at least now I know I was right to come here." He nodded. "That you *will* walk with us this afternoon, you *will* join us. Because that's exactly what this Peace Parade is all about—that same passion that *you* have to save human life. To refuse admission to waste and destruction. To turn back the agents of death for all the twenty-year-old kids, wherever they are. My God, Jonathan, I'm proud of you. I'm so proud that you're my son."

"Your son! *Your son?*" Jonathan thrust his hand through his hair—dark and wavy, the same as Merry's, the same as Pearl Milgram's—and pulling it through his fingers so tightly that the roots stood out, said, "You crazy bastard, you don't even know the meaning of the word."

"Jonathan! Please! Listen to me! *Don't* give in to private resentment. *Don't* let it stand in your way. I understand how you feel, but this is *so* much more important. Private bitterness can ruin everything, believe me, I've seen it. And so few things in life— Jonathan! Please! Wait!" But already he had sped off into a waiting elevator, and Ez was left speaking to air.

At the speakers' platform on Sixty-ninth Street, a folk singer was playing his guitar through the static and sinusy hum of the PA system, his voice either over-loud or almost inaudible, depending on the direction of the wind. The wind, too, was carrying off above the crowd balloons stamped STOP THE WAR IN VIETNAM NOW, and Abby Gerson, leaning against an enlarged photo of a ravaged Vietnamese mother and child, the picket sign that she had been carrying, said, "God, I'm freezing, I'm absolutely *freezing*. If he sings 'Where Have All the Flowers Gone' one more time, I swear I'll scream. It's not even Tom Paxton, I don't even know who he is."

"You've been here all day, Abby," Merry said. "You don't have to stick around anymore."

"No, I *want* to, I want to hear your father. Did you see his speech? Do you know what he's going to say?"

"Even *he* doesn't know what he's going to say before he says it. He only likes to speak spontaneously." And this was true. Ez always told people, "Oh, I'll see how I feel when I get up there." But considering the day he had just been through, Merry began to worry a little. Because exactly how good could he feel when he got up there today?

"Hey! Look, Merry! There's Rachel Polikoff! And look who she's with! That graduate student from the Film Society, Mike Spiegel. *I* thought he was supposed to be living with—you know, what's her name? Ellie Someone—she doesn't shave her legs and she's in Anthro?"

"I don't see where—" Merry started to say, as a loud,

crackling whine burst out of the loudspeaker.

"Well, he's got all these cameras and lights and things. . . . I bet he's making a movie of this. Do you think maybe Rachel'll strip? So she can be in it?"

The crackling continued, as if the folk singer were clearing his throat. Finally, hesitantly, he said, "I . . . I hope you'll all bear with me, because I've never done anything like this before—I mean, introduce someone who's not a singer. But, well, maybe in some ways he is—and I'll tell you what I mean. . . . A couple of months ago, a group of us were in Havana, and one day we were just sittin' around and eating and talking with this . . . this really wonderful Cuban poet. And suddenly he said to us, 'You know, my friends, I've been listening to American folk singers for years, and there's one thing that's always puzzled me. Why do you always sing folk songs from other countries? Why don't you sing your *own* songs, *American* songs? Because, you know, it's only when Americans sing their own songs, and realize the work they have to do at home, that we will feel safe—that the *world* will be safe from America!' . . . Well, I guess this is sort of a metaphor, but I kind of think of our next speaker as a man who's *always* been singing American songs. Friends, brothers and sisters, Ez Slavin."

There was applause, but it was really very scattered: the day had turned gray and chilly and people were tired. Ez moved over to the microphone, and holding up the newspaper which he had been carrying around all day, he waved it as if in greeting, and speaking very casually—just the way he would to friends sitting in his living room over paper containers of take-out coffee—he said, "I don't know how *you* feel about the *New York Times*—" and was instantly stopped. Because suddenly there was a traveling swell of laughter and appreciative booing and there it was: in ten seconds, Ez had captured his audience. "I don't know how *you* feel about the *New York Times*," he repeated buoyantly, "but I always think you can find . . . *something* interesting. Today, for instance, there was a little item—and by the way, always go for the stuff that's hidden away, that's how they let you know what's *really* fit to print—there was a barely noticeable one-liner informing us that eleven o'clock today at the World's Fair, the Westinghouse Corporation was going to be performing still another selfless corporate act. This one's for posterity." And Ez read out: "'The Westinghouse time capsule containing contemporary artifacts will be placed alongside the 1939–40 capsule.' Contemporary artifacts!" Ez repeated, and once again the crowd laughed. "Well, I don't know, what do you think they'll put in it? I mean, aside from Westinghouse appliances. Because after all, how would it look if they left out any of those? A few dishwashers, some air conditioners—all those products our fellow Americans in plenty down in Appalachia and right here in Harlem and Bedford-Stuyvesant are so intimately familiar with. And I certainly hope they're not going to forget a color TV. Because otherwise, *otherwise* who knows? All those people alive in future generations—if there *are* any future generations at the rate we're going—let's just say anyone still alive after the strontium 90 settles—well, they might just get the idea that the only people who made color TVs were Japanese. And my God! Japanese! Those are people with yellow skin and slanted eyes! And we all know what you do with them! Bomb the hell out of them, wherever they are! I mean, you can't *see* them. Not the way those skinny little sneaks go creeping around their snaky jungles! . . . Actually . . . actually, it seems to me that poor Westinghouse is at a certain disadvantage these days. If that time capsule were being prepared by the friendly folks at Dow Chemical, a much more fashionable outfit at the moment, then we'd *know* what would be in there—a roll of Saran Wrap and just a tiny little canister of napalm! Progress, my friends, progress has *always* been our most important product!" Ez paused, was forced to pause, because this time from

ance and a sense of enterprise, could *do* anything, *be* anything, succeed, *make good*. And if he didn't? If he didn't *make good?* What consolation was offered him? What dignity, what community? None. None at all. Only the undying judgment that he was worthless. Not luckless, as older cultures might have said. But worthless, utterly worthless. Less than human." Ez's voice broke and he was now crying openly. "It's a mistake to think we've suddenly just *become* a country capable of bombing innocent people. This is a country, a whole culture, that is cruel. And without compassion. And I'm not so sure I want anyone to think of me as a man who sings American songs." Ez turned away from the microphone, and for the few seconds before the thunderous applause broke out, people averted each other's eyes and the feeling of teary, awkward stillness was so intense that the only clear sound was the whirring of cameras.

One of these cameras was, in fact, Mike Spiegel's, and it was his film, the one which featured Ez's speech—*No More American Songs* (A Looking Glass Production)—that was shown at so many antiwar meetings and teach-ins all over the country, and even occasionally at art theaters. Of course, news cameras had recorded the speech as well, and that night Ez made both the six and the seven o'clock news. Ez had become, without in any way intending it, the Man Who Cried in Public, and it was only after that that he was so often invited to be on television panel discussions and interviews.

Apparently even Laura Spivak had seen some of these programs. Because when she called Merry back—*she* and not Jonathan—about that question of getting together, Laura said, "I wouldn't even want to speculate on what your needs are in this whole episode, Merry. I just want you to realize that probably for the first time in your life you're being responded to in a neutral and nonambivalent way. There's no double message here, there's no hidden agenda. This is reality. I just don't see—we just don't feel that the.e's any healthy purpose that could be served by your coming here. I mean, I understand that on your part there are obviously some strong elements of neurotic fantasy operating. But we're very firm about this—we will *not* be manipulated into any kind of collusion with pathology."

Had all this actually tripped off her tongue or was she sitting with a social work textbook propped up in front of her? Merry said, "Look, Laura, all I wanted—want is to see Jonathan and meet you and Adam. It doesn't *have* to be this way for us now. After all, Jonathan is my brother, Adam is my nephew. We could *change* things if we wanted. We're grown up now, all three of us."

"*Grown up?* Excuse me, Merry, but you didn't even get Basic Trust! And *that's* Stage One! And if we're talking about adult models, I mean, my God! Your father—and I'm not just talking about old patterns now, because I've *seen* him on television—your father is the most infantile, narcissistic personality going! He's manipulative, and paranoid with sociopathic trends. In fact, he's a perfect sociopath. Perfect!"

"Thanks very much, Laura. I can see that when my father wants a free diagnosis, he'll know exactly who to turn to."

"You see, Merry? That's exactly what I'm talking about! You're so *angry*. . . and hostile and defensive. I mean, I feel sorry for you, I really do. And it's not just your father. You had such pathetically inadequate mothering. That Isobel Rees, my God! I once had to read a novel of hers for a course, and the idea that a child would ever have to think of her as a nurturing figure—what an incredible distortion! I mean, that book! I couldn't get involved in it at all. And even the professor said that she had a cold intelligence."

Icily, Merry said, "The phrase that you're referring to is 'cold and luminous intelligence.' It does not mean what you apparently think it does. And it was said by a very well known critic."

Laura sighed. "This is sad, Merry. This is just really . . .

164

very sad. I mean, first you've had to form this really destructive identification. And then you were forced to pick up all those terrible defenses. But the fact is, they're not really working for you very well, are they? I mean, you are so out of touch that you still defend that woman! Do you *know* what you just said? Can you listen to yourself?"

"Yes," Merry said, "but I will not listen to *you* for one more second."

And this time, it was Merry who cried, but only in private.

# 10

AT just about the time when Ez had come into the period of his new fame, with *No More American Songs* being shown at teach-ins everywhere, and newspapers and television stations calling up for interviews, someone else in his family, Ffrenchy—Francesca Meisel, the older of his two daughters from his affair with Paula Meisel—was embarking on a brand-new celebrity of her own. It was not a widespread celebrity, true—in fact, at first it was only the other eighth-grade girls whispering and passing notes, and *staring* at her. But then she could see it had spread all the way into the high school proper. Because every time she went to the girls' bathroom, she would find herself so *bugged* by the most *incredible* and pathetic questions that just in order to get out of there, she had been forced to say—she, Ffrenchy, who *hated* lying—that she was allergic to cigarette smoke. And then finally, *finally*, out of all this really incredibly stupid, absurd and immature gossip, had come something *so* boss: she had been invited to a party by a girl who was a junior! Now, this girl, Tamara Dobkin, was not just *any* junior—she was well known—resented, in fact—for never inviting *anyone* lower than a junior. But not only that; even better, she had a twin sister, Gabrielle, who was a senior at Music and Art, and the two of them always gave parties together! So this meant that Ffrenchy, *eighth-grade Ffrenchy*, had just been invited to a party with juniors and seniors from Music and Art! This news was *so* boss, *so* terrific, that naturally she immediately flew off the phone to tell it to her mother. And that was her first mistake. Because instead of getting excited and happy, Paula had given her this very suspicious look and said, "Are your friends going? Was Janie Brecher invited? And how about little Carla Ohrenstein?"

"That's the whole point, Ma!" Ffrenchy had tried to explain to her. "*Nobody* else from my class was invited! That's what makes it so terrific! It's all these juniors and seniors and kids from Music and Art—and *me!*" Ffrenchy, as she told this story to Merry and Ez, in the Slavin living room for the first time in her life, was sitting with her legs tucked under her and eating a mango. Greedily, exuberantly, she sucked at its reddish-gold flesh, and as she leaned over it, her tongue lapping around it for quick but savoring licks—like a child with a melting ice cream cone—it seemed to Merry that the color of this fruit, its lush, melony inside ripeness, was exactly like Ffrenchy's own high reddish-gold coloring: they matched.

Ffrenchy said, "You know something? My mother would *die* if she knew where I bought this! She told me never to go into a bodega because the guys in there might— Ooh! Look what just happened!" Quickly she licked up the mango juice which had suddenly run onto her arm, and then noticing that it had run onto the couch as well, she said, "Oh, God! Look what I did! I'm sorry, I'm really *sorry*— Oh, I forgot! I don't

167

*have* to be sorry. Not with *you.* Not *here.*" Ffrenchy leaned back, and beaming at them both, said, "That's what's so terrific about you! You don't *care* about stuff like that. I mean, even if I didn't *know* it, I could *tell.* Just by looking around this whole place!" She happily held out two open hands, as if she were giving them a private benediction for the self-evident squalor, but continued beaming at them in an absolute euphoria of innocence. "Oh! Guess what I almost forgot!" She suddenly jumped up from the couch, and bringing over her schoolbag, said, "I've got these absolutely *fabulous* brownies! They're from William Greenberg's, so you *know* they're fabulous. I mean, a chocolate ecstasy and *totally* non-plastic!" Beaming still and offering them around as if it were *her* house, she said, "See, my father's office is practically across the street from there, so he's always sort of bopping in and buying stuff. Except *he* can't ever eat it because he's on a diet. And my mother can't eat it because *she's* on a diet. And Sunni—well, I mean, Sunni!" Ffrenchy grinned. "Like *she's* still the Oreo Kid! So-o, I guess really he brings them home for me. Except *I'm* afraid I might break out. I mean, I haven't so far. And my father says that if I haven't, I *won't.* Because I've already had this like really *precocious* onset of puberty. *That's* how he talks!" Ffrenchy giggled. "'Precocious puberty!'" She jumped up again, returning with a beautiful aquamarine Mexican shawl, and with great ceremony, draped it around her precocious shoulders. This gesture, and the shawl itself, reminded Merry exactly of the way Paula had once dressed, but since she had after all not even laid eyes on Paula for so many years, Merry only said, "Oh, Ffrenchy, that's beautiful!"

"It's my *mother's.*" Ffrenchy looked down at it critically. "But she doesn't know I have it and I'm not telling her! In fact, I'm not telling her *anything* anymore! *That* was my first big mistake—telling her about that party!"

Because Paula had just kept on bugging her about it, saying

things like: "But why were *you* the only one invited? What are *you* doing going to a party with juniors and seniors from Music and Art?"

"You *know* how serious I am about music, Ma! You *know* how much I love my flute lessons!"

"Your flute lessons! It's the only thing you've ever applied yourself to, God knows. . . . But then why wasn't that Armenian girl invited? Anahid? The one with the very soulful eyes. *She's* been taking violin lessons since she was practically an infant! And her uncle's a very famous composer!"

"What's it got to do with *uncles*, Ma? You're being so weird about this! I mean, my God! If I knew you were going to make such a big deal about it, I just never would have told you!"

And that was Ffrenchy's second big mistake. The biggest one, in fact. Because it had given Paula the idea—Paula, who had after all always been very open with both her daughters—for example, never acting like it was a secret about Ez being her and Sunni's *real* father, and Al Meisel, wonderful as he was, only their adopted one—it had given Paula the idea that there might be things here and there that Ffrenchy didn't tell her. Which had not only wiped out— actually *totaled*—the terrific trust that they'd always had going for them, but had just caused the biggest trauma and crisis of Ffrenchy's whole life! Because one day when her mother was making Ffrenchy's bed, changing the linens—a thing usually done by their housekeeper, Martine, who'd gotten into some incredible sick relative hassle in Haiti and still not come back—what happened was that Paula, taking off the bedspread, had found Ffrenchy's journals. (She did *not* call it a diary—that was just too childish, obvious and, well, Anne Frank-y.)

"It's so *shocking!*" Ffrenchy said to Merry and Ez. "I mean, it's so incredible! She had the nerve—she actually had the *nerve*—to pick it up and *read* it! I said, 'Ma! I can't believe it! How *could* you? How could you *do* a thing like that? I mean,

169

my God! Read something when you *know* it's private! It makes me feel so—so *violated*.'" But this was not the greatest word for Ffrenchy to have picked on. Because what Paula found out when she read those journals was that Ffrenchy was having an affair with her flute teacher, Alain.

"And you want to know what was the first thing she said to me?" Ffrenchy now turned to Ez, her face absolutely brimming with eagerness. "The very first thing? It's what gave me the idea to call you up! She said, 'Well, I guess I shouldn't be so surprised. After all, the apple falleth not far from the tree.' *The apple falleth not far from the tree!*" Ffrenchy repeated, giggling. And staring at Ez, she held out her arms and said, "Well, *I'm* the apple!"

Ez, who had been sitting very quietly and watching this daughter of his, whom he had not seen since her infancy—he was watching her with a kind of oddly tolerant, almost tender bemusement—now said, "Well, it's true, you know. She's got a point. Your mother tried very hard to be a whore. She *did* try. But she just couldn't do it. It went against her bourgeois heart, her bourgeois soul. . . . My God, that's it! *That* must be what they mean by the whore with a heart of gold! It never made any sense to me, that phrase, never! I always thought, what could it be but the most shallow sentimentalizing? To whom could it ring true? But now I see! *Why* is the whore redeemable? *Why* is she deserving of sympathy? Because at heart, she's just bourgeois!"

Merry began to laugh—there was Ez talking himself into a new piece, but he was right too. When had Ez been involved with Paula? How long ago had it been? Nicky had been a baby, perhaps a year old, so Merry would have been six or seven. And even now, so many years later, it was hard to visualize Paula Meisel with all her clothes on, though she was the first person Merry ever knew who loved clothes above all things. Her closets—huge, categorized and overflowing—gave out a clear and luxuriant scent of what Merry came to

170

think of as the Paula perfume; and the reason Merry knew what was inside those closets was that they were always wide open—Paula was never dressed. Rushing to the door in a half-fastened lavender bathrobe, she would stand at the threshold almost entirely naked as she let go of the robe to open the door. And other times, when Ez had had the key, Paula, who could hear it clicking in the lock, would sing out happily, "Here I am, come on in," and "here" would turn out to be Paula sitting on the toilet. Or Paula, surrounded by soaps and bottles, soaping and staring at herself in the bath. Because of the soapy film and the bubbles, as far as Merry was concerned, this bathtub routine was a big improvement; but often, Paula would half raise herself from the tub, and pulling Merry to her wet, naked body, would call out, "Well, look who's here! It's Cookie!" And that was the worst part of all: only her father could call her "cookie," and it was very stupid of Paula not to have figured that out.

"I left my cough drops on the table," Merry often said just to try and get out of there. But this fooled no one.

"Isobel," Ez would say, shaking his head. "You see? As if all those years with my mother weren't enough!"

But it was really Isobel whom her father blamed—thin, spare, decorous, straight-shouldered Isobel, who was private about her body, shutting the door when she went to the bathroom and actually wrapping herself in towels when she came out of the shower. The reason for this, Paula said, was that Isobel took no joy from her body. She did not really respect it. Which was the exact opposite of Paula. Paula, in fact, had so much respect for her naked body that she sometimes lay for hours on end in a special box, saving up, collecting—the way some people saved money or collected stamps—the special energy that could come only from her body. This energy, as she lay there, was helping to make her free, and was as precious to her, she explained, her arm stroking Merry's hair and back, as Merry, the child, was to

Ez, her father. Could it be that Nicky—drooly, crying baby Nicky—was precious, this precious, to Isobel? It was not a question Merry ever dared ask, because Isobel, it seemed, was always just waiting for Nicky to go to sleep. Otherwise, how would she ever be able to get any work done? This was why Merry and Ez went to visit Paula on weekend afternoons: Nicky was taking his nap, and it was only fair to give Isobel the time alone. Paula, on the other hand, did not have this problem: she had no children, and her husband, Al, whose name was still on the door, was now living somewhere else. *Finally*, Paula said. Because Al was another one—like Isobel—who not only did not respect the human body, but even worse, absolutely did not understand it. You *could* blame his mother, Paula called out from the kitchen, where, standing around in her bra and panties, she was making coffee, but in her opinion the real reason—the *real* reason—was that he was a doctor. Al Meisel hated the human body, his and everyone else's, and was afraid of it, and becoming a doctor was his way of getting back at it- -his *only* way. "Revenge against the body!" Paula said, carrying in a tray with tiny cups and saucers. "Revenge, pure and simple . . . It's *very* American," and saying this, she looked at Ez with the same exact smile as a kid in school who *knew* she had the right answer. "Oh, Cookie, little Cookie!" Paula clutched Merry's head to her cleavage, and sighing, rocked with her this way back and forth, back and forth. "Don't *ever* marry a doctor, promise me! If I ever have a daughter, that's the first thing I'd tell her."

Looking at Ffrenchy now, Merry suddenly wondered whether this particular advice had actually been passed on. But since Ez had just called Paula a whore—pronouncing it "hoor" in the old East Side way—instead Merry decided to say, "Ffrenchy, I think what Ez means is that once your mother wanted to be . . . Bohemian."

"But she's such a *hypocrite!* I mean, my God! *She's* the one

172

who was always telling me about eggs and sperms and how I shouldn't listen to what other kids hear from their parents because it's really all so *beautiful*. And I mean, she was right! It *is* beautiful! Alain makes me *feel* so beautiful! And *now*, now that she knows I'm doing it, she suddenly acts like it's—it's something *dirty*, something *sick*. You won't believe this, I know you won't, but *they're* trying to make me go to a shrink! Just because *I'm* doing what she does, *I* have to go to a shrink! I mean, *she* doesn't go to a shrink. Not anymore, anyway."

"Well, that's something," Ez said. "Maybe the voting rolls will show an increase."

"*Voting!*" Ffrenchy shrieked. "I'm thirteen, *I* can't vote! What's *that* got to do with going to a shrink?"

"I'm not really sure I should be answering that, Francesca. Probably you should ask your mother. *She's* the one who didn't vote for Adlai Stevenson because of an appointment with her analyst."

"Paula voted for Eisenhower?" Merry said. "You mean because they called Stevenson an egghead, she was afraid that he didn't really respect the human body?"

"Oh, no, nothing like that." Ez laughed. "What I mean is that Paula simply did not vote. It was a Tuesday—Election Day always is—but Tuesday, you see, was one of Paula's analyst days. Well! She had to collect her dreams, she had to collect her orgone energy, Tuesday was a very busy day for Paula, hectic. . . . Psychoanalysis imposes a burden of daily, and nightly, responsibility on its initiates that not all the rest of us can—"

"Ez!" Merry said. "That's from your beginning of 'Psychoanalysis and Everyday Life'!"

"And where did you think I got the idea from? Paula—Paula, my *zoftig* Muse!"

"*What?*" Ffrenchy cried. "What, what, what? *Tell* me! You wrote a thing about my mother going to a shrink? You *did? Really?* Ooh! I can't wait to *read* it!"

Ez said, "It's not about your mother, Ffrenchy. It's about *anyone*. In fact, in those days, it was about practically everyone."

"But you were against it, right? And you still are? Ooh! Let me just tell you the rest of it! And you'll see how *disgusting* they are!" Ffrenchy, hugging herself, rearranged her shawl, and ran a hand through her long red hair the better to show off both it and her dangling earrings. "See, one of their big things is that Alain—the name Alain is the same name as Allen. Meisel. So *that's* supposed to mean that what I *really* have is this big desire for my father. And that what I'm really *doing* is competing with my mother. Which is supposed to *prove* that I have to go to a shrink. Because it's this big, famous, classic conflict." Ffrenchy suddenly giggled. "I told it to Alain. And his friend Stuie was there. And *he* said, 'Classic Comic?' . . . God!" Ffrenchy said. "I have so much *fun* with Alain and his friends! I mean, we just laugh and laugh. All the time. And I certainly wouldn't call my *parents* Sam and Sally Breakup! *Especially* my father. Well, let's face it, he's not *really* my father. But okay, *say* he's my father, I mean, just for the sake of argument, say he's my father. He certainly *is* her husband. . . . Oh! And that's *another* thing! He's always telling me not to call my mother *her*. Or *she*." Ffrenchy screwed up her face and began a mimicking singsong: " 'Don't refer to your mother as *she*. It's disrespectful.' *Disrespectful!*" Ffrenchy repeated, giggling. "Well, I mean, I know he's old. But my God! Disrespectful! It makes him sound like something from—from *Thanksgiving!* You know, some—some *Mayflower* thing. With a *hat!*" She began laughing all over again, perhaps at the thought of her father actually decked out in Pilgrim garb, rushing down in the elevator to meet an Indian and shoot a turkey. "And he's the one—*he's the one* who's supposed to be finding me a shrink! Can't you just *see* it? I bet the shrink'll turn out to be some *Mayflower* number too!" And once more mimicking her father's voice, Ffrenchy said, "He's looking for someone 'with a special sensitivity for the conflicts of adolescence'! . . . Oh, God!" She was laughing so hard that her speech had become garbled. "You won't *believe* what they came up with the last time I went to a shrink! I mean, I was only around six, so I hardly remember it, but that chick weighed, I swear she weighed around nine thousand tons. And I don't mean *pounds*. I mean, the woman was an absolute *zoo* number, it was pathetic! She had, all over the place, like on little tables and everything—she had all these like giant coffee cans filled up to the top with peppermints and jelly-beans, and it was supposed to be for the kids, for the patients, right? Well, she used to sit there"—Ffrenchy was collapsing in laughter again—"she used to sit there with one hand scooping up the jellybeans and the other hand kinging the wrong checkers! That's the only thing we ever did—every week we played checkers, and every week she could never get it straight which way you were supposed to move. It was like the chick was color-blind, I swear it! Fat and color-blind and with these like little birthday-party paper napkins in the bathroom!" Ffrenchy reached into her schoolbag—a round-ish duffel bag of heavy, multicolored Guatemalan fabric—and sniffing back tears of laughter, pulled out a tissue. "God, it really cracks me up just to *think* about it! . . . I guess really *that's* the attitude I should have about going to a shrink. That it really is this total goof!"

Merry said, "Ffrenchy, they can't really *make* you go to a shrink if you don't want to go."

"I *know!* They can't really make me do *anything* if I don't want to do it. Except, see, the thing is—"

"Ffrenchy," Ez said, "why were you sent to a psychiatrist when you were six years old?"

"Well, I might have been seven. Or eight. I was like this—this *little kid*." And turning back to Merry, she said, "See, the thing is—well, I didn't exactly *promise* them, I mean, I *didn't* promise them. But I said—well, I mean, they were just *bugging* me so much that I finally had to say—well, I only *said* it—that I wouldn't see Alain again until I discussed it with a shrink. That I would 'honor their wishes, respect their concern,'" and having said this in her mimicking voice again, she also began laughing again.

Firmly, Ez said, "Francesca. *Why* were you taken to a psychiatrist? What was the *reason?* What was the presumed purpose?"

"*Then*, you mean? *Then?* I don't know! It was like a million years ago! How am I supposed to remember? I think it was some—some school thing. Like I couldn't read. Or I was having trouble learning. Something like that. Some bullshit."

"*You* couldn't read? You couldn't learn to *read?* You? Francesca? My *daughter?*"

"Hey! Take it easy! *God!* That was like a million years ago, I just *told* you! I mean, I can read *now*. In fact, a couple of months ago, I just read a book of yours! *Stranger in the Land*, that book about Appalachia? See, my committee was doing this report on Appalachia and poor people and stuff? So the teacher, Joel, said we should read *your* book and that book by Michael Harrington. And I did! I really did! Well, I didn't exactly *read* Michael Harrington's book, but I took it out of the library. I mean, it had all these *numbers* in it and everything. And statistics— Ooh, what? What's the matter? What did I say wrong? Is he like—like a friend of yours or something?"

"That's not the point, Ffrenchy," Ez began explaining, but the phone was ringing, and he jumped up, saying, "Oh, Jesus! That must be Jeannie! She expected me back yesterday!"

"Jeannie?" Ffrenchy whispered excitedly. "Who's Jeannie? Is she like his wife?"

"She's *like* his wife," Merry said, "but they're not actually married. He lives with her in Massachusetts."

"Oh, God, I think that's so cool! I mean, it's just *so cool!* Like even though he's old and everything, it's really like he's *not* old! I mean, he digs the chick, so he lives with her. Period! I bet he's practically the only old guy in the *world* whose whole life, whose whole *scene* is like so—so together! I bet he even turns on! In fact, *that's* what I'm gonna do the next time I come here! The next time I come, I'm gonna get ahold of some really great, great grass!"

Merry said, "You know, Ffrenchy, really, in a way what your mother did was much more unconventional—especially for that time. She had two children with him, openly, even though they were both married to other people."

"Well, that's *her* story. *Which*, by the way, she never shuts up about—even though it happened in like the year One! But *I* think—well, I mean, I *know* it—the real story, the *real story* is that my father had like this very low sperm count. So *I* think what she probably figured was like what's the point of making it with him? And so then, after, when she had me and Sunni, she decided to go back with him. . . . And I can dig that, I really can. Like he's a pretty good guy. I mean, he's very uptight and everything, but you know. . . ." Ffrenchy shrugged, and dipping into her schoolbag again, said, "God, I just *love* Marlboros, don't you? They are just like the best, best cigarette! I mean, I know you're not supposed to smoke and everything, and even my *grandmother's* trying to stop, and she's always been like this total *fiend,* this *addict,* but I don't know—I just think Marlboros are like so *good.* I mean, I know they're not good *for* you and Alain doesn't think I should— Oh, no! Oh, shit!" Ffrenchy suddenly clapped her hand to her forehead. "I just *remembered.* I *left* them! I left them on the table in the Art Room. Oh, I can't believe it—I just got this total picture in my mind. With every detail. Do you ever get that? Like you can just *see? Everything?* Like the colors and the plants and where everyone else was sitting and what the teacher was— Oh, *God!* I just hope Vera doesn't *find* them! Oh, disaster! See, her husband, Bruno—" Ffrenchy giggled. She said, "Oh, God, this *really* isn't funny. I *really* shouldn't laugh. But I can't help it. Every time I hear the name Bruno, I think of a dog! You know, a dachshund, with like floppy ears?" She started laughing again, and then, trying to make her face grave, said, "But he wasn't a dog, he was an abstract painter. Anyway, he died of lung cancer, so Vera became like this total antismoking . . . *nun!* I don't mean *that* kind of nun, I just mean she became like this—this *fanatic.* So that's why if she *finds* them . . . ! Oh, God! Now I *really* need a cigarette!"

"You can have one of mine," Merry offered, "but they're Kents."

"No, never mind, that's all right." Ffrenchy sighed, and plunging back into her schoolbag, bobbed up with a stick of red licorice. "Cookie," she said, sucking on it meditatively, "is Jeannie 'For Jeannie'? You know, 'For Jeannie'? On the first page of the book?"

It occurred to Merry that for Ffrenchy this "first page" was probably the most memorable one in the book. She said, "Yes, it's the same Jeannie, and in fact, it's really sort of a romantic story. Because that's where they met, when he was doing that book."

"*What's* where they met?" Ffrenchy asked, annoyed, apparently trying to puzzle out how Ez could have met someone inside the binding of a book. "I mean, like *where* did he meet her?"

"When he went to Appalachia. In some tiny, used-up mining town in West Virginia."

"Ohh! *I* get it! . . . She's gorgeous like a fashion model except she's very poor, right? *That's* why he called the book *Stranger in the Land*—I *get* it! Because everyone else there was like so hideous, wrecked and with no teeth and everything, and then one day he saw Jeannie and she was like *so* gorgeous that he went, *Wow,* this is *really strange!* Like this chick doesn't even belong here! . . ."

It was now clear that Ffrenchy had not read past the

dedication page. Merry said, "Jeannie isn't gorgeous like a fashion model, Ffrenchy. In fact, she isn't even especially pretty. But she *is* very nice. And she's very good to—"

"She *isn't* pretty? *Really?* Like you've seen her and you've really checked it out?" Ffrenchy's eyes lit up. "Wow, would I love to go up there and visit them! Do you think I could?"

Merry shrugged. "Jeannie's very *nice*, Ffrenchy. Above all, she's exceptionally good to Ez."

"Well, what's so strange about that? I mean, lots of chicks would be. I don't see why *that's* supposed to make her so strange and fabulous! Unless—do you mean—is she, is she like this incredibly zonked, totally weird natural head? Like this strange, strange—you know, no shoes and everything, and long, long straight hair—sort of stringy, but *long,* and she goes around in the woods picking wild berries and herbs and talking to animals? That's why he thought she was like so strange? That's how he came up with the title?"

How Ez had come up with the title *Stranger in the Land:*

In the cold early spring of 1960, I had been riding for days and days through the rutted back roads and wild, rocky hillsides of Kentucky and West Virginia. On the road map, there were many places called "hollows," but there, visibly hollow, were the bleak, charred, dot-like remnants of disused mining towns. "Ghost towns!" said Patrick, the young English journalist who was driving the car, perhaps happily remembering long childhood afternoons spent sprawled before Hollywood shoot-'em-ups. Still, Patrick was right— they *were* ghost towns: to the side of each one was a cemetery, the slanting gravestones marked mainly with Slavic names—all those men who once, in hope and brawny willing, had come to work the thriving mines. But the mines had become used up, and only the descendants of their owners were thriving—elsewhere. For now, in these hills and hollows, clearly no one thrived. Pasty-faced and emaciated, children and adults alike, their blank, guarded faces gave me the shivers and their eyes haunted me.

179

Patrick, in the meantime, from a short stay in New Haven, had acquired a passion for pizza. All through that raw, cloudy day, as we bumped along the narrow, rock-strewn dirt roads, he kept looking for pizza parlors, and I, growing queasier, colder and headachy, fell asleep. When I woke up about an hour later, still sour-mouthed and hazy, I was in a state of such chilly, dazed discomfort that I did not know where I was. Blearily, I looked out the car window, and it seemed to me that in the pattern of the dirt on the glass I saw two words—Hebrew words. Stunned, I looked again and there it was: in Hebrew, a language I had not read since I was a child, were the two words *ger shom:* a stranger there. And so indeed I was, I suddenly realized, all my inchoate feelings of unease finally crystallized. In this harsh, sad, alien land what could I be but a stranger? And the people whose gaunt bodies and denying faces so troubled me—in a nation of complacent plenty, an entire mighty continent of shopping-mall superhighways, they were surely strangers too.

In this book, this preface, set in italics and artistically indented, stood alone on the page, like a poem; it came directly after the page that said "For Jeannie." Merry said to Ffrenchy, "It wasn't Jeannie who was the stranger. It was Ez."

"Oh! . . . Far out! You're right—that really *is* romantic! God, I can't wait to come here with Alain! *He's* very romantic too. But that's because he's French. Well, I mean he was *born* in Belgium, but you know, he's like a musician and everything, so he's practically French. Anyway, he's this *totally* European type. I mean, *totally.* Like he just can't *stand* the things Americans are always getting hung up about. He says they're so *puerile*—" Ffrenchy's delight at using this word so overwhelmed her that she stopped, and looked up at Merry, beaming. "They're just so *puerile* that it really makes him crazy. That's why he thinks he might go to live in Cuba. Or Israel. In a, you know, kibbutz? 'Cause like they're not so, you know, like always watching *deodorant* commercials."

"*Who's* always watching deodorant commercials?" Ez asked, smiling, as he came striding back into the room. "You're not going to tell me your poor mother's been reduced to that!"

"No . . . Not my mother . . . Not *exactly*, anyway." Ffrenchy bounced up on the couch, and facing Ez directly, said, "See, it's what Alain says about Americans. That the reason they're always falling asleep at concerts and stuff is because the only thing they really *care* about is watching deodorant commercials on TV. Or like their idea of an important decision—now, here comes the *amazing* part— their idea of a really important decision in life is what kind of *car* to buy. Or what kind of *drapes* to get. And when he said *that*, I mean, it really blew my mind! Because, see, my room, my bedroom—well, it's Sunni's room too—but anyway, every time I came home and walked in there, I really thought I would puke! I mean, everything in there was so old and boring, I couldn't *take* it anymore! So I told my mother, and she has this friend, Bina, who's an interior decorator—I mean, interior *designer*. And *she* said that it was like probably not a great idea to get a whole bunch of new stuff at once, and why don't I first concentrate on curtains. So I did! I mean, I was really *thinking* about it, you know? Like that's what I *really* had in my head. So when Alain said to me—and this was like the same *week* and everything—how for Americans the big, big decision in life was what *drapes* to get, I couldn't *believe* it! I mean, it really knocked me out! It was like—like he could see inside my *soul!* . . . Oh, he's *so* terrific, Ez!" Ffrenchy said moonily, half pleading and half bragging. "You'd *love* him! He'd love *you!* Couldn't I bring him here so you could meet him? So he could meet *you?*"

Not at all nicely, Ez said, "Did you get your *drapes*, Francesca? And did the designing Bina get you a discount?"

"Oh, yeah! Of course! That was like a long time ago. I got all the other stuff too. Do you want to come and see it? Do *you*, Cookie? *Ooh!* You could come to my house and we could have all this great shit from William Greenberg's and Baskin-Robbins! Unless—if you—well, Alain says—well, *he* thinks that Baskin-Robbins is like truly repulsive. And that like a million years ago there used to be this TV show, *American Bandstand?* With all these like teen-age hits? And that's what Baskin-Robbins reminds him of. He only likes Haagen Dazs. So, I mean, we could have *that*."

Merry said, "Thanks, Ffrenchy. But I think if I came to your house, it would have to turn out to be awkward."

"I *know!* I know it! That's why I want Alain to come *here*. Oh, *please*, Ez! *Please!* If he could just . . . *talk* to you, hang out with you a little, it would be like such an *up* for him, I *know* it! I mean, he has all these huge, enormous, terrible *conflicts*. And *decisions* and everything! Like he doesn't know whether he should finish his Ph.D. in philosophy. Or whether he should just say fuck that, and *really* go with the flute. Which he loves. And then, *then* he has this whole thing with his *parents!* See, his father's in the diamond business—well, his uncle is too—but that's like in Belgium. Antwerp? Wait a second! How could *Antwerp* be in Belgium? I thought Belgium was like Brussels—you know, the sprouts? Anyway, Alain's their only son, and they—they like always expected him to do that whole *diamond* number with them! Which is *incredible*. I mean, it's incredible that he could even ever *think* about it. For a *second*. But his mother—well, she's like this—this *guilt* genius, that's what *he* calls her. He says his father's in the diamond business and his mother's in the guilt business. Get it? Oh, *God!*" Ffrenchy giggled, sinking all the way back. "He really cracks me up! I mean, he is just so *funny* and terrific and everything! Oh, *please*, Ez! *Please!* Couldn't I just bring him here? Just to hang out? *Please!*"

"Ffrenchy," Ez said, shaking his head, "you just said a little while ago that you hated lying and hypocrisy. That you *hated* it. So tell me, what would *you* call it if after promising your mother that you wouldn't see Alain—at least for a little

while—you brought him here? Without telling her? Behind her back? What would you say that was?"

"Oh, wow, I don't *believe* this! I don't *believe* it! Do *you* think you can—I mean, are you going to tell me that *you* never did things your parents didn't want you to? Or that you went around telling your *mother* everything? I mean, God! When you're on TV and stuff, and they introduce you, they're always saying how you were like this big *rebel* and everything! So am I supposed to sit here and believe that the first thing you did was run home and say, 'Hey, guess what, Ma? Want to see some of the great shit I just ripped off?'"

Ez sighed. He said, "No, I *didn't* tell my mother everything. You're absolutely right. In fact, I didn't tell my mother anything. At all. Because if I had, she wouldn't have understood. And I don't just mean that she wouldn't have been sympathetic. I mean that she literally would not have understood."

"You mean like because she didn't speak English?"

"That, and all that went with it. . . . That I was somehow . . . foreign to her, all her children were. We were from a different world. But just to set the record straight, Ffrenchy, she *did* speak some English, my mother. She was never really fluent and she certainly wasn't literate, but she managed."

Ffrenchy's outrage had passed and now she was simply curious. "But what language did she mostly speak? I mean, *really* speak? Like if she was talking to you and she wanted to tell you something really heavy? Because, see, I have this friend Anahid, and she has this like weird, weird truly ancient aunt—great-aunt? And I mean, the chick *can* speak English—even though she *is* a thousand and looks like this—this *mummy*, but when she wants to say something *really* heavy or like very private, she says it in *Armenian!* Which is just *so* far out! I mean, *Armenian!* Like I never even *heard* of it! So, I mean, if your mother was—well, say she was really freaking out about something. *Then* what language would she speak?"

Ez stared into the air, at an invisible audience, and for its benefit, repeated, "*Freaking out.* If my mother wanted to say something really *heavy* . . . Because she was *freaking out* . . ."

Hurriedly, Merry said, "Yiddish. She spoke Yiddish, Ffrenchy. That was her everyday language."

"Did you *know* Grandma, Cookie? Like you really *saw* her and everything?"

"I lived with her for a while when I was very little," Merry said, trying to just skim over it, because she was worried by this sudden Grandma-appropriation of Ffrenchy's and the terrible avidity in her face as she said it.

But Ffrenchy only said, "You really *did* know her! Far out! Do I look like her? I do, don't I?"

Amazed, Merry hesitated. "Well . . . she was very old when I knew her . . . But in a way you do, yes. You have the same fair coloring. I *don't* know if she ever had red hair."

"*Did* she?" Ffrenchy asked Ez. "Did your mother ever have red hair? Say, when she lived in like . . . Europe?"

Distant, dreaming, Ez shook his head. "She had blond hair . . . blondish, I suppose, really. When she married my father she had it shaved off, but then in America she let it grow back. And in fact, my first memory, the very furthest back I can go, is of my mother standing over my bed in the morning to wake me . . . well, to wake my brothers, really, I didn't go to school yet. She was standing over my bed with her one long, long blond braid and it would brush against my head, against my face. . . . That's how I always remember her—in the morning. . . . *You* had braids once, cookie. When you lived with her. Your two little *tzep,* do you remember?"

"Your *mother* shaved off her hair?" Ffrenchy shrieked. "She actually just chopped it all *off?* Shit, she *really* should've gone to a shrink! I mean, she must have been into a *total* hair-disgust! . . . Like I get *sick* of my hair sometimes, I truly do. Especially in the summer, on the Vineyard, with all the

*salt* and humidity and everything? I mean, it just gets me so *frustrated!* So I'm always getting into these enormous hair-hate numbers. Like I think maybe I should get it *cut,* or maybe I should get it *styled.* But *now,* God! Am I glad I didn't! Because Alain says—well, he really gets off on it, you know. The way it looks on the pillow, when it's like all spread out and everything. Especially in the dark. Except—well, *I* heard—well, I mean, Tamara Dobkin's sister's best friend *told* me—that it's like very middle class to make love in the dark. Is that true, Ez? That it's this really low, low, uptight, pathetic middle-class number?"

Ez, still completely in another world, said nothing. He didn't even look at her.

Merry said, "Ez's mother didn't get her hair cut off because she hated it, Ffrenchy. She did it because it's what all Orthodox Jewish women are supposed to do when they marry, and in those days it was very common. Now it's really only done by the *very* Orthodox. It's why Hasidic women wear wigs."

"Oh." Ffrenchy shrugged, and then she said, "*Ohh!* You mean those far-out little guys with the beards and the sort of weird, old-timey butcher stores? And they like dance? In Brooklyn? I once saw this thing on TV! Because my father had this patient with this like *weird,* weird blood disease? And he was like *one* of them! And then, after, he got into like such an incredible *grateful* number—because, you know, like he didn't die?—that he invited my father to his daughter's wedding! This really far-out weird-beard wedding! You know—everyone *there* was like one of them! Well, except for my father . . . Oh, *wow!*" Ffrenchy suddenly called out. "Was *Grandma* one of them?"

"No," Merry said, laughing. "She certainly wasn't."

"But she didn't have red hair? She really didn't? . . . *Well!* You know what my *mother* says about my red hair? About how I got it?" Ffrenchy bounced herself into a lotus position,

185

carefully, dramatically rearranged her shawl, and thrusting her body forward in Ez's direction, said, "See, like everyone in *her* family has this dark, dark hair—practically black, right? So she says the reason *I* have red hair, how I got it, is that in *your* family there was once someone who was raped—I mean, totally *ravished*—by this—this whole *horde* of Cossacks!" Ffrenchy's eyes had grown very wide as she spoke, and she looked right then, Merry thought, as if any Cossacks left in the vicinity could not arrive fast enough.

Ez said, "Well, it's *possible.*"

"But you don't know? I mean, like you don't *really* know. . . ." Ffrenchy frowned, but then she said, "Well, if *Grandma* didn't have red hair, then what about her mother? You know, your mother's mother. Like what color hair did *she* have?"

"I don't know that, Ffrenchy. . . . And *my* mother wouldn't have known it either." Sighing and distant again, Ez said, "She didn't actually ever know her mother, she was an orphan. Her mother died when she was . . . oh, I don't know—a baby, an infant. And her father was already dead; her brothers and sisters were dispersed—she never even knew who they were. So she was . . . she was *really* an orphan. Always being shunted around, taken in by various strangers, put out again when they couldn't afford an extra mouth. . . ." He shrugged his shoulders, and altogether, he seemed overtaken by a terrible, brusque hopelessness, as if the aching, wasteful misery of his mother's young years had been borne in on him for the first time.

Even Ffrenchy sensed this. Shivering, she said, "Whew! Was that because of like Auschwitz?"

Stunned, Ez said, "Francesca. *Anne Frank* was because of like Auschwitz. *Like Auschwitz* occurred in the nineteen forties. My mother was born in the eighteen eighties. That's the same time as—as Boss Tweed, as Sitting Bull. When she came to America, the President was Theodore Roosevelt. All

186

right, you don't like to read numbers. But didn't you ever read *anything?* Didn't you ever *learn* anything? Haven't you learned any history in school?"

"Well, see, we don't exactly have *history.* We have this— this double-period thing called MACC—well, it used to be called LOOP: Living On Our Planet? But then Joel left, and besides, everyone always thought it was like copying from New Lincoln anyway. So now we have MACC, which is . . . oh, shit! I always forget it! Because it's like new and every-thing! It's—it's—oh, *I* know! It's Man: Animal of Community and Creativity—MACC. So, you know, it's sort of bullshit in a *way*—well, Alain thinks it's bullshit. I mean, it really cracks him up. Because *he* says that the Community part is really History, and the Creativity part is really English, and why don't they just call it that and then they could charge less. God!" Ffrenchy began giggling again. "He is just *so* funny! I mean, stuff like that, shit! Don't you see what I *mean,* Ez? *Don't* you?"

"Oh, Christ, Ffrenchy! Who cares what they call the damn thing? What are they actually teaching you?"

"Oh! You mean MACC! Well, see, it's this individual study thing. And what's great about it—or anyway, what's *supposed* to be so great about it—is that you're *supposed* to be able to pick your own topic. Except—except that I couldn't. Les wouldn't let me. I mean, he just wouldn't let *me.* Like I'm the *only one.* He just *picked* on me. God! He is such a total, total sadist monster that no one even *believes* me. You don't know what it's *like*—I mean, they really *don't.* Because *they're* all in love with him," Ffrenchy said bitterly. "That's his trip, it's his *whole* trip. *He* just wants to get all the girls in the class to fall in love with him—well, not *all* the girls, but the ones he picks out." Tearful now, Ffrenchy narrowed her eyes, and with sudden surprising shrewdness burst out, "He picks out the *girls* he wants the way we're supposed to be able to pick out the *topics* we want. And I wouldn't *be* one of his little-girl groupies. I don't care! I just wouldn't! So—so he started to hate me from that"—she began crying—"But then, *then*, because *they're* always staying after school, and waiting for him, and *telling* him everything, so—so someone told him about me and Alain. And that's when he started—he started *staring* at me. In this way like he wanted to *kill* me, he wanted to *torture* me. So on the day we were supposed to come in with our topics, he just kept *looking* at me and *looking* at me for like a *whole* double period. And he called up everyone else but *me*, and then *finally, finally*—like the *bell* was ringing and everything—he got this like sadist smile on his face, and with his *bullshit* Creature Feature English accent, he said, 'Francesca Meisel. I have chosen your topic for you. Because I know it cannot fail to arouse your interest.' Like I'm not supposed to know what arouse really means? Like I'm supposed to pretend to be this *dummy?* . . ." Tears of rage were pouring down Ffrenchy's face; her nose was running and her eyes were swollen, and even so, even so, Merry saw, there was no way to mistake her inborn beauty. She pulled out a tissue, and crying into it, said, "So anyway, he *gave* me Emily Dickinson. Like *that's* how obvious he had to make it he was doing it for spite! I mean, my God! *Emily Dickinson!* Just because everyone *knows* that she never did it!"

"But, Ffrenchy," Ez said kindly, "Emily Dickinson, even if you don't really like her work, she's still a genuinely interesting figure in American literature. There's a whole *spirit*, a spirit of New England that she—"

"Oh, I don't care about *that*. I mean, I'll *do* Emily Dickinson, who cares! It's only little poems, it's not like I can't *do* it. I mean, okay, I was *going* to do gods and goddesses—you know, all that far-out Greek stuff? Myths? So big deal, instead—instead I'll read some grass and flowers bullshit, I don't *care*. But he—he just *hates* me so much!" she sobbed. "He just *hates* me! For no *reason!* He's so *nasty* to me all the time! And nobody *cares!*" Ffrenchy was now hysterical. "*No-*

188

*body! Nobody!* If I told my mother, she has this like *mean* streak and she—she'd just say I *deserve* it. And if I told my father, God, he's so out of it, he wouldn't even know what I was *talking* about. And I *told* Alain! I *did* tell him." She blew her nose, but still could not stop sobbing. "And all *he* had to say was that it wasn't really important. Because that's his whole *big-*brain European number! Like *nothing* is *important* unless it happens to a thousand people and it's this—this official *disaster*. Except when it's something that happened to *him!* . . . Oh, *God!*" Ffrenchy cried out desperately, suddenly flinging her book bag across the room and shuddering beneath her shawl. "Is this all you ever *get* in life? Is this *it?*"

# 11

THAT hurt and angry cry of Ffrenchy's early adolescence—
"Is this all you ever *get* in life? Is this *it?*"—was apparently the exact question that continued to plague her. Because
one day five years later, in 1970, when Merry was writing a
piece about the sudden upsurge of Eastern mystical-religious
groups, she climbed a steep flight of stairs to a commercial
loft on the Upper West Side, just above a bagel bakery and a
lingerie store, and there, sitting cross-legged on a mat, surrounded on all sides by silent, white-gowned devotees, their
eyes closed and their arms upraised in a trance-like spiritual
exercise, was Ffrenchy. Ffrenchy's arms were raised too, but
she was wearing a purple velvet jumpsuit, and her eyes could
not have been shut very tight because she instantly leaped up
from her mat, kicking it aside, and with her voice ringing, re-
sounding through that enormous snow-still room—it had once
been a ballet studio—she called out excitedly, *"Cookie!* Oh,

Cookie! Far out! I *mean!* Far fucking *out!*"

"Ffrenchy!" Merry embraced her. "What are you *doing* here? I thought you were in Providence! I thought you were going to the Rhode Island School of Design."

"Oh, *that!*" Ffrenchy said, as if it had taken place in another life. "God, that place was so low I don't even remember it! I like *totally* wiped it out of my head, you know? All those *down* art school vibes? Otherwise, it would *still* be bringing me down! And that was like *two months* ago! Shit!" She suddenly giggled and said, "Oh, wow, Cookie, you should have *seen* it! It was all these—these like pseudo-hippie *zeroes,* bopping around with their portfolios and—and hassling about *perspective! Perspective!*" Her giddy infectious giggle rang out through the loft as a slow, low-pitched chant was added onto the arm-raising. "I mean, *really!* Perspective! Like what they were *into!* It was incredible! I mean, I couldn't give a flying—"

"Radha!" A very thin, tall, sullen-looking girl who seemed to be leading the group—her tunic was gold and not white, and she was wearing a navel-length strand of orange and red beads—approached them. She disregarded Merry entirely, and glaring at Ffrenchy, she spoke sharply and with a British accent. "This is the second time today, Radha! The second time! You're breaking the Circle, you're breaking the Work! Our Work is one, our Energy is one, you *know* that. *And* you know as well that today is not an Open, so I just can't imagine what head games you think you're running when you invite a stranger!"

"Oh, but she's *not* a stranger! She's a *friend. Truly.* I mean, like she—she's my *sister.*"

"Of course, we'd be very happy to welcome her any day we do have an Open. She could feast with us and share our joy. But she can't hang out here now."

"No, no, no," Merry said. "Ffrenchy didn't invite me. I have an appointment with Jerry Solochek."

"Govind isn't here this week." The English games mistress

gave Merry a smug, stony look. "He's doing the *Sahra*."

"See, Cookie, that's like this—this *really* heavy fasting trip. I mean, like you can't even listen to *music!* So, you know, you have to be this *incredibly* high and advanced spiritual being to even try it. I mean, for instance, like *I'm* nowhere *near* it. But *Govind!* God, he is just *so* high and so *beautiful* that everyone thinks he was probably a *pretty* enlightened being at least one time before—well, you know, not *perfect*. I mean, he couldn't have been perfect or he wouldn't have come back. But, you know, like a *really* heavily spiritual person. When he was in another body." Ffrenchy turned to the gold-clad English girl, and with her broad, open, cheerful smile, said, "The same with Devi! Devi's incredibly high too. Like she has *absolutely* no ego! None! Because she was probably once a dakini. In—in—oh, shit! Don't tell me! What's that place in *The King and I?* Wait—I *know* it! Tibet!"

Devi acknowledged this with a distant, condescending nod, and Merry asked, "Do you happen to know if Jerry Solo—if Govind left me any message? He did know I was coming."

"I'll check," she said sourly, and with a swirl of her gold tunic, the games-mistress dakini disappeared into an office somewhere.

"Cookie . . . How come you call him Jerry? Solochek? I mean, *everyone* calls him Govind! Even his wife—well, actually they just split. Because like she is just not spiritual *at all*. But, I mean, even *Mimi*—when she calls him here to hassle him about something? Even *she* calls him Govind!"

Merry said, "Well, his cousin Julie doesn't. She's a friend of mine and that's how I got in touch with him in the first place."

"Julie Solochek . . ." Ffrenchy said. "Does she have this like *really* long, long black hair? And she's like *totally* into the guitar? I mean, the chick is still into this like *nineteen sixty-two* Joan Baez trip?"

"Come on, Ffrenchy! She's my *friend*, I just told you! Anyway, now she's in a women's street-theater troupe, she's their musician."

"Far out!" Ffrenchy seemed to perk up at this, but then she frowned and said, "Cookie, I don't think you should be friends with her, you know? 'Cause that like only *proves* how totally asleep she is! I mean, it's the same thing as her Joan Baez trip—ego, ego, ego! Like a chick who's into shit like that isn't even *trying* to wake up. I mean, like she doesn't even *know* it!"

"Julie's a *musician*, Ffrenchy. That's what she always wanted to be. I think she's the only person I know who's really always had the same ambition."

"Ambition!" Ffrenchy screamed. "Oh, *wow*, Cookie! I can't even believe you *said* that! I mean, that is just *so bad!* It is just *so low!* I mean, shit! *Ambition!* That's the same as—as *greed.* Or, you know, *pride!* And—and—oh, what's that other one? Not anger, that's in a whole different column. . . . Well, anyway, it is like *total* negativity. And illusion. *Total!* Whew!" Ffrenchy shook her head in outraged, pitying disbelief, and then suddenly, in a very sweet, disconnected voice, said, "Oh, hi, Vishnu," to a white-robed, blond-bearded boy who floated up beside her and began massaging her neck. He smelled very strongly of musk or incense, and with a look of cloudy, near-sighted ecstasy, said, "You know what I just flashed to? . . . Just now? . . . Your whole purple trip. That like . . . like maybe you *weren't* really trying to fuck us over. Maybe you *weren't* trying to do an ego number on our Energy center. Maybe . . . maybe what you were really doing was giving us a—a gift, an offering. . . . This—this really powerful shakti. And we were like all so uptight that we just couldn't let it in."

"Oh, thank you, Vishnu," Ffrenchy said in the same unnatural, high, good-fairy voice. "I mean, I just felt so like *obliterated* when the Circle came down on me! Like I felt—I felt that I was just, you know, *erased.*"

"Hey! Like that's . . . that's your dharmic lesson, you know? Like *our* dharmic lesson is to let in the shakti. And really *go* with it. And *your* dharmic lesson is like . . . like you have to *watch* the pain, *watch* the hurt. 'Cause it's just *out* there. In the Universe. And if you just . . . watch it, give it a little mindfulness, then you can let it go. . . . Then, then it'll be beautiful, you know? Like it'll just be . . . part of the flow."

Ffrenchy nodded, her smile and expression so radiant with vacancy that it was almost alarming. But she turned to Merry, and in a completely normal voice, said, "See, Cookie, our color of the day was purple. Like to meditate on, you know? But the thing is I am like *so terrible* at color visualization that I thought that if I—well, like yesterday, for instance, *yesterday* our color of the day was gray and like I just *could* not get my head into it, you know? I mean, I was *really* trying, but I just could *not* get my head into gray!" Ffrenchy shook her head as she said this, so that all her red hair came spilling around her shoulders: it made the very notion of grayness seem absolutely preposterous. "So anyway, when they said today would be purple, I thought probably that if I was *wearing* purple, I wouldn't have such an incredible *hassle* with the visualization. You know—like I'd really *feel* purple! And—and like *be* purple! Besides"—she suddenly fell into a whisper—"this is a brand-new jumpsuit! I just bought it—like two days ago! So, I mean, I *had* to wear it! I couldn't just leave it *hanging* in my closet. 'Cause then how would I be able to like *really* empty my mind? For, you know, Holy Work?" She gestured toward the center of the room, where the chanting had gotten louder, and said, "God, Vishnu is just *so high!* Like he is *definitely* the purest spirit in the Circle—well, in *our* Circle anyway."

Merry said, "Ffrenchy, how come you all have Hindu names? I thought this group was eclectic."

"Oh, no! We're *not!* We're not eclectic! We're not *any-thing*, Cookie! Like that's what's so terrific! What *we* do, like what we're really into, is getting together all the really highest, purest stuff from *all* the most truly enlightened beings. And like it doesn't matter where their external bodies

194

were! I mean, they could have been *anyplace! Especially*
beings who are so evolved! I mean, shit! *Their* external bodies
were probably—well, not *everyplace*, but you know—like
India, Asia, Tibet, Arabia—all those places. And—and
*Gurdjieff!* Now, this is *really* far out! Gurdjieff was in Paris!
And I mean, God! *Paris!* Like *everybody* knows how much the
French suck! Like when I was in Paris and I wanted some
butter? Those mothers kept making me repeat '*beurre,
beurre*' like eight zillion times, and they kept *laughing!* The
whole time! So, I mean, they definitely suck! But see, Cookie,
see, that's why it doesn't *matter* about like which *physical*
plane a truly enlightened being inhabits! Or like—like people
who waste their time hassling about which is the right *system.*
Or which is the right *guru.* Like it's just so *obvious!* The Spirit
is always *One!* The Energy is always One!'" Ffrenchy stopped,
but then suddenly clutching Merry's sleeve like a small child,
and staring into her face with troubled intensity, she said,
"Cookie, did you know that most people—*most* people—not
only are they asleep, which is like bad enough! But they're in
*prison!* And they like don't even *know* it! Because, see, reality
is a *prison! Truly!* It's this total jail! And like—like when you
think that you're thinking something? You're not! I *mean* it,
Cookie, you're really not! You're just doing this—this whole
mental jailbird number! And I'm afraid—well, I mean, I'm
not just *afraid.* 'Cause like I *know* it—that that's what
happened to *Ez!* He's in this total mental jail! It's *true,*
Cookie! It's true! Like that's why he's always *thinking!* And
like if I don't—if *someone* doesn't tell him, he could be in jail
*forever!* I mean, *really* forever—like even when he's in
another *body!*"

Especially with Ffrenchy staring at her like that, her
expression so strained in hungry and confused conviction,
Merry did not know what to say. She was about to offer up,
"Thinking is what Ez gets off on, Ffrenchy. That's his trip,"
when suddenly the downstairs door was opened, and along

with a burst of cold air, up floated an old childhood smell—
the wondrous, warm, oveny abundance of baking bagels and
toasted onions.

"Oh, *wow!* That *bagel* bakery!" Ffrenchy instantly leaped
into the air, beaming. "Shit, am I starving! I *mean!* Like I am
absolutely *ravenous!*"

"Me too," Merry said. "Come on, Ffrenchy, let's go! I'll
treat you to a bagel."

"*Cookie!*" Ffrenchy sounded horrified. "*Bagels!* Like they
are *so bad* for you! Don't you—"

"I did not say *cheeseburger,* Ffrenchy. I said bagel!"

"Yeah, but don't you *know?* Don't you *feel* what they do to
your body? I mean, bagels are so *processed!* They just
like—like totally fuck up your whole— Oh, shit! Here comes
Devi. I better go back to the Circle."

"Are you the press?" Devi said curtly. She was holding
finger cymbals and as they bounced against her prayer beads,
managed to look even surlier than she had before. "Because if
that's what you are, you can leave right now! You're not a true
seeker, and I can't imagine why Govind agreed to speak to
you at all!"

Ffrenchy said, "Oh, Devi, she's not the *press*. She just
writes these—these like *articles* sometimes. Like she works
in this poverty program with these little black kids? And she
wrote this thing about them that was *so* far out! Because like
she really got inside their heads! And I mean, little kids'
heads! You *know!* Like they are just naturally *so* spiritual
and—and *so* high! Especially black little kids!"

From the center of the room, everyone had begun ringing
their finger cymbals. Already turning away, Devi said, "You
*can* come back for an Open. *If* you're really into Consciousness. *If* you really want to wake up."

"Wow, she just gets into such *paranoid* spaces sometimes!"
Ffrenchy shook her head. "I mean, I know that she's always
like hanging out with these—these *incredibly* high beings.

But she—I don't know—*she* might really have a lot more karma cleaning to do! Like, you know, *she's* only done the *Sahra* once! And I mean, Govind's done it so many times that he could probably—well, I'm sure of it—he could even lead us through the Cave!"

"It doesn't matter, Ffrenchy. I have to go anyway. And besides, she's perfectly right—I'm *not* a seeker."

"Oh, but, Cookie! You *would* be! I *know* you would be! If you could just meet Dennis! If *Ez* could just meet Dennis! I mean, he could really *help* him. To get *free*. From his like, you know, *mind* attachment! I mean, Dennis is just so *totally* awake! Like the first time I met him? Well, I didn't even really *meet* him, I just *saw* him. We were just—just in the same *space!*" Ffrenchy grabbed Merry's arm, and peering into her face with that look of wide-eyed, pleading fervor, she burst out, "Oh, Cookie! This part is just *so amazing!* Because even though I hardly even saw him, I could just like *feel* my energy—I mean, I could actually *see* it—like, like completely *lifting* out of me and—and just *flowing* out to Dennis! And I don't mean some like bullshit superficial *sexual* attraction. This was just so—so *different*. It was like so . . . *incredibly* profound. . . . And—and ancient. And I mean, *truly* spiritual . . ." Ffrenchy stopped momentarily, caught up in wonder at ancient mysteries, and as Merry began edging toward the door, Ffrenchy walked after her, saying, "*Anyway*. When we were finished doing the Flame, he came up to me—I mean, I knew he would because it just *felt* so right—and he said to me, 'Are you a Jewess?' So, you know, *I* thought: Oh, shit! I don't *believe* this! I mean, like is he my fucking *grandmother?* But I just was *so high* from doing the Flame that I just said, 'Well, yeah, I guess so. But, I mean, like who cares?' And *then*, Cookie, and *then*"—Ffrenchy drew in her breath in an ecstasy of shivery wonder—"he *explained* to me why he asked me! See, he's English—well, anyway, his parents are English, *he* was actually born in India, which is probably why

197

he's so naturally spiritual. But anyway, once when he was in a different body—well, in *one* different body—he was in the Crusades! With Richard the Lion-Hearted! Which is *really* far out because his last name is Lyons. *And* he's a Leo!"

"Ffrenchy, I really *do* have to go. I have to—"

"Wait, Cookie! *Wait!* I didn't *tell* you yet. When Dennis was in the Crusades, and he went with them to—to, you know, wherever they went—the Holy Land? He fell in love with this like incredibly beautiful heathen princess. And that's me, Cookie! He knew it the second he saw me! It's *me!*" Standing at the top of the steps, her arms outstretched and her face glowing, Ffrenchy looked like a dancer or an actress in a long-awaited moment of triumph. She shifted slightly in the sudden burst of sunlight streaming in through the downstairs glass door, and frowning, said, "There's just this—this one thing. See, Dennis knows—I mean, he's absolutely positive that she had this like, you know, *totally* jet-black hair. And was named Rebecca. I mean, he *knows* it."

In the tone that Ez so disliked—in his opinion, it was both proof and symptom of how deficient she was of a sense of the utopian—Merry now said, "Oh, well, Ffrenchy, you can't have everything."

"Yeah, but you want to hear something *amazing?* Remember how I told you when he asked me if I was Jewish, the first thing I thought of was my grandmother? Well, when she was young, she really did have black hair! Like I can even remember it! But *wait*, Cookie! Wait! This gets even *more* far out! My grandmother's real official first name? Like the name that's on her checks and her driver's license and shit? Her actual, you know, like *legal* first name? It's Rebecca!"

"Don't worry about it, Ffrenchy. She's too old for Dennis."

"Oh, Cookie!" Ffrenchy giggled. "You're such a goof! You're just like Ez! He's always goofing too! That's why—why . . . Cookie, where are you going? I mean, are you—are you going to see Ez?"

"Ez is in Massachusetts, Ffrenchy. I haven't seen him for almost three months. Where *I'm* going—if I can get myself to do it—is down to the Lower East Side to buy some material. You know that torn sofa in the living room? Well, I can't *stand* it anymore, so I'm going down to some discount place and buy the material to get it reupholstered."

"Oh, Cookie! *Don't* get a sofa! I mean, *don't* get it reupholstered. What you should *get* are these—well, they're called zafus, and they're these incredible huge like pillows? See, they're really meditation cushions and they're from . . . from like Afghanistan? And you can *sit* on them, or *eat* on them—like you can do *anything* with them, but the *main* thing is they are just *so beautiful,* the embroidery and everything, that when you look at them, they just immediately get you *so high!* I mean, zafus are the only thing Dennis has in his whole apartment, and we *sleep* on them and everything, and I just always wake up feeling so *incredibly* high, so *incredibly* fabulous, that you just *know* that whoever made them had to be—well, I mean, that's why Dennis wants to go to Persia! Like he *will* be there, he's just waiting till he has a little more bread."

Looking up at Ffrenchy, framed beaming and rosy in the golden shaft of almost-spring sunlight, Merry did not have the heart to say, "Why didn't he check it out when he was in the Crusades?" Instead, she looked at her watch and said, "Ffrenchy, I really do have to go. But now that you're back in New York, why don't you just give me a call when you feel like it?"

"Oh, I *will!* I mean, I *would.* Except, see, well, like we do *have* a phone, but Dennis thinks—I mean, we're just not into phones. 'Cause like in India and Tibet and things? All the truly high and holy people, they—they always *know* like *when* you're coming and—and *why* you're coming and where your head is really at and—and *everything.* And I mean, it's like so obvious! It's because they just like *never* got into phones, so they could, you know, like really always tune in to

199

what's *really*— Oh, wow, Cookie!" Ffrenchy suddenly called out as the vibrations of a bell-like gong resounded down the stairway. "I better go back this second! I think that means we're doing the Garden!" And from the center of that odd pool of sunlight which had caught her lit up, emblazoned like the glare of a movie camera, Ffrenchy blew a jerky, child-like kiss and ran off.

Outside, the wind traveling up to Broadway from the river was so strong that Merry felt almost blown across the street, and right there, staring into the window of Zabar's, his shoulders hunched and his ears flaming, was Ez. He was wearing only a thin gray windbreaker, and beside the lavish display of the store window—enormous hanging hams and sausages from Italy and Denmark, barrels of caviar from Iran, trays of glazed apricots from Australia, Italian espresso machines, French bain-maries, German coffee grinders and Swiss salad spinners—beside all this and the endless in-and-out thrust of determined, laden, smug-looking shoppers, for whom this was no lazy, sunlit Sunday stroll, empty-handed Ez, in his peering unease and obvious physical discomfort, could not have looked more out of place. Also, and maybe it was only the frayed gray jacket, as if he had "gotten into gray"—just what Ffrenchy had been unable to achieve—Ez looked suddenly old: not frail, not sick, but somehow diminished, as if there were something wrong.

"Ez!" Merry said. "What are you doing here?"

Turning around with the slow, squinty confusion of someone just barely awakened from a deep and disorienting sleep, he said, "Oh! . . . Merry! I . . . I'm not staying at the apartment. I'm just . . . just staying with a friend."

A friend: since when was Ez embarrassed about his girlfriends? And since when was a new affair a matter for such evasive, sheepish confusion? "No, no," Merry said, "I meant what are you doing *here*? At Zabar's?"

"So you know about it too." Ez nodded, half mournful,

half accusing, and nearly dislodging a long French bread from the arm of an exiting customer, he said, "I suppose you want to be like *them.*"

"It must be the bad values you brought me up with." Merry smiled. "What else could it be?" To the side, the woman with the French bread was giving Ez a hard, annoyed look, but then her expression changed. "Larry!" she whispered excitedly to the man beside her. "Look! Isn't that— No, not *there!* You're not looking where I'm looking—right over *here!* That's Ezra Slavin! You see? That's exactly what the girl by the coffee beans was saying! Whenever you go to Zabar's, you always see somebody famous!"

"Famous!" said the man, who was trying to juggle his Zabar's shopping bags and already walking away. "I wouldn't exactly call him . . . I mean, to you, you see somebody once on television and bingo!"

This whole interchange was lost on Ez. He had turned back to the store window, and staring at it intently, he took on the mournful, melodramatic tone he had always ridiculed in his father, and said, "What was it that Socrates always said to himself whenever he walked through the marketplace, when he passed by the stalls and displays? 'How *many* things there are here that I do not want!' "

Merry immediately started to laugh: it was one of her earliest memories of Ez. On weekend afternoons when Isobel was working, Ez often took Merry to the five-and-ten, and holding her hand, he would stride with her through the long aisles of Woolworth's, declaiming, "What does an honest man say when he sees the display of the marketplace? He looks around and happily says to himself: 'Ah! Look! How *many* things there are here that I do not want!' " But this was not what Merry said to herself on those Woolworth afternoons; they bred in her a lust for almost anything—dollhouse furniture, magic slates, multicolored pencils, and on one occasion, bright-red nail polish. "Do you remember how you always used to say that to me when you took me to the five-and-ten?"

Ez nodded, smiling, and for the first time that afternoon, it was a genuinely happy, nostalgic smile.

"Well, you know what it did for me? It made me want every Goddamn thing in sight!"

"But, cookie!" Ez said, astonished. "Talk about bad values! You were only a kid! What did *you* know? You once wanted *lipstick*, for Christ sake!" And as this memory—the enormity of her infant crimes—grew in his mind, he turned on her, shouting, "My God, Merry! You once wanted—actually *wanted*—a Mickey Mouse watch!"

"And not only that—my favorite food was peanut butter."

"Yes! Precisely! You see that? You see what I mean? Doesn't that *prove* to you what that kind of indiscriminate wanting can lead to?" Because to Ez peanut butter was the great American sludge food; it was the symbol, the code word for all that was worst in American popular culture, and he used it the way many people used "white bread" or "corn flakes."

Merry said, "Well, you must have wanted something in Zabar's. Otherwise why would you be here? And by the way, Ez, what did you mean before when you said, 'So you know about it *too*'? *Everybody* knows about Zabar's! Are you trying to tell me you didn't? You're pulling another one of your Rip Van Winkle acts?"

"Rip Van Winkle!" Ez said bitterly. "Do you know— sometimes that's exactly what I feel like! Sometimes . . . sometimes it's as if there were *nothing* familiar here anymore! As if it weren't my city anymore! . . . I don't know. . . . If I were a landscape painter, I'd never be able to find myself returning to a known spot, a familiar view. I . . . it would all have to be from memory."

But he was not a landscape painter, and besides, that's what he had always loved about New York: that it was always changing, always making itself over into something different, something new. This broody bleakness was so unlike Ez that Merry was now certain there was something really wrong. Was he sick? What was it?

"Ah! I see you find me inconsistent." Ez grinned, instantly enlivened by the scent of combat. "And of course, for *you*, inconsistency—what was it that Emerson said about consistency? The hobgoblin of small minds?"

"Well, I was just wondering," Merry said, smiling. "Because everyone knows what *you* think! Change and flux are life: America! But stasis and ugly permanence, reverential monuments? That's death: Europe! And even in the case of Sweden—now, take Sweden, for instance. Or better still, the new towns of England. Change, yes, but not spontaneous. So what wins out? Sterility. An impoverish—"

"That's right! Go ahead! Mock me!" Ez said happily, clearly back in stride. "My own daughter! Reduce me to a College Outline Series!"

"Listen, Ez." Merry laughed, pointing to the door of Zabar's. "Were you actually planning to go in? Or is this a Silent Vigil?"

"*Planning* to go in? *Planning?* I've already *been* in. And do you know why I went in? Do you know why I came here in the first place? No? Well, I was informed by a *brilliant* young historian, the classiest new Ph.D. in all of Western Mass., that I, above all people, would *love* Zabar's. And why? Because according to this Ivy League hotshot, in Zabar's I'd be able to find all the favorite foods of my childhood! So just now, I went into Zabar's and asked for tomato herring. And do you know what I got? You know what those arrogant bastards handed me? A three-dollar can of fish imported from Scotland! With a picture of a guy in Highland kilts and a bagpipe! And when I didn't want that, you know what they showed me next? An even more expensive can—imported from Scandinavia!"

"That's Zabar's, Ez. That's its reputation. Maybe you should just try someplace else."

"You're damn right I'm going to try someplace else! I'm going down to the Lower East Side!"

"You are? Really? Now?"

"Yes! *Really! Right* now!" Ez mimicked. "So why don't you just call up Isobel and tell her? Go ahead! Call transatlantic immediately! Why spare the expense? After all, old Rip Van Winkle never *bought* you anything, so why should you continue the deprivation? Why should you *prevent* yourself from—"

"Ez, what are you *talking* about? Why would I want to call *Isobel?* What's it got to do with Isobel? I only asked you because *I* have to go to the Lower East—"

"What's it got to do with Isobel? I'll tell you what it's got to do with Isobel! It's that *sneering* attitude of yours. *Straight* from Isobel! 'Oh,' " Ez taunted in a high-pitched, thin-lipped voice. " 'Are you *really* going down to the Lower East Side? Now? Are you really going right back to the gutter? How interesting!' "

"Ez! I *only* said—"

"And your wanting to shop in a place like *that!*" He stabbed out at the display window. "That's also Isobel! With her foreign imported gourmet foods! It's probably why she married that fancy Wop in the first place! Fontina forever! I suppose she thinks that's what Danilo Dolci sits around—"

"Ez, *please!*" Merry said, grabbing his arm. Because all around them, people were beginning to stare.

"Oh, goodness me! Oh, dear! Oh, my! Am I creating a scene, a public row? Heavens, how inexpressibly vulgar! How right Henry James was! No wonder he shuddered when he saw those—those 'inconceivable aliens'!" And taking long, angry strides, Ez began heading off toward the corner. "And after all, who could blame him? Why would he want to 'share the sanctity of his American consciousness' with *them?* Those 'dowdy Jews,' that 'swarming of Israel'! Really, a man like Henry James! Isobel's *favorite* American writer! Do you know that when he went to the Yiddish theater, he couldn't even stand the smell? Why don't you ask Isobel about *that* when you call her?"

But Isobel's favorite American writer was Willa Cather. Merry said, "Which novel is *that* in? You don't read novels. When did Henry James write about the Jews?"

"It's not *in* a novel! It's in *The American Scene!* When that poor, precious, quivering man *forced* himself to visit the Lower East Side. And since that's where *I'm* going right now, we might as well just say good-by right here!"

"Oh, for God's sake, Ez! That's just what I've been trying to tell you—*I'm* going down to the Lower East Side now too! I have to get some—"

"*You're* going down to the Lower East Side? *You?* How were you intending to arrive? By taxi?"

"Oh, no," Merry said, though she hated subways and Ez knew it. "I was just waiting for my chauffeured limousine. Or better still, my horse and carriage. The way Henry James probably went."

"Poor Merry!" Ez said happily as they crossed Broadway. "The trauma that awaits you on the subway! The hideous screech of the trains, all those awful crowds, the pushing, the shoving, the elbowing!" And he was smiling so broadly now, with such high, wild, boyish delight, that it was almost impossible to believe that this same man, about ten minutes earlier, had looked as if he were standing around waiting for his own funeral. Even his walk was cheerful—that long-legged, buoyant, arm-swinging gait that Merry remembered from childhood: he used to reach the corner so far ahead of her that running behind him, she had always worried he would cross the street without her, simply forgetting she was there. In the game Simple Simon, "Take a giant step" had always meant for Merry the way her father walked. And even now, on dusky spring evenings, when she heard this cry, "Take a giant step," from children playing outside, five floors beneath her windows, it gave Merry back her earliest sense of Ez: Ez walking, musing and distant, with his broad, hopeful strides, nearly sliding up the block.

"Ez, I just saw Ffrenchy," Merry said, because it had troubled her. "She joined some crazy mystical group, and she—she actually seems to believe that in a former life, she and her boyfriend knew each other because he was in the Crusades and she was a heathen princess."

"Ah, Francesca! Paula's little apple—Paula's little *golden* apple . . . Do you know that she's been writing to me? She wants to change her name to Slavin. Legally. But I don't see that it's at all fair to Meisel, and that's what I told her." He shrugged as if it were all beyond him and said, "I'm sorry, I know she didn't like my answer. She still keeps writing me these— Oh, Christ! What's the matter with that tree? *Look* at that! Just *look* at it, will you!"

"It's a sycamore!" Merry said dreamily, recalling suddenly what had once been her favorite tree. On those long walks of her childhood, on Sunday afternoons when stores were closed, Ez would take her off to strange neighborhoods, sometimes even on long subway rides to far-off boroughs. They would walk through small parks or quiet, leafy streets lined with one-family houses, and there, as Merry hung back in the slow, hazy trance of imagining she lived in one of those sturdy, sunlit houses—a bike-riding, red-jacketed child in a life and family totally different from the one she had—Ez, in a burrowing trance of his own, traced over leaves and barks with his fingers, and taught her the names of the trees. It was what he once learned on "nature walks" in a settlement house camp. "The big, bare sycamore tree is beautiful even in winter," said a book in Merry's school library, and having lit on it, she had sneaked this book out, keeping it hidden in her desk for the rest of the year. What else remained from those long-ago walks? That somewhere in the Bronx, somewhere near a church or a convent—there were always nuns walking around, nuns whose faces were the same iridescent blue-white as Isobel's when she was angry or tired—they had found a bench-lined square entirely planted with gingko trees, gingkos which came from China.

But all this was not what Ez had in mind. Pointing to the heavy spike guard rail which surrounded the tree and had grown into it, he said, "Oh, cookie, it's a *dying* sycamore! Don't you see how these spikes have eaten into the trunk so that it's rotting? They just grew into the bark and now the whole *tree* is rotting! The whole tree, my God! Why didn't someone on this block do something about it when it first started? Now there's *nothing* you can do about it. Now it's just too late. . . . My God!" Ez called out, looking up and down Seventy-ninth Street from Amsterdam to Columbus, a block so crowded with massive, gloomy old apartment houses that though it was in fact a broad crosstown thoroughfare, it had a look of being forever hemmed in, forever sunless, a street of wintry, decayed Weimar splendor and absolutely no sky. "My God, how many trees *are* there on this street that people could just let this happen? What were they *doing*? Going to Zabar's? Or were they too busy buying tickets for—for lieder recitals? Merry, where I am up there in North Darby, you can't turn around without falling into an entire Goddamn forest. But here, how can you take a tree for granted? How? Here, on a street like this, a tree . . . a tree is—it's precious."

The agony in his face, in his voice, was unmistakable; but it was a railing agony and admitted no solace. Like all his old disappearing acts, Ez just walked off so rapidly, so far ahead of her, that for a minute Merry had the old sensation of being left behind, forgotten, just as she'd had as a child. But she was not a child. Bitterly, Ez turned around, shouting, "But what do *you* care? When was the last time *you* ever noticed a tree?"

"Is that Isobel's fault too? Or do you want to blame this one on Henry James directly?"

Ez smiled. "I'm sorry, cookie. It's not your fault. Really, it isn't. I'm . . . I'm just— Oh, *look!*" His hand suddenly shot out toward the towers of Central Park West, which they were already approaching. "That's Dave Roizman's building, isn't it? Now—now *there's* a man who certainly took his paternal responsibilities seriously, wouldn't you agree? I mean, *his* daughter never missed out on any Mickey Mouse watches, I'm sure of it! After all, growing up in a building like *that!* Look what *her* father gave her! Doormen and elevator men and maids and housekeepers—and would you like to know what Nina Roizman is doing now? Would it interest you? She's living in Switzerland, working full time for the Maharishi!"

Merry shrugged. "You know what I think of Nina Roizman. She was always silly and full of pretentious—"

"And how about Abby Gerson? Your *good friend* Abby Gerson? All that Park Avenue and summers abroad and more charge accounts than she could keep track of, and she's the one who dropped out of social work school to join a witches' coven! Isn't that what you told me, Merry? A *witches' coven!*" Ez was now so beside himself with delight that he bumped into a woman walking four beribboned miniature poodles. "Oh! Pardon me, madam," he said as if he were drunk. "I'd apologize to the dogs too, but I believe they're French-speaking."

Merry said, "I never should have told you about Abby. You were always looking for something to nail her with. You just can't forgive her father his window shades!" But they were both laughing.

"And then there's Ffrenchy! You were upset about Ffrenchy. Just think of poor Meisel—rushing into the operating room every day at sunrise just so that he could keep that girl in William Greenberg brownies! And what did it do for her? And what does *she* believe? That she's the reincarnation of—of a *what?*"

"It's not exactly reincarnation. It's—she believes—"

"Maybe I *didn't* buy you Mickey Mouse watches. Maybe you *didn't* have elevator men to—to press your buttons. Or doormen to open your doors. But for Christ sake! At least *my* daughter knows which end is up! Oh, excuse me, young man," Ez said as, this time, he knocked straight into a kid standing in front of the subway entrance with a stack of leaflets and End the Draft petitions. As the green leaflet sheets scattered on the sidewalk, Ez faced the boy with an open, disarming smile and fixed him with that intent, locking look he had perfected in public debates. It suggested a rare and particular personal connection—that luxurious intimacy-of-the-mind look with which he addressed girls he'd just met and touchy, unconverted students. He said, "I'm *terribly* sorry, really I am. Tell me. Please. How can I make amends?"

The boy, not more than sixteen, startled out of his first-wind antagonism, began stammering, "Well, well, you could —you could *sign* the petition."

"Certainly!" Ez said grandly, and swept the clipboard and pen right out of the boy's hands.

"Ez! *You* can't sign that!" Merry whispered. "It's to your congressman. *You* don't vote in this district!"

"Cookie"—he waved her away—"where I vote now, all they've got to sign petitions are cows and professors. And if you think I fit in with either of—"

"Oh, wow! Ezra Slavin!" the boy suddenly called out excitedly. "What a far-out thing to happen! I just think—I mean, my parents have all your books—and I just think you're *so cool!* I mean, shit! It really blows my mind that I'm meeting you!"

"I'm very happy to meet you too." Ez extended his hand and nodded solemnly. "*Very* happy. Because I know, I can see, that for as long as it turns out to be necessary, *you'll* be someone we can count on! And for as long as it turns out to be necessary, you'll be standing right here!" And as the boy stood there blushing, Ez grabbed Merry's hand, and almost pulling her down the subway steps, said, "Stick with me, cookie. The way *I* go to the Lower East Side, you don't have to change trains! And not only that—for *you*, we'll get off at Fourteenth Street and take the bus that goes right down Avenue A into Essex Street. *You'll* see! *That's* where I'll get my tomato herring!"

But on Essex Street, when they got off the bus, Ez began looking around cloudily and turning disjointedly in the narrow, crowded street like a kid who'd been blindfolded and whirled around for a game of pin the tail on the donkey. Finally, pointing eastward, he said, "I could show you where I used to go swimming when I was a kid. But in this weather, in this wind . . . I don't know . . . I guess it's too far."

Merry knew perfectly well where he had gone swimming as a kid: he had jumped off the rotting piers to swim in the sludge of the East River. Once, hitting his head on a piece of steel piping, he had almost drowned; once, he had stowed away on a boat and been missing for days; once, at the age of five, still in his wet bathing suit, he'd followed his older brothers and their friends, hiding with them in the back of a moving man's horse-drawn wagon, but too small to jump off as quickly as they did, Ez alone had remained on the wagon and Ez alone had gotten lost. All of these stories which Ez liked to tell in the high spirit of boyhood adventures always left Merry with a feeling of orphaned, panicky sadness: so much getting lost, so much desolate confusion, and above all so much precariousness—a precariousness that Ez still celebrated and would not give up.

On the corner of Essex and Rivington, Merry now followed Ez's eastward gaze—it forced her to look in the direction of the house she'd lived in with her grandmother—and said, "I *know* where you used to go swimming. Maybe we'll walk over there later."

"*Later? Later?* It's late enough now! You just don't want to go there! And it's not only the river—you don't want to go *anywhere* around here! I could show you . . . I could show you the block that had the best bonfires on Election Day. I could show you the old Sephardic cafés on Allen Street—all those strange Oriental old boys sitting up there on the second floor playing cards and smoking their narghiles. . . . I don't even know if they're still there. . . . But *you* won't come with me. You won't come *anywhere*. I can see it in your expression—you can't bear the smell."

"Ez, it depresses me around here," Merry said. "Why can't you understand that?" Because even though the neighborhood was crowded with double-parked suburban cars and their bustling, Sunday-bargain-hunting owners, there now was a grayness, a windy rawness in the day that blew around the streets like an ugly, cheap-clarinet sigh of absolute hopelessness. Here and there, lights went on in apartments above the stores, but they had neither the quickening, sudden excitement of tall, ranging city streets proclaiming themselves in premature twilight, nor the intimate childhood allure of unknown, cozy rooms lit up and lazy for a cloudy Sunday. It had nothing to do with the weather. Watching the occasional lights go on, Merry felt the bottomless bleakness of a dream from which you wake up crying. "For me, the Lower East Side is just depressing. All it ever reminds me of is funerals. Funerals, poverty and failure . . . You know what I mean." And because he didn't respond at all, bitterly Merry added, "You *do* know what I mean. It's—it's the lullaby with which you sang me to sleep."

"*Lullaby!*" Ez spit out this word, making such a face that a little Puerto Rican boy sitting astride a fire hydrant nearby pointed and yelled out joyfully, "*Mira!* Dracula!" "With which

I *sang* you to sleep!" Ez said. "My God, Merry! *Who* wasn't influenced by Isobel?" And he plowed through the crowd toward an appetizing store in a way that made Merry suddenly think of the word "irregardless"—it was the word Ez used to make fun of immigrant English usage—and called out, "How can you let a sentence like that come out of your mouth? *Whose* daughter are you?"

"But it's true." Merry followed him into the store. "You brought me up to worship failure."

"*Failure!* If what you mean is that I didn't—"

"Take a number there, mister! Take a number!" the counterman cried out, seeing Ez just range through the line of waiting customers as if they didn't exist.

"Number!" Ez said with extreme distaste. "What's going on here today? Why is it so crowded? And why are people *buying* so much?"

The counterman, a sharp-featured, impatient-looking man, pushed back the yarmulke which had slipped onto his forehead, and looking up briefly, said, "What are you, mister? A comedian? You don't know what it's like here before a holiday?"

"Holiday?" Ez frowned. All around them, there were people carrying cartons of matzos, and the countertops were lined with outsized jars of red and white horseradish.

Merry said, "It's Passover, Ez. Next week is Passover."

"Passover? . . ." Ez repeated in a voice so puzzled and distracted that once again Merry began to wonder if he was sick.

"Thirty-four!" the counterman yelled out. "Let's *go*, thirty-four! Do I know where you are? *Talk* to me, thirty-four! Don't just stand there dreaming!"

"Thirty-four," Ez said sourly as Merry reached up for a number. "When I was a kid, around here you *never* heard anyone called by a number. It would have been unthinkable. Unimaginable. I can't even . . . I mean, it's just so . . ." He

shrugged and then abruptly turned away, so that all Merry could see was the side of his head and one prominent, red, red ear. As a child, watching him shave, the white, snowy morning lather beside his bright-red, beet-red ears in the bathroom mirror had seemed as hypnotic as a fairy tale, but later the extreme redness of his ears always came at her like a shock, a rending private sign. It made her think of ears frozen in the snow: the story of Ez's father as a child in Siberia running out in the snow with his dog, running and running to meet visiting cousins, and finally finding their bodies frozen in a wagon in the middle of a howling, drift-filled woods.

In a flat, miserable voice, Ez finally said, "Cookie, Jeannie's pregnant. The baby's due in two months. I'm sixty years old, I have a son in his thirties, and Jeannie's pregnant. . . . Oh, Christ!" He suddenly pushed himself forward in the crowd. "*I* don't see any tomato herring here! I'm certainly not going to stand on this line if they don't even *have* it!"

"Take it easy, mister!" the counterman said. "Whatever you want, if it's appetizing, we have it. I guarantee you—we have it. Only first, *here,* there's one rule: don't aggravate yourself."

"Rule?" a man in the crowd called out genially. "Where do *you* come to making rules? Listen to him! *Yeder momzer a melech!* Every bastard's a king! *That's how he's making* rules!"

All through the packed appetizing line, people laughed. They moved and breathed a bit, and looked at each other with exactly that feeling of easy belonging that Ez so much longed to restore to city life. But now, in the midst of it himself, his face remained tense and his tone abrasive. He said, "I am looking for tomato herring. And I *don't* see it."

"You still don't see it?" The counterman pointed behind him to a shelf lined with Del Monte cans, and handing one to Ez, said, "You see? You just didn't know where to look. That's all it is and that's the whole story."

"A *can?* You, too? Here, too? Do you think I came all the

way down to the Lower East Side to buy something in a can?" But he picked it up and turning it in his hand, lashed out, "This says *sardines*. 'Sardines packed in tomato sauce'! What do you mean by giving me a can of sardines! I told you I was looking for herring!"

The counterman sighed. "You're a very excitable person, mister, I can see that. Listen to me. What *we* always called tomato herring—you, me, your mother, my mother, *everybody*—we all called it tomato herring. It's true, we *called* it that. But what it really always was officially, technically—you understand what I mean—the fish technical name, it was always really a sardine. And not only that, it *always* came in cans. It always came Del Monte."

"*This is not* what I want." Ez practically threw the can down on the glass countertop. "You clearly don't *have* what I want, and yet you shamelessly go on trying to sell it to me! Well, there's a name for what you are too! Officially! Technically! Because what you are, *mister*, is a cheat!"

"*Please!*" the counterman called out as Ez stalked off. "You really think that for sixty-nine cents I would cheat you? For a lousy sixty-nine cents I would bother to make up a lie? I'm only telling you what—"

"Ah *hah!*" Ez turned and pointed his finger in triumphant accusation. "You admit it yourself! Of *course* you'd prefer a higher profit! Of *course* you only wish you could cheat on a larger scale! Well, let me tell you something. It says in *your* Talmud that when a man dies, the first question asked of him is: How were you in your business dealings? In *your* Talmud!" And once again "irregardless," Ez dove through the crowd and slammed out.

"*Well?* Why don't you *say* it?" Ez demanded. "I've *shamed* you again! I've *embarrassed* you again! I've made another public scene!"

"Oh, Ez, why don't we just get into a cab and go home? You're much too—"

"Taxi! What else? Of course! Just run out into the street and yell taxi! Is there any other way of going somewhere that you would ever think of? Because—because in your pathetically deprived childhood, your father never *let* you take a taxi, so just go ahead! Take a taxi! Don't let me stop you *now!*" He pushed past a group of clumsily laden shoppers—a surburban family, probably; they were rushing toward a double-parked car—and glaring at them, he called out, "After all, you're the only child of the fifties who never even *had* a car! Denied, denied! All the delights of suburban living! You didn't have a *lawn* to play on! You didn't even have a picture window that would look out on it! You didn't even have a television until you were almost— My God!" Ez said, suddenly staring straight across the street. "That's DeWitt Cameron! What the hell is *he* doing here? And who is that—that *stick* with him? *Quick*, cookie! Turn around and walk fast and maybe he won't see me!"

"That short, bouncy guy with the Irish cap and the big package is DeWitt Cameron? I always imagined he'd be—"

"*Irish* cap? *Irish* cap? I'll have you know, my dear, that that cap is the very mark, indeed the very mark of an English country gentleman! An *academic* English country gentleman! Because, as you surely *know*, my dear, those of us in the higher reaches of—"

"Slavin! Slavin! Ezra!" boomed a carrying, hearty-in-fellowship voice from the other side of the street. "Hello there, friend! Hello there!"

"Goddamn it!" Ez said, but he turned around, and as the two men came across the street, he smiled tightly, saying, "Hello, DeWitt. I didn't know you believed in crossing the Massachusetts state line."

"Rarely do these days, rarely do!" DeWitt Cameron continued booming cheerfully though they were now practically on top of one another. "But now that I have, just see what I've done! Think of it! I've bearded you in your lair! Here you are—the man in his natural surround! . . . Ah, hello, my dear." He turned to Merry, smiling. "How nice to see you again. The last time I saw you, you were . . . you were . . . it was . . . Goodness, when *was* that?"

God only knows who he's confusing me with, Merry thought. Jeannie? A girlfriend? A student? But she said, "I don't think we've actually ever met before, Professor Cameron. I'm Merry Slavin."

"Well, of course you are, my dear. Of course you are! And this is my old friend Tom Selkirk. Managed to drag him up all the way from Washington. Rather a feat!" Cameron was beaming. "Rather a feat!"

For a second Merry thought he had said, "Rather effete." Because this Tom Selkirk, "the stick"—tall, thin and immaculate—managed to look aloof, grayly patrician and surprisingly ill at ease all at the same time. He said, "Now, that's not a bit fair, DeWitt. I was in New York only last week, dining with a client."

"Client!" Ez muttered under his breath. "Which one of the Greek colonels was it?"

"Oh, these legal fellows!" DeWitt Cameron pealed out, expansive and oblivious in his deafness. "I daresay my father was right. Up to town to dine in one evening! And then, there *we* are, snowbound with our books and our papers, so that we . . . we . . . Well, of course you do get up rather often, Slavin. But then this is all your . . . your . . ." And smiling, he made a sweeping motion with his arm that ended in a corner clogged with uncollected garbage.

Tom Selkirk said, "Do you know, Miss Slavin, I think it was that same evening, on the shuttle coming up, that I came across an article of yours. About ethnic radio stations, wasn't it? An unusual subject, I'd say, but interesting. I did find it interesting."

"Well, of course she's good!" Cameron said bluffly, smiling at Ez. "Her father! Her father! Now, I don't know what our social science friends would have to say, but just think of the genes!" And pointing to Ez, he said, "Think of it! The man himself!"

Ez turned away. He kept turning and twisting on that chilly corner with the bitter, body-strained hopelessness of a man whose sleepless night would never end. He said, "No. No, she's not like me at all. She's like her mother. She has a feeling for the left-out that's totally unsentimental. It's just like her mother. *If* you want to talk about genes."

"Why, I'd forgotten all about that, my dear! Your mother! Of course! Isobel Rees! My wife's a great fan of hers, you know. Great enthusiast. Now, why don't we all stop in for a drink? Slavin, what would you suggest? Can't say that Selkirk and I noticed anything awfully promising."

"Isobel!" Ez practically pounced on him. "If you imagine that Isobel Rees could ever in her life have a feeling for anyone or anything that wasn't—"

"Isobel Rees was my *step*mother," Merry said quickly. "That's not who Ez meant."

Cameron said, "How about that drink now, Slavin?" at the same time that Tom Selkirk, his eyes turned toward some distant point—as if mentally searching out that familiar, far-off place where the streets would stop yielding such unrelieved meanness—said, "Do you know why it interested me, Miss Slavin? You see, I do quite a lot of traveling, and it's always puzzled me. Disturbed me even, I'd say. Because over there in their own countries, those folks are always so helpful and friendly. But when you meet them here, why, they don't seem friendly or interested at all! They do the job, I'll say that for 'em, but they certainly don't seem awfully eager to . . . Well, just as you say, Miss Slavin, they've even got their own *radio* stations!"

"Just imagine that! Their own radio stations!" Ez said. "Why, I'll bet those folks actually speak their own language, play their own music, and even advertise their own foods!"

"Now, Ezra, what about that place across the street?" DeWitt Cameron asked, pointing in an uncertain direction. "Do you see where all those empty taxicabs are parked? This typewriter's beginning to feel awfully heavy, and I wouldn't be surprised if those cabbies knew something! Why don't we have a drink where they're drinking? Might as well have a drink with a little local color!"

Merry tried to figure out what Cameron was pointing to: what the taxis were parked in front of was the Garden Cafeteria.

Ez's face told nothing, and he only said, "Oh, no, DeWitt, I'm afraid that just wouldn't do. They haven't got a liquor license."

"Run into trouble, did they?" Cameron said with interest, and stepping off the curb to get a better look at this rowdy metropolitan sight, was nearly run over by a double-parked car in the process of pulling out.

"Oh, my God, Artie!" The woman inside rolled down her window, screaming, "Would you look at what you're *doing?* My God, you're not on the L.I.E. here! You're in a city! With *people!*" The driver slowly, grudgingly got out of his car, and looking at Cameron, said gruffly, "I'm sorry, I'm very sorry, mister. Are you all right?" And then, still standing right there, not even waiting for an answer, he immediately bellowed, "If he just walks right out in front of me, that's *my* fault? *That's* my fault too? Tell me one thing I did right today according to you! Starting from breakfast, let me hear one thing!"

"Goodness!" Cameron said. "I don't know when I've seen so many cars of this size! All these . . . these great-finned Cadillacs and what-have-you. Why, I don't even know what they *are!*" He smiled. "In our gentle hills, we just don't see them. Gentle hills, gentle cars—would you say that's it, Ezra? A certain innate moderation, a modesty from the landscape itself."

Ez said nothing. Cameron persisted. "I know this sort of thing's much more in your line of country, but, well, all this hurly-burly that city people seem to . . . seem to . . ." He motioned to the streets, busy with package-laden crowds. "Such a great deal of getting and spending. I don't know that I . . . that I . . . Why, just now, for instance, just now when I went in to buy this typewriter— Do you use an electric machine, by the way, Slavin? No? Of course, I never have either, but my wife . . . my daughter . . . Well, you know how it is when they gather up and join forces against you—and my daughter . . . my daughter—not Julia. The little one. Oh, she's cagey, Sally is. She just took away her old dad's old typewriter, hid it somewhere and left me a booklet, some sort of consumer listing, I gather, stores where you might find things more . . . more reasonably priced. Of course, I'd never been into one of these places before, so I . . . so I . . . Well, good Lord, Ezra! The crowds! A tiny little place, but filled to the brim, just filled to the brim! Whole families! And repeaters too! Because the storekeeper seemed to know some of them—actually asked a young fellow ahead of me how his *rabbi* was feeling! You wouldn't think that in a city of this size with so many . . . so many . . . that—that . . . Now, where was I? I seem to have lost my train of thought."

"Getting and spending," Ez said in a voice of such chill that even distant Tom Selkirk looked up at him.

"Oh, yes! As I say, there were entire families in that little place, and each and every one of them buying something! Even the children! Why, there were teen-age girls in there younger than Sally, and goodness, what they were buying! Electric hair setters or—or hairbrushes or something of that sort . . . Reminded me of the first time we took Julia down to Swarthmore, and her roommate, the Kirschenbaum girl— father owns a chain of *furniture* stores somewhere in New Jersey, I believe—why, that child had so much to unpack that

# 12

Not long after the birth of her daughter, Mountain Spring, Ffrenchy, who had been resentfully keeping her distance, suddenly called up, sounding breathless and triumphant. "Merry, you won't *believe* this incredibly dynamite thing I just heard from my *mother!* You know how she's always doing her like bullshit volunteer number at Channel Thirteen? Well, I mean, it's total bullshit, it really is, it's just her whole, you know, chic-East-Side-lady-into-culture trip —oh! I forgot! I didn't tell you—we moved to the East Side. I mean, *they* moved to the East Side. Well, *anyway,* my mother was doing her usual Channel Thirteen number, and you know they have this program, it's called—it's called *First Impressions: An American Album?* And it's like this—this interview thing where they follow the person around? Well, Ez is gonna be *on* it! Next *Wednesday!* And I mean, they always have these like—these really famous people! Like—like, you know, what's her name—that old lady, she once went to New Guinea to live with these like far-out Indians and now everybody always sees her near the Planetarium with this—this like giant stick? Well, *she* was on it! And I mean, James Baldwin was on it! And—and Allen Ginsberg!"

And Erik Erikson, and Edward Steichen, and A. Philip Randolph, and Martha Graham. "I know," Merry said. Because at the time of the taping, Ez, pleased but uneasy—he kept drumming his fingers on the chopsticks in the Hunam restaurant, where he and Merry were having dinner—had said, " '*First* Impressions'? They ought to call it '*Last* Impressions, or Beat the Undertaker'!"

"Come on, Ez!" Merry had said at the time. "Robert Lowell? John Kenneth Galbraith? Isaac Stern? They're *all* younger than you are!"

"Oh, I don't know, cookie. It's not that. . . . It's the way—the way he kept on *looking* at me. As if every time I opened my mouth, he was staring into the face of—of hoary wisdom."

"You mean the interviewer? Carl Springer? You've seen him before, Ez. That's what he *does.*"

Ez sighed. "Well, he's a very pleasant fellow, Springer. And God knows he certainly did his homework. But Jesus Christ! No matter what I said, he just . . . he just—well, he made me feel like a Goddamn Chinese fortune cookie!" And picking one up, a leftover from the table beside them, he crumbled it in his hand.

On the telephone, Ffrenchy now said, "I didn't *mean* whether you knew he was gonna be *on* the program! Like I figured he told you *that!* I mean, naturally he would tell *you!* But this is like something *he* might not even know! They changed when he was supposed to be on, *that's* what I heard from my mother! Like they had some—some bullshit technical hassle, so *now* they're putting him on on Wednesday! *Next*

*Wednesday*, Merry! Aren't you—I mean, doesn't it just blow your *mind?*"

Because Merry hesitated, Ffrenchy immediately drew her stepchild conclusion, and very bitterly said, "You already *knew* about it, didn't you? He *told* you! Oh, shit! He probably called *you* up the second he found out about it!"

"It wasn't *like* that, Ffrenchy," Merry said. "I found out about it because I called *him*—and about something entirely different. My brother in India is very sick—*seriously* sick—and his mother asked me to tell Ez."

"Oh," Ffrenchy said, completely uninterested. "That's the one who—who he's into this like really boring music professor trip and he limps?"

Which was not so different from Ez's reaction the day before when Merry had called him. "Oh, God. *Nicky!*" he said. "How the hell in this day and age did that kid get malaria? *Malaria!* Christ almighty! I tell you, Merry, if *he* went to Central Europe, *he'd* come back with bubonic plague! I don't know. . . . What am I supposed to say? You want to tell me? Because whatever the hell it is, I can't say it. That's it. I just can't."

"It's not a matter of what you're supposed to *say*. Isobel just thought—"

"Oh, I *understand*. I understand perfectly. Isobel delegated you to break the news to that well-known monster his father. Well, you did it. And now you can report back that the monster responded in characteristic fashion. Absolutely true to form. Tell her! That'll cheer her up, you'll see!"

"Stop it, Ez! Just stop it! Isobel thought you ought to know because you *are* his father. And because he almost *died*. My God, they think he'll have permanent kidney damage! And they still don't even *know* yet when—"

"Permanent *kidney* damage, permanent *leg* damage! Do you realize that that kid is—"

"And they still can't even tell when he'll really be out of

*danger.* Isobel only found out because there was a European doctor there who sent her—"

"*Ah!* A *European* doctor! Of course! How could some strange, dark barbaric Asian be trusted to minister to *Isobel's* son? Isobel's pale, thin, fine-featured son? Well! I'm certainly glad to hear the doctor is European. Now Isobel can stop worrying and go right back to one of her perfect and—what is it?—*luminous* sentences."

"Ez, Isobel is in India by now. She called me in the middle of the night from the airport."

"From the *airport? Isobel?* Do you mean to tell me Isobel was actually *flying* to India? Isobel was taking a *plane?*"

"She flies now, Ez. You know that."

"Yes," he said gleefully. "But she *hates* it."

"So do I," Merry said. "And for that matter, so do *you.*"

"Well, I do. . . . That's true . . ." Ez said slowly. "But you know, I sometimes think—I've sometimes had the feeling that a real case could be made for the airport as a kind of—well, as a kind of great democratizer. *Because* of its sterility. *Because* of its placelessness. For all the reasons I hate it. But it becomes . . . it becomes a kind of forced crucible—you know, everything else falls away. Like people stuck in an elevator, that kind of thing. It might sound crazy to you at first, Merry, but the next time you're in an airport, take a good look around and see if I'm not right. You *could* make a case for it."

"*You* could," Merry said. "For some reason, I can't seem to put my mind to it at the moment."

"Oh, Christ, cookie! I'm *sorry.* What do you want me to say? I admit it—I don't *feel* what a father is supposed to feel at a time like this, I just don't. Not for Nicky. And I never have. All right, so I'm deficient as a father, I admit it. I am. But I just— Oh, look, Merry, he's always seemed like *Isobel's* child to me—not mine. Not mine at all. In any way. I don't know. . . . I can't—I could never even have a *conversation* with him. He's so Goddamn uptight!"

"All your children are uptight, Ez. *Jonathan's* uptight, *I'm* uptight, *Nicky's* uptight. The only one who isn't is Ffrenchy. Your child of nature, the shining exception."

"Well, she *is* an exception! She is! She has a genuine spontaneity, a certain innate feel for—for—oh, Christ, cookie! Do you know what that girl said to me the last time I saw her? That Jeannie wasn't really *free* because she shaved her legs!"

On the phone now, Ffrenchy said, "Merry, what are you gonna do when you watch the program? I mean, like are you gonna have a big party and everything, and all these *people* will be there, and everybody'll like bring something *different*, and they'll all be standing around grooving and talking and eating all this really *great shit?* Because, I mean, I make this truly *dynamite* zucchini bread, I really do, and I could make a whole lot of it—I mean, not *too* much, because then people might think I'm like really into excess. Or—or else, wait, I've *got* it, Merry! I could make tabbouleh! It's this—this really incredible Assyrian salad thing, and it's really very simple and very *healthy* and everything. I mean, it's just bulgur wheat, and really all you do is soak it and add some like vegetable shit. And then, when I bring it over, I could—"

"Ffrenchy," Merry said finally, the image of Nicky, fish-like and feverish, tossing on a string bed somewhere in India so fixed in her mind, "if what you really want to know is will Ez be here when I watch the program, the answer is no."

"No, no, I just meant—well, I mean, I *could* watch it here, I really could. 'Cause like we just got this new—I mean, *they* just got this new really incredible color TV. Like *I* just thought it was cute, but *Peter*—do you remember Peter? Honig? Well, I mean, he is really *heavily* into, you know, *fine* equipment. Like that's what he really gets off on. And he—he

225

really freaked out when he saw it! So, I mean, I *could* watch it here, but like *they're* gonna be watching it here, and I just *know*, Merry, I just *know*—the vibes are gonna be *so bad.*"

"Well, I'm not having a party, Ffrenchy. I'm just watching the program."

"*That's* cool. I didn't mean that you like *should* have a party, I just meant—well, I mean, I just wanted to *talk* to you anyway. And—and I want you to see Spring! Because, oh, wow, Cookie—I mean, *Merry. Merry.* I *know* you don't like me to call you Cookie, only *Ez* is allowed to do *that.*"

"It's not a question of *allowed,* Ffrenchy. It's not a *name,* and it's not my nickname either. That was just the old mistake your mother always made, and you were only repeating it."

"Oh, well, my *mother!* Let's not get into *that!* Shit! But I mean, like you have to see Spring! She is just such a trip! She's like this little, tiny total *trip!* And I mean, you're—you're like her *aunt*—well, sort of. Even though Ez was such a total motherfucker about it. I mean, you are—you are *kind* of her aunt."

"What do you mean? What did Ez say?"

"Well, that's *one* of the things I wanted to talk to you about." Ffrenchy suddenly began whispering. "But not now. Because my mother just came in, and the walls in this apartment are *to-tal pa-per. Total.* Oh! I forgot! I was supposed to tell you that my mother says hello, and that she sends her best and, you know, all *that* shit. And that if you want to have lunch with her sometime—I mean, I don't see why you *should* want to have lunch with her sometime—*any*time. But I mean, *especially* now, since her mastectomy, she has just been *so freaky,* so *weirded out!* Like that's why we had to move and everything! She couldn't even stand to stay in the same—"

"Ffrenchy! Your mother had a *mastectomy?* I had no idea she was sick. I'm really sorry to—"

"Oh, well, I mean, it's really not *like* that, Cookie. It really isn't. Like she's totally okay. *Totally*. You know—like it hadn't really *spread*, and they *got* it and everything. . . . But I mean, shit! Her *head!* Whew! And that's *another* thing Ez was really—he was really—well, I mean, I *told* him about it because she was like really freaking me out every time I just talked to her on the phone! And I mean, I was at Carob then, and Spring—Spring was just *born* and everyone was—well, they were really getting on my case about how *bad* it was for Spring. And they were—like I'm really glad they said it! 'Cause they were totally right on. I mean, she just kept on *crying* all the time—this totally beautiful, perfect, dynamite little *baby!* So I told Ez, and he—he got this like *super-*serious look on his face, and he said in this—this *voice?* About how *sorry* he was that Paula was sick! And I mean, *sorry?* Shit! You know—like how sorry could he really be? I mean, for him she was like this—this one-year stand! And then, *then* he went into this whole heavy bullshit boring rap about how when you're *young* you never think about the like limitations of your *body.* Or being *sick.* And there was like no reason why you *should,* so he could *sympathize* with me. But then, when you got older and you saw all this bad-vibe sickness shit happening to your friends, people your own age, it like really changed your head and—and I don't know! He was standing there doing this—this whole Old Man of the Sea number! I mean, he didn't *really* sympathize with me *at all!* And that's only one examp— Oh, shit! I have to *go,* Merry. The *baby's* crying—I mean, it's not bad vibes or anything, she's just hungry. *Yes, I know, Mother! I am coming! I am not deaf!"* Ffrenchy suddenly shrieked, and dropping her voice again, said, "See what I mean? She's a total freak show! That's why I— Anyway, I'll come early. *Before* the program. So I can tell you all the— *Ma! I said I am coming! God!"*

Quickly, Merry said, "Listen, Ffrenchy, is there anything you want me to have in the house for the baby? Juice? Milk? Anything?"

"Oh, *no!* Shit, no! I mean, I am *totally* together! It's—it's like *zero* hassle! Zero! Truly!"

"I just thought if there was something I wouldn't ordinarily—"

"Oh, *wow*, Cookie! You just sound so *freaky!* I mean, if you're worrying about your brother, you shouldn't. I *mean* it—you really shouldn't! Like if *I* was gonna be sick anyplace, I would *definitely* pick India. Definitely! Because—because in *India*, if you get sick they are *truly* mellow about it, they really are! I mean, Darcy told me—do you know my friend Darcy Greenblatt? Well, *she* was in India for like—like *four months!* I mean, she wasn't just *in India*, she was in an ashram. Well, anyway, when she was there, there was this girl there from . . . from like Sweden? And she was so gorgeous and like super-skinny and everything that it really made Darcy feel like—well, that's a whole other thing, really. 'Cause that's just Darcy's *head*. But *anyway*. The girl from Switzerland got sick—and I mean, I don't know what she *had* or anything, but she was sick for like a really long time, and then she died. And Darcy said everyone was just so incredibly *serene* and—and *peaceful* about it that it was like the most beautiful experience of her whole life!"

Zero hassle: At seven o'clock on the following Wednesday evening, a good two hours before *First Impressions* was supposed to go on, Ffrenchy's voice came through the intercom. "*Merry?* Could you—could you like come down and help me carry up some shit! I mean, I've got *Spring* and everything and—and like I *forgot*. You don't even have a *doorman!*"

Downstairs, there was no one in the lobby and no one in the vestibule either. But outside, directly opposite a schoolyard basketball game—its customary high-jumping, joyful progress now suddenly interrupted—there was Ffrenchy, Ffrenchy with her long red hair streaming all the way down and a bright yellow tie-dyed T-shirt pulled all the way up: right there in the middle of the sidewalk, she was nursing the baby.

"*Ffrenchy!* My God! Couldn't you—"

"Oh, hi, Cookie." Ffrenchy beamed, and speaking in her very high, sweet, good-fairy voice, said, "Isn't she just—just *beautiful?* I mean, she's so *happy!* Doesn't she look . . . *blissed out?*"

"She's not the only one, Ffrenchy. Why don't we—"

"I know!" Ffrenchy crooned. "I *love* feeding her! I always feel so—well, everyone even *says.* I get this like *total* glow!"

"*They're* glowing too!" Merry indicated the other side of the street. "Let's just go upstairs! *Fast!*"

"What are you *talking* about? Those—those *kids? They* don't—I mean, *I'm* not— Oh, shit, Merry! Spring *likes* eating outside! Look at her! She *loves* it! I mean, when we were at Carob, I never fed her inside! *Never!* And now, like even in the middle of the night, I always try to take her out on the terrace!"

"But there's a difference, Ffrenchy! Don't you see the difference between your own private terrace and the middle of the street?"

"Oh, I don't *believe* this. I cannot believe you're even saying it. Shit! It's—it's—I mean, you're doing this *total* Ez number! Like we were in the bus station in Springfield? And—and I mean, I didn't even *want* to feed her there! 'Cause it's like so *grungy* and *disgusting.* And the *people*—oh, my *God! Ugly! Depressing! Low!* Like it's this whole, you know, it's just this whole super-repulso bottom-of-the-barrel scene! So, I mean, I really *didn't* want to feed her there. But she was like really hungry, so I *had* to. And I *mean!* The *rap* that Ez went into! Like—like that I was *offending* other people, and they were my fellow *passengers.* And I mean, shit! Fellow passengers! Tops, we'd be on the same bus—and it's *only* the same bus—for two hours! So like why should I give a fuck where *their* heads are at! Besides, they were like these—these *obvious* pigs!" Ffrenchy stopped, and pointing to a large striped Mexican straw bag that was propped against the doorway, she said, "Cookie, could you take that? It's like all this—this *baby* shit. Oh—and some garbage my mother sent. She's really gotten into making all this— Ooh, what's the *matter*, Spring?" she suddenly crooned. "We're going *upstairs* now. We're going in the *elevator*. But there's *no* nice man here to help take us up. In *our* house, we have *Hector*. And Hector *loves* you, doesn't he?" She turned to Merry and in her ordinary voice, said, "He really *does*, Cookie. I mean, he's so like *caring* with her. And *gentle*. I mean, everyone's always saying how Spanish guys are only into this big macho trip? Well, I don't know, I guess they *are*, but I don't know. . . . Like I really always *liked* Spanish guys. I mean, I always sort of thought . . . you know, that if I could like ever really get it on with one of them, it might—I mean, maybe I would sort of get into this— Well, like *Hector*—I mean, he is just so totally *sweet* with kids! He has this—this little daughter and she like comes to hang out with him in the lobby after school? And I mean, you know, she sits there in her little *Catholic* school dress, and does her *homework*, and I mean, it's like—like—well, it's really *sweet*."

Looking at Ffrenchy's sudden wistful and almost teary confusion in the dim upstairs hallway, Merry unlocked the door and said, "My God, Ffrenchy! You're talking as if you were an old lady . . . as if it were all over for you. You'll do a lot of different things in your life, you'll go through a lot of different scenes. And who knows?"

"Yeah, well, I guess you're right, Cookie. . . ." Ffrenchy was half laughing and half crying. "But I don't know. . . . Sometimes—sometimes I just . . . Well, I'm not really *down* or anything, I'm really not. But sometimes . . . sometimes people—well, like *Ez?* That time in the bus station that I was telling you? Well, I mean, I *only* said—well, I mean they were like these absolute *grunges* that were sitting there. Like—like *fat* and—and you know, *puffy*, and wearing these like . . . *grotesque* clothes. So I just said that I didn't care if I—I offended them. Because it was totally obvious that they were pigs. And I mean, my God! Ez almost went *insane!* He got like so *angry* at me, Merry. He just went into this *insane rap!* That—that *I* was the one who was always talking about being *free*, and—and what did I think freedom *meant*. And that *I* was the one who was choosing to live this like, you know, nonbourgeois life-style, so that I was supposed to be more—more—oh, *I* don't know! I mean, I don't even *know* what he thought I was supposed to be! Like it was just so *crazy!* It was this whole . . . whole insane like all-about-*poor*-people rap. And I mean, nobody there was even black!"

"It's not a *color* issue, Ffrenchy. It's not a question of black and white! It's—"

"Oh, I *know!* Like a black person could be a motherfucker too. I know that! Like the nurse in Dr. Weisbrod's office? I mean, God! Every time I take Spring *in* there—well, I mean, I would *never* tell anyone at Carob, I *do* take her to a pediatrician! *Ne-ver!* Like they would just—I mean, they are like so *totally* against—well, I mean, not just pediatricians. *Any* doctors. And I mean, they are totally right! Totally! Like I am just *so glad* I had her at Carob and not in some, you know, like bad-vibe hospital! 'Cause like I *know*—I mean, I really *know* it, Cookie—that that's why she's so perfect and healthy and everything! And why she'll totally never need Dr. Weisbrod! But you know, my *father* said—well, you know, he's just so *into* being a doctor and everything and like he really—well, I mean, especially because I *didn't* have her in a hospital, he just really got into this whole number about how she— Oh, *Cookie!*" Ffrenchy suddenly called out excitedly as she walked into the living room. "You got a new sofa! Far out! I really like it! I mean, I *love* the color! It does this—this truly *up thing* for the whole room!" And putting the baby down on one of the cushions, she cooed, "Look, Spring! Look at the *beautiful* blue sofa! Doesn't it make you *happy?* Wasn't it a really groovy thing for your Aunt Merry to *get?* 'Cause *you're* gonna remember it all your life! *Whenever* you see your Aunt Merry. And she *is* your aunt, Spring. She *really* is. Even though Ez was just *so* mean about it."

Merry said, "What did you once start to tell me about that, Ffrenchy? *How* was Ez mean? What did he say?"

"Oh, well, I mean, he was just a total motherfucker, Cookie. It was incredible! I mean, I *told* him that *now* it was like really important for me to change my name to Slavin. Like *vital.* You know, so that Spring could have the name Slavin too. And I mean, he just—"

"Why should *Spring* be named Slavin? Why shouldn't she have Peter's name?"

"*Peter?* Peter *Honig?* Why should she—I mean, why should he— Oh, wow, Cookie! You mean you thought that he—that Peter and I were still— Oh, shit! That is just so far out! It really blows my mind! I mean, I've known Peter for like—like *two years! More!* And I mean, I love him and everything, I truly do, but he's just *totally* this, you know, this like old, old friend! *Don't* you remember that time when— when he came to Ez's house in Massachusetts? And—and he brought all his cameras and shit? Because I'm pretty sure that that was the time—I mean, I *know* it—like it *was* the time when Ez said all that stuff about abortion and how he was *against* it and everything, and—and how it was like *killing?* 'Cause like when I told that to *Rob,* he—he kind of really got *into* it. I mean, he doesn't always—well, he totally *admires* Ez and everything, he really does, but he doesn't agree with him about—about how, you know, that demonstrations should be like . . . nonviolent. I mean, I think he thinks they *should* be. Violent. And—and I mean, Ez really isn't into that, is he? Like he's really not into throwing things up. Ooh!" Ffrenchy suddenly cried out, clapping her hand to her mouth. "I mean *blowing* things up, blowing things up! Shit!" She giggled in amazement. "That was like a—a Freudian slip, wasn't it?" Ffrenchy frowned. "Ez doesn't believe in *that* either, does he? I mean Freud. He doesn't believe in Freud or—or any of those ancient shrink types. Like I think my mother once told me that—that they used to fight about it or something. Well, *anyway*. That time that Ez said all that stuff about abortion? Well, that's just another reason why Spring *should* have the name Slavin! 'Cause like that was one of the reasons—I mean, it *was* the reason—shit, it definitely *was*—that I decided— well, I mean, Rob and I *both* decided—that it might be, you know, this like really cool thing if I did *have* the baby! And I mean, he already knew people at Carob who were like totally turned on to having kids."

"Rob," Merry said. "Rob is Spring's father?"

"Oh, right, I forgot, Cookie. You never met him. Well, I mean, he's just totally sweet, he really is. He has this, you know, like this whole kind of totally *gentle* farm-boy look. D'you know what I mean? Like blond hair and very tall and sort of—sort of—well, like Darcy"—Ffrenchy started to giggle—"Darcy used to call him Wonder Bread. But that was really just because he didn't—well, they just never really— see, she actually thought he had this like really low sexual energy. Which is *not true!* I mean, it is just *so* not true that it's like—like *amazing!*" Ffrenchy beamed. "But he does kind of have a Wonder Bread look, I know what she means. He looks—he looks—well, when you look at him—when you look at his face?—you can like totally tell—I mean, you can just *see* him when he was a little boy! You know—that whole kind of real gentle sweet look? I mean, like I sometimes think *she* really looks like that, like him," Ffrenchy said, smiling moonily at the baby. "*Don't* you, Spring? *Don't* you? You look like Rob. You know, Cookie, I bet he'd really get off on that!"

"Then why shouldn't she have *his* name, Ffrenchy? Rob's name?"

"Oh, *wow*, Cookie!" Ffrenchy said, exasperated. "You are just being so—so—I mean, *Rob* isn't into that! He truly isn't! I mean, he is just totally not into possessiveness. Like that's what's so *beautiful* about him! He really understands why that whole, you know, possessing-*people* trip is even lower than—well, I mean, it's *much* lower than possessing *things*. And I mean, he's not into *things* either! *At all!* Because his parents—shit! Like they were always laying this really heavy right-and-wrong trip on him? Like everything *he* did was wrong? Bad? And that he was always—always *embarrassing* them and—and bringing *shame* to their *family*. Really weird shit, you know? And like it *totally* never occurred to them—I mean, Rob said *ne-ver*—that what was truly *wrong* was their whole possession trip! That they thought they could like possess *him* and his *sister*, and—and that all they were really into was—was owning more *things*. And—and so, you know, that's why the whole scene at Carob was just so really right on for both of us—I mean, *all* of us! Spring too. 'Cause like at Carob, it just wasn't—well, I mean, nobody was into owning. People *or* things. And I mean, *my* parents are pretty heavily into things too, they really are, but they would never—I mean *never*—hit me with some—some *sick* right-and-wrong number like *Rob's* parents! God! I mean, I don't even *know* anyone else whose parents are into anything like *that*. It's so—I mean, it's just *so* fucking *morbid*. . . ." An odd shadow came over Ffrenchy's face, as if it had crept in with the word "morbid." "Cookie? . . ." she said uneasily. "You want to know this like really . . . weird thing about Rob? Well, I mean, it isn't . . . it isn't really *about* Rob. It's just—it's just—well, you want to know what Rob's *name* is? His last name?" She looked away, and taking a deep breath, said, "It's Stranger. Robert Stranger, that's his name. And I mean, I *thought* about it and everything, I really did, and—and I wouldn't want—I mean, I couldn't *stand* it." Ffrenchy began to cry. "I just couldn't *stand* it if—if she were named

234

Stranger. I mean, my beautiful little *baby? Stranger?* Oh, God!" She sobbed. "It just made me so *crazy* to even *think* about it that I—I couldn't—well, like suppose when she goes to school? Well, I mean, maybe she *won't* go to school. 'Cause like everyone at Carob was just *totally* down on school, *any* school. *At all.* But—but just say suppose—suppose sometime she *does* go to school, I don't know. Like she might even *want* to—I mean, *I* did. When I was little. And what if, you know, some teacher or—or like other kids, if they started—I mean, like it's *true* that little kids are really motherfuckers sometimes. It's—it's not just a thing that people say to dump on kids. 'Cause like my sister? Sunni? She—she was *always* coming home from school crying. 'Cause she was always, you know, this little chub. And I mean, what if Spring—what if they saw the name Stranger and they—and they—" Ffrenchy began to sob all over again, crying out, "Oh, why couldn't Ez just do this *one thing? One thing!*"

"Did you tell him? Did you tell him the *real* reason you—"

"Oh, I couldn't tell him *that,* Cookie," Ffrenchy said tearily. "You don't know how *weird* he is with me! I mean, he is just . . . *so weird.* Like—like he tells me to look things up in the *dictionary?* I mean, for like zero reason, *ze-ro,* he tells me to look something up in the fucking dictionary!"

"You mean he gets impatient with you?"

"*No!* It's *not* impatient. I mean, like impatience . . . that's—that's something I can totally get into. You know, like when my mother starts one of her bullshit raps? I mean, I am *definitely* impatient. Definitely. So I mean, it's *not* that. It's—it's—well, *okay.*" Ffrenchy leaned forward and narrowed her eyes. "Cookie, what's totalitarian? I mean *au*thoritarian? No, I mean *to*talitarian. Well, *anyway,* isn't it—isn't it—it's like the police, right? Like when you say the cops are Fascist pigs. I mean, I don't have to look that up in the *dictionary!* Shit! And—and like I totally don't know how he could've said the whole thing in the first place!"

235

"Where'd you call a cop a Fascist pig, Ffrenchy?" Merry asked, immediately envisioning Ffrenchy in her pulled-up, tie-dyed T-shirt, squatting on the sidewalk of the main street of North Darby, nursing her baby as the one town cop glared and drove by.

"I *didn't!* It had nothing to *do* with the cops! Nothing! Totally! That's why it's so— I mean, that's why I can't even— See, what *happened*—well, I mean, *nothing* happened. *Nothing!* That's why the whole thing is just *so* fucking weird! *Anyway.* Ez came over to Carob. For a visit. Like I *wanted* him to. I *asked* him to. I mean, *everybody* wanted him to, even though a lot of people . . . a lot of people—well, you know, they're really not that cool to having parent types come around. But I mean, Ez is different and—and we all *talked* about it and everything. In a Community Meeting? And everyone really—well, maybe not *everyone.* I mean, *Melinda*—see, she's like really heavily into astrology? And she just said that she like *knew*—I mean, she was absolutely *positive* that no male Capricorn should ever come to Carob. *Ever.* And that like she, personally, would never *trust* one, and that Nixon *is* one. . . . But I mean, people like *Brad* and—and *Margo* and *Jesse*—all the really *major* people at Carob? They . . . *they* really wanted him to come! I mean, they were truly getting off on it! 'Cause, you know, they wanted to rap with him and everything. And they *did!* And I mean, *that* part—*that* part, Cookie, was just—God, it was just *so cool!* I was just *so happy!* Truly!" Ffrenchy, so wistfully recalling the brevity of her Eden, was becoming teary again. "I mean, you know, he came over and he kind of walked around—with *me.* And then, then he rapped with people—I mean, he rapped with a whole *lot* of people. He didn't just hang out with the heavies! Like this guy once came from— from, you know, like an underground paper in Boston? And I mean, he *only* hung out with Margo! Like he took her *picture* and everything, and everyone—everyone really got into this whole—well, I mean, the vibes just got *so bad* that some people actually left Carob! Like they really would *not* come back! But I mean, the scene with Ez was just so *totally* different—like he was just *so* mellow and really rapping with people and everything that everyone kind of—well, they really *wanted* him to come to this—this Community Meeting that was going down. And I mean, *visitors* . . . Shit, visitors are just *never*—I mean, *never*—invited to Communities! 'Cause like all they *really* ever do is just kind of suck off our energy. Which is like a big high for *them* but, you know, *nowhere* for us! And even this one—well, she was this really *dynamite* radical feminist therapist and—and the *other* times, when she was just like rapping with some of the women? She was *definitely* giving out some incredibly high energy! To *us!* Like she was telling us all this stuff about male incest fantasies, Cookie? About how it's really fucked us over for centuries? And—and *oppressed* us? And like I never really thought about it before, but when Tzipporah *said* it, wow! I just *knew* that it was true! I just *knew* it! Like I even think"—Ffrenchy narrowed her eyes and looked out at Merry with a kind of sly challenge—"I even think that the *real* reason Ez got so weird when I was nursing Spring? In the bus station? You know— that whole poor-people rap? Like what was *really* going down was, you know, when he *saw* me, he just like totally *desired* me. So he had to hit me with this—this male-incest-oppression respect-your-fellow-passengers bullshit! I mean, that was just the trip he was laying on me! It was really just—just his *head,* you know?"

Merry said nothing, wondering which was the greater marvel: the open-hearted crudeness of Ffrenchy's innocence or the callow, garbling greed of her sophistication.

"Cookie, do you think . . . do you think I should like *confront* him? I mean, just sort of be really upfront? Because at Carob, in Community Meetings—see, a lot of people— well, *some* people—like before they came to Carob? They

237

were like really heavily into encounter-type scenes, so they always—I mean, we *all* always—well, you know, we just got right into these *totally* honest, dynamite, no-bullshit raps! That's why it's just so *incredible*, Cookie—I mean, it's just so fucking weird—that Ez, when he like came out of that Community Meeting? And I mean, it wasn't even *over* yet or anything, but I figured he probably had to go someplace, so, you know, I just went out to say good-by to him? And he just stood there and he gave me like this *look?* This like weird, sick, *wasted* look! And he said he couldn't stay in there for another second because—because . . . well, I don't *know* why he couldn't stay in there! But *that's* when he said all that—that authoritarian totalitarian stuff! Can you *believe* it, Cookie? Can you *believe* it? Do *you* think—do you think he's like getting senile?"

"No," Merry said firmly. "I think he really disagreed with whatever went on at that meeting." And purposely turning away, Merry suddenly noticed the time. "Oh, Ffrenchy! The *program*'ll be on in a few minutes! Let me just quickly get you Spring's present."

"*Disagreed?*" Ffrenchy cried out. "There wasn't anything you could like *disagree* with! You don't *understand!* It was just—just—see, Singing Sky had this rash? Or like a bite or something, you know, an insect bite? And *Naomi*—that's Singing's mother—Naomi was just getting into this—this whole like Western medicine *panic!* That it was *spreading* and it was going on for *weeks*. And I mean, she just got like *so* freaked out behind it that she called up her *mother*. Who's this—this *dermatologist!* And I mean, everyone *told* her— well, you know, people were being really caring and every- thing, and I mean, shit! Naomi's mother sent her this salve with—with like *chemicals* in it! So—so people just *really*— Oh, Cookie!" Ffrenchy jumped up, beaming. "You got her this like whole little *outfit!* Far out! It's really beautiful! Oh, wow! *Look,* Spring! Look what your Aunt Mer— Oh, she's *sleeping*, Cookie. Isn't that sweet? Wow, she *is* just like Rob! *He* was always getting wiped out too!"

"Do you want to put Spring in the bedroom? So the television doesn't wake her up?"

"What?" Ffrenchy said distantly. She had sat down on the floor, and like a child engrossed in an arts and crafts project, was, in dreamy, languorous abstraction, carefully folding and shredding the ribbons and tissue paper from her daughter's present. "Oh, Spring? No . . . no, it doesn't matter. She . . . she won't really . . . Cookie?" She looked up uncertainly. "Can I—can I ask you a question? I was just, you know, thinking about presents and shit and—and—Cookie? What did you get Ez for Father's Day?"

"*Father's Day?*" Merry said, astounded, trying not to laugh. Because in a family where no one had ever given presents for any reason at all, this question had the distinctly topsy-turvy, high lunatic charm of some benign science fiction. "I didn't get him *anything*, Ffrenchy. I never do. He doesn't—"

"You swear? I mean, you really swear it? Because—because, see, when Ez came to Carob, like when he first got out of the jeep? I went over and I gave him this—this tie that I made. You know, that I wove? On a loom? And he went into this—this whole—well, I mean, he just started laughing and laughing *so much* that, you know, like everyone figured he and Brad were probably turning on in the jeep. But then—then like when he was finally finished cracking up? He sort of looked at the tie, and he looked at *me,* and he said didn't I see what was funny about living in a commune and giving Father's Day presents. Because—because, you know, that Father's Day is like this big bourgeois commercial *number.* And I mean, shit, Merry! Like the whole thing—the *whole thing* was that it *wasn't* commercial! You know, I *made* it and—and the *dye* was natural and everything. I mean, when Darcy was in India, she got into these incredible plant dyes and berry dyes, and she just does these—"

239

"Ffrenchy," Merry said. "It's nine o'clock, and I am *not* going to miss the program. Not even the first few minutes."

And especially not the first few minutes. Because this was how the program began: Over the theme music, the most familiar section of *Applachian Spring*, the sound of a camera clicking in quick rhythmic bursts to match on screen the dizzyingly juxtaposed photographs of past guests: *click-click*— an architect sitting on a park bench—*click-click*—a poet licking an ice cream cone; then the title, FIRST IMPRESSIONS: AN AMERICAN ALBUM, and finally, as the music diminished, but still not a word had been said, there would be the Great Man of the month engaged in the homely, humble authenticity of his daily early morning routine. So a psychologist had walked barefoot along a windy beachfront as gulls called and waves lapped; an economist had, with private, scrupulous delight, brewed tea as the wintry dawn light of Cambridge filtered in through his kitchen window; a very near-sighted biologist did yoga exercises without his glasses while his two giant Labrador retrievers stared menacingly into the camera; and an elderly musician, grabbing a child's umbrella, rosily rushed out into an apparent blizzard to buy bagels. Of all these, only the musician had spoken. "One onion," he had said to the cheerless, mustachioed bagel baker as faint strains of *Appalachian Spring* continued on in the background and the eerie white light of the snow obscured the neon-lit storefront. And then, "Wait a minute, wait a minute. Make it a bialy."

What would Ez do in the magically serene silence of *his* televised early morning? Spoon up some instant coffee and with the same spoon still in hand, stand in front of the open refrigerator and dig into a dish of left-over tuna salad? Stare off bemusedly as the kettle whistled on and the water boiled out so that ending in amazed frustration, he would swear and fill up his cup at the hot-water faucet? But exactly as if Ez himself had made that whole ritualized, other-worldly hush impossible, there he was on the screen in his old gray windbreaker, walking in fitful, impatient strides somewhere on a sunny open country road. The sun was bothering him; usually he wore a hat against it. "You know that music you use as the theme for your program?" He squinted at Carl Springer and stabbed at the air.

"Oh, yes." Springer nodded soberly. "*Appalachian Spring.*"

"No, no, no, I've always very much *liked* Copland, that's not what I mean." Ez smiled. "I'm talking about the particular *section* that you use—the Shaker song." And as Springer stood there beside him, eager but confounded, Ez suddenly leaped into a shady spot and sang:

> " 'Tis the gift to be simple, 'tis the gift to be free,
> 'Tis the gift to come down where you ought to be,
> And when we find ourselves in the place just right
> 'Twill be in the valley of love and delight.

You see that, Carl? You see what I mean? Love and delight, love and delight!" Ez shook his head, beaming and enlivened from the relief of the shade and the avidity of argument. "There it is—the essential American mistake! The *quintessential* American mistake! I mean, my God! Just look what it runs through! Look what it encompasses! The Shakers— and all those other early utopian communities, Hollywood movies and popular magazines, psychoanalysis and—and whatever it is they call themselves—therapies? Religions? And then, of course, there's the traditional bourgeois family —notice I don't call it 'nuclear.' " Ez grinned at Springer. "I don't call it 'nuclear'—because *that's* a bomb! Well"—he started to laugh—"I guess you could certainly say the same for the family. . . . Anyway, there's the traditional bourgeois family, and right alongside it, the kids in communes. And it's all that same—that same Goddamn pursuit of happiness!"

"Oh, shit, Cookie!" Ffrenchy burst out from her lotus position on the floor. "He *is* senile, I swear it! Like he is just fucking *demento!*"

On the screen, Ez and Carl Springer were just coming to a turn in the road which Merry recognized: in the distance, the Berkshire hills, in the nearby small meadow, grazing cows, and just at the very side of the road, a clump of aspens. "I'll show you how you tell an aspen, cookie!" Ez had excitedly said to Merry when he first moved to North Darby. "When the wind blows, the leaves quiver. They actually quiver." And suddenly momentarily embarrassed, he had shrugged, saying, "Well, it's a nervous tree. Like a kid who stutters." Which had instantly reminded them both of Jonathan, so that they had continued walking down that road saying nothing. Now, on the screen, Ez stopped in front of these aspens, not yet in full leaf, and looking genuinely troubled, said to Springer, "You know, I sometimes even think—I know it's an odd thing to say—but I really do sometimes think that there's a way in which it's even responsible for the war in Vietnam. I mean, it's our national obsession, the pursuit of happiness. And we're just so smug about it, or if you want to be charitable, so naively certain, so much in its thrall, that like the whole-hearted adherents of—of any irrationality, we've just got to go *spreading* it. And what is it really that we're spreading?" Ez looked up at the tree-sloping Berkshires. "What?"

A plane buzzed overhead, and Carl Springer faced the camera and intoned, "Ez Slavin. Author, critic, teacher, thinker, pacifist and fighter. Controversial all his life, he continues to surprise us with his contradictions, arouse us with his questions, and more often than not, provoke us with his responses. He is not an easy man to follow, yet his views are more and more sought after; he can be prickly and relentless in his impassioned grappling for the truth, yet he is much loved. He's been accused of trying to subvert the national interest by some, and of being hopelessly American by others. Certainly he's a man who's always been ahead of his time. Born and raised on New York City's Lower East Side,

Ez Slavin owes much of his feisty energy to the fierce electricity of his native city and the eager rough-and-tumble of its neighborhoods and streets. But he's been very critical of contemporary urban life, and in fact, though he's been called the 'subway Thoreau,' for some years now he's been living up here in tiny, rural North Darby, Massachusetts." Springer now gestured to the broad, solemn country vista behind him, instead of the intimate Tobacco Road shambles which was just to his side. "Here in the peaceful shadow of these calm old Yankee hills . . . Tell me, Ez," Springer said jovially, as the camera jumped to the torn screen porch where they were now both sitting. "What's an old city boy like you doing in a place like this?"

Ez smiled, but he looked wary, as if a mosquito were flying around somewhere. He said, "You know, Carl, I'm not sure it's such a good idea to mythologize *places* in the way we do—Americans do. I don't go in for that. For one thing, it's false. It sets up these—these terrible adversary stereotypes and they're very destructive. You know—the country against the city, or the—the inherent characteristic superiority of one region as opposed to the equally beloved characteristic superiority of another. The wonderful, lovable, tight-lipped, granitic New Englander against the wonderful, lovable, open-hearted, cheerful Midwesterner. It's all crap anyway, and it panders to the most terrible, blind provincialism—it's the beginning of every right-wing movement. . . . But if you're asking me in a more direct, personal sense, I don't really know that—that . . . Well, my father—my father spent his whole youth in Siberia. And every time he went to the library, I remember he used to stand there poring over the pictures in reference books, geography books. And the only thing he looked for was pictures of frozen, snowy lands. Russia, Canada, Alaska—it didn't matter to him. What he was looking for was the landscape he knew best." Ez shrugged. "I suppose that was just nostalgia for his youth. . . . Anyway, that's what my wife used to say . . ." and Ez smiled slightly, a shadow of nostalgia passing over his face too. He said, "I guess what I'm really saying, Carl, is that in my own family, mine is the first urban generation. And that that holds true for very many children of immigrants. In fact, there's even a whole body of Yiddish poetry, written in America, that is *about* this cut-off from nature. And it's all a poetry of loss. It memorializes country life, village life—you *could* say that it romanticizes it. My wife always did, she thought it was a *terrible* romanticization. It used to make her so sore." Ez smiled, his whole expression lightened at the quickening memory of old angers. "She once . . . she once dragged me to a Yiddish movie— Do you know, Carl, you're really taking me back to my salad days! This goes back—oh, God, I don't know—it goes back to somewhere in the late thirties. . . . Anyway, she once dragged me to a Yiddish movie called *Grinneh Felder,* it means 'Green Fields' and it—"

"Greenfield!" Springer burst in. "Say, isn't that the name of the big town around here?"

So abruptly snatched out of reverie, Ez stared at Springer as if he were looking at a Martian. "Yes," he said finally, and fighting back the torpor of incomprehension, he leaned forward in his chair, toward Springer, and smiled. "Well!" he said. "As I'm sure you realize, as you've gathered from the title, the movie was about this same—same nostalgic re-creation of East European village life, and it just made her so angry that after about twenty minutes, having dragged me in, she dragged me right out again. . . . But you see, Carl, talking about urban generations, she herself was from a little town, a little village in Poland. In fact"—he began to grin—"all my wives have come from little towns, hamlets, the country. All of them!"

Springer never asked personal questions on these programs; it was not his style, so that this unsolicited venture into the near sordid clearly alarmed him. "Are you saying,

then"—he sailed in instantly, smiling with nervous haste—
"do you feel, really, that you're a country boy at heart?"

"I'm sure you don't mean do I *disown* the city," Ez said
with his slightly cranky charm. "Because of course I don't.
You *know* I don't. A lot of the feeling against cities—well, it's
really just the old rural prejudices, the Know-Nothings. It's
what I was talking about before. I mean, I *value* privacy,
anonymity and—and the personal freedom which, oddly
enough, often seems to flourish best when you've got crowds
and heterogeneity. I value them *wherever* I live." Smiling
again, Ez said, with that look of innocent surprise, as if it had
just occurred to him, "Maybe what I *really* am, Carl, is an
urban provincial!"

Springer smiled too, dutifully, but he was obviously puzzled. "But you've been *very* critical of urban life . . . the
dehumanization, the impersonality, the—the—"

"The loneliness." Ez nodded. He was tracing over the rim
of his coffee cup, his long, narrow face lowered and in profile;
through the evening-like shadows from the warped screen of
the porch, he could not have looked more lonely or cut off
himself. He said, "In fact, I've just been reading *The Secret
Agent*. Some of my students were assigned it in an English
course, and they wanted to talk to me about it. And you know,
Carl, I didn't think it was a novel about politics at all—at
least, not about political *ideas*. It's about big-city loneliness. . . . Not that I think loneliness is limited to big cities.
Or that it can be avoided in life—or even that it *should* be
. . . But yes, I have been, I *am* critical of urban life. When
anonymity, impersonality, descends to brutality—the easy,
unthinking brutality of so many city encounters—that girl in
Queens who was murdered while her neighbors stood there
watching—when any sense of community, connection,
brotherliness—an old-fashioned word, brotherliness, isn't
it?—when all that is so far eroded as to seem a—a relic of a
past only old fogies like me can remember, well, then, yes, I

certainly *am* critical of city life. But not in the adversary sense of placing country life above it. Because let me tell you something, Carl." Ez leaned over to Springer and grasped his elbow. "When Karl Marx talked about the 'idiocy of rural life,' believe me, he wasn't just whistling the *Internationale!*"

This time Springer laughed, genuinely laughed. The tension fell away from the wide white clouds of his face, and he said, "You know, when I first heard about that phrase, I was a high school kid in Elkader, Iowa. And while I guess it wasn't rural exactly, it sure was a real small town. And I was just so relieved, so happy that there was someone—and someone *famous*—who had thought that before me and *said* it! It sort of buoyed me up. Because I was just itching to get out of there, so many of us were. We felt that town was so confining for us. And boring too."

"It's a funny thing, Carl, isn't it? Because the myth . . . the *myth* about country life is that because you are so far removed from all the frenzied external stimulation of the city—the inauthenticity, really—you're freed to develop *internal* resources, a deeper and more varied internal life. But it doesn't often seem to work out that way, does it? I mean, maybe it *is* true for farmers, although even there, technology has encroached so far—and I'm not just talking about the farm kids who race their motorcycles to drive-in movies and—and McDonald's. But there you are." Ez suddenly smiled. "I guess *that's* what happened to Old McDonald and his chick-chicks!"

Carl Springer was drinking coffee, and he almost choked on it in surprised, overeager laughter. In the country distance, a dog barked harshly, and Springer said, "Where I come from there really aren't even any more small, family farms. Or hardly any. It's all become corporate farms, sort of farming conglomerates."

"Do you know what amazed me most about the farms around here?" Ez said with that look of Rip Van Winkle excitement he always got when he came upon something new. "They have these—I don't know—mechanical, automatic hay balers! There's no such thing as a haystack anymore! It's all just neat, mechanical, rectangular bales of hay. Uniform, uniform . . . And apparently—I'm sure you know this— there were once even regional differences in the way hay was baled, but no more . . . no more . . . Still, it's not at all fair for me to talk about farm life. It's something I genuinely know nothing about."

"But you've written, very recently, about what you called 'the new myth of the land,' and you certainly stirred up an awful lot of people. What was that all about?"

Laughing, Ez said, "Well, that takes us back to the 'idiocy of rural life,' and I'm afraid a lot of people felt I was saying that some of my best friends—or their children—are idiots. Have *become* idiots. And it's true, you know. I *was* saying that, I was! But in the original Greek sense—that an idiot is someone whose devotion to private life, to the trivia of blind private concern, is total. And anything, *everything* public—political life, social life—well, an idiot just doesn't have to bother! By definition he's not supposed to. All he has to do is grow his own vegetables and—and bake his own bread. And what I see around here so often now—people who've moved to the country, come to the land in search of a simpler, more honest life—well, that's the myth. Because the reality, which swallows them up very fast—just like the black hole of bourgeois success from which they are presumably fleeing—the reality turns into the boredom of property and property-owning. Repairs, additions, bills, plumbing problems, wiring problems, and where should we plant the zucchini, my God! For one thing, it's boring and puerile in itself, and when you hear them talking about it, what you hear in their voices is that very dubious quality—the smugness, the pride of ownership—I don't know. . . . If they heard suburban people talking this way, they'd be the first ones to disparage it.

247

And they'd be right, too! Because how could it be any more noble or admirable in one place than in another? You know, I'll tell you something, Carl. Every time I hear that—that *tone*, I'm always reminded of what Jefferson *originally* wrote: that what every man was entitled to was 'life, liberty, and property.' All right, he later emended it, but that was what he first wrote. And I sometimes really wonder . . . Maybe Americans are a hell of a lot closer to the Jeffersonian spirit than they realize."

"But he *did* emend it, of course," Springer said. "He emended it to 'the pursuit of happiness.' And you've been critical of that too. Why?"

"Yeah! Right on! I wanna hear *this* one!" Ffrenchy suddenly assailed the screen. "I mean, how could he—why does he just want everyone to be *down?* Like that is just *so* fucking freaky!"

Ez sighed. "I know what it must sound like, Carl. That at the . . . the perpetual Christmas feast of American life, I'm the sour old geezer who stands there muttering, 'Bah! Humbug!' But somehow, you know, I really—"

"Oh, *no*, Ez!" Springer broke in in alarm. "That isn't what I meant at all! Perhaps I should—let me rephrase the question. . . ."

"You don't have to, Carl. You don't have to. You want to know why I'm against the pursuit of happiness, I'll tell you." Absently, considering his answer, Ez began stroking a kitten which had just come padding into the room.

"Far out!" Ffrenchy said. "I didn't know he was into cats!"

"I think it's probably Jeannie's," Merry said, inhaling, as she sat on her own new sofa, the stench of old cat food and cat urine which so overwhelmed the small damp house in North Darby. Exactly like Ez's own mother, all Jeannie's housekeeping ways bore the sad, lingering smells of lifelong poverty and absolutely no expectations.

On the screen, the kitten bounded up into Ez's lap, and

248

looking at it in mock hauteur, he said, "Ah! *Buenos días, Señor Gato.*" Which was a line from a children's story, *Perez and Martina:* probably he'd been reading it to Sammy. "You know, Carl, I've sometimes thought we'd all be a lot better off if Jefferson *hadn't* emended it. If he'd left it at 'property.' Because that's so empty, you can't idealize it. But 'the pursuit of happiness'—because you *can* idealize it, because we *have*—well, it seems to me that as a vision, as a goal, it's just been very damaging. And the damage is everywhere. Wherever you look. Public policy, private life, everywhere!"

"But don't you think there's a bright side to pursuit? Even if we, as a nation, have lost touch with it?"

"Oh, yes!" Ez said enthusiastically. "If you were to say the pursuit of possibility, the pursuit of what might be, I'd go along with that one hundred percent! Absolutely! But when you say the pursuit of happiness . . ." He shook his head. "You see, for *me* that implies the end of pursuit. And as far as I'm concerned, that's the whole aim of life. That's *it!*"

"Ez Slavin, you *are* a utopian!" Springer declared ringingly, and glowed with relief.

"Sounds good." Ez raised his eyebrows. "But why is that a better thing to be? Mostly—anyway, as far as I can see— mostly, that just gets us right back to the wrong end of pursuit again! No, I'll tell you where I see the—the bright side of pursuit in American life. I've been rereading Theodore Parker, an old enthusiasm of my youth." He grinned. "You might say I've been returning to the scene of the crime. . . . And Parker said—this was somewhere in the eighteen forties—Parker said, 'We have this characteristic of genius: we are dissatisfied with all that we have done.' And as long as that remains true—well, true in a good sense—then that's the *spirit* of pursuit that I'm happy to be for."

"True in a good sense," Springer repeated, smiling. "Do I hear a nagging doubt?"

"Well, of course!" Ez practically snapped, impatience

curdling his whole expression. "You can see how double-edged that is! I mean, dissatisfaction with all that we've done can very easily turn into let's make bigger and better bombs. Or—or let's put absolutely everything about absolutely everyone into the biggest and best Goddamn computer of them all. It's the old American mousetrap syndrome, except graduated—*graduated* from the triviality of gadgets!"

"Oh, God, Cookie!" Ffrenchy yawned loudly and began stretching. "This is just *so-o* bor—I mean, heavy. Heavy. It is *definitely* heavy shit. I'm gonna see where I put my grass." And rummaging around in her giant striped wicker tote bag—she hurled out of it stacks of Pampers, opened cigarette packs, two pairs of sunglasses and a container of baby powder—with all her commotion, Ffrenchy almost drowned out Carl Springer's next question.

"You don't see yourself ever making a separate peace with technology, do you, Ez?" Springer said, looking at Ez with exactly that air of refined, eager reverence which Ez had complained of.

"Hey, far out!" Ffrenchy called out happily. "I still have these really dynamite pistachio nuts, Cookie! Look! Want some?"

Ez laughed. "Well, you know, Carl, even if I ever wanted to, I'm afraid I just really couldn't. It's—it's a kind of inborn allergy, I think. I'm a kind of natural, unconscious Luddite. I mean, I don't actually have to *smash* a machine. All I have to do is go near one. Phonograph knobs come off in my hand, light switches stick when I touch them. . . . In fact, my daughter told me only recently that she was buying something in an appetizing store. And just as the man was about to staple the price tag onto the bag, the staple gun flew out of his hands. And my daughter—well, *being* my daughter, she instantly jumped back, away from the counter, so that the man looked up at her and said, 'What are you jumping for? What are you afraid of? It's only a machine.' " Shaking his head, Ez repeated, "*Only* a machine!" and as Springer now beamed at him in the ease of shared understanding, Ez said, "So you see what I mean, Carl. It's a characteristic I've even passed on. It's—what can I call it? I guess it's my unfortunate legacy."

"That's *you*, Cookie, the daughter part, isn't it?" Ffrenchy said bitterly. "Oh, shit! He even tells about you on television."

"But it happened in Zabar's, Ffrenchy," Merry said quickly, "and that's something he *won't* tell on television!"

"Why not? Did *you* ever have their Russian coffee cake? God, like that is just *total* bliss-out! And these *pistachios* are from Zabar's, and they are truly—" Ffrenchy suddenly stopped, because on the screen now, Carl Springer, standing alone on the road, his back to the Berkshires, was saying, "If Ez Slavin is worried about the unfortunate legacy he's passed on to the young, his students don't seem to share his apprehension."

"Students!" Ffrenchy burst out. "What are all those *girls* doing there? I thought where he taught was a *boys'* school! And—and how come they're all in his *house?*"

As if answering her directly, Springer continued, "Even within the ordered confines of a lecture hall, the lively enthusiasm and stubbornly questioning spirit of both teacher and students are apparent. But it's here, in the informality of his own living room, that the passionate give-and-take which Ez Slavin has always believed in can really have free rein."

In the informality of Ez's own living room, students with soda cans and paper coffee cups sat sprawled out on worn strips of carpet on the floor or else they lounged back on various pieces of cast-off furniture: the two torn, faded wing chairs and a crumbling club chair, some beach chairs that looked as if they'd been left outside during a particularly severe hurricane, and worst of all, that ugly brown, flowered sofa whose springs and upholstery buttons popped out from

251

under as soon as you sat down on it. The window with the torn shade and no curtain still had the same torn shade, but now a piece of curtain material, unsewn and utterly different from the other curtains in the room, fell drooping from a rod at what was meant to be midpoint. On the floor below it was a plastic laundry basket half filled with sheets, towels and clothespins—Merry could smell the mildew as the camera lit on it—and layered above the linens, a toy telephone, some blocks, and other bits and pieces of Sammy's toys. The students, surrounded by their notebooks and bags of potato chips, looked perfectly happy; but Merry, staring at this room of her father's on television, and as if seeing it newly, felt a rage that rose up and lodged in her mouth with the taste of a bloody toothache. Ez didn't care how he lived, he didn't care how he looked, he didn't care what he ate: all those old childhood privations were so natural to him that he lived with them still, carrying them aloft as if it were a matter of principle. But it was not a matter of principle; he really just didn't care, and in his not caring, any small pleasure or sweet comfort that could be wrested from life was made to vanish. He has taught me nothing but austerity, Merry thought bitterly, and with the blood taste still in her mouth, she said, "He can't *drive*, Ffrenchy. That's why they all come to *his* house. It's just easier for him that way."

"Well, someone could come and pick him up. *We* did. At Carob."

On the screen now, a boy sitting on the sofa was eagerly leaning forward and saying, "But, Ez, I don't see why we should pay *attention* to De Tocqueville! I can't even get into why you think we should *read* him! I mean, *De Tocqueville!* Like he—"

"You're *not* going to say irrelevant, Brian." Ez smiled. "Not to *me*. That's Committee of Public Safety talk—and you *know* what I think about that!"

Everyone laughed, and Brian, not the least bit put off—he

was laughing too—said, "No, I wasn't, Ez. But it's—it's like *very* relevant that you said Committee of Public Safety. Because—because—well, I mean, De Tocqueville was an *aristocrat!* And like you *know* he was really into that whole trip. No matter *what* he said! Because he was an official of the French prison system! Like that's even why he came here! I mean, talk about power elite! *He* came to America to check out the jails!"

Ez said, "Well, first of all, I think you're being very unfair to De Tocqueville, both in misinterpreting his position and his purpose in coming here. But even if you weren't—and as you all know, I certainly have my own misgivings about what De Tocqueville had to say—but even if you weren't, Brian, even if you weren't, don't you find it possible that someone whose attitudes and background are totally different from yours could still have something valuable—or interesting—to say?"

A tall, curly-haired girl, carefully rethreading one of her earrings, said, "Well, I think he *did* say some true things, I really do! Because I found this thing he said about how like when Americans meet each other in a foreign country? That even if they didn't know each other or anything, they still get very friendly right away just *because* they're Americans? And I mean, like I *know* it's true. Because when I was in Greece last summer and I was on this sort of ferry—and I mean, I was really in *super*-bad shape. Because I'd just been through this like really *horrendous* scene with my boyfriend, and then I got so sick on the ferry I thought I would die! And these *people* on the boat—I even remember their name, the Glattsteins—they just came right over to me, and like they were *so* nice. They really kind of took care of me and everything, and they didn't *know* me at all. I mean, they said stuff like I reminded them of one of their nieces and like that, but *I* think that was probably just their way of, well, acknowledging that we were, you know, American. And in a way, the *really* funny part—which sort of backs up De Tocqueville—is that if I met them *here*, I know I'd think they were really gross! Like they were from Great Neck or something!" she finished, laughing.

The rest of the class laughed too, and a blondish girl in granny glasses said, "Robin! You went to *Greece?* How *could* you?"

"Well, that's when I was with Tim," she half whispered. "And he was into this whole archaeology num—"

"What a stupid story!" Ffrenchy immediately said. "Just because she puked on a boat! I hope Ez gives her an F!"

On the screen, Ez was nodding pleasantly at the girl. He said, "I don't mean to dismiss your experience, Robin, and in fact I share your agreement with De Tocqueville on that point, although"—he suddenly broke into an inward, mischievous grin—"although I think your story may be an illustration of—of—well, I do think there's something else involved. But don't let me get sidetracked, *please*. Because what I'd really like us to get back to is the question I asked Brian before. And I guess, really, it's not unrelated to what Robin just said about her—her shipmates from Great Neck. If you knew that someone came from a background which you disapproved of or held certain views with which you disagreed, would you consider it impossible, I mean would you dismiss out of hand the chance that somehow, somewhere, a person like that might still have said something valuable? Something you might, in any case, want to think about?"

There was a sudden dive for the potato chips and the cookies, and students rustled papers or shifted around in their chairs. One boy said hesitantly, "Well, my grandfather . . . I mean, like he's practically Genghis Khan! You should hear these raps he gets into! That America's the greatest country in the world, that he had nothing when he first came here, that . . . that he would go out to vote even if he was like really sick . . . So, I mean, I really don't agree with him about

254

*anything*, but he really is this sweet old guy. He's definitely a whole lot mellower than my father."

Ez said, "I'm sorry if I misled you, Jason, but I wasn't talking about personal relations. That's different—or, if you're lucky, it *can* be. I was talking about ideas."

The uneasy rustling and shifting resumed. Ez leaned forward and said, "Well, look, I'll give you an example. There is a quotation that I keep hanging over my desk." He looked away, so that his face was nearly hidden, and in a faraway voice that trembled with private revelation, he declaimed, " 'Most of the time we were solitary adventurers in a great land as fresh and new as a spring morning, and we were free and full of the zest of darers.' "

This time the silence was absolute. Finally, one of the boys sitting on the floor said shyly, "That's really heavy, Ez. I mean it's . . . you know . . . Like it's beautiful."

"It *is* beautiful," Ez said slowly, almost sadly. "I've never failed to find it beautiful; that's why I keep it hanging up there. . . ." He stared off for a few seconds, and then he said, "But it was written by a man named Charles Goodnight, and by the end of his life he was a very rich man, a cattle baron. And I can't imagine that he and I would have had very much in common. Or that we would have thought alike about the issues of his day or mine. But when he was a young man, a kid really, he was a cowboy in Texas. And he blazed trails for the cows all the way from Texas to Cheyenne, Wyoming."

"Oh, *that's* not the one I like," curly-haired Robin said. "I like the *other* quote you have hanging up in your study. *You* know—the Chinese one! About authority!"

Ffrenchy said, "Shit, Cookie! How does *she* know what he has in his study?"

Because the camera was now focused on the semicircle of students, you could not see Ez's face. He said, " 'Love labor, hate lordship, and seek no intimacy with those in authority.' "

"Right on!" The granny-glasses girl raised her fist, and near her, someone called out, "*Very* Buddhist. That is definitely a true Buddhist head!"

Ez smiled. "I can see why you say that, Douglas. But actually it's from *Ethics of the Fathers,* a collection of rabbinic observations from the first century. And I don't suppose you'd agree with everything *they* had to say. Or for that matter, that I would either!"

As the class laughed—and it was a relaxed, comfortable kind of laughter—on the screen, once again, Ez and Carl Springer were walking along a hilly country road. Springer was saying, "So all those words with which we seem to have boxed ourselves in, words like 'generation gap,' 'dropout,' 'irrelevant'—would you say, Ez, that they don't, in fact, describe anything real?"

"Well, they just don't describe anything *new.* I mean, Tolstoy—yes, Leo *War and Peace* himself—actually dropped out of Moscow U., because . . ." Ez started laughing. "I guess he was a history major. Because what he said was: 'History is like a deaf old man who keeps answering questions that were never asked.' Well, it's *funny,*" Ez said, still laughing. "It *is* funny, you know, but it's not true. . . . And I'll tell you something, Carl—these days I sometimes feel as if I'm the deaf old man he had in mind. Because every time it's brought home to me how profoundly cut off so many kids are from the *sense,* the *feel* of anything that came before them— well, my God, that is disturbing, *deeply* disturbing. First of all, it's dangerous. But aside from that, can you imagine—*can you imagine,* Carl, how *boring* that must be!"

Springer smiled uncertainly. "Does that relate to your frozen-orange-juice theory? Can you explain for us your— your 'three generations of the orange'?"

"Ah *hah!* I see what you're after, Springer! Ez Slavin, the cranky old man of the Berkshires! Well, I'm not going to deny that I said it." He smiled. "One day . . . I guess, really, I was just feeling blue. . . . Anyway, I told my students that they were the frozen-orange-juice generation. And what I meant was that in *my* parents' generation, in Europe, an orange was so rare, such a luxury, that it would be bought only if someone—a child, say—was very, very sick. Then, by the time I was growing up in America, oranges were quite common; they were neither special nor expensive, but you ate the *whole* orange, you didn't just wring it out for its juice. Later on, of course, in the thirties, those glass juicers came around, and people did make orange juice, but they made it *from, with* the actual orange. But in my students' generation, orange juice was always something you just popped out of a can in the freezer."

Springer frowned. "Do you mean, then, that a society that's only shown its children instant food, instant consumption, instant obsolescence—well, that these same kids would *have* to grow up wanting instant change, instant revolution, instant gratification?"

"Oh, no!" Ez said. "That's not what *I* meant at all! I was talking about how much kids miss when they have no sense of the past—when it can't, doesn't *naturally* stand peering over the shoulders of the present for them. But what *you're* talking about is impatience. And *that*—well, that's a *characteristic* of the young." He smiled. "It's my *favorite* characteristic of the young, Carl. And I wish they could keep it. Hang on to it. *Always*. Because sometimes . . . sometimes when I talk to my students, or other kids, I begin to think that my worst fear for them is the same as their own: that they'll turn out to be not very different from their parents. A slightly different set of conventions, of orthodoxies, if you like, but not very different in the end." And looking down from the ridge, Ez, his face lengthened and in shadow, seemed to be staring out at trees and hills that held no more promise than people.

"I know you've often said that this is a particularly difficult time to be young and American. And I wonder whether—"

"No question about it. *Very* difficult." Ez nodded. "But you know, Carl, once you accept that, once you *really* understand that that's so, well, then there's something very exhilarating about it! Because it *does* connect you to what's come before. Especially *here*, so near Springfield, right in the shadow of Shays' Rebellion. It's a perfect reminder of how *American* it is to struggle against your country's wrongs!"

"Shit, *Springfield!*" Ffrenchy called out, laughing. "Like that place is so *hideous!* Did *you* ever see their—well, what *they* think is downtown?"

Carl Springer sat down on a ledge, and looking up at Ez with the slow sobriety of hard-won thought, said, "I wonder if it's just that special double sense you have, of both the difficulty *and* the exhilaration, that's allowed you, almost more than anyone I can think of, to keep the lines open with—with so many angry young people. . . ."

" 'Guru to the disaffected young'?" Ez said, raising his eyebrows.

"Well"—Springer smiled—"so many kids have *come* to you, *turned* to you at a time when there's just been—"

"Oh, Carl, what good is it if another generation grows up wanting gurus?" Ez cried out bitterly. "How would that be different from their parents? Does it matter if they chose Freud or Marx or Norman Vincent Peale? If what you want in this world is a guru, how the hell will you ever be able to go against the grain?" And *click-click* went the sound-track camera. It was the last impression for *First Impressions:* Ez, his shoulders hunched against the wind or betrayal, standing by himself on a Berkshire ridge.

# 13

MEMORIAL SERVICES
Slavin—Ezra B. A memorial tribute will be held in the
auditorium of the Donnell Library Center at 20 W.
53 Street in New York City on Monday, March 20, at
11 A.M.

Hopping on and off the sidewalk in front of the Donnell
Library on Monday morning, Sybil Roizman had a divided,
eager look. She rushed over to the taxi which Merry was
getting out of with Isobel and Charlotte Barro, and briefly
embracing her with the gravity of bereavement, Sybil immediately said, "Merry, darling! What in God's name is the
*matter* with you? Don't you realize that practically *everyone*
else is here already? Of *course* I understand how disorienting
it is, mourning and grieving, and you can't work it out
overnight, but *this!* Really, darling, you're just so late!"

259

"I know. I'm sorry, Sybil," Merry said.

"Oh, no! Oh, no!" Charlotte, stumbling on the curb, clapped her hand to her breast. "It's *my* fault, all *my* fault."

And it was, too. Because early that morning Charlotte had called up—in fact, woken up both Merry and Isobel, saying, "*Don't* worry, I have it figured out perfectly! This is how we'll do it—I'll pick you up in a cab."

"Charlotte," Merry had said groggily. "You're coming from SoHo, we're coming from the Upper West Side. What *sense* does that make?"

"Oh, *no*, dear! My teeth! I have to be on Ninety-sixth Street! Would *I* ever leave my brilliant, wonderful Sol? The best dentist in the whole city?" She paused and said, "Well, of course, *really* he's a painter, but the Depression forced some people to make terrible choices."

But as it turned out, one of brilliant Sol's painterly virtues was that though he did *make* appointments, he could not feel bound by them, so that Merry and Isobel stood downstairs waiting and waiting for Charlotte's taxi, and when it finally arrived, there was Charlotte, with the left side of her face swollen, and her heavy black eye makeup so smudged that she looked as if she'd been in a fight. "What am I going to *do*?" she moaned, opening the door. "Sol couldn't get it. After all that pain and agony, he *still* couldn't get the roots in the last canal! He gave me Percodan, but he says I'll have to go to an *endodontist*! Ohh, ohh," she called out pathetically. "What am I going to *do*?" And clutching at Isobel's hand, she suddenly cried out, "Oh, *Isobel*! Your *hands* are so cold! Poor Isobel . . . How can I—how *can* I burden you at a time like this?"

Isobel was giving the eulogy; she was almost rigid from anxiety and fatigue, having spent the night before pacing back and forth between her scribbled Alitalia notes and Merry's typewriter. Isobel's pacing and all her nighttime activity reminded Merry of those times, so many years ago, when Isobel had spent nervous, sleepless nights; and this childhood memory gave Merry such a sense of comfort that each time she was half awakened by the sounds of Isobel's typewriter, she felt a dream-like, unseemly happiness and forgot that Ez was dead. But Isobel did not forget for a second and it showed in her face: after so many years of being divorced from Ez, years during which she had seen him maybe twice, she now stood outside the Donnell Library with a look of such tense, pale, translucent-skinned vulnerability that even Sybil Roizman noticed.

"Isobel, darling," Sybil said, and leaning forward to embrace her, in the end had to settle for only grasping her hand. "I can't tell you how *grateful* we all are to you for coming so far. And for making—for *volunteering* such a wonderful, generous contribution. I just *know* how enriched we'll all feel."

Isobel took a step backward, and though her face said: You have just made it sound as if I were buying Girl Scout cookies, she simply smiled and nodded politely.

Anxiously, Sybil said, "You know about not going first? Dave explained it to you? I mean, of course, if we were being strictly formal, you *would*, but since when have *any* of us ever been concerned with empty—*Isobel?*" But Isobel had already begun walking into the building, so Sybil turned back to Merry, darkly saying, "Oh, darling, the *tricks* the unconscious plays on you at times of stress! *All* the old insecurities! Of course, I know it's ridiculous, but I just can't get over the feeling that that woman doesn't like me. I *know* it's ridiculous. . . . Well, of course, I could never warm up to *her*. And I never understood what *Ez* saw in her. Or how he could have been married to her for all those— Oh, my God, Merry!" Sybil suddenly cried out in alarm. "Paula Meisel is here! Wasn't she the one—I mean, didn't Ez—wasn't it Isobel who he was married to when—"

Merry said, "Naturally Paula's here, Sybil. Why shouldn't she be? I'm sure Isobel wouldn't in the least—"

"Merry, darling! For a very intelligent young woman, you

are being extremely obtuse! There are two conflicting sets of feelings here! *Conflicting!* And to compound the problem, Paula brought her daughter! And *that's* the daughter that she had with Ez, isn't it? *Wait* a minute, Merry—didn't she have *two* daughters with Ez? I always thought there were two of them."

"It's probably the older one who's here," Merry said. "Ffrenchy." Because only two days before, Ffrenchy had called up, saying, "Cookie? I have this—this like *dilemma*. Oh, God!" She suddenly giggled. "That's such a total, you know, like College Boards *vocabulary* word. And I think I got around three hundred. . . . Anyway, I don't know if I should go to the—you know—if I should do that whole memorial meeting number."

"I can't tell you what to do about that, Ffrenchy," Merry said irritably. "Nobody can."

"Yeah, but see, my mother keeps saying that I *should*. Which like probably means I really *shouldn't*. I mean, you should *see* her! Like she's just crying all the time and everything. And saying how bad she feels for *you*. 'Cause now you're like this total orphan. And I mean—" Ffrenchy stopped suddenly, and then she said, "Cookie? If you—if you're a *total* orphan, does that sort of mean—I mean, could you sort of say that I'm this—this like *half* orphan? *Could* you?" But because Merry didn't answer, nearly mesmerized by this ability of Ffrenchy's for stumbling, happy discovery even in the face of death, Ffrenchy said, "Oh, wow, Cookie, I didn't mean to hit you with such heavy shit, I really didn't! I just—well, see, my mother said that at the memorial thing—well, she said that what they *are* is that everyone gets up and says how great the person was. You know—like for *them*. And I mean, everyone *knows* that Ez was great and everything, like he was even famous! But you know, like he wasn't always that great to *me*. Well, he was *sometimes*. But you know, *I* couldn't—like how could I—I mean, I really

think it just totally *sucks* when you can't be upfront! And like I
don't see how I can—what I could— *Cookie?* What are *you*
gonna say at the thing?"

"I'm not saying anything, Ffrenchy. You don't *have* to. It's
for people who feel they—"

"You're *not?* Really? You swear it, Cookie? Far out! You
know what my mother said? This weird thing? That the reason
Ez like loved you best was that he had this—this whole *guilt*
thing about your mother. You know, like because she *died?*"
And the amazement in Ffrenchy's voice seemed to measure
exactly the distance she felt from such an unlikely emotion.
"Well, I guess I'll see you Monday," she said. "I mean, I *will*
see you Monday, and like maybe I'll bring Spring. I mean, I
*would.* Except my mother would probably have this total
heart attack— Ooh, shit! I'm sorry, Cookie. Like Ez really *did*
have one— Oh, shit!"

To Sybil Roizman, Merry now said, "Did Ffrenchy bring
her baby?"

"*Baby?* What *baby?* Merry, darling, we have no time for
this! Not *now!* Why do you think I'm so distressed that you
got here so late? We have *things* to talk about! *Important*
things!" And briefly turning around, Sybil caught a glimpse of
Charlotte, who was covering her face with her hands and
leaning against a car in a near-swoon. "What the hell is the
matter with *her?*"

"She's got some big root canal problem," Merry said. "The
dentist just gave her a painkiller."

"Painkiller! *That's* what I want to talk to you about. Really
*Dave* wanted to talk to you about it, but you got here *so* late
that he had to go inside and at least get things—well, all
right. . . . *Look*, darling." Sybil put her arm around Merry,
and peering at her, her face furrowing in concern, she said,
"Merry, dear, you *cannot* kill your pain. You cannot bury
your grief. And if you try, if that's how you attempt to master
it, all you do is make terrible trouble for yourself later on.

*Believe* me! Believe *Dave*—it's his *business!* That's why he feels so strongly, Merry, that it's *necessary* for you— imperative, darling, *imperative*—to just get up and say *something!* Two sentences, four sentences, you don't have to make a speech. Just—just verbalize whatever you *feel.* Because otherwise, what are you *doing* with the feelings? You're allowing yourself to lose touch!" Sybil shook her head. "Don't think I don't understand the temptation. You want to ward off the pain. Of course. But it just doesn't *work* that way, darling. The unconscious is much too clever to— Oh, my God!" Sybil suddenly called out. "Is that woman actually *fainting?* From a *toothache?* When the rest of us are genuinely *grieving?*"

"Look, Sybil," Merry said. "What I feel now is not something I want to get up and talk about publicly."

"*Publicly!* Merry, what are you *talking* about? *Darling!* If we didn't all love Ez, would we *be* here? Just look at all the people who've come! I only hope there'll be enough room for them all now! This is a very *intime* setting, that's why Dave chose it. Shestak kept pushing for the auditorium at Hunter—of course, he *teaches* there. But it's enormous, so Dave said inappropriate, absolutely not, and he wouldn't even— My God, Merry! Look! There's Stewart Saunders! I just hope there won't be any trouble."

"Why should there be any trouble? Isobel told me he had particularly asked to come and speak."

"*Really,* dear! Do you think *anyone* here has forgotten that he worked in the Johnson administration? Of course, we all know he had *nothing* to do with Vietnam, *nothing* to do with foreign policy, he was only concerned with domestic issues—*and* he didn't last very long. But still! To be so close to the source of destruction! . . . Merry?" Sybil cocked her head to one side. "Do you think it's *true* that he was . . . involved with Jacqueline Kennedy?"

Merry shrugged. "All I know about Stewart Saunders is that years ago, before he was such a big shot, he was once Ez's editor."

"You see what I mean, darling? He *loved* your father! *Everyone* here loved your father. That's the purpose of our coming together here—so we can all feel less *isolated* in our grief. And that's why it's *so* unfortunate that Ginny isn't here. Although I suppose it makes things an awful lot easier for Isobel!"

"Ginny?" Merry said. "Who's Ginny?"

Sybil was staring at Merry as if all those unverbalized feelings had already begun to exact their predictable, hideous due. "*Virginia*, darling! In Massachusetts! Your father's *wife*."

"Oh, *Jeannie*," Merry said. "Jeannie really didn't *want* to come, Sybil. She was never a part of Ez's New York life, and she knew it. I think she felt that if she *did* come, she would just be uncomfortable."

"But, darling! What a *mistake* that is! What a *terrible* misperception! How could she *possibly* feel uncomfortable among people who all loved Ez? What we all *need* now is this—this ritual of remembering." Shaking her head, Sybil said, "I just hope she isn't *denying* her need. Because of course she has it too."

But Jeannie was not denying her need. "He just went into the ground so cold," she said in her sad, thin voice of Ez's prayerless burial, and hardly daring to look at Merry, explained that she was taking Sammy with her to a prayer meeting: she had just joined an evangelical church on the outskirts of a nearby town. This church was real old and real small, she said, and made her think back to the churches of her childhood.

Sybil said, "Look, darling, I don't want to *push* you. I *know* that you're stubborn. Your father was too, and I *honor* it. But just promise me—*promise* me, Merry, that you'll keep your mind open and if you decide you *do* want to share your feelings, just get up and say whatever you want. Of course, Dave's been passing around a sheet for people who want to say something, but *you* don't— Oh, Merry! I almost forgot to ask you. Did Dave speak to you about the music? 'Fanfare for the Common Man'? You don't have any objection, do you? After all, darling, we would *never* want you to feel that just because Dave and I organized this, you don't have a very prominent voice in it! That would be the *worst* thing that could— *Darling?* I just thought of it! Where's Isobel's son? Why isn't *he* here?"

"Nicky's in India," Merry said, and saw no point in explaining anything further.

"Oh, that's *wonderful!*" Sybil beamed. "Nina's in India too! Dave isn't so happy about it, really, but she's become absolutely *fascinated* with— Oh, *hello,* Reva, darling." Sybil embraced a round, gray-haired woman, swathed in a purple shawl. "I'm *so* glad you could come. Carolyn said she'd be here too, but with Art's schedule, it's so difficult for them to—"

"Excuse me, Sybil," Merry said, having caught a glimpse of Abby Gerson sheltering in the library doorway. "I think I see a friend of mine."

"God, Merry, it's just so weird to be standing here like this," Abby said diffidently. "The last time I hung around the Donnell Library was cutting classes in high school!"

They both laughed, and Merry said, "I thought your big cutting hangout was the Cloisters."

"That was only on Tuesdays, when they had the concerts. All those Gregorian chants . . ." Abby shook her head. "Shit, it makes me feel so old! I mean, then I was this . . . little avant-garde high school girl, and now I'm a grown-up social worker? Oh, Merry? You know who's here? Who I just saw before? My supervisor! The world's biggest bitch, Laura Spivak."

"*Laura Spivak* is here?"

"You *know* her, Merry? How do *you*—"

"Come, children!" Sybil called out, dragging in her wake the shawl-clad Reva. "We can't put it off anymore, and really, in the service of health and life, we shouldn't even want to."

Downstairs, in the dim auditorium, only Ffrenchy was

standing up. "Hi, Cookie!" she called out happily in a stage whisper, and waving and gesturing frantically, mouthed, "Look! I saved you a seat!"

The timpani and triumphant clear brass intervals of "Fanfare for the Common Man" sounded through the auditorium, and Dave Roizman, not solemn, but a bit uneasy, moved to the center of the stage. Smiling, he said, "Once again, Ez, you've brought us all together, as you had the joyful gift of doing so many times in the past. And for you, for you above all, we play 'Fanfare for the Common Man.' Because as Walt Whitman wrote, and you yourself illumined for us: 'Ever the most *precious* in the common.' "

"*How* can he call Ez common?" Charlotte grasped Merry's hand, infuriated. "That's why psychoanalysts are so bad for creative people—they just have *no* appreciation of any of the—"

"Cookie, is he a *shrink?*" Ffrenchy turned around, whispering. "Because I think Darcy's sister was going to him, and *she* said that he was like totally—"

"Shh!" Paula, sitting beside her daughter, nearly wrenched Ffrenchy's shoulder, and in her half turn, fixed Merry with a heavy, mournful, crumpled smile.

"My God, how *sad!*" Charlotte clutched her swollen cheek, whispering. "Isn't that Paula Meisel? *Look* at her, Isobel! Doesn't she look absolutely *awful?*"

On the stage, Dave said, "I know, I'm aware that I've been saying 'you.' As if Ez were really here with us right now. And of course we all know, we all understand that that's a common defense against loss. But I think I'll always feel that Ez is with us at times when we need him. Perhaps for each of us the moment, the occasion will be different. But those of us fortunate enough to have known him will find, in the months and years ahead, that we've incorporated some part of Ez's extraordinary spirit. And that incorporation is as valid and authentic as any other aspect of our personalities, and for many of us"—Dave now peered into the audience with his

267

professional smile of empathic seduction—"for many of us, perhaps the only aspect to arise from an influence so wholly constructive."

There was a slight stirring in the audience. Charlotte took Merry's hand, and sighing deeply, nodded up at the stage. "Oh, he's right, dear," she whispered in a half moan, her enormous kohl-rimmed eyes rolling. "He is *so* right. . . . Even after all these years, I still feel my husband's presence at the oddest times!"

Every time you take out your checkbook, Merry thought—Charlotte's husband the real estate magnate—and almost giggling, realized that here was an aspect of Ez's wholly constructive personality that she had incorporated so long ago.

Dave, on the stage, seemed more relaxed now. He said, "Because we'll each cherish memories of Ez that are different, specific to our individual needs, perhaps the encounter or interaction that was most meaningful to us, I'd like to share with you now a memory of mine—the first time I met Ez. And it's particularly appropriate to this setting. Because the first time I met Ez it was in a public library. Not *this* one"—Dave smiled—"but the Seward Park branch on the Lower East Side. *I* don't know if it's still there, but if Ez were here, *he* would." Oh, Rip Van Winkle! Merry thought: he would *assume* the library was still there, and could easily have found himself returning a book to what had years ago become a Cuban-Chinese restaurant. Smiling still, Dave said, "I was fifteen years old, and Ez was probably . . . oh, seventeen or so. And in the way of those old extended-family neighborhoods, we each knew who the other was, even though we'd never actually spoken."

"Oh, I don't believe *that*, do you, dear?" Charlotte whispered. "Ez was so gregarious, he always talked to people when he *didn't* know who they were. That's how he and *Isobel* first—"

"I remember that day," Dave continued, "because it was Yom Kippur, and what I have to reveal to you about myself is that my family was very Orthodox. My father, particularly, was such a rigid, inaccessible, authoritarian man that even though I was, of course, no longer caught up in his compartmentalized system of beliefs, I didn't dare *not* fast or *not* go to synagogue with him. So there I was in the synagogue, in the middle of all that endless droning, wearing my bedroom slippers—as some of you may know, that's the ritual footwear for Yom Kippur—and suddenly, my instinctive healthy aggression just asserted itself. Because I ran out. But still, *still*, I was so overwhelmed with all the guilt and anxiety which had been instilled in me that I felt I had to hide. As if I were a criminal."

In the audience, people laughed sympathetically. "And exactly as if I really *were* a criminal, I went sneaking into the library. I hardly even dared look around," Dave said, beaming in removed, nostalgic appreciation at this one-time folly so cleanly excised. "But then, just as I was about to sit down at a back table and hide my face with a book, I saw that there, right opposite me, was someone who might know me. Well, I'm not proud of it"—Dave shook his head—"but I did actually jump—in alarm and amazement. I said, 'Ezra Slavin! What are you doing in *here?*' He just sat back, and looked at me, and then he pointed to my bedroom slippers, and said, 'David Roizman! What were you doing out *there?*' And when I looked blank and tried to stammer out some answer, Ez said, 'Don't you know that famous story of what Thoreau said to Emerson when Emerson came to visit him in jail? My God, Roizman! Don't you know *anything?*'"

Dave stopped because everyone had started laughing.

"Cookie!" Ffrenchy said excitedly. "You mean he always talked to *everyone* like they were these—these *cretins? Everyone?* Not just *me?* Oh, far out!"

Dave smiled. He said, "Well, that's how I knew we'd

become friends. . . . But I didn't know then it would turn out to be perhaps the most valuable friendship of my life, a friendship that would always validate me for myself, and at the same time, delight me with its unique otherness."

Unique otherness, Merry thought. That Roizman, sleek now in his white turtleneck, smiling and smug in the small-minded ease of his decorated ten rooms, could look out at the famously brilliant Ez Slavin and take pleasure, pure pleasure, at the sight of so much disorder. So that if he ever woke up in the middle of the night to the milky, far-off lamppost lights of doubt, or else found himself nodding off from boredom in his appointed chair behind the couch, how much more validation and delight could he ask for?

"Merry, darling." Sybil, hovering in the aisle, now crouched down beside Merry's seat. Perching on the armrest, she whispered, "Sweetheart, if you would just walk up there right now! Just go on up there! *All* you have to— Oh! You see that? Someone's there already!"

On the stage, a young man in dungarees and a fatigue jacket walked uneasily to the center. He said, "My name is Larry Sorkin, and Ez was my teacher. . . ."

"Oh! Larry Sorkin!" Sybil whispered happily. "He wrote that *wonderful* book! It's called something like 'Superman,' but it's really about Cuba. Mark gave it to us for Christmas!"

Merry sat back, away from Sybil's grasp. The book was called *Up from Super-Cop: Alternative Directions for U.S. Foreign Policy in Latin America;* it sat beside a toy fire truck and a straw basket on the telephone table in North Darby.

Larry Sorkin said, "I . . . I guess it sounds sort of anomalous to make a statement like that, because I was in school for so many years. But in all my other classes, even in seminars, those guys . . . they were always . . . *professors.* And Ez was *never* that. For *any* of his students. He was a teacher and he was a friend. And from the day I heard that he died, every time I get on a bus or a subway, I just keep thinking . . . I can't help thinking that I *see* him . . . that some man on the bus is *him*. . . . Well"—Sorkin nervously passed his hand through his hair—"I'm not really good at this, so what I . . . what I'd like to do is read a poem by Pablo Neruda."

"Pablo Neruda!" Charlotte whispered rhapsodically. "That *marvelous* poem about Spain! I used to do it at dramatic readings! Remember, Isobel? 'Come and see the blood in the streets, come and see the blood in the streets!' "

"It's called 'For Everyone,' " Sorkin said. "Or in Spanish, 'Para Todos.' Which can also be translated 'For All.' And that's what seems really *right* to me. Because Ez really *was* for everyone, he really *was* for all." He took a deep breath, and in the tone and jerky movements of a child uncomfortable before an assembly program, began:

> "I cannot tell you at once
> what I ought to be telling you.
> Friend, forgive me; you'll know
> that although you don't hear my words,
> I neither wept nor went to sleep,
> that without seeing you I'm with you
> for a long time now, and until the end.
>
> "I know that many are thinking,
> What is Pablo doing? I am here.
> If you look for me in this street,
> you will find me, with my violin,
> prepared to break into song,
> prepared to die."

Sorkin's voice wavered.

> "It is not a question of abandoning anyone,
> much less those ones, or you,
> and, if you listen well in the rain,
> you will be able to hear
> that I return, or leave, or linger.
> And you realize I must leave.

271

"If my words are not aware of it,
do not doubt, I am he who left.
There is no silence which does not end.
When the moment comes, wait for me,
and let them all know I am arriving
in the street with my violin."

Sybil, her eyes tearing, squeezed Merry's hand very hard, and Ffrenchy turned around, saying, "Cookie, Ez didn't *really* play the violin or anything, did he? I mean, like that just makes him sound so—so, you know, *Fiddler on the Roof-y!*"

Charlotte screwed up her face, staring. "How awful, Merry! Is Paula Meisel's daughter . . . *backward?* I think that's just so sad. Did you *hear* her, Isobel?"

But Isobel, clearly lost in her own thoughts, now jumped in precisely that taut violin string way which Ez had always made fun of. Quickly looking straight ahead of her, she said, "Look, there's Stewart Saunders. He doesn't seem to change at all, does he?"

"Ohhh," Charlotte sighed. "As far as I'm concerned, that's the most glaring inequity of life, and I don't know why the Women's Lib people don't *do* something about it! Why should men always have that advantage?"

Sybil snapped a handkerchief away from her face. "Well, of *course* he hasn't changed, Isobel! That's exactly what I said to Dave! I don't care *how* many petitions he signs, *how* many letterheads Stewart Saunders gets his name on! You'll never convince *me* that he's changed! And how he has the gall to even *appear* here is just be—"

"Friends . . ." Stewart Saunders smiled and held up his hand. "I hope you'll forgive me if I begin by borrowing something I learned from Ez—by starting with an item I found in this morning's newspaper."

"Well, that's *it*," Sybil said. "I am *sick*. And I just feel terrible for *you*, Merry, darling, that at a time like this you should have to be *subjected* to—"

272

"So often," Saunders said, "Ez began with something in the newspaper that had made him angry. Because he never stopped being angry; he never turned a blind eye. And if we did, if, unwittingly, we let something slip by, he reminded us. He was our unflagging conscience. And that's why, when I opened my newspaper this morning, and I saw this particular sentence, I couldn't help thinking of Ez. It's in an interview with Marcel Ophuls, the director of the film *The Sorrow and the Pity*, which is about the responses of the French to the Vichy government and the Nazi occupation. Well, that's just what Ophuls was explaining to the interviewer, and here's what caught my eye. He told him this: 'People who just lived—that was one of the themes of the film.' *People who just lived*," Saunders repeated, shaking his patrician head. "Well, if there was ever anyone in this world who *didn't* 'just live,' why surely that person was Ez Slavin. Because for him, I'm sure, that would have been the definition of *not* living. Of not being really alive. Yet he was not one of those sham 'heroic figures' who, in order to feel connected to life, look to danger, war or violence. He was enraged and anguished by war and violence and oppression wherever it occurred, no matter who the perpetrators or who the victims. For him, this was a personal thing and very simple: if human life was being violated, so was his; and where human dignity was affronted, his was too, no more or less than the victim's or the aggressor's. Because always he taught us, he reminded us that no matter what the outrage, no matter how near or far away the injustice, because of our shared humanity, we were *all* of us compromised, we were *all* of us victims. And for him this was not an abstraction, but a matter of passionate personal belief. . . ." Saunders paused. Clearly a man at home on a podium, he now pulled at his collar as if he were about to loosen his tie, but he wasn't wearing one. A rumpled English-style tweed sweater covered his long, long torso; he, too, had dressed for the occasion. In the homey but theatrical

273

adeptness of this gesture, Saunders seemed to Merry like someone thinking of running for office.

"I hate to say this, darling"— Sybil leaned over, whispering—"but I think I'm going to have to eat my words! I never would have *believed* that he could—"

"I've said that Ez was our unflagging conscience," Saunders continued. "He was also our truth-teller, and that can sometimes mean a lonely voice, a voice not in chorus with all the popular clamor of its own time, but a solo that persists separate and fervent, often unappreciated or misunderstood. Well, that was all right with Ez. Even from the very beginning. Because he didn't *believe* in timidity. He believed, always, in taking an unflinching look at what others might have preferred to pass over. And he believed in asking questions. Whether he was writing about Vietnam or Appalachia, the city or the country, a book or even an apparently ephemeral observation, I think his question was really always the same one: What in hell are we *doing?* Meaning: How should we live? Luckily, this was a question he never tired of asking. Of course, he never found one answer, but more important, he never fell prey to the cynicism that pretends it's not worth the asking. There's an ancient Chinese saying, which according to Albert Camus is a curse: May you live in interesting times. When the times were *not* interesting, Ez made them so—not just for himself, but for everyone who knew him, anyone whose life he touched. And when the times *were* interesting in the sense that that Oriental sage intended—that is to say difficult, confusing, painful—for those of us who were lucky enough to know Ez, when we talked to him or read something he'd written, we felt—*I* felt—that for a little while, in some measure, the curse was lifted. We live in a time—and in a world—which assumes that political power is where it's at. Ez knew better. He had no political power. He didn't need it and he didn't want it. Because what he had, what he gave us, was a unique moral energy, and it's that energy, that vision, which has infused generations and will surely continue to do so for generations to come."

Oh, it's your America, Stewart Saunders, Merry thought. And how the hell do you know what Ez might have wanted from it? There you are: craggy, handsome and just now a little pensive from this chastening brush with someone else's death, but soon you'll go out and have lunch. Eat up, Stewart Saunders. You've praised the lonely outsider, your "truth-teller." Alive or dead, he was never any competition for you.

"Cookie," Ffrenchy said. "Is he—is he like a senator or something? Or is he one of the, you know, *old* guys on the six o'clock news?"

Sybil glared at Ffrenchy, and leaning all the way over, said, "Isobel, darling, I think it's *your* turn now."

Isobel stood up nervously; she never gave public readings. Once she had read at the Ninety-second Street Y, but it was a torture for her and it showed.

"Here, dear, take an herb candy," Charlotte whispered. "They prevent your throat from tightening and they're *much* better than Valium. I promise you I absolutely *depended* on them because they just have the most— *Isobel!* You mustn't sit down now!"

But Herb Shestak, looking oddly unkempt, was already on the stage. He didn't walk to the center, and he didn't even wait for the audience buzz to subside. Shakily, he began, "In primitive societies—I mean, in what we *call* primitive societies—there was always a person whose established role it was to criticize. And I—I've often thought that that's what Ez did for America. Only America didn't understand, didn't accept it. But that's not . . . it's got nothing to do with what I came up here to say. . . ." He took a deep breath. "What I want to tell you about is something I've never told anyone, not even my wife. And I—I hope she'll forgive me even though it means bringing back memories that are still . . . still painful for both of us. . . . As some of you know, twenty-two years ago we—we had a son. He had a congenital neuromuscular disease and he died when he was nine. And as a result of the disease, among many other problems, he was—he became retarded. Naturally our friends complained and worried as they raised their perfectly healthy, normal children, while our lives, in those years, were a constant and agonizing round of doctors, hospitals and special school facilities. We felt helpless and angry and *I* felt—I always felt terribly ashamed. Then, of course, I would feel guilty, but that was how I—that was how it was for me then. Above all, I dreaded meeting anyone I knew. . . . Well, one day I was taking Michael home from some doctor—it was somewhere on the East Side—and while we were waiting for the bus, we ran into Ez. I remember it was a warm day, perhaps May or June; Michael had a Mickey Mouse balloon the doctor's receptionist had given him and he was wearing a Yankees polo shirt. I have no memory at all of what Ez and I said to each other, whatever brief civilities we exchanged, but as I stood there struggling, drowning in my own feelings of hopelessness and shame, Ez turned to my son and said, 'Tell me something. Which do you like better—your balloon or your shirt?' 'Shirt!' Michael yelled out. For us, it was always a struggle to get him to take it off at night. Ez immediately shook his hand and said, 'Oh, I'm so glad to hear you say that. I can't stand Mickey Mouse myself. To me Mickey Mouse is silly.' Michael began to laugh uproariously; it was the first happy sound that had come out of him all that day since he had known he was going to the doctor. He jumped up and said, 'Silly! Silly! *Very* silly!' 'You said it, Mike!' Ez waved to him because our bus had just come. '*Very* silly. And the next time I see you, you'll have to tell me what's so good about the Yankees.' " Herb smiled as he reached this, but it was a deeply inturned, painful smile. He said, "There are so many good things I could say about Ez, he had so many extraordinary qualities. But what I keep thinking of over and over again is what

expression softened as the audience laughed. She resumed, "But however faraway he may have seemed, suddenly he would stop, his face alight with amazed pleasure. What had caught his attention? What had fired his eye? A construction site, a store, a lamppost, a billboard sign: it was never anything remarkable, but because in his eyes it *was*, as you listened to him it became so. Taking a walk with Ez was an Arabian Nights of the everyday. But who would ever have dared tell him that? For Ez protested—too much, I think, and always with that particular edge in his voice—against poetry, against what he would derisively call 'the finer feelings.' Those were really *his* feelings, and his longings; he wrestled with them within himself, and expressed them, perhaps under cover, in his singular imaginative empathy for American places, the American past, and a certain sense of wildness—a spiritual wildness. It was his equivalent of poetry, an equivalent of the heart, and it was there in his attitude toward people as well. Once, in teaching a class, he reminded his students of the Socratic admonition: 'The unexamined life is not worth living.' 'And how do *you* know?' a young, belligerent student responded. This—" Isobel stopped because the audience had begun laughing. Quickly, taking off her glasses, she said, "But you see, Ez *didn't* laugh. The girl's response electrified him. Suddenly so wrenched out of an old attitude, a habit of mind he had never thought to question—and Ez, of course, delighted in just such wrenchings—at that moment, I imagine, even the furniture in the room must not have seemed real to him. He felt that this student had unwittingly initiated him into a truth about most people's lives that was at least an equal truth, and he was dazzled and grateful. How many teachers would have had that reaction I can't say, but that Ez did accounts in some part, I think, for his special attraction for and attachment to the young. Of course, it's been the fashion recently, especially in the United States, to hold the young in heightened regard and even awe. But Ez, in his own way, always did, and this was *not* because he was ahead of his time. Rather, in this sentiment, I've always thought of him as old-fashioned. He believed, in that stirring and romantic phrase of Ibsen's, that he 'was in league with the future.' Romantic and innocent, as Ez thought of it. For unlike ideologues, he had no program for the future, no twenty-five-year plans, but saw it, especially in his most optimistic moods, as an open and unknowable promise, and the clear, sunlit possession of the young. That was his attachment to the young: they *were* the future.

"But Ez was not always so optimistic; there were other, darker moods that perhaps none of us really understood, pretending, as he partly wished us to, that they did not exist, or that they arose solely from the bitter exigencies of a troubled and troubling world. In this way, he's often seemed to me an authentically Old Testament type: a cranky, restless, thundering prophet, so impatient and unconsolable in his frustrations, so stern and single-minded in his griefs. 'And when I heard this thing,' says his namesake, the biblical Ezra, 'And when I heard this thing, I rent my garment and my mantle, and plucked off the hair of my head and of my beard, and sat down appalled.'

"But if Ez often 'sat down appalled,' at bottom that's not how I think of him. What I think of always is the young man I met one evening in the summer of 1939, who sat so perilously perched on the very high sill of an entirely opened fifth-floor window. It was a perch of daring and insouciance, and though it seemed to me then, provincial girl that I was, emblematic of the city itself, that has remained the view of Ez Slavin most deeply lodged in my mind, and the one which comes to me unbidden now and whenever I think of him.

"It was Henry James, not one of Ez's favorite writers, who said that being an American is a complex fate. Sometimes I think that Ez understood that better than anyone I've ever known, and sometimes, that he hardly understood it at all, but always with the spirit of the bold young man who sat on the high sill, simply lived it out in a way that confounds understanding. He confounded *my* understanding, and I will miss him."

Isobel took off her glasses and walked off the stage, and Duff Adair, the folk singer who had introduced Ez at the antiwar rally in 1965, now stood before the microphone. With self-conscious absorption, he kept tuning his guitar and readjusting the microphone. Finally, slinging his guitar over his work shirt, he looked out at the audience and said, "For a whole lot of years now we've . . . we've really been through a time of dying. Going all the way back to Kennedy and Martin Luther King. And Vietnam. And Joplin and Hendrix . . . It's like . . . it's like it's just been a whole . . . *season* of dying. So I just want to say that even though I didn't really *know* Ez, it was . . . it was good to be on this planet at the same time he was." He paused awkwardly, and then said, "I—I'm gonna sing a song for Ez, and anyone who wants to join in—well, that's what it's all about." He took a few steps away from the microphone, and half closing his eyes, began singing,

> "To every thing, turn, turn, turn
> There is a season, turn, turn, turn
> And a time to every purpose under heaven
>
> A time to be born, a time to die
> A time to plant, a time to reap
> A time to kill, a time to heal
> A time to laugh, a time to weep
>
> To every thing, turn, turn, turn
> There is a season, turn, turn, turn
> And a time to every purpose under heaven
>
> A time to build up, a time to break down
> A time to dance, a time to mourn
> A time to cast away stones
> A time to gather stones together

To every thing, turn, turn, turn
There is a season, turn, turn, turn
And a time to every purpose under heaven

A time of love, a time of hate
A time of war, a time of peace
A time you may embrace
A time to refrain from embracing

To every thing, turn, turn, turn
There is a season, turn, turn, turn
And a time to every purpose under heaven

A time to gain, a time to lose
A time to rend, a time to sew
A time to love, a time to hate
A time of peace, I swear it's not too late

To every thing, turn, turn, turn
There is a season, turn, turn, turn
And a time to every purpose under heaven."©

The folk singer put his guitar down, and looking out at the audience directly, repeated in his rough, unaccompanied voice, " 'And a time to every purpose under heaven.' "

"Oh, darling." Sybil put her arm around Merry. "I'm just so glad for your sake that Dave decided not to play the 'Fanfare' again at the end. Duff is exactly the *right* way to end it, the right spirit." Sighing deeply, she patted Merry's hand, and eagerly got up from her uncomfortable perch on the armrest. "My God! There's somebody *else* up there now!" Sybil suddenly cried out. "There wasn't supposed to be! I *know* there wasn't supposed to be! Who the hell is it?"

On the stage, a dark-haired young man was walking toward the microphone. Even in his bearing—the defensive, sullen tilt of his head, the vexed, resentful hunch of his shoulders—there was still that old awkward, aggrieved look: Jonathan, Jonathan Spivak. He opened the book he was carrying, and staring into it, his head down and his voice uncertain, appeared to gulp out, "I'm going to read the Kaddish."

"Oh! Allen Ginsberg! What a wonderful *idea!*" Charlotte whispered. "I don't know if I told you, Isobel, but I saw him on the street the other day, and I really didn't think he looked at all well."

"*Yisgadel v'yiskadash shmey raboh* [Jonathan read], *b'olmoh di vroh chirusey,*

"*V'yamlich malchusey b'chayeychon u'v'yomeychon, u'v'chayey d'chol beys yisroel, ba'agoloh uvizman koriv, v'imru omeyn.*

"*Y'hey shmey raboh m'vorach l'olam ul'olmey olmayoh.*

"*Yisborach v'yishtabach, v'yispoar v'yisromam, v'yisnasey v'yis' hadar, v'yisaleh v'yis'halal shmey d'kudshoh, b'rich hu, l'eyloh min kol birchosoh v'shirosoh, tushb'chosoh v'nechemosoh, da'ami-ron b'olmoh, v'imru omeyn.*

"*Y'hey shlomoh raboh min sh'mayoh, v'chayim, oleynu v'al kol yisroel, v'imru omeyn.*

"*Oseh sholom bimromov, hu ya'aseh sholom oleynu v'al kol yisroel, v'imru omeyn.*"

Jonathan finished and rushed off the stage, his desperate adolescent gait and pained expression so instantly reminiscent of his angry flight from Ez into the elevator at Mount Sinai.

But there was no awkward silence: people immediately began picking up their coats and craning around at each other, so that within seconds, all the milling and buzzing in the aisles gave the stark auditorium the look of a cocktail party.

"I don't *understand* you, Sybil!" Bea Shestak pushed her way up the crowded aisle, storming. "How could you and Dave possibly have allowed something so—so *barbaric!*"

"It's a *prayer*, dear," Charlotte said in one of her most ethereal, other-side-of-the-moon voices. "I remember it now because when my husband died, someone—ohh, who could it have been?" she moaned, covering her face with her hands. "Could it have been the rabbi? Could it have been Abe's nephew? Ohh, I was just in such a *haze* then. I don't think I can even remember. . . ."

"Merry." Isobel leaned over, frowning. "Was that Jonathan?"

"Yes," Merry said. "And I'm going right over there now to see if I can speak to him."

"*Darling! You* can't go anywhere now!" Sybil cried. "People will be coming over *here!* To speak to *you!* And, Bea, darling, really! I'm surprised at you! How could you even *imagine* that Dave and I could be responsible for anything like—"

"Excuse me, Sybil," Merry said, and making her way through the crowd, found herself suddenly halted.

"Hey!" An enormous, barrel-chested man gripped her shoulder, and handing her a glove she didn't know she'd dropped, he jerked his head back like a conspirator in a gangster movie, and said, in a flat voice, "You're Pearl's kid, right? I'm your cousin. Ira. Sorry about your old man."

Merry looked up at him: he had the burly, red-faced look of Ez's older brothers, the wide forehead and heavy, broad cheeks—those cheeks which had always made Merry think their tongues were also raw and heavy, and that was why they talked so little. She said, "Are you Bloke's son or Menasha's?"

"Bloke, Bloke. Menash . . ." He shook his head. "No one knows what the hell happened to that son of a gun. Well—he didn't want no one to know, don't kid yourself. . . . Shaiky's around, though. He comes around sometimes. He didn't go for it in Florida. He had the dough, ya know, he just didn't go for it. He's got a good pension there, that crazy Shaiky, if he don't piss it all away. That's a good union, the Teamsters." He nodded slowly. "They take care of 'em. Take care of 'em a helluva lot better than what my old man gets from the TWU. Or what I'll ever see. Well"—he smiled, and suddenly there was Ez's tricky charm alive on Ira's Slavin face—"who knows how long I'll stick?"

Staring at this transformation, which had already come and gone on her unknown cousin's face, Merry said, "I didn't know Shaiky. He's the one I never met."

"Naah." Ira shook his head. "It's Menash you never met.

283

He was . . . he was always *sore*. Like the zaydeh. And he wouldn't forgive no one no matter what. Just like the zaydeh's brother. Avrum. That's who I figure he *really* took after. You know that business about the passage money? The thirty bucks? How Avrum somehow got it in his Russky head that the zaydeh cheated him, so when he finally got here, he just walked himself right off that pickle boat and wouldn't even—"

"Merry, darling!" Sybil, exultant, was suddenly beside her. "Darling, I really *do* have to change my mind about Stewart Saunders! He's just invited us all to lunch at Le Clos Normand! It's right here, right around the corner, so just get your coat and let's—"

"Sybil," Merry said, "this is my cousin, Ira Slavin. Ira, Sybil Roizman."

"Oh, are you Ez's nephew? Well, then why don't you join us?" Smiling broadly, Sybil offered him her arm, and said, "Come on!"

"Naah," Ira said. "I gotta go to work, I gotta pay off my kid's Sweet Sixteen. Or her mother'll put me in jail again. She'd do it, too. 'Cause when you're dealin' with a dumb guinea broad like that, logic just don't come into it." He shrugged, but said all this conversationally, without any particular animus. "I mean, if I don't have the dough, how the hell is jail gonna put it in my pocket?"

Sybil drew in her breath, and taking a step backward, seemed transfixed by the huge gold *chai* which hung around Ira's neck. Barely able to speak, she finally came up with, "What is it that you *do*, Mr. Slavin?"

"Now?" Ira said, and smiled Ez's smile again. "I'm in one of the classy hotels around here. I'm in the security operation. It's a big operation they got there, lemme tell ya. *Very* big."

Sybil shook her head. "Oh, it's so sad," she said. "I know just how *anonymous* that must make you feel. . . . Big operations are exactly what Ez spent his whole life fighting against."

"Aah, it's all a crock." Ira shrugged. "I don't pull down more than a deuce a week." He took a cigar out of his pocket, and fingering it, said, "I *got* opportunities. But ya know how it is, I'm tryin' to keep my nose clean."

Sybil's eyes darted through the crowd. "Oh, *there's* Dave," she said. "Excuse me, Merry, darling."

"Well, I gotta get into my uniform," Ira said, "so I guess I better say so long." He nodded brusquely, and already walking away, said, "I'll tell my old man you're all right. He remembers you, ya know. From when you lived with the bubbah on Rivington Street."

"Oh, I remember *him*," Merry said, and grabbed Ira's arm with a rush of feeling that had nothing to do with this cousin she didn't know, nor an uncle to whom she'd barely spoken. "And your mother too. I guess the last time I saw them was when they sat *shiva* for bubbah."

Ira frowned. "*My* mother never went to no *shiva* for the bubbah. Are you kiddin'? She wouldn't even go to the funeral."

"But I *remember*, I'm positive. They sat *shiva* in Brooklyn and it was at Bloke and Nettie's."

"Oh, *Nettie!*" Ira laughed. "My mother got rid of him way before Nettie. She *had* to. Well—Nettie hadda get rid of him too. He was no good, he gambled away every penny. He still does. It's what he lives for. Ponies, pinochle, football pools, any Goddamn thing." Ira shrugged. "I dunno, they say it's a sickness, but what the hell—I think it just runs in families. Like these lousy Dumbo ears," and he tapped at his own large crimson ears that were so much like Ez's. "*Your* old man didn't gamble, though, did he? He didn't go in for anything like that?"

"No." Merry smiled, and in the midst of the dim library auditorium, suddenly imagined thin, angular-faced Ez with his sallow skin and cranky smile, a rakish hat on his head and a folded-up racing form in his pocket. In a way, this was the burnt-out Bickford's bum look that had always so much frightened her. And why, really? No rakish hat had ever really sat on his head nor loser's racing sheet stuck out of his pocket, but forever defying the fragility of illusion, Ez, with that first-generation disease, had believed himself to be self-generated. Hellbent on winning a private, impossible sweepstake, a prize you could never touch, he had put all his money on an idea of America he had just gone ahead and made up. And so what if it had come out of libraries instead of race tracks. It was what he had lived for: a horse with such long odds it would never come in.

"No, not really," she repeated, and following Ira out into the raw city wind which Ez had always brazened through in a thin jacket, felt her eyes tear from an answer that was entirely different. Isobel's daring young lover had sat on a high sill, but Merry's disappointed, self-denying father with his lousy Dumbo ears—the whorled, beet-red, blood-red ears that had so long ago in the shaving mirror flamed like blood in the Siberian snow, this Ezra Slavin, whistling up to place his bets, had nearly gambled away every penny.

**7**

**DAY
BOOK**

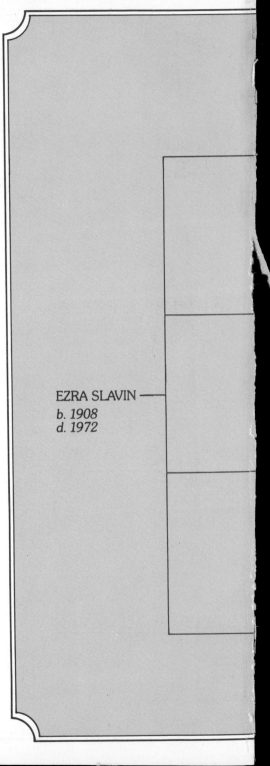

EZRA SLAVIN

*b. 1908*
*d. 1972*